I0699818

Kingdom Seat
Princess Embla
Princess Emenda
Prince Ayxian
Prince Noxian
Prince Roxalus
Prince Maximus
Princess Elodie
Prince Loxias

Also by

Veil & Shadow Series
**The Breaking*
**The Bleeding*

(**Prequel** to *The Anavrin Series*- Stand Alone)
**Little Red Rising*

The Anavrin Series
**A Kingdom Of Crowns And Malice*
**A Throne Of Chains And Fate*

Eventide Series
**Falling Even*
**Rising Tide*

A Kingdom Of Crowns And Malice

Author's Note:

Some Trigger Warnings

This book is a work of fiction. Any likeness to that of actual beings, living or deceased, is coincidental or embellished to tell a fictional tale.

It contains scenes that may be uncomfortable for some readers.

Including, but not limited to... violence, blood, explicit sex, alcohol abuse, and implied and/or unwanted sexual advances.

Some characters in this book are based off of real-world placement and classical works but do not strictly adhere to any one folklore.

The creative uses of such are fully fictional and not to be taken as fact.

ANEXA O. SAPHIRE

Chapter One

Ah, palace life. Nothing like the boredom and tedium of faux civility.

Everything was much simpler when I lived with a pack of wolves. Now, I feel like prey that has wandered into a den of monsters.

The undoing of that wretched curse was the end of my life in the wilds of the Lupian Forest. If mother could only see me now.

I've been in the faery lands of Anavrin for nearly six months and getting used to being fae has been quite a struggle. I'd had no idea who I was before being sucked into this gods forsaken realm.

The beauty of the land is unmatched, but their way of life confounds me. Even the kinder fae have an underlying mischief about them.

I've always said "please, thank you, and sorry" on a regular basis but here, these tricksters turn every misspoken word against me.

Currently, there is a contest for the king's throne. That's why we're all gathered in this banquet hall in the kingdom seat palace.

It is an ongoing challenge set for thirteen months from the Festival of Luna, which was when I'd arrived here in Anavrin.

I'm complaining a lot for someone seated at a table that hosts all of the princes and princesses from every court across the land. It's all just so ridiculous.

No one should have to strap themselves into a tight-laced corset and low bustline dress just to witness royals gossip and snip at each other over hearty meals.

The last six months haven't been the worst experience of my life... but they certainly haven't been the best either.

At the Festival of Sol, a new king or queen will be crowned. That's still seven months away from now but it's not the biggest worry on my mind.

With each challenge, the King Regent, Maximus, tallies the points of every prince and princess but tells no one the outcomes.

It's as frustrating as it is exciting, but I've never been one to sit on a razors edge and enjoy the slide of a blade.

It may be that he doesn't want the fae of the land to be swayed by the events. Or it might simply be that he feels these spoiled royals will act poorly if they know where they stand in the rankings.

I admit, I find it both fun and unnerving to watch the competitions while mingling at each revelry. As long as I'm here, I might as well learn to play their games, right?

Max has been... Sorry, King Maximus has been as helpful as possible to all of us who were sucked into Faery land, otherwise known as Anavrin.

His great-granddaughter, The Deliverer, cast a spell to bring the fae back to their homeland and bar them entry to the human realm.

She'd made a promise to one of the princes at this very table and kept it, breaking the long-standing curse over the Spring court fae that kept their power dampened and their mates unable to find their other half.

Reworking the magics, she didn't tell anyone until afterwards, that she'd be locking them away from their favorite toys.

Homes have been found or built to accommodate most of us. We've been given the opportunity to spend time figuring out where we fit best and what our new callings may be.

It's been a trying time for a lot of the newly found faeries. Myself included.

Some left friends, family, and lives that we'd genuinely loved behind. None of us had a choice in the matter. One minute, going about your day. The next, "Hey, guess what, you are a faery!"

Learning that you have fae blood is wild. Finding out, like I had, that I was a full-blooded faery, turned upside down everything I'd ever thought I knew about myself.

With the curse that had been placed on Anavrin's people lifted, all elemental gifts in the land were now back to full power.

I never knew that I could switch between my true panther shift and my werewolf shift. Or that I had the ability to slow time around me and sense true intentions. That had been a surprise for sure.

These lands magics made it easier to be who I truly am. I'd been hiding from myself for far too long.

Six months in and I still can't figure out the whole slowing time thing. It's only happened twice so far, and I don't know how to summon the gift or control it yet.

Feeling other people's emotions has been overwhelming, but I am starting to be able to dull it down to a bearable point. At least, I'm trying to.

Looking around the table, I feel bitterness, and happiness, envy and something else I can't put my finger on.

None of it is mine. It's all coming from the princes and princesses... except maybe the envy.

When I first came here, learning all of the princess's and prince's names was a daunting task. There were just so many of them.

Fae had difficulties when it came to having children but the late king, Zyoden, was able to have four children with each wife.

He wouldn't have married Queen Leyashna if Queen Ombriana hadn't been murdered by his former mistress, the First Witch, Mab. Who... dun dun dun... is my long lost ancestor.

As it is, I've learned the names of the royals because they each have a court that is named after them.

When I looked at the map in the library of this palace, it all finally clicked in place. Lands have been easier for me to memorize than names for as long as I can remember.

Queen Ombriana was the Royal Queen. It was her throne. Not King Zyoden's. He only assumed it after her death. Which was why he had to take another wife.

The fae of the land insisted, or else he would have had to pass the crown down to Maximus at the next solstice.

Maximus is the oldest. Then Roxalus. Followed by the twins, Embla and Emenda.

I'm told that Queen Leyashna knew going into the marriage that there would be no love from the king. She gave him four children anyway.

Ayxian is the oldest of her children. Then Noxian, whom I haven't had many interactions with, but he has been genuinely kind for the ones that I have. Elodie is Queen Leyashna's only daughter. She's possibly my favorite. Next to Max, of course. Then comes the baby of the group, Loxias.

I find myself laughing along at his jokes. Smiling at his quips. And enjoying his company when he is around. Something that Inara says is *just the strangest thing.*

He really has changed from the brooding, arrogant male we'd known for years to a laid back, happy-go-lucky prince of his people. All because he could now be free to find his mate someday.

My thoughts drift to my mother. She may not have wanted my feline side revealed to anyone, especially faeries, but I was no longer bound to her wishes for an unremarkable existence.

Early along in my teen years, she'd had a vision. She never spoke of it to me but made me promise to become a wolf when the first shift came. That was back when I'd thought myself a simple shifter, back in the Lupian Forest.

After she'd spoken to my Aunt Eowyn, she'd told me that I was to fit myself into my cousin Inara's pack when the time came.

"Blend in and be quiet, Peppercorn," she'd say. I'd thought maybe when I was older, she might tell me what was so terrible about her vision, but she died before I'd circled around the sun even one more time.

"What are you so deep in thought about over there, Piper?" Maximus asked casually, shifting in his chair and drawing me back to the present. Never having a father figure, sometimes I'm caught off guard by his genuine concern. "You look troubled."

Eowyn had been his mate. Her death had devastated him.

Inara, who is my cousin and best friend, had never known who her father was until after I was sucked into Anavrin. Being The Deliverer's grandmother had its perks apparently.

Faelan had added a loophole into the containment spell that allowed her and Inara to stay with their wolf pack back home. It was in relation to her direct bloodline.

Max has teleported me back to see Inara several times, but it's different from being able to be there for her whenever she needs me. We'd always been closer than two sisters could ever be.

I smiled up in his direction. Over the time I've been here, he's been kind and just, never acting with what I have come to know as fae deviance.

Occasionally, I'd catch him twist the words of a thief or wrong doer when they were brought before him for judgement. A hint of fickle fae there and gone from him before I could blink.

If I hadn't been an observer my whole life, I would have missed it.

It was fae nature to have cruelty, or at least mischief, as our undertone. His sentences were always fair, though, even if some of them had that fae twist on them.

Like the one thief who'd stolen five sheep from his neighbor and Max made him eat the grass from their overgrown field for five days.

That made me laugh more than I expected. It was times like that which gave me pause. Realizing how deeply fiendishness was ingrained in my fae DNA.

My mother's passing had gripped me and shook my foundation all those years ago.

I'd become a quiet observer. Only speaking when something truly needed voiced, though it was never quiet inside my head. Sarcasm bounced off the walls of my skull, begging for an exit, nearly my entire life.

Here in Anavrin, I've found myself quicker to laugh or lash out with a retort. It's been more difficult to hold my tongue, and honestly, I like myself more this way. It's freeing.

"I was remembering my mother's words... and those of Aunt Eowyn." Max's smile fell for the briefest of seconds before he plastered it back on.

The loss of one's mate is said to be an all-consuming ache that never fully goes away.

"I know that you are Inara's cousin, but somehow, I always fail to make the connection readily as to why that is." A twinkle in his eye gleamed obviously with Aunt Eowyn's memory.

Maximus lifted his glass, and I lifted mine in response. "A toast," his voice carrying down the long table.

The other royals who were gathered around the half empty dishes and low burning candles lifted their glasses and all of the courtiers followed suit.

"To the friends we call family. The family we call blood. And to the love that spills between the two."

Everyone sipped from their glasses.

Everyone except Roxalus. The prince who'd been set to take the throne when Max had disappeared and was presumed dead.

I found his cold gaze, once again in the last several months, landing on me.

Bitterness indeed.

Chapter Two

"Well, dear brother." Roxalus put his wine back onto the table, nearly knocking over the half dozen candles in front of him.

Clearly the quality of the wine wasn't the problem.

He swayed slightly and his glassy eyes stayed locked on mine as he addressed the King Regent without once looking away.

I was trapped in his gaze. Try as I might to look away, I couldn't make my eyes heed my command.

The prince was devastatingly handsome, like most fae. His dark hair and sharp jawline cut through me with precision. Those eyes though. Damn magnets.

"I suppose it would be ill advised for me to cheers to the blood that runs in both of our veins when yours holds that of a coward." The last of his words came out in a slur as he got to his feet.

Princess Emenda made to grab his arm, but he slipped through her grasp.

Gasps and whispers ran the circle of the chamber through the courtiers in attendance. Oh how they loved dinner and a show. This would be the highlighted talk of their week.

If King Maximus doesn't address his brother's statement, he'll be seen as weak. These fickle fae won't follow someone who would allow such disrespect.

Though if Max does punish Roxalus for his statement in his drunken state, he'd be seen as a draconian ruler. They'd say that mere words could hurt him.

It was a no-win situation for Uncle Max.

Thankfully, Prince Ayxian stood and clapped Roxalus on the shoulder. "How about we get you into a night shift and tuck you in, aye brother?"

A nervous energy shudders throughout the room. I dropped my eyes briefly when he released me from his glare but couldn't keep myself from joining in on the unfolding drama.

In all my time here, I'd never seen Roxalus out of sorts. Always controlled. Always uptight. But never a drink beyond his faculties.

His sleeve made short work of the red liquid that had dribbled down the sides of his mouth.

"Or maybe," grabbing his glass, Prince Roxalus drank deeply before continuing. "I'll take a poke at that fair lady there."

Even if I didn't feel every eye in the palace on me, I'd have known where he was pointing.

Heat radiated down my neck, and my hands began to shake. My long, black hair fell forward covering the sides of my face.

Lifting my head to look at him in his drunken state, I held my chin high in defiance.

There were those here in Anavrin who thought the fae brought back by The Deliverer's spell to be beneath them. Poppycock in my opinion but winning them over wasn't going to be easy.

"You flatter me, Prince Roxalus. I could never be worthy of your company. Forgive this lowbee for even attracting your eye." I said, hating that term. It had become a slur for all of us newcomers.

Roxalus didn't care for his own people, much less anyone who had resided outside of the realm before the retrieval. That much I've gathered over in my time here.

I still can't get a feel for his intentions with my new gifts. This male is an enigma. Locked up tighter than a cryptex with only one code.

Catching him looking my way, either in mild perversion or slight annoyance, I can't be sure, has become my new norm whenever all of the royalty are gathered.

Ayxian shoves him back down into his chair with an audible thud. Wine spilling the length of the table, smoke from the extinguished candles rising in small plumes.

"You will have no part of her!" His tone brokers no room for argument.

I shifted slightly towards Max unconsciously at Ayxian's raised voice. He was my uncle by fate, not blood, but over the last several months, it felt like he'd become true family.

That may have been what his toast had been about. It hadn't crossed my mind before now. Way to be observant, dunderhead.

Roxalus obviously had let the words take root and offense.

"Are you now her keeper, brother? Does the flower smell that much sweeter when the fruit has spice?" He slurs each word without taking his eyes off of me.

Ayxian's shocked face was mirrored by many around the room, including my own.

Though no one ever seemed to notice Roxalus' poetic words like I did. Even when they weren't kind and lacked warmth, they'd always held a depth that spoke to me.

In this moment, they brought me up short. They laid me out bare. "No one here has ever smelled my flower and tasted my spice. I am not sure if you have been told otherwise, but if that's the case, you have been misled."

Smoke was practically coming out of my nose; I was fuming so hard at the insinuation.

Faeries can't lie, but talking around truths is our specialty. And I am a quick study.

I had spent some time with Ayxian when I'd first arrived here. He is strong and well-liked by most of his people as far as I can tell.

It made it easy for me to forget that he is just one of many vying for the crown.

With all of his training centered around fighting, I'd felt that I should visit with Leif for the duration of the competition. He is Max's son who had taken over his court in his absence.

"So says the lowbee." Embla came to Roxalus' defense. As usual.

Max is the oldest, but Roxalus is known to have the same way of thinking as she and her twin, Emenda.

They prefer those higher in royal rankings not mingle with commoners unnecessarily. And those of us who came from the human realm are far below even the commoners in their eyes.

King Maximus raises his hand to quiet the crowd, and the other royals fall silent as well. He looks to Queen Leyashna, his stepmother, before proceeding. With her slight nod, he continues.

Relinquishing her control to Max has been a blessing for her. There is no animosity between them.

In fact, they had been close friends for many centuries before he'd gone missing. His deference is respect. Not permission.

"That term Lowbee is most unbecoming, sister. If you thought yourself to be truly better than others, wouldn't your words and action follow along those same lines?"

Ensnaring her in a word trap, her downturned lips said that she knew he'd bested her.

If she uses the term, people will see her as unworthy of her station now. Max is brilliant.

Princess Embla pursed her lips, but no words followed. Emenda patted her arm and glared at me like I'd slapped her sister.

I couldn't contain the wide grin spreading across my face.

The twins anger crinkled at the corners of their eyes but nowhere else. Public view during these thirteen months is crucial and we all know it.

Drawing the attention of those in the room once again, Max indicates a small table to the left of the chamber.

On it sits a crystal chalice filled with small, folded pieces of paper.

"The tally as we head forward to the Festival of Sol is at an even pace. In that chalice lies pieces of paper with a number, one through seven, on it."

The smell of fresh baked bread still hangs in the air from our supper. I am full to bursting, but that doesn't mean I can't snatch a loaf to have for a snack while I read tonight.

As my mind wanders to thoughts of butter and sweet jams in my comfy pajamas with my newest book in hand, a servant retrieves the chalice and brings it to stand before the king.

He addresses the princes and princesses and I kind of tune him out before I remember that we're about to learn of the next competition.

I miss the first part of what he's saying but focus as he continues to relay their set tasks.

"Each one of you will draw a number. I will tell you what they mean after, so as not to encourage cheating," he says, gesturing towards the chalice.

And cheat, they would. Anything for a leg up.

His sibling's hymn, haul, and mumble but take a piece of paper out of the cup as the servant brings it to each of them in turn.

"Now that your numbers are drawn, show them to the crowd."

He whispers something to the servant, and she scampers off, only to return a few seconds later.

"Callalina here will be recording who the numbers are assigned to once you reveal them." Nodding in Ayxian's direction, Ayxian looks as Roxalus opens his own paper.

A chuckle escapes from the large muscled male who towers a good half foot over his brother. "I have three and Rox has five."

The drunk prince tries to pull his paper out of Ayxian's grip, but he holds it open to show the court.

"I could have told them myself! I do not need led around by the nose hairs." Clearly, Roxalus is beginning to sober some, but isn't nearly as put together as we are all used to.

After turning ten shades of red, he sits back down and takes a long swig from the bottle that has been placed on the table beside him. So much for sobering.

His eyes brush over my body, and I shudder. I've been weirdly obsessed with seeking him out at all of these gatherings.

He is fear and ruthlessness incarnate. Handsome beyond anyone I've ever encountered. And I am oddly attracted to his dark side. Though I've never admitted that to anyone, even Inara.

He comes off as menacing, but I've glimpsed beauty and depth there, lurking in the shadows of his mask.

Luna, save me. Don't lust after the nefarious prince, Piper! Geesh.

"I have two." Prince Loxias tells the servant, showing his paper to the crowd with an exuberant smile.

He has been easy going since I arrived here in Anavrin.

I'd been fully expecting him to be right back to his usual arrogant self, but when the curse was lifted and he had his full powers back, he'd been contented to live and let live.

The change in him is something to behold. All smiles and zest for life.

I'd been skeptical of his claim that he'd only wanted the ability to find his mate. With a power like his, the world could be made to bend to his will.

Having his full abilities back, not once has he used them nefariously... at least, as far as I can tell.

Others in Anavrin were just as contented. Some because they feel whole again. Some because they can now find their soulmates.

None of them appears bother that they can no longer leave this realm for the human one. That's only bothersome for us lowbees.

The twins look to be having a silent argument. Max has to ask them three times before they finally realize he's been talking to them.

"I have number one and Embla has number four." Emenda's smugness rubs me wrong instantly.

Princess Elodie looks at the twins and back to Max. I have come to learn that her gift is seeing through things.

Not like a looking glass, but of intentions. It is a gift remarkably similar to mine.

While I only receive a mild sensation of what someone is feeling in their hearts at any given moment, Elodie can decern emotions, sense deceits, and see through illusional magics.

"I have six. And I don't know if this matters, but the twin's switched papers after they looked at the numbers." Her tone is reproachful.

She has been the kindest fae I have encountered yet. Even Max and Leif can't hold a candle to her non-assuming character.

She doesn't hunger for power and is just in every word she speaks. Honesty sits in her lap like a well-cared for cat.

Sometimes it comes off as harsh, but that isn't her intent. I can feel her words when I've spoken to her. They come from a deep well of forthcoming and I find that refreshing here in this land.

Max raises an eyebrow but smirks. "Thank you, Elle. It's fine. Now that it's been recorded, they can't change again."

The twins stare daggers at their younger sister and hiss in whispers behind their hands about Max.

"That leaves Noxian with the seventh and final spot before the Festival of Sol. Each number represents the next court and game we will play."

Max catches my eye and motions towards me. My stomach bottoms out when everyone else looks my way. What is he playing at?

"Lady Piper will be a guest in each of your kingdoms from the end of one competition to the beginning of the next."

My stomach does a full-on summersault. I never liked roller coasters, and this is one with a big drop.

I start to protest but stop when I notice the angry stares and murmurs passing from royal to royal, courtier to courtier.

"Is this some sort of joke?" Embla's tone gets the better of me.

My tongue quicker than my self-preservation, I lash out without the ability to hold it in check.

"A joke has a punchline, Princess. I honestly don't see anything funny about wasting ... your time in my presence."

I hate kowtowing to these people, but royalty is royalty, and I am just a commoner with the title of Lady because of the First Witch, Mab.

The brother standing next to her chimes in his two cents. "As much as I like having Piper's company, there is a kingdom on the line."

Ouch. Ayxian isn't wrong, but to hear him voice that he would do better without me around stings.

Max isn't bending. There has to be more to the *why* than he's letting on.

"Let me put it to you this way... Piper is going to be in each of your lands for one month. It is my advice that you do your best to be, not only accommodating, but welcoming. I will say no more on the matter. I will send word of the challenge that will be played two weeks before each one is to take place. That will give you two weeks prior to get to know the company you are keeping."

Lifting his glass, all around the hall glasses are raised in response.

"I look forward to seeing you all in Princess Emenda's court on the first of the month."

Chapter Three

If I didn't know Max better, I would have thought this was some sort of cruel punishment.

While everyone else is filing out of the dining hall after the feast, he motions for me to stay put.

The darkness of the hour makes the retreating figures look eerie against the flickering of torchlight.

After the chamber is empty, I follow him into a cozy sitting room off the side of the throne room. It smells of rich alcohol and cedar.

"Have a seat." Motioning me to a plush blue couch next to a large bookcase, he sits in the comfy chair opposite from me. "I know you have questions. I don't plan on giving you answers to them."

Well, that was as forthcoming with vagueness as the oceans being wet.

"I don't understand. Did I do something wrong?"

Leif and I have gotten along famously. Most of the people of his court respond well to me. I can't think of anything that I may have done wrong.

I've settled into a nice house just outside of the castle grounds and have begun to make personal touches with a small garden and decorations of shells and stones.

"Of course not, Piper. I need you to do this for me." A wooden box lays on the side table that I don't notice until he opens it.

Taking out an unusual looking necklace, he held it out for me to see.

It's heart shaped but only abstractly. There is a shimmer of color that disappears when I try to look at it for more than a few seconds. There is a beautiful stone wrapped in a wire setting with seven small diamonds around the sides and point.

"I have been tasked with finding the best king or queen possible to reign over Anavrin." After a quick nod in affirmation for my consent, he places the necklace, which hangs down to settle between my breasts, around my neck. "I can't see my siblings without the goggles of our past. I want to be fair, but I find myself lacking."

I suppose it makes sense. Inara and I grew up together. It would be difficult for me to separate who I've always known her to be from how the world may see her.

"What would you like me to do?" Observing others has always been one of my strong suits but spying is different. It feels intrusive. "I don't want to put them out while they're trying to concentrate on winning a kingdom."

Pouring two glasses of amber colored liquid from a carafe sitting on a shelf by the door, he hands me one and I cautiously take a sip.

Since coming to the fae lands, I've learned that every cup you are handed shouldn't be drank from. Not all intent is nefarious, but neither is it honorable.

I danced for two full days after the first time I wasn't careful enough with my actions. Ayxian found humor and Roxalus found displeasure in my foolish naivete.

When a courtier tried to get a bit friendly on the dance floor, I still remember the darkening glare of Prince Roxalus. He apparently didn't like the idea of someone with stature dancing with a simple lowbee.

Maximus would never do anything to me with food or drink, but the lesson is so ingrained in my mind now that it's hard to push pass without pause.

"This is precisely why I need you in this position. I need to know how they react to pressure. How they treat their subjects when there are obstacles. I need to know if their temperament's will be balanced enough to provide a just and fair rule."

We both sip the honey mead for another quiet moment, the sweetness edging off the sting of the alcohol.

Max has done so much for me in making my adjustment here tolerable, I can't be selfish and say no. Even if going into some of these courts unwelcomed will be uncomfortable.

Gods, Embla's will be horrible. She hates me already. That is one princess I'd like to avoid like a plague.

"I don't want you to do anything other than be yourself. And I must ask that you wear the necklace at all times." I started to ask why but he held up a hand to stymie my questions. "It's best that every fae in the kingdom be ignorant of the details until the Feast of Sol."

That doesn't sound ominous or anything. I trust that Max has his reasons though.

If he would have wanted to remain king, he'd have made an amazing one. But with missing out on Inara and Leif's lives until recently, he simply wants to be a good father and prince to the people of his own court.

With seven brothers and sisters, being the oldest and losing his mate along the way, Max deserves to be happy.

"So, all I have to do is live in these kingdoms for a month. Be myself. And attend the competitions at the end of each? Then you want me to move on to the next kingdom after each revelry?"

That seems easy enough. I know that it won't be. Not with Emenda and Embla. And most definitely not with Roxalus. A girl can dream though.

Taking another sip from my glass. The subtle hint of smokiness has been infused with the sweet honey undertones. I don't know how the fae make this, but it is divine.

"That's the gist. I need you to observe them, Piper. Just as they are. Just how they treat others... and you. You don't need to do anything else."

"Other than wear the necklace." Arching an eyebrow in his direction, he doesn't see it as studiously gazes out of the tall window at the back of the room onto the gardens below.

Chuckling softly, he turns back towards me. "Right there. That's the observing fae that I need you to be. Nothing ever escapes your scrutiny. I'm counting on it."

It's been a long day. The axe throwing competition, along with the number puzzle challenge, had both been entirely too early in the morning for my liking. I crave the sweet oblivion of sleep.

"Okay. I'm sure Emenda will be ever so accommodating this month." Taking the bottle from him and pouring another glass, the liquid stings with the long swig. The honey and smoke scent hits the back of my nose just as the sting catches in my throat. "You're going to owe me... big time."

His returning grin is reassuring. A silent promise. "I'm sure I will be paying you back for the next century to come. You'd better go get some sleep."

Heading towards the door, he stops before he gets there. "One other thing... if you, at any time, feel unsafe or need me right away, place your thumb on the back of the pendant. I will be alerted and teleport to your location. Only your thumbprint will activate the signal. It's just a safety measure but I wanted to make certain that you had a way out if you should need it."

"Thank you, my King."

Calling Max my king feels natural. I'd expected my human raised side to protest the formality when I'd first gotten here, but it doesn't feel awkward at all.

Max was born to be king. He doesn't want it, but that doesn't mean that he isn't great at it.

"I'm hoping to not need it, but it helps with my peace of mind." I won't use it except as a last resort, but that doesn't mean I'm not grateful for the *out*.

"Sleep well, Piper. The kingdom will be better for it."

Chapter Four

Waking up has never been my favorite thing to do, but the sun shining through the window of my enormous guest room in the Anavrin Kingdom Seat Palace helps ease me into the day.

The sky outside is a beautiful shade of blue, one that is not seen in the human realm. It is dazzling and has an opalescent sheen to it, almost like the magics in the air somehow shimmer in its very being.

I've gotten use to the weather being near perfect most of the time here. Anavrin is the Spring court, or so I'm told. That's a whole other can of worms to open later down the road.

If it rains, it does so in showers where the temperature remains mild, and the sky is never grey or dismal. This land doesn't get cold enough to snow.

Max and I had discussed the weather at length on one of my visits with Inara. He'd said that it will snow if the gods are stirring. It's only happened a handful of times in his long lifetime.

He and Eowyn lived together in the Lupian Forest and when he'd returned to the Kingdom seat to tell his father of their union, the king had thrown him in the dungeons for more than three decades.

She was not of royal blood. Worst of all, she was a descendant of King Zyoden's banished mistress, the First Witch, Mab.

Max spent thirty-seven years imprisoned under the castle. His siblings all thought he was missing or dead.

Other than King Zyoden, only Queen Leyashna knew where he was. She was helpless to give aid to her stepson, even though she wanted to with all of her heart.

After the first decade, the queen visited less and less often. Before his escape, she'd stopped visiting all together.

When he'd returned from the human realm after two hundred years, Elodie told him it snowed for two months straight a few years after he went missing. Then for over three decades Anavrin had become a winter wonderland.

After that, the weather turned warmer, but it rained for an entire year before returning to normal.

The gods must have had issue with King Zyoden placing his eldest son in the dungeons for asking to wed his mate. And it would seem they'd wept when she died too.

I put on my robe and slippers out of habit. Faeries rarely feel the need to cover themselves from prying eyes and the floor isn't chilly like I would have expected from stone.

The bathing chambers adjacent to my room hold a large tub, a chamber pot, a wardrobe full of beautiful dresses and several pairs of shoes, and a rather large vanity covered with the kind of make-up I've only ever heard about in fairytales when I lived in the human realm.

There was a bottle of perfume sitting next to the brush on the vanity with a bow and note attached.

Max is the sweetest uncle. It doesn't surprise me that he'd think of everything.

The scent is divine. I can't place the floral notes, but the spicy undertones are that of ground peppercorns.

As I reach for the note, I notice the rose that has been placed beside the bottle.

I hope you find this to your liking. May it compliment you in a way that I never seem able to.... X

What an odd note. No signature. Just an X. All of the male princes have an X in their name, so that's no help. If Max left it, he would have simply signed it Uncle, as he has in the past.

The rose was overly thorny, and I prick my finger the instant I pick it up. "Ouch!"

Sticking my bleeding finger into my mouth, I look around for something to bandage the wound but find nothing that will suffice.

Getting use to no paper or plastic products here has been a wakeup call, for sure. Books, tomes, and stationary are the only papery things produced here.

The bathing chamber door opens, startling me enough to drop the note. I'm still not accustomed to being waited on by the servants.

"Good morning, My Lady. King Maximus has sent me to attend to you." The handmaiden sets down a tray filled with fresh fruits, baked pastries, and...

"Yes!" Coffee, not tea. Thank the stars. "The king truly does spoil me."

Now my happy dance is in full swing inside my head. If I could climb inside this dark water and swim, I would in a heartbeat.

Tea is the beverage here for morning, afternoon, and evening meals. I need my coffee habit to keep me sane.

Max has seen fit to obtain a year's worth of coffee beans for me. Cutting my intake down to one or two cups a day hasn't been easy.

"Oh, My Lady," she sighs. "If I may speak freely?"

I'm still not used to being doted on but not allowing her to do her job is an insult, so I nod my affirmation, and she continues.

"King Maximus still grieves his mate. Finding his daughter and her family, it has brought him some semblance of solace. You are his extended family and as such, I believe he would grant you any comfort you wished." Lowering her eyes, she curtsies as if to soften any forwardness she may have shown.

I've thought about that too. I don't want Max to feel taken advantage of by anyone, let alone me for silly little things.

"What is your name?" It only feels right to address her with her given name, but she looks shocked that I'd asked. "I don't mean to ask for your true name," I say, shaking my head. "I only meant to know what to call you."

The fae guard their true names. If anyone knows the true name of a fae, they can use it to make them do their bidding.

She recovers her composure and grabs the brush off of the vanity. "I'm called Sienna, My Lady." Her smile is weary, but I try to give her my best smile in return.

"Alright, Sienna. How do you think I should wear my hair for traveling to Princess Emenda's kingdom?" Her smile falters for just a fraction of a second, but I see it. "Speak freely. I'm not use to all of this formality. I'm just a lowbee after all."

Her hands fly up to cover her mouth. "Oh, no My Lady. You mustn't say such things. You are revered by many throughout the courts. Including a few princes."

Heat rushes to the surface of my face and a pink blush creeps across her cheeks as well.

"I can't say that I feel worthy, but I certainly can say that I am not accustomed to Anavrin's class statuses. It all feels so fantastical."

I've lived in the forest my entire life. I've stayed with Inara a lot but mostly, I was contented enough to sleep in the den with the rest of my pack of werewolves.

Only Inara knew that I wasn't one by birthright. My cousin had taken me into her pack once she'd become alpha. After my mother and Aunt Eowyn had died.

I am the last living panther shifter, and I've suppressed that side of myself for longer than I've been a werewolf.

My mother's vision plagued my thoughts during most of my quiet time throughout the years.

The only thing that I'd overheard were a few clipped words as she'd told Aunt Eowyn. Something about a fae prince. A cage. And a war.

That's all I could glean before she'd caught me spying and chased me away. The next year, she was gone.

Aunt Eowyn said when the time was right, that she would tell me, but a few years later she'd died too.

Sienna slowed her braiding of my long, dark locks. "I couldn't imagine living in the human realm. I don't think that you realize how jealous of your strength they are."

Picking up a ribbon, her deft hands threaded it through the intricate braid twice. I'm thoroughly impressed with her work.

With a moment or two of silent thought, she lowers her voice conspiratorially. "I do believe that is why they refer to those who'd lived in that realm as lowbees. It gives them the illusion of power over their singular mind set."

Interesting. Frankly, that makes quite a lot of sense.

I don't trust the fae as a whole, but I have met many here with whom I feel a genuine connection.

I never forget their nature though. My nature... but this is now my home.

I am going to have to make friends at some point. Sienna seems like just as good a place to start as any.

"Thank you for your council. I will remind myself of that whenever I am feeling low."

Her lips turn up, and the pink color returns to her cheeks again. Making the servants blush has become an unintentional specialty of mine.

That thought brings a smile to my face. "You shall have to remind me whenever I falter in my recollections."

Sienna curtsies and takes the half empty tray from the room as she leaves.

A gentle breeze filters in through the opening in the curtains. A whisper of the morning dew kisses my skin as the sun shines across the open space.

Alone with my thoughts, my mind drifts to the perfume's note.

Who would like me enough to send it? If it wasn't Max, will accepting the bottle make me indebted to the gifter?

Stupid faery politics! Why do they make everything ten times more difficult than they need to be?

Checking my appearance one last time in the looking glass, I latch the necklace King Maximus has asked me to never take off around my neck.

The pendant settles low, nestling between my breast, close to my heart.

Flattening the wrinkles from my dress, I grab the cup of coffee as I make my way out the door.

Sienna packed a few containers of it in my bags. It will definitely be a long few months, but it will feel even longer with no magic beans.

Sighing a little at the thought of leaving, I close the door and don't look back.

Chapter Five

As I enter the main hall of the castle, Max stands with former Queen Leyashna.

Princesses Emenda and Embla are hunched over a fruit bowl to the side of the large entrance doors. With their heads bent towards one another, those cheeky bitches hide behind cupped hands, giggling every few minutes.

"Ah, Lady Piper. How lovely to see you, my dear," says the queen. "I hear you are to accompany Princess Emenda to her kingdom today."

Her hair is platinum blonde with pure silver strands mingled throughout. The pale color of her skin is a direct result of her introverted lifestyle.

It is well known around the lands that the queen mother loves nothing more than lying about on a comfortable chaise and losing herself in a book.

Over the many centuries, she'd sent fae servants to the human realm to retrieve books from every genre. So many books, that if she were human, she'd never be able to read them all in her lifetime.

As an immortal, she will chew through them within the next few decades and be craving new ones.

Since coming here, I've found out that the fae have only a handful of writers in all of Anavrin. Her supply of fresh material will become a problem in the future if more faeries don't take up the profession sooner rather than later.

While Max can cross the barrier into the Lupian Forest until Faelan and Inara come to live here permanently, it would be considered rude to ask royalty to play fetch.

The queen and Max are friends, so he might bring back a few anyway, but a few won't last long for a true bibliophile.

When I'd arrived, Leif had asked me what I would like to do. I honestly had no clue.

After living in the Lupian Forest and sleeping in the den for so long, it had never crossed my mind to think about a trade.

Food was readily available to hunt. Clothes weren't a problem because Inara loved to sew and make them.

I've never had to think about the constraints of living in society, but I've always had a knack for storytelling. Maybe being a writer will be a path that brings me joy.

When this competition is over, perhaps I'll give it a go.

Inara and Faelan will love that. They both love to cozy up to a good book. If I think it's good enough, they'll be the first to read my works.

At some point, they will be coming to live in this realm, too. The fae live for several millennia.

When everyone they know passes away, the plan is to assume residence here in Anavrin.

Faelan will bring her mate, Wylder, when she comes. With a soul bond, these lands will help him live an extended faery lifetime, or so I've been told.

With so much time stretching before me, I'll need to find something I can be passionate about. Life will get boring quickly if I don't.

Oh crap. She'd asked me a question, and my daydreaming got the better of me. Shit!

I hurry to answer. "Yes, Your Majesty."

Curtsying, I keep my chin low and eyes downturned. It wouldn't be proper for me to act as familiar with her as I do with Max.

"I look forward to seeing more of the realm. Princess Emenda's court will be a splendid place to start."

How I choked out those truths around the unpleasant feelings about Emenda herself confounded even me.

I've learned the omissions and word twists that make lying an artform. Without the ability to give false information, it's necessary to my survival here.

Emenda snorts and Embla's nose turns up in disgust. I can't understand why Max thinks my presence will matter in the prince's and princess's courts, but I will play my part.

Voices echo from behind us. The tall stone walls shimmer brightly, bouncing the sound from the floors to the cavernous ceilings and back.

Twisting my head around, Loxias and Noxian enter the foyer with Quill not far behind.

Being more observant than most, to me it seems Loxias' personal guard is obvious in his desire to be closer to the prince, but no one else around me ever notices. Maybe it isn't common knowledge.

Perhaps my gifts allow me to register what the others don't sense about Quill. Interesting.

I'll file that tidbit away for later. Maybe confer with Elodie? Get her thoughts on the matter.

"Your Majesties," Noxian inclines his chin towards the king regent and queen mother.

Looking my way, I don't sense any distain at my presence. He hasn't shown any since my arrival, and I don't know why I'm always waiting for it.

"Lady Piper." It is a surprise when he takes my hand and places a gentle kiss upon my knuckles.

I giggle. I actually giggle. It's just so... gentlemanly.

"Prince Noxian," I say as I attempt a decent curtsy. I'm not very good at it yet. "Are we all to leave the castle for our separate roads at once?"

It will be a day's journey for some, and a couple of days for others.

I'm supposed to spend the two weeks prior to each competition traveling to and being with each prince or princess before all of the others arrive at each court for the final two weeks. My nerves are a little frayed at the thought, but I'm doing my best to quell them for Max's sake.

The competitions always involve revels and feasts and merriment for days before and the evening after each event.

"It would seem so," Loxias says as he steps forward and kisses my hand as well. "Max wants us out of his hair apparently."

Looking at the king regent, a twinkle appears at the corner of his eye. This must be part of his secret plan.

If I was a less observant person, I would have missed the mischief that played there on his face.

The sound of servants reaches our ears and there are loud shouts from the corridor just off the foyer.

Ayxian and Roxalus are in a heated discussion as they round the corner.

Stopping their argument at the site of us all, Ayxian makes a beeline straight to me and Roxalus' features draw tight.

"Lady Piper. You are a vision of loveliness." He, too, kisses my hand.

I've become accustomed to this world a lot faster than I thought possible. From a forest sleeping wolf to a Lady of the court in basically a wink of an eye to the fae.

Though I still prefer running on all fours in my new panther form, fur for my coverings, it's nice to be seen as civilized here.

If I'm not careful, I'll forget the warning vision my mother had had.

I just wish I knew what it was about. Aunt Eowyn knew what it was, so perhaps she'd written it down in that grimoire Inara is so fond of.

Making a mental note to ask her to look next time I see her, I turned my focus to Princess Elodie as she enters the room.

Beautiful is an understatement. All fae are good looking, but her beauty radiates from within. It shows like pure white light.

Awestruck as I am, no one else looks at her like I do. Honesty and pureness radiate straight from her soul.

If I didn't know any better, I'd think she was a goddess trapped in a fae body.

Her smile lights up the foyer as she inclines her head my way.

I don't know the full extent of her gifts but how embarrassing would it be if she'd just heard me fangirling over her? Gah.

The longer I live with the fae, the tighter I try to hold on to those years I've spent in the human realm.

Slipping into a pattern of etiquette and out of a pattern of immodesty is the fae way. It creeps in on me from all sides. Worst of all, I find myself liking it.

Gone is the Piper of the Lupian Forest. I've shifted into a werewolf only once in the last several months. It took all of my concentration to achieve the task.

I have, however, shifted into my natural black panther form several times without any trouble. Sometimes I've shifted into it before giving myself the conscious thought to do so.

My mother would be so disappointed. She wasn't ashamed of our feline side. She just didn't want me using it because of whatever that stupid vision was that she'd had.

Finding out I was a faery and having to live among them now, I care less about her vision and more about learning my natural magics.

Whether that's due to coming here or because I am done hiding, I don't know.

All that I know was that no one is ever going to make me feel small again.

Outside of the royals, that is. Even the humans have that problem.

Roxalus watches Ayxian's and my exchange with pursed lips and rolls his eyes.

He watches me a lot actually. I've felt uncomfortable about that for long enough.

It's not in a creepy way but with not being able to read him, it always feels like a weight pressing down on my being when he's around.

This is my life now and I'll be damned if I am going to cower under his gaze, lowbee or not.

"Prince Roxalus," I say, watching his lip twitch at the sound of me addressing him directly. "It is nice to see you again." Arching his eyebrow, all I receive is a slight incline of his head. "Would you care to escort me to my carriage?"

Squirm princeling. It'll make my day. A true smile stretches along my lips. The thought of bringing him discomfort this time is a rush I'm not prepared for, and I nearly let a laugh slip out into the wild.

Dear Luna, what am I becoming? These fae have brought out all the little dark places in my mind and dance them to the forefront.

His eyes meeting mine hold me captive. "I would, My Lady," his rough, husky tone makes it clear he thinks the very proximity to me is distasteful. "But I must be off without haste."

I don't miss the glance in Ayxian's direction. With a quick bow to Emenda and Embla, he's gone without a backwards glance. Rude.

Elodie hooks her arm around my elbow and marches us towards the open doors. "We're losing daylight. Let's get this show on the road."

Giggling at her choice of words, maybe I'm rubbing off on her as much as the royals are rubbing off on me. I've never spoken so much in my lifetime as I have since coming to Anavrin.

It's refreshing and freeing to have lower inhibitions here. It's also scary as hell.

Without another word, we march out the front doors and to the waiting carriages.

Waving over my shoulder to Max, his returning smile falls as he turns back towards the hall.

That isn't what I'd have expected but perhaps he knows that my next few months won't be easy and that lays squarely on his shoulders.

Touching the necklace for a moment, I sigh with resolve.

Climbing inside the carriage and settling on one of the bench seats, I give one last look to the castle before the horses take off at a gallop.

Next stop, Emenda's domain.

Chapter Six

It's been a long day. We stopped only twice. Once to take lunch and once to stretch our legs and relieve ourselves.

Princess Emenda had pointedly ignored my presence each time.

My stomach is protesting loudly at its emptiness, growling with hunger. I long for a full belly, a bath, and a nice sleep.

The sky is in it's transition from day to twilight. As I step out of the carriage, a gentle breeze carries the scents of lavender to me from a field at the edge of the road.

The purple flowers against the backdrop of the orange and purple sky make the surroundings devastatingly beautiful.

My mouth refuses to close as I stare in awe. It's breathtaking.

Faintly aware of the princess's entourage making fun of me close by, I want to care but simply don't.

The castle isn't quite as big as I'd expected, given Emenda's ego, but it is still large.

Guards standing at the entrance, one hand on the hilt of their swords.

A small dip of their chin is all Princess Emenda receives, and I am ignored completely. If I look like a threat, they don't show their concern.

As we climb the front stairs, there's intricately carved woodwork along the railing.

It must have been done somewhere else and brought here afterwards. It's an inlay that is almost seamless.

The stone railing is exactly the right size to house the artwork, and it strikes me as odd they used wood rather than carved stone in this instance.

The effect is masterfully fluid, but I can't place why it stands out to me so much.

A soft, feminine voice drifts through my awareness, bringing me out of my musings. The servant must have been trying to get my attention for some time.

Her lips are pressed together against whatever sharp remark she wants to throw my way. I can also *feel* her anxiety.

Maybe it's because of how Princess Emenda keeps throwing glances our way.

"Lady Piper, are you well?" she asks since I still haven't replied to her out loud.

For so long, I've kept my thoughts inside. My voice only used to convey the bare minimum.

Here, in Anavrin, I've used my voice in the last six months more than I have for the last sixty or so years.

Being made to fill every silence with words has never been my forte.

Nodding in her direction, she prattles on. "As I was saying, my name is Amalie. I will be your handmaiden during the duration of your stay. If there is anything that you require, allow me the opportunity to assist you."

Clearly waiting for me to respond, I wonder if this is her first job. Her curtness is either a court trait or inexperience.

The she can't have been a handmaiden for very long. Her impatience sings out of her every pore.

The fae don't age like humans so it's hard to guess at her age, but something about her speaks of youth in the way she holds herself. The rebellion of a young adult blazes in her eyes.

"That is most kind, Amalie. I will be grateful to have you." My reply is with a genuine smile.

Her eyes sparkle briefly before recovering their outward appearance of indifference.

"If you'll follow me, I will get you all settled in, and we can change you into something more appropriate for dining with the princess."

At this, a tinge of annoyance settles in. I want to eat in my room and go to sleep. Of course, I can't just ignore the haughty princess like I want to. I have to play my part. Max is counting on me.

Shoving my retort down and inclining my head as acceptance washes over me, I plaster on that fake smile I've grown accustomed to using over the last few months. "Lead the way."

Without anything more than a half-assed semi-curtsy, Amalie begins walking. She never looks to see if I am following or not. Something could be said for the ignorance of youth.

Smiling internally at my *growth*, I find myself slipping more and more into my human realm ways, at least inside of my head.

Oddly enough, being in the land of faeries is bringing out my repressed side. Faelan would be proud.

The thought has me giggling into my hand and Amalie looks back at me over her shoulder. That's becoming an embarrassing habit but I kind of like it. It's just so wickedly fae.

My cheeks hurt from stretching my lips up so far. I give her a weak smile, but playful before she turns back around.

The kitchens must not be too far from where we are because the smells of fresh baked bread and some sort of stew permeate the corridor.

My stomach gives an enormously loud growl just as we reach my rooms. Amalie slides the key into the lock and enters without so much as a glance back.

I entered the smallish room a moment later.

It has only a tiny window that is too high up on the wall for me to see out of fully. The bed is what they would call a twin sized mattress in the human realm. There are no ornate carvings on the four poster columns or pictures on the wall.

Touching the bed and giving it a little bounce, it's soft and lush enough for a good sleep. A nightstand sits to the right of the bed.

The room is clean, and a fire blazes in the underwhelming fireplace, but it isn't a room fit for a Lord or Lady.

If Princess Emenda thinks I will complain about the accommodations, she will find herself sorely remiss in her assessment of me.

The Den isn't exactly a grand suite at the Plaza. Finery is something I have adapted to once I'd gotten here because it made Max happy, not because I needed it to make *me* happy.

There is a wardrobe in one corner and a vanity on the wall, just outside of the bathroom.

Venturing into the space, there's a chamber pot and tub too small to lay in. It's meant to be sat up in. No luxury here.

When I turn to come out, Amalie stands waiting for my reaction. I don't know if she is reporting to Princess Emenda or she simply wants to gauge my character.

"I do love a cozy sleep," I tell her. "And the kitchens close by will make midnight snacking so much easier."

From the way she tilts her head, only ever so slightly, I gather that she is trying to figure out whether or not I mean the words that I say.

"Amalie, do you think it would be possible to get a lantern that's bright enough to read by for my nightstand? I enjoy a good book before bed most nights."

The corners of the female's mouth turn up. If she was expecting me to through a fit, maybe that explains her shortness with me earlier.

I've discovered over the years that when expectations of anger or annoyance enter the mix, people tend to put forth a harder demeanor to counter them beforehand.

"Yes, My Lady." Her curtsy is deep this time. A smile still plays at the corners of her eyes. "I will see to it after we have you dressed and put you on your way. I wouldn't want that hungry tiger growling in your stomach to force its way out and eat me."

At this I laugh. I knew it had been loud, but I guess with fae hearing it must have been shouting; *Feed me!*

"We don't want that, do we?" After another moment, I say, "By the way, Amalie... it's not a tiger. It's a panther."

Her eyes widen at the remark but don't push for more information. I *feel* her admiration and find myself easily liking this young fae.

After a quick bath, Amalie helps me dress in a formal pastel blue dress. It has a modest neckline and tapered waist. The corset is tight, and I absolutely hate wearing them, but the royals do love their formality.

She helps me with my make-up and places my hair in a lose single braid that flows over the side of my left shoulder. After putting a few flowers throughout the braid, she steps back.

"You look radiant, My Lady." Amalie isn't dainty but she is feminine.

A genuine smile spreads across her face, and I smile back.

"You do good work," I say with a wink. "If I looked half this good back where I used to live, I don't think I'd have been single for too long of stretches as I was."

Walking a few steps behind, I follow her to the door. "If I may speak freely?"

"Of course, talk away." At that she giggled.

Yup. A fae trait for sure. The sound is like tinkling bells set off by a group of dark ravens.

"Princess Emenda isn't nice, but she can be kind. I think that the life she'd envisioned for Prince Roxalus makes her resentful. Faeries don't cope well with change. It's almost like dealing with death, a loss."

I took a moment, thinking through what she was saying. She could see that her princess had her faults, but she also could empathize with the *why's* behind those faults.

"Tha... that helps." I had started to say *thank you*. I learned the hard way early on when I got here not to make that mistake again. "I will keep it in mind during the course of my stay here."

Without another word, she leads us the way out and, while I appreciate her honesty, my nervousness at going down to the dining room churns through my system.

If I am going to make any difference in whatever plan Max has cooked up, I have to keep an open mind. I only hope that doesn't come at the expense of my newfound assertiveness.

Seeing these princes and princesses from their subject's points of view will be precisely the right strategy.

We walk down corridor after corridor, turn after winding turn, until we come to a halt outside of a grand set of double doors. These are as intricately carved as the art in the foyer. Absolutely beautiful.

When Amalie opens them, a grand banquet filled with courtiers sitting at a long table greets us. The room goes completely quiet and still.

At the head of the table, Princess Emenda sneers in my direction.

"Oh look, Lady Lowbee..." she spits the word and stops herself. Max's words from earlier must have had an impact. "Pardon, Lady Piper. How good of you to join us."

There is a lone empty chair that sits as far away from the princess as possible at the opposite end of the table.

"Have a seat. I'm sure you are starving for good company as much as food." Snickering to herself, she must have heard my stomach rumble when we'd left the confines of our carriages.

This is going to be a long month. "I would be honored, Your Grace."

Her lip curls at my addressing her back. My not letting her snips get to me ruffled her feathers.

Indeed, it was going to be a very long month.

Without further comment, I sit down a dig into the feast without any thought for manners.

As I chew, there's the drumming of fingers on the table over the cacophony of voices all around. It's so loud to my ears that I am surprised no one else has noticed.

Lifting my eyes from my meal to find the source, a pair of cold blue eyes stare back at me from the seat just to the right of the princess.

Prince Roxalus.

Chapter Seven

My first thought is that I am imagining things.

Why is he here? He isn't supposed to come to this castle for another two weeks, when the others will arrive too.

My second thought is that something nefarious is afoot.

He and the twins are close. They have that same haughty, better than everyone, air about them.

If Max sent me here to learn more about the princes and princesses individually, then this isn't a good way to start that journey.

Now that my attention is focused on the prince, his eyes light darkly.

"Perhaps my sister has underestimated how hungry you are, Lady Piper." Prince Roxalus' smirk belies the true nature of his concern.

I can feel the intent behind his words. There isn't any belittling of my appetite in his heart, but by all outward appearances, he was mocking me.

The princess's face beams with twisted delight at her brother's poking.

The courtiers around the table give little snickers and whisper behind their cupped hands. Any type of comradery that I'd felt with Amalie is lost on these fae.

Their mischievous ways and cruel merriment make my stomach churn.

To be fair, I had picked up a large turkey leg and was making a mess as I devoured the greasy bird.

Setting down the remaining bones and wiping my mouth on a cloth napkin, I take a long drink of my wine before I address the prince.

If I had been like any other human realm raised fae, maybe I wouldn't have bothered with semantics, but I've always been the quiet observer.

The less a person speaks or fills the silence with useless chatter, the more chance they won't lash out irrationally.

Smiling at the arrogant prince has its benefits. I wait for him to begin opening his mouth again before speaking, thusly cutting off whatever it is he's about to say.

"I won't deny my animal like feasting habits, Prince Roxalus." He arches an eyebrow, but I swear there is a smile in his eyes. "I rather love that side of my nature."

"Is that so?" he asks mirthlessly. "Do wolves even have use for utensils?"

I am beginning to loathe the way he looks at me. If he would just show his hand, let the resentment ooze from his heart, it would make life easier.

Not everyone in life is meant to like you. And once you figure out a person hates you, not putting effort in to trying to change their mind makes things simpler.

This fae, however much he puts on a front towards me, his heart doesn't match his efforts.

If my gifts hadn't *felt* his contradictory emotions, I may have believed his farce.

As it is, I can never get an accurate read on him. And that makes him extremely dangerous.

"Maybe they do. Maybe they don't." I hold my glass high in a mock toast. "As a panther myself, I have no ...... dog in that fight." I let the jest fall from my tongue as I turn towards the other fae at the table.

A gleam sparkles in the prince's eye. Whatever he had thought to say was lost in the next breath by the entrance of dozens of servants clearing away dishes and placing desserts along the long table.

Not to be outdone, Princess Emenda turns her attention my way.

"A panther, you say. I don't believe that I have ever seen a panther shifter." The taunt is there in her voice. She knows I am the last of my kind. My mother's declaration for me to become a wolf was the last brick in the panther shifters line. "Would you care to give us a demonstration?"

She poses it as a question, but it is most definitely a command. As the sovereignty of this court, I really have no choice but to do as she asks.

Standing and stepping away from the table, making sure that every single pair of eyes follow my movement, I begin running towards the princess.

Her scream is such a satisfying sound. Her terror pulls at my fae wickedness in a delicious tug.

Before I am ten feet from her, my shift is complete. My four heavy paws landing softly with a quiet thud in front of her.

Sauntering up to her legs and brushing my chin against her ankles, I scent mark her as I wind around her legs. That should really piss her off.

A panther's purr is said to calm even the most anxious of hearts.

The princess is putty in my hands as she reaches down and runs her fingers through the fur at the back of my neck. Fascinated and mesmerized, she lets herself forget who and what I am.

Snapping my large jaws in her direction, a pitiful cry escapes her lips.

Internally, I'm smiling, but I know I'm now on her shit list. Even more so than I was before.

A monarch can't be seen as weak. These fae are nothing if not wicked.

She knows it. I know it. And Roxalus, sitting there with the most irksome look on his face knows it.

"That's quite the parlor trick, Lady Piper." Her voice is strong, but I can see her hands still shaking.

After a few seconds, she returns to rubbing the fur just behind my ears.

Well played, Princess. Damn it.

Still in panther form, I stride towards my seat. Shifting back from one blink to the next, my nudity is on full display.

Pack life left me with no modesty. I am proud of my body and don't give a second thought to the glares of the courtiers around the room.

Perhaps it isn't proper etiquette for a royal dining room but the fae mischief side in me thrills in the exhibition.

Reluctantly gathering my scraps of clothes from the floor, I put them on quickly as best I can.

When I glance towards the end of the table, Roxalus face is torn between amusement and anger, and I'd be lying if I said that his attention didn't stir something deep inside.

Sitting back down, I dig into another spot of food. Shifting always makes me so hungry.

Roxalus' strange eyes darken slightly as he glares in my direction but that's par for the course from him.

I can't read his emotions clearly. With him, it's always a mix of things going on under the surface. If he's impressed, he doesn't show it.

Leaning over to whisper in his sister's ear, there's not an ounce of amusement or hospitality on either of their faces.

These two royals came to play a game, and I've just evened the odds. If I'd thought it'd make me feel better, my self-preservation doesn't know it.

Digging into my dessert, I give it my full attention. The cherries and cream burst in splendid flavor over my tongue.

Sweet with just a hint of tartness, the cream whispers a subtle breath of lavender that compliments the dish quite nicely.

Fully immersed in the magnificent concoction, the sound of someone clearing their throat draws my attention from the decadent three tier masterpiece.

Lost as I was in it, I hadn't heard anyone approach.

"Lady Piper." I look up from my plate and find the prince towering over me.

His dark, deep blue eyes give away nothing. There's a storm brewing behind them, but it's muted in the lines of his face. No smile. No smirk. Just a simple stoic blankness.

Holding out his hand to me, I take it without thinking. "Will you please accompany me to the study so that we may have a word?"

Wiping the cream from my mouth on the napkin, I stand in one fluid motion. I might not be regal, but I am still fae, and every courtier at the table is watching this exchange.

"I would be honored, Your Grace." It occurs to me that I've never been alone with Roxalus before.

A smidge of fear runs along my spine as I stand. He is known for his wickedness and his self-righteous attitude.

If he thinks I dishonored his sister, he might possibly want to punish me for the offense.

A shiver goes through me at the thought. But if it's fear or... excitement, I can't say.

We walk through the double doors and down a long hallway that leads to another set of double doors.

These ones are carved with intricate designs too. As if a story can be read through the pictures it depicts along the sides and ending in the center.

"What do these mean?" I ask as I run my finger over each carving.

When I look back, Prince Roxalus is staring at me with an intensity that brings goose bumps to my neck and back. "Forgive me, Your Grace."

He cocks his head to the side. I don't know what else to say. The silence is starting to feel awkward.

I keep my head bowed until he speaks again. The method has never failed me.

"You mustn't taunt Princess Emenda like that." He reaches a hand forward towards a piece of my hair that escaped its braid but stops short of touching it, curving it into a fist, dropping it to his side. "She will retaliate in ways that will be most unpleasant."

I'm shocked he'd taken his time to give me that warning. I'd have thought he'd enjoy in my suffering his spoiled sister's retribution.

After another moment, he pushes the doors open and walks inside, not bothering to see if I am following.

Arrogant sexy enigma. Brutality oozes off this male the way water trickles from a stream. Fluidly and beautiful.

When I enter the cavernous room, I realize the "study" is actually a massive library.

The smell of books and old tomes infused with leather and coffee wrap me in an immediate hug.

It has several large, arched windows that look out over the lavender fields I'd seen on the way in. In the moonlight, the gentle swaying of the flowers is a soothing lullaby.

Glancing around, there are bookshelves that reach the ceiling on both sides of the room. Comfortable looking chairs and couches all along the center.

It doesn't have that academic feel. It's more like an oversized, cozy reading room. Now I could understand why he called it a study and not a library.

"This is amazing," I blurt out. "I don't think that I've ever seen anything like it."

Still looking at every nook and cranny, I hadn't seen the look Roxalus wore right away... but I *feel* it now.

Turning around to face him, he's staring at me like I am some simpleton that has never seen splendor and doesn't know how to act.

Irrationally irritated, I come to stand directly in front of him. Probably not the smartest move but he brings out a wickedness in me that I've never let myself indulge in.

If I wasn't already feeling a bit out of my league, now that I am looking up at this royal, I might as well be as insignificant as a weed in a garden of roses.

"If you're going to continue to stare at me like a bug under your thumb, maybe I should retire to my rooms for the night." I don't know what else to say, as annoyed as I am.

Before I have the opportunity to make my escape, he leans down, wrapping his arms around my waist, pulling me close.

My breath catches in surprise. The small gasp of breath I exhale is all that hangs between us.

Taking my chin in his fingers and lifting my face to look at him, he brushes his lips to mine.

Chapter Eight

Shock reigns through my head and body. I pull away after a few seconds, taking a huge step back from his towering figure.

He looks as aghast at his own actions as I feel.

"Your forgiveness," he whispers in the fae way of an apology.

Dipping his chin and averting his eyes, the door opens, leaving me alone in the empty room without so much as a look back in my direction.

I am left standing in the middle of the room, with butterflies and stinging bees floating in my stomach, looking after the most perplexing individual that I've ever met.

In the time that I've let slip by unnoticed, a female figure assumes the space at which I was blankly staring.

Amalie must have been saying my name for a few minutes because she was now gently shaking me, worry lines appearing between her brows.

"Lady Piper, are you well?" There's a note of anxiousness in her tone. "I saw Prince Roxalus leave the room in a fluster. When you weren't responding to my calling, I became concerned."

It takes me a few seconds to realize that she's babbling due to fear. She thinks that I'll have her punished for shaking me.

I'm sad for her in a way I don't fully understand. The necklace over my heart warms briefly and pulses once before returning to normal.

"I'm fine, Amalie." She doesn't look reassured. "I promise. I'm exhausted and I need to get some sleep."

Heat floods my cheeks, and a smile tugs up the corners of my mouth. The embarrassment coloring my face works for her. Fae don't make promises unless they mean them.

And I am a fae. Even not knowing it before coming to Anavrin, their ways affect me all the same.

Adjusting the bodice of my dress, I follow her out the door and towards my small room by the kitchens.

The noise of clanking dishes and raucous laughter fills the corridor. The feast must have ended and now the cleanup crew is doing their part.

A smile plays at my lips as I think about how vexing it must be for Princess Emenda.

She thought I would complain about the room she assigned me. I didn't.

She thought that making me shift into my panther form would humble me. It didn't.

Then she nearly lost ground to fear in front of her own people when I'd snapped at her. I'm going to venture to say that put a bit of distance between her high horse and the ground.

If I was a betting person, I might be weary of what she will try next.

As it stands, I am actually looking forward to seeing her in her element, here, amongst her people.

If life has taught me anything, it's that there's a kernel of good in every soul. Just like there's a spot of wickedness too.

What you show to the world is whichever one you feed the most.

Amalie snuffs out all but one torch along the walls. Setting a night shift on the bed, she's turned the covers down and fluffed the pillows before coming over to help unbraid my hair.

It's never stopped astounding me how my hair goes back to whatever style it was in before I shift. Puzzling, really.

"May I speak freely, My Lady?" The softness of her young voice surprises me.

She'd been so boisterous and forward when I'd first arrived.

"Always speak freely with me, Amalie," I say. "I'm not one for politesse. I'm just Piper." Her cheeks blush pink.

"Okay, My La... Piper. In this room only." The handmaiden winked at me. "It's well known that Prince Roxalus is arrogant and wicked."

I wait for her to continue. I don't know if she saw what happened or if maybe she was guessing at his fleeing expression.

She hesitates again before finding her voice. "He is, but there's also a side to him that is loyal and cares for his people.

It isn't seen outside of his and the twin princesses' kingdoms often, but it's there."

Laying back in my bed now that she's finished with my hair, I crawl under the covers. The bed is soft and plush, even if it is smaller than the normal size meant for Lords and Ladies of the court.

"Why are you telling me this, Amalie?" If I'm going to fulfill Max's request, I need to listen to everything anyone will have to say about the royals, but that doesn't mean I'm not curious about why they feel the way they feel.

Lighting a lantern and placing it on the bedside table, she turns her back to me as she snuffs out the last lit torch on the wall.

"I didn't want you to think ill of him. You have the king's ear, and it appears that Prince Roxalus has taken interest in your part of this competition."

Unconsciously, I let my fingers brush along my lips. The feel of his barely there kiss lingering just under the surface. "Is that a good thing or a bad thing, do you think?"

In the low light coming from the lantern, it's difficult to see her expression. Not saying anything, she heads towards the door.

"What I think isn't important. What is important is that you get some sleep. I will bring you your breakfast at first light."

Wondering at the sudden evasiveness, I call to her before she can exit. "Amalie, where is the prince's rooms? I may want to avoid going in their direction if I wander the castle."

Not fooled by my words, her smirk says everything that haven't. "He's left, My Lady. He won't be back until the rest of the royals arrive for the next challenge."

With that, she shuts the door behind her, leaving me alone to my bewildering thoughts.

I don't know why I feel disappointed. Prince Roxalus is an enigma. A dangerous one at that. I would do well to steer clear of him.

So, why do I feel like that is exactly the opposite of what I want to do.

Chapter Nine

Amalie brings in my breakfast in the morning, as promised. I've only woken up a few minutes before I hear the tap on the door.

Still in bed, I stretch the ache from my muscles as she sits down the tray. It's filled with bacon, flapjacks, and a few fried eggs.

There's no coffee, but there is hot water brought for tea. Cream and sugar sit beside the kettle.

"Would you please get the bag of beans from my chest. I need to make my coffee."

If she doesn't understand what I mean, she doesn't let on.

Searching through the chest, she finds one of the bags of coffee beans, a French press, and the mortar and pestle I have to use to grind them.

Getting used to having no electricity has been the biggest change I've had to make since arriving in this realm. Max told me that magics interfere with electrics.

We had a solar panel for the few lesser comforts at the den and Inara's cottage ran with a full set of panels to provide electricity there.

Amalie watches on, fascinated by the process. Something in her wonderment tells me that she'll want to give it a go tomorrow.

Lips turning up in a grin at the thought, if I can get more people hooked into my obsession, perhaps I can convince Max or Faelan to bring a few coffee plants here to try and cultivate.

Then I'd be able to keep my addition alive throughout the centuries.

I'm find myself ever the more grateful that Princess Emenda has chosen Amalie to be my handmaiden.

Even if she did it because she thought that a young, under trained one would peeve me, the reason behind her gift won't diminish the value of it.

After I add the cream and sugar, handing it to her. "Would you like to try some?"

Taking it without reservation, her lips curl up into a mischievous smile. If I knew her better, I'd say she thinks we're doing something we aren't supposed to be doing. Wicked little fae, this one.

As the first sip caresses her tongue, a twinkle sparkles in her eyes, lighting up her entire face.

It's how I feel every single time I drink these magic roasted beans.

"It's delicious. I've never tasted anything quite like it." She tries to hand the cup back to me, but I motion for her to sit down on the edge of the bed as I make myself a cup in the smallish bowl the eggs came in.

Her eyes widen when I dump the eggs and bacon on top of the flapjacks. Maybe they don't do that sort of thing here, but I have no etiquette when it comes to my grub. The faster it goes in, the better.

"That cup you're holding wouldn't be big enough for my addiction." To that, I earn a giggle. Her twinkling laugh is like sunshine on a rainy day.

I can *feel* all of the goodness she has within her soul, and it makes my heart happy to be the one to bring out that small amount of joy.

After finishing my breakfast and coffee, Amalie helps me get dressed. When she bends down and slides a knife sheath up along my thigh, I gasp in surprise.

She holds out the hilt of an exquisitely decorated blade. It has the elegant scroll of the fae language on it.

I've been attempting to learn it since my arrival, so I recognize the symbols for strength and sureness. The handle is plain wrapped black leather.

"You can never be too careful around the royals, My Lady." I've told her to speak freely, but I didn't anticipate how her forwardness would make me feel so exposed.

I nod, not trusting myself with the hundreds of questions that are flittering around my head.

Taking the blade from my hand, she quickly bends again to put the knife in its sheath. After straightening back up, she takes one look at my bed head and tsked.

"Did you not sleep well, My... Piper?" Grabbing the brush from of the vanity, her hips sashay as she makes her way back over to me. I like her renewed confidence. I must have imagined yesterday's evasiveness about the prince.

With deft hands, she pulls my hair in several directions. Her quick fingers move through my messy nest with small tugs of the brush.

After an ample amount of some sort of cream, the finished product is amazing.

The looking glasses here aren't quite like the mirrors in the human realm. They are a magic enhanced stone that shows your image back to you the way the others see you.

It was extremely disorienting at first. I'd tried to put on a spot of make-up using the inverted stone when I'd first went to Ayxian's court. I hadn't wanted to trouble any of the hand-maids or maidens.

Having not been a make-up wearer back in the forest, it looked as if a painter, with only the notice of how a face looked, had slathered my face for my funeral.

It proved harder than I'd expected to match my hand up to the correct eye and my lips felt out of place as I'd attempted to smear the lip color on.

After that, I called in one of the waiting handmaids. They snickered but did a splendid job fixing me up proper.

When I went back to Max's court with Leif, I didn't bother with the face paint anymore. No one seemed to care if I was made to look regal or stayed smudge faced from digging in the gardens.

Amalie did a great job on my hair. The intricate braiding is beautiful. There were many thin strands wrapping individually into braids and then those braids were braided into one long one that was swept to the side of my head.

She made a tiny circle of small wispy braids at the crown of my head that holds a few lavender flowers and baby's breath. It's an elegant display. Her work exquisite.

"It looks wonderful. Your skills are amazing." My praise beams through in her radiant smile.

With one final look at my appearance in the looking glass, we walk out the door to face the day.

Taking he long way around the castle to see the sights, I can't help but marvel at all of the fine craftsmanship. All of the decor is lovely.

Beautiful paintings hang on most of the walls between each stretch of corridor. Glassless windows let in light and gentle breezes as the scent of lavender infiltrates the cold stone of the castle walls.

We finally arrive at the front doors and this time I do linger to admire the designs that run up and down the entire foyer.

"It's awe inspiring, isn't it?" Amalie grins. "Every piece. Every design. Each one overseen by my Princess. She loves when her people thrive in what they do. That's why she has so many different artist's works throughout the building."

"It's incredibly beautiful. The entire castle is a work of art." My voice must hold all of the emotions I feel because when I look to my handmaiden again, tears rim her eyes.

Sometimes, I forget how my gifts affect others. I don't just *feel* other people's emotions. I can *inspire* or *incense* their feelings with my own.

I spent months working with Max on how to control that particular part of my gift.

Inara, on the other hand... all my best friend offered in the way of advice was to keep my lust contained until I *really* wanted to use it.

Gah. I hadn't even thought about how that could be... interesting.

Leif often took the brunt of my blunders those first few months when I'd arrived back from Prince Ayxian's court.

He was patient and caring but if I were angry or upset, he'd feel that emotion as his own and would storm about the place until I'd realize it was my influence that needed reined in.

Inara found that part hilarious when I'd told her. She and her newfound brother had already taken to the sibling dynamic withing a few short months.

They'd bicker. They'd laugh. They learned quickly to love and protect each other too.

I am happy for her. She's been my best friend since childhood. Not jealous at all.

Okay, maybe a little bit.

The fact that she is currently a fae princess who runs around the Lupian Forest as a wolf and is an endless source of entertainment to some of these crass faeries notwithstanding.

She's taken it all in stride when she visits. Mostly.

Until one afternoon, when we'd been visiting the kingdom seat together instead of Max's princely court.

A group of courtiers snickered as we'd walked through the dining area. My nerves were frayed from an encounter a few days prior.

With my anger at the forefront, I'd accidentally insighted her with my own unchecked emotions.

She'd lunged, shifting between one blink and the next, straight at the courtiers. Teeth snapping an inch from the face of a snobbish Lord.

Max had rounded the corner just as she'd lunged. Catching her wolf form around the middle, he had teleported them back to where I stood, ten feet away.

Inara teased me repeatedly for that instance for weeks afterwards. It was her way of getting me to work on my behavior and my gifts.

It had been the kick in the ass I'd needed to get myself under control. And I loved her for her gentle pushing ways.

Looking now at the emotions filling Amalie, I realize I've unintentionally let loose the restraints on my gifts in my state of oblivious admiration.

Reining them back and locking them tightly behind that imaginary door I've built in my mind, she regains her composure.

Linking my arm with hers, we walk out into the fresh air.

As much as I dread what's to come next, it's time to face the princess.

Chapter Ten

As we round the corner where the other courtiers are milling around, Amalie falls a step or two behind me.

Adverting her eyes from their looks, she acts every part of a well-trained handmaiden. She is going to do great at her position when they finally give her a chance.

Her youth isn't an issue, like I had first considered. There has to be some other reason the princess assigned her to me. Possibly to annoy me with her forwardness.

Ha! If that was the case, I'm glad her plan had backfired.

Some of the other courtiers notice our arrival. A few Lords bow slightly, and Ladies give a casual dip as I walk by them, but no one approaches.

Looking around to see if I can spot any friendly faces, I can *feel* their unease. Plenty of false smiles and curious looks, but not one of these fae tries to make me feel welcome.

If that's the princess's doing, I will simply have to be extra charming.

A niggling voice sounds in my mind. I've not heard it very often since coming here, but it used to be my constant companion. It's one that developed around the time I started needing a sounding board to counter my mischief when I'd first joined Inara's pack.

Maybe they are a tiny bit afraid of the panther with large teeth and snapping jaws who rushed their princess.

Well Damn. Perspective's a bitch, huh?

The thought hangs in the forefront of my mind for another few seconds.

It makes sense. If these fae actually do care for Princess Emenda, I can see their point.

I'm getting ready to turn and leave the area, maybe to head to that study Prince Roxalus had shown me or perhaps to take a stroll in the lavender fields, when two males approach me cautiously.

Of course, both of them have that faery beauty, but something about them sticks out andI can't put a name to it though.

"Ah, Lady Piper," the dark-haired male says. He's the more regal of the two. "It is a pleasure to meet you."

It's straight forward. No tricky wording or taunt to his tone. Since fae can't lie, I take that as a good sign.

"I am Lord Davian. And this is my mate, Nydin."

Nydin dips his chin but never takes his eyes off of me as he kisses my proffered hand.

"It's a pleasure to meet you both." I look at Nydin again and see that his body is leaning, ever-so-slightly, in front of Lord Davian.

Realization smacks me in the face. He sees me as a threat. Interesting.

I so rarely feel like a force to reckon with. That's how I see Inara... but me? I've only ever played as a backup character in my own life's story.

Giving him a conspiratorial smile, I wink. "I wouldn't know the protocol to deal with a lowbee like me either."

Lord Davian rolls his eyes at his mate, and I giggle. Their relationship is so lovely that an ache forms behind my ribcage.

I can *feel* their mating bond. It's been accepted and made whole. It's like two sides of an electric cord, connecting in the two spots where the length of cords touch, making them a complete circuit.

There's also some kind of tattoo on Nydin's forearm. When Lord Davian notices my perusal, he rolls up his sleeve and shows me his. They aren't the same, but they do match. Mating marks. They're beautiful.

"I must confess, Lady Piper. I was the one who wanted to meet you. Nydin advised against it." His mate looks at him like he's thrown him under the bus.

I suspect that Lord Davian is simply taken with my charms, as Max says, and doesn't see me as a threat the way the others do.

"Oh my. Nydin, I promise not to harm you or Lord Davian." Promises made by fae are worth something. Binding.

I don't fully understand the magics, but I've felt their tug when I've accidentally invoked them.

Nydin straightens and gives me a weak smile. "You can never be too careful when dealing with a powerful fae."

His words flash brightly in my mind's eye, warming my chest.

All of these fae believe I'm powerful. I've shifted and approached their princess without hesitation.

Now I am getting it, why they are being so stand-offish. I've acted like a wasp in their beehive.

"I assure you; I am not all that powerful. I didn't even know that I was a faery until coming to Anavrin with the rest of the human realm dwellers."

This doesn't have the impact I think it will as Nydin glances over at his mate and Lord Davian gives a small nod.

Had I not been so observant, I would have missed it.

"Then you are a fast learner, My Lady." Lord Davian's smile conveys sincerity. "It takes some of our kind more than a few decades to control their abilities as masterfully as you've displayed since arriving in our court." Gesturing towards a path, he asks, "Would you care to take a walk in the gardens with us?"

Turning to tell Amalie I'm going with them, she's nowhere in sight. Well, goodbye to you too. Geesh.

Facing the two males again, I nod pleasantly. "That would be lovely, Tha..." I almost thanked a faery again. Ugh. "Shall we?"

Lord Davian's smile is just as wide as Nydin's at my faux pas. "You learn quickly, my dear. I'm glad to see it."

We head towards the inner gardens. The pleasant scent of the lavender blooms waft through the air, filling me with an uncanny sense of calm.

The weather is perfect, as usual. Not too hot. Not too cold. Sunny, but enough big, puffy white clouds to cast teasing shadows over the whole of the land.

Reaching the center of the fields only takes a few minutes. There are courtiers, servants, and commoners throughout the fragrant flowers.

They're all enjoying picnics, taking walks between the rows, or chatting by a gazebo that I only just now notice. And perched on a plush swing on in the center of the gazebo sits Princess Emenda, laughing.

Her subjects aren't giving her the space that etiquette usually dictates for someone in her position. And it *feels* like... they are genuinely delighting in her company.

If I hadn't seen it with my own eyes and felt it with my own gifts, I'd have never believed it.

Once she spots me, her laughter stops. The others around her turn and spot me too.

Lord Davian and Nydin gently steer me in her direction. I don't dig my heels in, but I'm not exactly rushing to her side.

"She won't bite, Lady Piper," Lord Davian leans down and whispers. My fae hearing doesn't miss the amused sound in his tone. "She's actually a pleasant person. If only you'd show her your charming side, I wouldn't be surprised if you became the fastest of friends."

With a quick wink, he ducks out from under my glare. Nydin smiles but follows his mate up to the gazebo.

"Your highness." Lord Davian bows at the waist and Nydin's bow is even lower.

These two males like her. Genuinely like her. They liked me too. That must mean something, right?

I guess it doesn't matter. I'm here to help Max. I need to keep an open mind, whether I want to or not.

Still staring at the mates, trying to figure out what made them stand out to me when I first saw them, it hits me in the face like a branch swinging back as you walk down a trail in the forest. They truly, whole-heartedly love each other.

I've never met a mated pair before. Max loved Aunt Eowyn but I didn't realize that was true for all mates.

I'd often thought of it as not having a choice in who you were meant to be with. As a shackle that the fates threw to you in case you wanted to embrace amplifying your magics.

It's so obvious now that I'm looking at them standing in front of their sovereign. They emitted it in their aura.

My gifts felt the pull towards them before my mind had caught up. It was telling me that there's goodness here.

With a sigh, I begin my walk towards the gazebo like I'm heading to the gallows. The princess is watching my every step. Stopping a few feet shy of the steps, my curtsy is as sincere as I can muster.

Open minded. That's how I'm going to have to approach these next few months. Better start now.

"Lady Piper. How nice of you to join us." She sounds anything but pleased. "I wondered if you'd find your way to me today."

She never intended for me to see her being so carefree with those around her.

I realize that a moment before I open my mouth. Pursing my lips to trap the smart retort that pushes at the back of my teeth, I refocus.

The king needs me to see the royals as they are, not how outsiders perceive them.

With that thought held tight to the forefront of my mind, I begin again.

"Princess Emenda. You look as lovely as always." Her eyes tighten at my words, no doubt trying to decipher any hidden meanings.

There are none. She is beautiful. "I am so honored to be a guest in your lands. My room is perfect for late night snacking. You are most gracious."

Trying for my best smile, I let sincerity seep into my eyes.

A tinkling laugh meets my ears. Looking up at her fanning her face, she takes a sip from the iced tea in her glass before she speaks. "You truly mean that, don't you?"

Maybe there is some claim to Max's nonsense about my winning charms. Maybe it's a hidden gift that I've yet to understand. Either way, I'll use it to my advantage whenever I can.

"I do. I am grateful for the cozy room and your selection of handmaiden." Inclining my head towards her, I put as much feeling into those words as I can.

Standing from the swing, she descends the steps gracefully. Looping her arm through mine, she draws us to walk back towards the fragrant purple plants.

"You know, I wasn't sure what to make of it when Max decided to send you to each of our lands before each competition." Keeping quiet, I let her talk. "I thought that he was planting a seed of discord, you being from the human realm and all."

Stopping mid-step, I raise an eyebrow, but still say nothing.

If talking is a rope, then genuine people use it as a lifeline while disingenuous people hang themselves on its length.

"Oh, don't give me that look. If you were still in the human realm, running around with the wolves, and your pack leader brought a faery in to *just observe* without telling you why, I know you would have the same misgivings."

Her words strike a chord. Looking at it from her point of view, I can picture exactly what she's talking about. Facts are the truth, but perspective always plays its role.

Maybe if I let her see *me*... not as a lowbee, not as a fae coming to her land to steal homes and jobs from her people.

As an actual living, breathing soul with thoughts and feelings. Just maybe she'll be more inclined to show the same warmth and compassion to me that I glimpsed from her earlier with her people.

Thinking over my next words carefully, I choose the only ones that will matter.

"Princess Emenda, I had a life outside of Anavrin. I was ripped away without any warning. Starting over in a strange land with a species I was taught to avoid wasn't some decision I'd gotten to make... but I *am* making the most of it."

I have to give her credit. She's actually contemplating what I am telling her. I can *feel* my words stirring within her heart and mind.

With an exaggerated sigh, I press my luck that she'll listen and take in what I'm saying. "The lowbees, as some of you have referred to us, are just lost in a sea of uncertainty. We're not trying to gain anything that isn't earned or given freely." Looking her in her beautiful face. "Can't you please just let us try to find our way without prejudice?"

"Do I come off that bad?" The impishness in her tone makes my heart thump. "I have lived a privileged life for its entirety. I love my subjects, Lady Piper. Sometimes I forget that all of Anavrin are my people." I let her continue so I can see how that rope will be used. "I know that being queen will mean representing all fae. I will try my best to push my biases aside."

Huh. I'd hoped, but I didn't truly expect this level of metanoia.

Her sister won't be pleased by it. That much, I'm sure of. They may have nearly the same face, but Embla's attitude towards commoners and lowbees is ingrained deep within her character.

Smiling at her feels more natural now that I can feel her heart ring true with her words. "That's all I'm sayin'."

It's her turn to raise an eyebrow at my human realm sarcasm.

A tinkling of laughter meets my ears again and I realize we have an audience. We walked in a circle and came back to the gazebo without my noticing.

Lord Davian, Nydin, and the other courtiers are lounging on benches and poufs, sipping tea and cocktails, and chatting easily with one another.

At our approach, all heads swivel in our direction. "Well, make room. Lady Piper and I would like to have lunch here on the swing."

Servants scurry and courtiers glance between the two of us. That's all of the approval they need for me to be welcomed into the fold.

More and more come forward to introduce themselves or give the princess the local gossip.

And oh my, does she like gossip. The mischief beams from her eyes with every new detail she receives.

The afternoon flies by in a pleasant blur. The beautiful weather with the gentle breeze continually drawing the scent of lavender through the air, keeps my mind pleasantly serene.

I've eaten my fill of cucumber sandwiches and drank more butterfly pea tea than I have ever before. And after my third helping of croissants drizzled with lavender honey, I am ready for a nap, but I'm not ready for the afternoon to end.

As the sun begins to set, I feel the weight of the pendant at my neck. It's nestled above my heart and every once in a while, its metal will warm or cool.

It's mostly when the princess does or says something clever or mischievous.

I can't be sure if the king regent's goals are going as plan, but then again, I'm not supposed to be "in the know" anyway.

That day's events carried on throughout the next couple of weeks.

More days lounging by the gardens. More genial conversations with a rascality to their undertone. More lighthearted *feelings* floating through me from the fae about their princess.

Lord Davian and Nydin sit amongst us nearly every day. I've felt friendliness, if not acceptance, with several of those who've hung around us throughout the two weeks since I'd arrived.

A note came on the twelfth day by way of a messenger whose enormous dragonfly like wings were a fantastical sight to see.

The other royals will be arriving over the next two days.

The competition won't be straight forward. Max and his fae deviance never fail to make me giggle at these events.

There will be a poetry reading from each royal. They must write their own words with no outside help. The poem must be about what being a ruler means to them.

As odd as it is, I can understand why the king set them this task.

We are about to see how much their tempers will stir and how high on their priorities list following rules are.

I wonder if it is as obvious to them as it is to me.

Chapter Eleven

Princess Embla is the first to arrive. Her entourage is fairly small, about twenty people. That's still a lot of accommodations if each of the other seven royals bring that many.

The commoner fae throughout Anavrin who travel to the courts for the competitions either stay at one of the inns or with family or friends.

She's brought seven trunks of personal items. Each fae with her had been allowed only one trunk.

It makes me wonder at how her subjects feel about that. Is her vanity the main seat of her reign?

Twins usually have similar personalities, likes, and dislikes. I hate thinking Princess Embla might not be as loved by her own people as her sister is.

"Lady Piper," she says with a sneer the moment she catches me staring. "How good of you to be on the welcoming committee."

Princess Emenda comes up behind me before I have a chance to retort. That's probably a good thing.

The longer I'm in this land, the more prone I've become to making sarcastic remarks before thinking them through.

I'm beginning to understand Inara's granddaughter, Faelan, a lot better. Wicked quips and all.

We'd always thought that shifters lived an extended life simply because of the magics. Our family had been gifted extended lives beyond that. *Blessed genes*, Inara would say.

When Faelan discovered that our family was full-blooded fae, it all clicked into place.

I'd spent many hours turning over the events of the last months leading up to me arriving here. Everything fate had lined up. Every nudge and hint along the way.

Inara being a grandmother in the first place made me tease her mercilessly over the years.

We're the same age... old, but neither of us look more than a few decades at most. I would razz her endlessly for the glamour she used to wear before Faelan found out she was a shifter... well, fae.

That elderly old lady get up was a sight the rest of the pack found infinite hours of entertainment in.

Apparently, Faelan's sarcastic wit is a family trait that I am grasping with both hands now.

With all of the years I have stretching before me, there's no way I'm going to make myself small again.

"Sister, don't be catty. Lady Piper has been a most enjoyable guest during her stay here." The twins exchange a look that I don't understand but in the next moment, it's hidden away behind false smiles.

Princess Emenda hasn't been mean or bitchy to me since that first day.

I know there have been jokes made at my expense while we were gathered each day, but there were jokes made at everyone else's expense too. It was the fae way.

Now that Princess Embla has joined her, I suspect her kindness may not continue to be genuine.

That thought brings a touch of sorrow to my heart. We aren't the best of friends, but over the course of the last couple of weeks, I'd begun to let myself believe that she actually liked me.

Keeping my guard up is exhausting. Perhaps that's all I can expect from this new life now. Fake feelings and a weary soul.

No, damn it! I'm not going to let negative thoughts or people make me into someone I'm not. Shake it off.

I am the girl who tries to see things from every angle. I am the person who found kinship with a pack of werewolves. I am a fae who is no longer afraid to claim her birthright as a panther shifter because of some vision that my mother had.

Keeping my chin high, I reply with a bit of playfulness. "Princess Embla has every right to be catty, Princess Emenda." I winked at her. "After all, it's a large cat that's said to be queen... pardon me, king of the jungle."

The courtiers around us gasp and whisper behind their hands. Lord Davian and Nydin give a small laugh.

Princess Embla looks at her sister to see if she should take what I said as a threat. The smallest of chin dips tells her that yes, she should and I can't be more pleased.

"Well, aren't you a clever one." Princess Embla sounds as if she actually means that. There's a spark igniting in her deep ocean blue eyes.

Before she can make any farther remarks, another carriage pulls up in front of the castle.

The sight of Prince Loxias makes my heart race involuntarily.

He was the Hunter of my worst nightmares for so long when I lived as a wolf shifter. The thing that all creatures living in the Lupian Forest were weary of. He hunted magical beings for sport back then.

Since coming to Anavrin, not once has he been cruel or even interested in me. My trepidations are of my own making.

The fact that he'd been the one to hunt Faelan down and drag her back here to face the former king brings me undue anxiety and puts my body on high alert in his presence.

Max told me once that Loxias had looked up to him in his youth. He'd missed him terribly in his absence. And that him being Inara's father, and Inara being my best friend, would endear Loxias to me.

I hadn't believed it at the time. I still have to remind myself that he's not the hunter anymore, but honestly, he's a really likable guy.

I should be giving him the benefit of the doubt. Damn logic... always making things clearer than I'm ready for them to be.

"Princess Emenda, Princess Embla." His curt nod holds no familial warmth. Catching sight of me, his lips stretch into a wide grin. "Lady Piper, I see you have fared well here in your time amongst these thorns."

There's a distinct impression that his words are more of a jab at the twins than they are a compliment towards me.

"I have, Your Highness. Princess Emenda has been a pleasure to have as company." There's a slight warming in the necklace as he takes in my reply.

Embla looks at her sister with unrestrained disgust, but Emenda gives both me and Loxias a faint smile.

She either doesn't want to disappoint her sister, or she is still trying to play the game she knows Max has in play.

Either way, I'm grateful when Lord Davian hooks his arm in mine and addresses the elephant in the room.

"Prince Loxias," he says with a bow of his head. "We're glad to have you here. If I may be so bold as to ask, what have you chosen to do with your time now that you are not permitted to hunt the trophies in the human realm any longer?"

Giving my arm a gentle squeeze, it eases some of the tension I'd allowed to fill me since the prince's arrival.

"Oh, I still hunt." My eyes widen but his eyes crinkle with a smile playing at his lips. "Only now I hunt for my other half. There will be nothing stopping me from finding my mate." He winks in my direction and a small laugh falls from my lips unwillingly.

I've never glimpsed this side of him before. A weight truly was lifted from his shoulders after Faelan broke the curse that her great- grandmother, Max's mate, had put on the fae.

It was one that blocked the bonding of mates. And with Aunt Eowyn's curse now gone, Loxias appears to be a renewed male.

The sound of hoof beats growing closer draws our attention away from the moment.

There is no carriage, and the entourage is small. The lead horse stands a full foot taller than the rest of the other eight in the party.

As they get closer, I can see why.

Prince Ayxian sits upon the saddle of the massive steed. His hulking form diminishes the horse's size to that of a normal one as they approach.

It's fitting that his ride be oversized. The male is a specimen of broad shoulders and corded muscles.

When he jumps down, the others in his party follow suit, but only he approaches our gathered group.

There is an arrogance to his features that I hadn't noticed before. A way to how he looks down on those around him. I don't even think he is aware that he's doing it.

"Sisters, brother." That's all of the greeting that they receive before he strides past them, takes my hand, and brushes a chaste kiss across my knuckles. "Lady Piper. I've missed your company."

Taking my hand back as nonchalantly as I can, I give the prince a small, clumsy curtsy.

Emenda snickers and begins speaking to Embla in whispers behind her hand. Even with my fae hearing, I can't make out what they are saying.

As it is so often with twins, they have their own language.

"How lovely, Prince Ayxian." My mind still too focused on the twins.

Nydin pokes me in the ribs from a step behind and I realize he's trying to discreetly prompt me into giving the prince a more regal greeting.

My curtsy isn't a gracious bow but a meager, barely there dip. "Your absence has been felt as well."

There's no way for me to say that I'd missed him too. I'd been enjoying myself in Emenda's court and hadn't given him much thought. Fae can't lie but we can speak circles around the truth.

When I'd first arrived in this realm, Ayxian showed me around, trying to make my transition easier.

Quickly figuring out for myself that his attentions were geared more to his goal to win the crown than he was in putting in the effort with me.

We'd kissed a few times, but I'd remembered Inara's words with perfect clarity. *"If a person wants you, then they want all of you. And if they want you to change something about yourself or you are not their priority, they're not the one."* She'd been right, of course.

That's when I left his court and went back to live in Max's, which is currently being run by his son, Leif, while he's in the kingdom seat castle.

Max had recently discovered Leif was his son around the same time as he found out he had a daughter with his mate.

Inara has a brother. She and I are closer than sisters, even though she is my cousin. Once I'd come to that crossroads in my head, the only logical step was to get better acquainted with my bonus brother.

"I find you a refreshing breath of clean air in this land." Ayxian gives his sisters a look that says it's a jab at their leadership. Offering me his arm, he asks, "Would you like to show me into the castle?"

I start to give him a reply when I hear a disdainful huff of laughter. I hadn't even noticed the approach of a lone rider. No one had.

Prince Roxalus sits high in the saddle of a beautiful black stallion, looking down on us all. It's a magnificent sight against the backdrop of the powder blue sky.

"And why would Lady Piper deign to do that? Surely, even a doltish brute, such as yourself, can find their own way to a building right in front of them." His tone is sardonic, but his eyes hold a note of true pondering in their depths.

I'm not sure if he's upset that Ayxian is touching me or if he is razzing his brother because I am a lowbee and seen as lesser by many of the fae.

The last time I had seen Roxalus, he'd been fleeing the study after our unexpected kiss.

Now that we are out in the fresh air and daylight shines all around, I can't fathom what had made us succumb to our entanglement.

Except... there is an allure to him I can't shake.

There's that inner voice again. Loud and clear. *Surface level princes are not worthy of your attention. You deserve depth.*

Giving my head a little shake, I address Roxalus before Prince Ayxian has a chance to reply. "Oh goodie. Prince Roxalus has arrived alone and not a moment too soon to save me from the pleasant conversation with the handsome prince on my arm."

Lord Davian snickers from behind me and Nydin kicks the back of my shoe. Some of the gathered courtiers gasp.

Before I can shrink from the improper comment I'd made to a royal, Loxias laughs. His entourage following along.

Only his right hand, Quill, shows any concern for the prince's safety. From what I understand, Roxalus had been cruelest to him out of all of the royal siblings in Max's absence.

I should probably feel guilty about addressing a royal family member like it's my right, but with Ayxian's well-muscled arm linked in mine, I can't muster a single bit of fear.

Besides, there is something about Roxalus that pulls at me. Placing him in the friend or foe category is blurred whenever we are in close proximity.

There's that voice again. *Don't be so quick to make choices that can strangle a kingdom.*

"Princess Elodie, Prince Noxian, and King Maximus aren't due to arrive until tomorrow," Emenda hurries forward to take control of the situation. "Shall we all freshen up before dinner?" She gestures towards the open front doors.

It is her courtyard, her small part of the kingdom. She doesn't want to appear weak in front of her subjects.

The fae and the games they play have me rolling my eyes most of the time. If we had been in the middle of my stay alone with her, she'd have laughed along with Loxias.

The calming scent of lavender dances pleasantly on the gentle breeze, reminding me to keep an open mind as well as a level head.

Sighing, I draw my eyes away from the still staring Prince Roxalus. Turning my body fully to face Ayxian now, a huge false smile plays at my lips.

He doesn't see anything amiss and smiles down at me with a genuine one. "Shall we?" Even though I know all of the fae present can hear me just fine, I make my voice loud enough to carry. "I do hope that you will save me a seat at dinner. I would love to catch up."

As we walk towards the door, I swear I hear a faint growl.

Chapter Twelve

I didn't take Princess Emenda up on her offer to *upgrade* my room after that first day in the gardens. I like the cozy size of the one she gave and its proximity to the kitchens.

Besides that, I don't have to talk to anyone in the corridors if I want to escape to my rooms and read. There's no one but servants down this way.

It's so far out of the way that no courtiers ever come this far into the back of the castle.

It doesn't take me long to bathe, dress, and let Amalie fix my hair up into a complicated braid. Ribbons of sapphire blue are woven throughout my dark tresses.

She pats the seat in front of a vanity that holds all of the make-up and a large, handheld looking glass. This not being my favorite part, I sigh loudly.

Her lips twitch but she doesn't comment on my lack of enthusiasm.

I had told her on that second day I was here that I'm not fond of make-up. It feels like hiding who I am.

She knew, through gossip and whispers, some of my life's story. Taking a small step back, she'd mulled over what I'd said.

After a moment of quiet reflection, she boldly gave me advice I hadn't asked for. *"It's not the same thing as hiding your panther behind your wolf."*

She got it. Smart young thing. I hadn't voiced my underlying concerns, but she'd picked up on them anyway.

And that was that. She went to work making my face look exactly the same, only slightly more enhanced.

Each time she tends to me, I know it's going to be harder to say goodbye when the time comes. I've really grown to like this sassy young faery.

Maybe I will ask Princess Emenda to extend her a leave of absence to come with me to each kingdom as I go.

Only if Amalie wants to, of course. I'm not going to force her to be my handmaiden, no matter how much I like having her around.

"There," she says. Her finishing touches done, she stands back to admire her own handiwork. "With the blue ribbon and understated make-up, this dress really pops on your figure."

Brushing a bit of lint from my shoulder, she twists her fingers, indicating that I should twirl for her.

I giggle but give her my best slow spin. Clapping her hands together, she looks pleased and I find that her joy brings me happiness too.

I miss my friends, my pack, but I've stolen moments of elation over the last few months from these types of interactions.

The last couple of weeks here at Emenda's court have been some of the best since I came to Anavrin.

Chancing a glance in the larger looking glass, glaring at the points of my ears. The longer I'm in the fae realm, the more pronounced they are becoming.

They're not exactly ugly. I just don't remember they exist until each time I catch a glimpse of myself in a reflective surface. Silly as it may seem, it shocks me every time.

"I guess we should get this show on the road. I wouldn't want to keep all of the royals waiting." Pulling up the skirt of my long dress, I slip my feet into a pair of one-inch heels.

I hate heels. It's been a battle every day.

Amalie won't allow me to wear flats in the presents of her princess. So, this is our compromise.

As we enter the dining room, Prince Loxias and Quill have already arrived. Several courtiers have taken their places at a few separate tables from the main one but Lord Davian and Nydin sit in the middle of the royal's table.

I suppose it makes sense that each prince or princess would allow only their Right Hand and a guest at the table. There isn't enough room for all of their entourages to sit and dine with the royals. Maybe I should sit at one of the other tables too.

Still standing at the entrance, deciding whether or not to take a seat at one other guest tables, a sense of heat flushes my skin.

A shiver runs down the center of my spine. A presence at my back. My body shudders involuntarily.

Prince Roxalus' breath breezes over the bare flesh of my exposed neck, just behind my ear. "Quo perii," he whispers across my skin.

I not sure I was meant to hear it, and I have no idea of what it means in any case. That doesn't stop my nipples from pebbling beneath the band around my chest.

He's already walking away, over to take his place at the right of the table by the time my mind refocuses.

With his eyes averted, I chance a glance at him, not understanding why I feel the need to. My mind is screaming at me... *Danger. Danger...* but my body isn't catching on.

I've unconsciously taken two full steps in his direction when Ayxian sweeps in from the door beside Roxalus.

Snapped out of my inane stupor, I give my head a slight shake. There's the bustling of dishes being set in the center of each table. Chatter filling the room.

Others have come in and taken their seats while I've been distracted. The scent of roasted pig, steamed sweet corn, and yeasty bread rolls fills the dining hall.

Taking back my self-control, I start towards the tables in which the other courtiers of each party's entourage sit. They are opposite the royal table in the front of the room.

"Oh, no you don't." Princess Emenda takes my elbow and steers me to the seat next to Ayxian, speaking low in my ear. "You are an honored guest, Lady Piper. I won't have you sit where I can't delight in your impiety."

A wicked grin touches the corners of her lips. Speaking aloud for all to hear, she turns to the two brothers on her right. "Make room for Lady Piper."

Oh, this mischievous vixen! She and I are going to have words later. I'm certain she's throwing me to the wolves to be the gossip of her gazebo tea session tomorrow.

Ayxian scooches over one seat, leaving the seat beside Roxalus open. I look back at the princess and that wicked grin has grown into a full-blown smirk.

Her amusement at my predicament is rubbing my fur the wrong way. I might just have to shift and take a few snaps at her for good measure later. Tea indeed!

If we were in the human realm, I would be hearing the cackling of the witch from the Wizard of Oz.

Glaring at her, she's unrepentant. She knows damn well I am fighting an internal battle, but the fae value entertainment more than sympathy.

I'm learning how to play the game, but I'm not as ruthless as them... yet.

Being in the land of Anavrin is bringing out my fae side more and more each day. A chilling realization, for sure, but I refuse to let my baser instincts rule my character.

Noticing my less than grateful grimace, Lord Davian takes up the charge of steering the conversation. "Prince Loxias," he says. "I've heard that you've turned over a new leaf. With respect, what would make a never changing fae do such a thing?"

Loxias doesn't look upset at the question. On the contrary, he looks pleased. "I'm glad that someone has been paying attention."

Quill averts his eyes as the prince speaks. His hand is white knuckled on his fork as he stabs at the meat on his plate.

"I've said it for years. The only reason that I hunted was to find a way to break that awful curse. Think what you may of me but having access to your other half means being able to discover new things about yourself. Immortality does become tedious at times," he says unabashedly.

Loxias had been a thorn in the side of the creatures in the Lupian Forest for a long time but seeing him lay himself bare before everyone in attendance cracks a sliver of my heart open to his former suffering.

"Oh, dearest lonely brother. How you ever managed to live past the weaning of the teat is a mystery." Roxalus' words are deliberate and drawn, irrationally grading against the nerves of my newfound acceptance of the youngest prince.

Quill shifts in his seat but remains quiet and poor Loxias loses some of his confidence in the wake of his brother's teasing.

Ayxian is no better. His radiant smirk drips with cruelty. I never noticed that wicked streak of his in those weeks that we'd spent together.

He'd hidden it well, but now that I've seen it, I can't unsee it.

Trying to regain his composure, Loxias ignores Roxalus' comment and speaks directly to Lord Davian. "As I was saying, I am contented now that I have accomplished my goal. And with another goal ahead of me, it has brought me an inkling of peace."

After reaching for a roll, he turns to me. "Lady Piper, how are you enjoying your new life in this realm?"

My mouth is gracelessly full of some of the most delicious food I've been served since coming to stay at Princess Emenda's castle and that's saying something.

All of the meals have been beyond scrumptious here. Her cooks have out done themselves for this feast.

I've never been one to hold back while I eat, but I've been gorging on the tasty morsels from the second my backside hit this chair.

Every eye at the table presses upon my skin. The pressure is a physical thing. Uncomfortable. Daunting.

After swallowing the huge bite I have in my mouth, letting it tear at my throat with it's under chewed size, I take a cleansing breath to compose myself.

"It's been wonderf..." the lie sticks in my throat. I had to change tactics. "It's been interesting."

I hadn't wanted to leave the Lupian Forest. It wasn't my choice. Trying to make my way here in Anavrin has its challenges but I am beginning to feel like I belong. Sort of.

"We have all heard different accounts of what happened to King Zyoden. The Deliverer has broken both the mating curse and the power binding curse. Would anyone care to tell the story of what actually happened at the castle that night?" Nydin finishes asking and Lord Davian puts his firm hand in his mates, giving it a gentle squeeze.

Nydin doesn't usually speak in front of the royals directly. With no title himself, he tends to relay his thoughts or questions through Lord Davian.

If and when they ever marry, I suspect that will change. He'll be a lord then. With all the bells and whistles that go with it.

As far as I know, neither of them have agreed to marrying yet. As mates, they don't need to be wed but most mated pairs like to make it official anyway.

So, when he asks his question in front of the whole table, it puts me a bit more at ease. He is throwing me a lifeline, and I'm grateful for it.

Prince Roxalus sneers. Ayxian gives an amused smirk. Princesses Emenda and Embla were too busy with their whispered secrets to acknowledge the question.

Wondering if no one will tell the tale, the quiet stretches into tension.

Just when I start to speak up to change the subject and spare Nydin the gaze of the room, Prince Loxias blows out a long, sighing breath.

"I'll tell the tale. Be it known from my lips, the truth to be spread across the land." His proclamation is lighthearted but bares weight.

I don't understand what is happening. The fae have their customs and rituals but magics are a binding thing. Words have meaning. They hold people accountable.

Plucking a steak knife from off the table, Prince Loxias slashes a cut across the palm of his left hand.

I gasp but I'm the only one. No one else finds this out of the ordinary.

Squeezing his fist, letting the blood drip, he holds it over a candle in front of him. A sizzling sound engulfs the atmosphere. The dining room has fallen silent.

Looking towards the other tables, expecting them to be turned in our direction, they are all staring directly at their own table's center.

A moment later, when Loxias begins, I understand why.

Chapter Thirteen

As the prince begins his tale, images appear before us. We aren't hearing Loxias tell the tale.

We are witnessing it, voices and all. Everything is from his perspective, but there is no interpretation other than what each of us takes away from it.

The Deliverer, Faelan, enters the throne room in shackles beside Loxias. Quill and Leif stand just behind them and two more guards behind those two.

The king mistakes Faelan for his former mistress, the First Witch, Mab. Things happen quickly and Loxias is losing control of the situation.

Faelan has step forward to speak. She drops her glamour away from those other guards and Prince Maximus stands staring at King Zyoden and Queen Leyashna.

Shock and murmurs run through me and around the dining room. Only the royals, here in attendance, don't react because they've already lived it.

Prince Roxalus sends an ice spear, aiming for Faelan. Maximus melts it before it's halfway to her.

A fight breaks out between the royals as Inara, Faelan's grandmother/Max's daughter, is brought up from the dungeons and Roxalus throws his ice at her this time.

The king is in an agitated state. His mind is addled.

Another fight breaks out between more of the royals.

Faelan teleports to Inara and then out of sight.

My eyes glance sideways to Roxalus as he picks up his wine and sips it and looks away from the memory playing out in front of everyone.

He's not thrilled that we are bearing witness to his failure, that much is obvious.

I can't understand why he dislikes his siblings so much. Other than the twins, he doesn't appear to like anyone very much.

The scene has turned to chaos once again as Queen Leyashna says some words that sound like a spell of sorts.

The king slumps in his chair and doesn't move again.

She declares Max King Regent for the next thirteen moon cycles during these competitions.

Max makes an oath to end anyone who tries to harm or command the harm of those from his bloodline.

I am taking all this in when the scene changes again. I notice Quill tug at Loxias's arm, but he ignores him and continues anyway.

Max, and Faelan's mate, Wylder appear in the next instant. Loxias clings to Max's back on the side of Ritual rock.

My form is there, in the circle, beside Faelan.

Roxalus glances in my direction this time. As does Ayxian.

Loxias had jumped the teleport when Max and Wylder left the palace.

Faelan doesn't stop the full blood moon ritual that she's performing.

Inara is still too weak from her time in the dungeon to be of any help, so Faelan reads from the book of shadows without pause.

The pack tries to stop Loxias's approach, but he puts his hands on me, and I bent to his will, turning on my brethren.

Low growls hiss from both sides of me and Loxias has the good sense to look abashed, even as his mind continues reliving the memory for us all to see.

Faelan finishes the ritual and Loxias is drawn back into Anavrin from the force of it.

So was I but I ended up at Max's court. Loxias ended up back in his own. Or so I'm told from other's experiences of the fallout.

When the tale is over, the images fade and the lights around the dining room brighten again. No one speaks. The air is somber with the truth.

Realization that Prince Loxias has, in fact, facilitated the end of the curses runs in hushed whispers around the room.

Gazing to my left from under my lashes, I find Roxalus has slipped out of the room while everyone's attention was elsewhere.

Ayxian takes my hand in his and brushes his lips across my knuckles. "If you are through with your meal, I would like to take you for a walk in the gardens, My Lady."

It isn't quite a question. It's more of an announcement that he is taking me out to the lavender fields.

I can say no, but that'll be seen as denying a royal and I don't have it in me tonight to argue.

"After dessert," I say, scooping a fresh helping of the trifle that has been set in front of me.

He smiles as he notes that I still have the ladling spoon in my hand.

"I do love a female who likes to eat." His voice is velvety... throaty even, and I almost unwittingly lean in. "I'll retrieve you after you're through."

Standing abruptly, the prince is through the chamber doors without even glancing back.

In his wake, the full effects of what he probably wants from me brings heat to my cheeks, a small breath catching in my throat.

I am no prude but the fact that he is aroused and wanting, and I hadn't caught on quicker, makes me question my attraction to him.

Ayxian is beyond handsome, with dust colored hair and striking hazel-colored eyes. Kissing him those first couple of weeks had sent my stomach into flutters.

After his interests fell more to the crown than to us, I let my feelings for him fall away as well.

Perhaps revisiting them would be foolish. He hasn't changed his goals.

But a girl has needs, and making out with a hot prince can't hurt. Can it?

Setting my fork down and rising from the table, Nydin catches my gaze and winks. Aw crap, I've been busted.

Cheeks heating with embarrassment, it won't stop me from seeking out a little fun time.

Before I can think twice about it, I excuse myself from the table and head out the same doors that Prince Ayxian left through... only to run headfirst into Prince Roxalus.

Chapter Fourteen

My first thought is to step back, but he catches me under my elbows before I can fall.

I haven't forgotten how hard his stomach is. I haven't forgotten the heat of that kiss he planted on me in the study. His smell is intoxicating, like peppermint and pine needles.

Gathering my composure, his strong arms gently, but unwillingly hold me steady. A snarl sounds deep in his throat. Why does he hate me so much?

Before I can apologize for walking into him, he turns on his heels and flees. There is no other way to describe it. He is a blur and then nothing.

There's cold sensation gathered around my head and chest, a thin layer of ice coating my skin.

I'm not sure if he meant to harm me or if it had happened from the sudden shock of my attack. His power danced from my elbows, up my arms, and down the course of my stomach to my core.

Not being able to read him is driving me mad. I don't want to meet him in another dark corridor anytime soon. Ugh!

Turning in the opposite direction of the one he fled, I make a beeline for the double front doors.

A bit of heat from Ayxian will be just what I need to warm up the chill Roxalus has left in his wake.

The gardens are far from empty. Courtiers stroll through the fragrant rows and servants come to and fro with snack trays and faery wine.

Many of the frolickers are already giddy with drink. Jackets discarded. Shoes left behind... Shirts lay strewn about.

The fae are nothing if not wildly lecherous creatures. Passion and pleasure aren't shamefully hidden away in this realm.

Here in Anavrin, debauchery is the norm, and modesty is the unusual.

A hulking figure stands in the shadows cast from a tall oak tree on the far side of the gardens. Even with my superior fae eyesight, I can't make out the face.

Moonlight slices across the male's shirtless chest, and I can see his firm abs lead to the vee just above his manhood. The back of a head pops up from where my eyes had just been fixated.

It's still too shadowy to see below the vee, but I have a feeling I don't want to know who is servicing the unknown male.

Just as I turn to head in the other direction, someone calls my name. "Lady Piper, you came."

It was the shadowed figure. Ayxian pulls up and buttons the front of his pants, stepping out onto the walkway. The female who had just been with him is nowhere in sight.

In the shock of the situation, I forget everything else.

He had asked me out here and when I didn't immediately come with him, he'd found another partner? Rude.

Finally remembering myself, I dip a slight curtsy towards him. "Prince Ayxian."

It's all I manage to say while he stares at me like I am a puzzle in need of solving.

I find that I don't like it very much. It's intimate, raw even, and it leaves me feeling exposed.

Taking a step forward, he makes to catch my hand, but I step back without thought, and a menacing growl erupts from his chest.

His gifts are ones of a warrior. Strength, sure footedness, certainly. The thing that strikes me in this moment is his beastly primal side.

When I moved away, all instinct screamed *prey* to him. As an animal shifting fae, I should have known better, but I don't want him near me right now.

The sweet gardenia scent of the faery who'd just been sucking him off still lingers on his skin.

"I am finding myself in need of some sleep, Prince Ayxian." Putting my shoulders back and holding my head high, I take another step backwards.

Growling again, his head cocks to the side and his eyes darken. There in their depths I can see his predator instincts in full control. The Ayxian I know isn't checked in.

Maybe because he's let his other baser needs be sated or maybe I am seeing this side of him because I know it firsthand from an animal's perspective, but he's never felt like a threat to me before now.

Another growl rumbles through his chest and he shakes his head to clear the cobwebs. My words must be working their way into his conscious thoughts because light is starting to re-enter his eyes.

Holding my hands up, palms open, I take another step backwards. The prince inhales deeply, in through his nose and out through his mouth.

"I was hoping you'd stay," he says with silky heat radiating in his voice.

Almost leaning in, I stop short at the other female's floral notes on his skin. I don't need to take myself off the top shelf because someone can't reach my standards.

Thanks Inara! Gods, I miss her constant tidbits of wisdom. But here, her voice is as clear as crystal in my memories.

With him reaching for me again, I take one more step back, tripping over my own two feet and his discarded shirt.

I don't hit the ground like I was expecting, landing against a muscular chest. A strong arm snakes around my waist, holding me firmly. The scent of peppermint and pine needles engulfs me.

"I'm pretty sure Lady Piper told you that she'd like to get some rest." Roxalus' is a coil of tense muscles.

His heart at my back beats a steady rhythm, helping my own heart to slow its frantic pace.

Finding my courage, I look up to his face. His eyes burn with derision. He's been staring daggers at his brother but has said nothing more.

I'm hyperaware of each point of contact our bodies make. The way his breath tickles the bare nape of my neck. The press of his splayed fingers against my stomach.

Gathering his thoughts, Ayxian snaps out of his lust induced primal haze. I'm surprised he has no retort to throw his brother's way. Maybe he's genuinely embarrassed?

"Yes, if you'll excuse me." He gives a dip of his chin, turns in the direction of the gazebo, and leaves me standing alone with Prince Roxalus.

Once the other prince is out of sight, Roxalus drops his arm and pushes me away like a hot coal.

An ache in the center of my chest pounds behind my ribcage as he puts his hands into his front pockets and begins to walk away.

The sight makes me irrationally angry. "Well, thanks for your help!"

Shit! I just thanked a faery. A dangerous faery who hates me. My sarcasm is apparently lost on him.

Turning back around to face me, he's only two strides away from where he'd been at my back a second ago.

"I accept your thanks. A boon you will owe me. To be used as I see fit. At a time that I decide." The air shimmers with magics. A binding contract. Fuck!

Creasing my eyebrows, my teeth worry at my bottom lip. Why the hell is this particular faery able to get under my skin in a way that no one ever has in all my days? Stupid sexy asshole!

"You should return to your rooms, Lady Piper." Towering over me, he glares down his nose, like I'm a weed amongst the beautiful fae gardens. "We wouldn't want anything to happen to an honored guest in my dear sister's court. Welcomed or not."

Without a single glance back, he's gone. I'm standing in the gardens, alone, confused, and ... unsatisfied? Well, shit.

The sounds of passion from all around the gardens grows louder with each passing moment. My feet move towards the castle of their own accord.

As my mind runs through today's course of events, I'm left seething. Everything that's happened since leaving the dining room playing on repeat in my head.

First, not picking up on Ayxian's cues. Then, running head-on into Roxalus. Followed by finding Ayxian with his pants around his ankles. His predatory advances towards me. and ending with Roxalus' defending me, then pushing me away... it's all been too much for one afternoon.

I make my way back to the castle, down the long corridor towards the kitchens, and end up in my bed.

Laying here... wide awake, staring at the ceiling, unable to sleep. I started to read another book, but my lack of concentration is making it impossible to take it in.

The smell of Roxalus still wraps around me. I'd taken a long, hot bath and yet, it still persists.

The sight of Prince Ayxian's abs on display in the gardens. The head that appeared from below his navel. The growls he'd thrown my way when I'd made to get away from his advances... ugh! Unsatisfied indeed.

The longer that I lay here, the more my mind runs over the events from the day. Then it hits me. The feeling I couldn't place before.

Hurt. Prince Roxalus had hurt my feelings. And for the life of me, I can't understand why he, of all people, matters.

My self-esteem has never been tied to what others did or thought of me. Not once in my life have I felt the need to look pretty or be accepted by people who don't care for me.

Either Anavrin is changing me more than I want to admit. Or there is something more to this arrogant male that my mind hasn't let me in on yet.

Huffing in frustration, I punch the pillow to try to get more comfortable. Morning is only a couple hours off and Maximus, Elodie, and Noxian are due to arrive today.

As I begin to finally drift off into an uneasy sleep, my hand making its way between my legs. The building heaviness finding a small fraction of comfort from my ministrations.

With the two princes dancing behind my eyelids, my dreams are likely to be brutal.

Chapter Fifteen

Princess Elodie and Prince Noxian arrive just after break-fast. They both bring smaller entourages of maybe ten people. We have all just finished lunch and Maximus still hasn't arrived yet.

During the previous competitions, he would often be late in attending. Several times he'd shown up with Inara in tow. A few times, Faelan and her mate, Wylder, were with him.

Faelan is able to teleport, just like her great grandfather, but her abilities of particle manipulation are the reason.

That's not from Max's side. It's from the First Witch's side. It's what makes most fae in Anavrin weary of her and her gifts.

"Lady Piper," Princess Elodie says as she walks through the study doors. I'm so caught up in my own head that it takes me a moment to register her presence. "How are you finding my sister's hospitality?"

I can't tell if it's part of the game or if she is generally interested in my well-being and I rub at my temples.

Elodie's a straight shooter though. At least, from everything
that I've seen from her. I'm not here to play the game. I'm here
for my honesty.

"Better than I suspected." Her eyes search mine for any
half-truths, but she can *feel* my sincerity. "I'm not saying that
I've been welcomed with open arms."

Smirking in understanding, her chin gives a slight dip.

Her sisters aren't the friendliest fae, not to anyone they feel
beneath them, but especially not to those of us who came from
the human realm. Full-blooded or half-blooded.

"Princess Emenda and I had a chat at the beginning of my
stay and though I've found myself the butt of many of her
jiving's, her subjects also took their fair share of ribbing." Her
smirk intensifies as I squirm under the pressure of her glare.
"What?" I throw my hands up in mock exasperation. "It could
have been worse."

With that, the corners of her mouth turn up. "Yes, that it
could. I'm pleased that you're not running for the hills from all
of us in the royal family. We tend to overwhelm even the most
patient of our kind."

I start towards the back of the study to return the book I had
borrowed earlier in the week, pleasantly surprised when Elodie
chooses to walk with me.

It's a comfortable silence. Faeries don't tend to feel the need
for incessant chatter. Immortality gives the soul time for quiet
reflection and, knowing it or not, that's exactly what they do.

"Lady Piper, do you mind if I ask you a question?" Nothing comes for free with the fae.

She knows, in asking me a question, I will be owed a debt of some kind. She's asking anyway.

A small nod is all she gets from me. "What was it like to leave everything and everyone behind? I've been curious since it happened, but I didn't want to further any of my people's trauma in asking them too soon."

"My trauma is alright though?" With an arched eyebrow, I wait for her reply. Dumbledore had it right.

Staring patiently, without speaking anything more to provoke someone's answer, often leads to their discomfort. And discomfort tends to make people fill in the space with words they might have held back otherwise.

With a pensive look upon her goddess-like face, she takes her time before answering me. "If I were to take a guess, I would say that you feel like you're fitting in more and more each day here."

I'm not surprised that she sees me with that way about her. I'd feel fully exposed if it was anyone else.

Perhaps it's her gifts leading her, but Elodie is thoughtful and calculating. She doesn't rush head long into a situation or argument.

I can almost see the clockworks of her mind. I've heard that some consider her to be too forward, too honest. I find her to be smart and witty.

Sure, maybe tact isn't her thing, but it is refreshing in a land where half-truths and omissions too often take center stage.

After another moment, the corners of my lips turn up. Somewhere along the way that little spot of dark, wickedness inside me started pushing its boundaries.

It feels good to be free of human connotations. I'm still me, but I am no longer suppressing the parts of me that have been hidden away for so long.

Whenever I catch myself reaching for the cruelest responses, it never fails to bring me up short.

Arriving at the study, I give her a true smile as I open the doors. "I am adjusting. It hasn't been easy."

I don't know how much I want to reveal to her. She's practically a stranger, but sincerity glows from her skin. "I miss Inara terribly. The next few decades will be agonizingly long I suspect."

"So, Max's daughter still plans to come live here after Faelan's mother passes?" She says this with intense interest. It doesn't sound like plotting.

I haven't talked about it with any of the other fae because the games they all play are too conniving. Too exhausting to keep up with. It's been better to keep things to myself.

Elodie and Leif are different. I feel as if I have a true kinship with them.

Friendship comes with a price when it comes to the fae, but theirs seems natural to me. Leif is family and Elodie, I can *feel* her heart. It's pure light. If there's any dark wickedness in there, I can't sense it.

The scent of dust motes and parchment hits me the moment we walk over the threshold. If breathing in the books is a drug, then I am an addict. My heart skips and an instant calm overtakes my senses.

Smiling, her face is the kind of beauty that great painters captured for all to admire. All fae have a perfection to their looks, but Elodie's is exquisite.

"She does. She would come sooner, but her daughter has outright refused to acknowledge any magics."

Grabbing my arm to stop our progression, her shock is apparent. Angels shouldn't wear that look. I'm taken aback by her sudden sorrow.

"Wait, are you saying that Max's granddaughter will see the final season in that short time?" Her eyes hold all of the pain of loss that I'd felt myself.

Inara's daughter is pure fae, but growing up in the human realm and refusing to accept the truth of the supernatural world is her choice. Magics demand balance.

She is aging slowly, but only just. She will probably live to one hundred thirty or so. In human terms, that's an extremely long life. To the fae, that is still at the older end of an adolescent child.

Her sadness for the great-niece she's never going to get to know is etched in her down turned lips and glistening in her eyes.

Patting her on the shoulder, I'm not really good at consoling people, but something about Elodie pulls me to do just that.

"It's her choice. No matter how Inara or Faelan approach the topic, she shuts them down and refuses to allow them to get more than a few words out."

Placing the heavy book that I've been toting back onto its shelf, we head towards the back of the room.

There are few copies with interesting titles are down this way. I'd found them when I had wandered the room last week. I want to read them before my time here is up.

"Faelan doesn't want to leave her mother or her pack. Wylder isn't fae... well, not technically. All shifters come from the First Witch's line, so they have fae in them, but you know what I mean. He's already well over a century old. I suppose he'll live for at least another two or so, but Faelan will lose her mate at some point."

Her face is so full of despair that I unconsciously wrap my arm around her shoulders and bring her in for a hug.

I don't have any experience with the topic of mated pairs other than Max and Eowyn, and now Lord Davian and Nydin.

From what everyone has told me over the last few months; Max had come back different. More hollow. They say he is the same male, only diminished somehow. Like a whisper of who he'd been in the past.

Faelyn and Max will be in the same boat. "Wylder and Faelan may choose to come live here after her mother passes but poor Wylder. A werewolf living here, with all of us fae? I don't envy him."

Elodie's been quiet. Contemplative and mindful with her thoughts. I had expected her to push the issue but instead, she simply sighed and changed the subject.

"To answer your question from earlier." I paused in my perusal to look at her. "No. Your trauma isn't okay."

Arching an eyebrow, I wait for her to elaborate. A faint smile lights her face, and she winks. "I feel you. I mean, I *feel* your strength."

Linking her arm in mine, we walk back towards the lounging chairs. There are refreshments on the low table at the center. Tea and pastries sit on a tray and the smell of cinnamon floats in the space all around the room and awakens my appetite tenfold.

Elodie takes a seat on one of the chaises and I plop down on the comfy chair across from her.

"I'm not sure what you mean by that," I say. "Most days, I am lost here. I don't know where to go or what to do with myself."

Picking up the kettle, she pours us both a glass. I like that the princess doesn't ask one of the servants to do it. It's a small thing, but it speaks volumes about her character.

It must be chamomile tea. I'm still not familiar with all of the different types, but this one has an herbal smell, and the taste is mildly sweet. Amalie told me that combination usually turns out to be chamomile.

Shoving an entire cinnamon dusted croissant in my mouth, the flavor explodes over my tongue. It's beyond delicious. My insides tingle from the tip of my nose to the curl of my toes.

"You may want to ease into that," she says. "Those are euphoria pasties. I'm sure you're feeling the effects already." Reaching over, she snatches the second one from my hand. Nibbling a small bite from the tip, putting the rest back down on the tray. "In small doses, it's wonderful to take the edge off. In larger doses however, I find that helps take the clothes off."

Her wink brings the heat of embarrassment to my cheeks. It's such an Inara thing to do that I can't help myself from laughing.

Faeries often want to mess with you, and I can't tell if she's pulling my leg or not, but with the tingling still making its way around my system, I believe her.

I **am** one. A Faery. Coming to realize that I possess a dark kernel of mischief in me almost makes me shy away becoming my true self. Almost.

"You know, of all of the human realm transplants, you're the only one who doesn't give off vibes of being afraid all of the time," her tone matter of fact. "I would be surprised if fate doesn't have a great purpose for you, Lady Piper."

Standing up, I hold my palm open for the pasty in her hand. "Alright. Enough faery cakes for you." When she laughs, I laugh right along with her.

The doors to the study open when we're so far into our fitful laughs that we're nearly falling from our chairs. Loxias and Quill walk in smiling and enjoying their conversation. The way that Quill's face lights up every time Loxias glances his way sends a bit of joy through him. Loxias doesn't appear to notice but Elodie and I do. We can *feel* it plain as day.

They stop talking as they sit down in the other chairs around the low table.

"So, what's on the agenda for today, ladies?" Loxias' tone is light but there's an undercurrent to it.

He isn't using his gifts. Power can feel power, but his intention is obvious. He wants to know if we are working together. The rules Max set for this part of the competition are clear.

The princes and princesses have to write their own poem about their Rule. About how and why the kingdom as a whole will benefit from them taking the throne. And they have to write it alone, without any help.

"Oh, you know," Princess Elodie says with an airy wave of her hand. "Lady Piper and I, we're looking at books so that I can plagiarize some long dead poet and win myself the kingdom."

Quill stiffens but Loxias laughs at his sister's not-so-subtle poke. "How much of the Euphoria pasties did you consume, sister?"

Relaxing at the prince's ribbing, Quill settles himself into a chair and grabs a pasty. Maybe he's not so uptight after all.

"Not nearly enough..." her words hang there as the doors to the study open again.

The strong wintery scent of peppermint and pine needles wafts through the room. Roxalus enters and the entire dynamic changes.

Loxias sits straighter. Quill looks like he is ready to grab him and make a dash for it. Elodie pouts out her bottom lip like a kid who's been told *no more cookies*. And here I sit... staring.

As he draws closer, the torches hanging around the room throw his face into stark relief. His eyes find mine and I can't look away. I feel like a deer trapped in headlights.

Distantly, I registerer Elodie making a concerned clucking noise, but I haven't been able to break away from his glare.

As he approaches our little group, the heat from his proximity brings the hairs on the back of my neck to stand on end.

"Is this the meeting of the small and inconsequential? You know, helping each other is breaking the rules." That smirk that lifts one corner of his mouth? Gods, how those lips torture my memories.

I've tasted them, and the most awful things often came out of them. How can they taste so sweet and speak with such sour notes?

Before I know what I am saying, my voice rises above the startled silence. "Are you just upset that you have no friends to help you, Prince Roxalus? Or are you afraid that you aren't worthy of friendship in the first place?"

Chapter Sixteen

R oxalus instantly crosses the short space in two long strides. Standing in front of me, he bends over at eye level, and I bite back all of the fear that swells to the surface. I won't let him see me afraid.

"Buzz.., buzz..." His throaty voice is low enough for only me to hear if I were human, but every fae around me will understand his meaning as it reaches their fae ears.

Heat rushes to my cheeks, and I can't take my eyes off of this completely flummoxing male.

Loxias shifts uncomfortably while Quill pretends not to hear. Elodie stares at her brother like he should be pitied. Interesting take.

Straightening up, he brushes down the front of his shirt as he stands. "Come on then. Where shall we start?"

Princess Elodie opens her mouth to set him straight but the doors to the study clang open loudly for a third time.

King Maximus and Prince Noxian come in with a whispered conversation happening between them, but at the sight of us all sitting here, they clam up.

Elodie glances in my direction, and I give her a knowing look. We can both feel the tension and angst coming off of them in waves with our gifts.

"Princess Elodie, Prince's, Lady Piper," Noxian says with a dip of his chin as they approach.

He ignores Quill entirely. Whether that's because of Quill's station or because of Quill as a person, I'm not sure.

Noxian and I haven't had many interactions. I hope to get to know him better when I go to his court for the competitions.

"I'm glad to find you all gathered here already. We're only waiting on Prince Ayxian and the twins." Max's distressed state is obvious. Ringing his hands and pacing, his eyes fall to the pasties on the table, and he snatches one up.

After a few bites, some of the tension visibly leaves his body, but I can still *feel* it barely contained beneath the surface.

"I need to fill all of you in on some things that have happened in the kingdom over the last few months. This room is better than the throne room. I don't want what I'm about to say to travel outside of us here."

"Do tell, dear brother." Roxalus' flippant attitude hides true concern beneath his cool composure.

"We should wait for the others. I don't want to re..." Max starts but the doors to the study open yet again.

Ayxian strolls into the room with a princess on each arm. Emenda and Embla don't look put out by his company, but I know they don't have the same devotion to him as they have to Roxalus.

I haven't seen him since his primal state took over last night. Swallowing a breath as quietly as I can, knowing that those around me can hear it, I try not to draw attention, but Roxalus straightens in his seat, shifting ever so slightly towards me. No one else would have noticed but I am hyperaware of everything the arrogant prince does.

I'm sure everyone can hear how my heartbeat has picked up. First at the sight of Ayxian. Then again as Roxalus moves closer.

Standing to face Max, I'm preparing myself to leave. I'm not a royal and I don't want him being accused of nepotism. "I'll see myself out."

Quill looks to Loxias but his prince is still staring at Max. I've seen that same look on Max's face before. Every time he looks at Inara or Leif. Familial love and devotion.

Max is his favorite brother who went missing for centuries. The eldest brother of the eight fae siblings and rightful heir to the throne. The one who holds the balance of the kingdom in his hands.

The reverence for his oldest brother shows through the wonderment in Loxias' eyes.

It's touching. So much so that Elodie clears her throat to dispel the emotions hanging the air.

"I would like you to stay, Lady Piper. This affects you and it would make me feel better if you were in the know." His concern seeping into me like a heavy weight.

Staring at the king's face trying to decipher what he's silently trying to tell me, I come up short.

"As you wish, My Liege." I say, dipping my chin in deference before remembering my etiquette and curtsying.

Technically, we all should have stood when he came in. In this informal setting, it's easy to forget that Max is the king and not just Uncle Max or their brother.

Ayxian takes notice of me then. Taking a step in my direction has made his behavior last night come rushing back to the forefront of my mind.

I'm not sure whether I'm afraid or excited and that terrifies me.

An involuntary swallow sounds loudly from my throat. The next moment there's a light tug on my skirt from behind, but I don't turn. I can't show fear to these cruel royals.

When I don't move to sit back down, Prince Roxalus stands. His hard chest brushes up against the back of my shoulder. His peppermint and pine needle scent assaults my nose and my senses, and I shudder at the close proximity, but my eyes stay glued to Prince Ayxian's.

"Lady Piper, how good to see you." He takes another step in my direction, and a faint growl reverberates off the shell of my ear.

No one else hears it. No one acknowledges that it happened. Maybe I'm losing myself to the anxiety I'm feeling, but it sounded so real.

Finally looking away from me, he notices Roxalus standing close to me. His eyes widen and his hand goes to the sword at his side. "If I may have a word after this meeting?"

I want to run and scream. I don't know where to, but anywhere has to be better than here, under the scrutiny of all these royals.

The prince in front of me and the prince behind me both make my insides squirm. I can't be sure if that's a good thing or a bad thing, but either way, I feel trapped like prey.

"Oh brother, you will have to get in line," Princess Elodie's tone is lighthearted, but I know she *feels* my consternation. "Lady Piper has promised her afternoon to me."

Roxalus relaxes his posture ever so slightly, but Ayxian attempts to double down.

"It will only take a moment. I will have her back to you before you've arrived at the gazebo for afternoon tea." With a flash of his crooked, rugged smile, my heart does a backflip.

Elodie picks up on that too because she inclines her head in acknowledgement. My teeth sink into my bottom lip, not sure if that's what I truly want.

"Hold on," Princess Embla holds out a finger on each hand in protest. "I thought that Lady Piper was here to get to know Princess Emenda this go round. Why should you be promised her time?" The wicked gleam in Embla's eye tells me that she's up to no good. Elodie sees right through her. "It's only fair that she spends the day with us."

Feeling emboldened by Elodie's save, I direct my attention to Princess Emenda, ignoring Princess Embla altogether.

"I'm sure there is enough room in the gazebo for us gals to have a pleasant teatime." A ping of approval hits me in the feels from Elodie. Directing my next statement towards Embla, it's game on. "As you said us, I will assume you mean all of us girls."

Emenda's lips are so thin, they look painted on. I've ensnared her sister in word play in front of Max and she knows it.

She fights hard to not twitch the corners of her mouth, but I see them curl up ever so slightly. Check and mate. At least she appreciates that I've got game.

Embla is livid. It wafts off her like seawater dashing across a cliffs face. I've effectively tied her hands.

If she claims there's no room, she'll be lying. If she denies Elodie a seat, then she'll be overstepping Emenda's rule here.

I have left her with no other option than to agree to the terms that I've set and she knows it.

Roxalus tsked, then returns to his seat. I can't tell if he's annoyed that I've gotten the better of one of the twins or if maybe he is impressed.

It shouldn't matter to me which. If I was as smart as I've always thought myself to be, I'd leave well enough alone and stay far away from him.

The other's now all sit in the seats around the low table. Max asks Quill to leave but he knows that Loxias will tell him whatever it is that we discuss here. They all will tell there trusted second's in command. Of that, I'm sure.

"I've asked you all to gather so that I can tell you of the deaths that have occurred during the last several months." He's frazzled, worn down. There are dark circles under his eyes, and a weariness emanates from his soul. "I had hoped that it was only a couple of isolated incidents, but last night's murder has confirmed all of my suspicions. Someone is killing the human realm fae transplants."

Meeting my eyes for a split second longer than the rest, he looks at each of the other's faces in turn.

My guess, he's trying to gauge their reactions and hopes Elodie or I might pick up something. He once told me that of all his siblings, he trusted her without a doubt.

"There are too many fae in this land anyway. So what if a few of the lower class get picked off?" Princess Embla has an axe to grind but I can't *feel* any malignity coming from her.

She truly feels she is above the lower classes of Anavrin and doesn't understand what the big deal is if some of them are killed off. Rotten to the core, that one.

"Now, now, sister. We can't be good rulers and not look out for all of our subjects. That's what it means to be a good ruler." Ayxian winks at me from across the table. Looking to each of them in turn, he says, "This means we all must be on our guard. I will send word to my court after we've finished here."

I still have lingering effects from those euphoria pasties, and the room is swaying slightly. Good thing I'm sitting. Without my carefully crafted walls, I'm picking up emotions from all around me and it's seriously overwhelming.

Roxalus brushes his fingertips against my arm but pulls them away when he catches Elodie noticing. She glances to and then back to Max.

"Where have these deaths happened? If it's contained to one place, perhaps we can concentrate our efforts in that area."

Sighing dreamily, I can't help myself. She'd make a wonderful queen. Thoughtful. Devoted. Beautiful...

Shit! I'm fangirling again. The haze brought on by these damn cakes coupled with all of these emotions feels like I'm riding a roller coaster. Focus damn it!

Her point has merit, but somehow, I don't think that Max would be addressing all of his siblings if he knew which one of their lands the killer hailed from.

"Our first half of the competitions were held in the Kingdom seat. That's where the first eight murders occurred," Noxian reveals. Gasps go up around the circle.

"Eight? There have been eight murders and none of this has reached our ears?" Princess Elodie's incredulity is mirrored on all of their faces.

Loxias is scrubbing his hand through his hair and Roxalus is seething from the chair beside me. They are all in their own personal states of concern.

"And why have you only just now brought this to our attention, dear brother?" Ice coats his fingertips, and in response, fire plays at the tips of Max's.

"There will be no fighting in my study!" Emenda says, now standing between the two. "This is my favorite part of the castle, and I will not see it destroyed."

Once again, Ayxian's hand has gone to his sword. He doesn't appear to be as taken aback by the news as the others. His poker face is intentionally neutral, and I find myself drawn to his calm as much as I am afraid of what's lurking beneath the surface.

With a pointed clearing of his throat, Loxias does his best to break through the tension that hangs thick in the air. "What conclusion have you come to, brother? Should we be sending messengers?"

Glancing in my direction, I can *feel* Loxias' concern for me. Max is his favorite brother, and I am Max's daughter's best friend and cousin. After coming to realize how much I like this version of him earlier, it doesn't surprise me at all. It's in his character.

A lump forms in my throat. I'm touched by his caring. I didn't think to try and make friends with him before but now...

I guess I never really considered things from Loxias' point of view. I'd always seen him as the Huntsman. The one who came to the human realm and made trophies of the creatures who resided in the Lupian Forest.

He's the youngest sibling. He's been picked on for being the baby even before Max's disappearance.

My uncle has a soft spot for him and when he wasn't there to stand up for him, Loxias had been at the mercy of all of his older siblings. His adoration for Max now extends to me and a warm-hearted sensation fills my chest, the metal of the necklace heating above it.

"This is the first competition outside of the seat and the murderer has come here. It means that it is someone amongst us. Perhaps one of our very own entourages." Max tilts his head. "Give me a moment."

Teleporting away and back in the blink of an eye, his hands aren't empty when he arrives back in the room. There's a person held tightly in his grip. "What were you doing listening at the door?" he demands.

A light from one of the wall torches casts a flickering light across the male fae's face and I gasp at who Max has captured.
"Nydin?"

Chapter Seventeen

Nydin dangles from Max's grip, his eyes are wide, with fear radiating off of him in droves.

"What have you to say for yourself?" Roxalus' hard voice rumbles through the room.

"I swear, I wasn't..." Nydin starts, but Ayxian snatches him from Max's grip and tosses him across the room.

Books from the shelf he slid into come crashing down around his head and Princess Emenda shouts, stomping her feet.

"Enough, enough, enough!" she screams. "I will not have my home, or my subjects disparaged."

Lifting the hems of her skirt, she walks over to where Nydin is crumbled on the floor. Extending her hand, he takes it hesitantly. There's fear in his eyes and concern in hers.

"I swear, Your Highness, I didn't mean any harm. I..." He falters after glancing around the room at the other royals.

Walking over to him, I place my hand on his shoulder. Maybe it isn't my place but standing there while someone I've come to care about is tossed around the room isn't my style.

Hearing Max, Ayxian, and Roxalus all make sounds of disapproval, my anger turns to them.

"Is this what it means to be a good leader?" I say, disgusted at their lack of decency. Nydin has been nothing but kind to me. The situation makes my inner panther growl at the injustice. "Do your subjects not get a voice when accused of an allegation?"

Max's expression softens. Sometimes it's easy to forget that his wicked fae side exists. That seed of darkness that all fae possess. It only flourishes if you feed it.

I, personally, have been keeping mine starved. The longer I'm here, the more it fights to grow stronger. Almost as persistent as a weed growing through the crack in a sidewalk.

"You're right, Lady Piper. Perhaps we would all do well to remember that." Max says, motioning for Nydin to come forward.

My hand remains on his arm, but I don't stop him from following his liege's request. Inara would do the same.

"Nydin, tell us why you took it upon yourself to listen at the door," he pauses and then adds, "knowing that this is a royals only conversation?" Raising a brow in my direction, I don't miss the meaning.

I had just overstepped but I am more than willing to do that to defend an injustice and hold the princes and princesses accountable. I'm certain the king and I will be having a talk later.

If he thinks I'll feel bad about it, he really doesn't know me well at all.

Embla looks Nydin up and down in a clear dismissal and Elodie's face is full of woe. Emenda hasn't left Nydin's side either.

Most of the euphoria pasties effects have burned off. I'm still not able to distinguish individual emotions as well as I usually do. Talk about frustrating!

Tension sits heavy throughout the room as we wait for Nydin to find his courage. Ayxian takes a menacing step towards us and ice appears at the tips of Roxalus' fingers in response.

It's odd to me that these siblings are all so quick to fight. I have no blood siblings of my own, but Inara is my sister none the less. We've argued from time to time but never have we come to blows. It's unconscionable for us to even consider. Crazy fucking males, I swear.

"The fae that was murdered was my cousin's daughter," he says, wringing his hands until the knuckles stand out white against his dark golden complexion.

Despair fills my chest. Now I know why Elodie's saddened. Her gifts allow her to see the things she *feels*, were as mine only give me the feelings in general that someone is feeling at the time.

"I didn't mean any harm, I swear it." His words are directed at Princess Emenda. "I feel lost, Your Highness. I don't know how to contain the sorrow in my heart. I... I..."

Princess Emenda wraps her arms around him and Roxalus makes a sound of distain. He clearly thinks comforting someone from a lower class is not something the princess should be doing.

The double doors bang open, and her second comes rushing into the study. Ayxian's hand goes to the sword at his side instinctively and Loxias' hand rests quickly on the axe that hangs from his belt.

"What is the meaning of this?" Prince Noxian demands firmly, but more calmly than I'd thought the royals capable. "This is a closed meeting, Lord Davian."

Max speaks instead. "Nydin is his mate. Nothing would have kept me from Eowyn if I'd felt her distress while within range." He turns back to Nydin. "Forgive us for our overzealous assumptions. I'm sure Lord Davian would like you to leave with him. I shall allow it," he says with a small dip of his chin. "Lord Davian, take the afternoon off to comfort your mate. See to it that he doesn't interfere with our investigations again."

Princess Embla and Prince Roxalus tsk at the same time. Unfeeling assholes!

"It must be nice to have no accountability," Prince Roxalus sneers. Walking towards the doors, he turns, staring daggers at Max. "No worries. Justice always finds its mark." His boots make no sound as he swiftly leaves without another word.

I can't believe how mean he'd been. Nydin has lost a family member, and the prince is acting like he's the bad guy for listening at the door.

Anything I had been feeling towards him turns laden with distain. Cruel bastard. What was I thinking? That he can be good? When will I learn to stay in my lane?

My stupid inner voice smacks me over the head as always. *Or maybe your safety and that of the kingdom means something. Change doesn't happen overnight. A candle can lead the way in the blackest of nights, but the darkness won't be breached with no air to breathe life to the flame.*

Ayxian and Loxias stand in hushed conversation. I can't make out what they are saying but Loxias doesn't seem happy about whatever it was.

Max comes to stand next to me. "Thank you," he whispers in a hushed tone.

I think he's mocking me at first and I glare at him. He'll owe me a boon if I invoke the magics.

"I mean it. Sometimes I forget to be me while I'm here. Eowyn would have had my balls if she'd have seen how I'd acted back there."

That makes me laugh. Inara might still have his balls after I tell her. She and her mother were so much alike, it makes me miss my aunt greatly.

"She was always fair. I learned a lot from her when I was growing up." After my own mother had died, Eowyn had taken me in without hesitation.

Smile sad, I know he misses his mate. Never having experienced the mating bond myself, it's from an outsider's point of view, but my gifts give me an insight to his pain.

"She was. I need to keep her in the forefront of my mind more often; ask myself what would Eowyn do?" This time, his smile's genuine. It lights up his face. Crinkling lines appear at the corners of his eyes. "I must go inform Leif of the situation. I'll be back for dinner." With that, he teleports away.

Just as I reach the doors, a presence behind me has my senses on alert. A shadow falls over the entrance to the study, and a shiver runs down my spine.

The smell of earth and cedar creeps through the air, and for a second, I relax a fraction. I know that scent. Over a month's worth of it had crept into my nose not so long ago.

Ayxian places his hand against the small of my back without preamble and I shudder again.

"Lady Piper, a word." His tone makes it clear that it isn't a request.

He's ruggedly good looking with long, wavy hair that hangs to one side in a messy braid and eyes that have a darkness barely hidden in their depths.

Starting to head left down the corridor towards the gardens, he steers me right. My confusion must have shone on my face.

"I would like to speak with you in private, without prying ears." That raspy, deep voice of his sinks beneath my skin, tightening my core.

"Of course, Your Highness. Should we return to the study? It's empty now." My heart picking up speed.

I don't want to think about his actions from last night but right now, the flashing **DANGER** sign in my head won't go away.

He isn't in that same predatory head space he'd been in last night, but I can't help the fear and the excitement that still takes up space in my mind equally.

"No. I would prefer to speak in here." Giving a slight push to the bottom of my back, his massive hands slide down an inch towards my ass, and I step away from him as we enter a dark, anti-chamber in the south stairwell.

The only light in the room is coming from several windows, high in the air along the wall. They don't quite reach down far enough to see out of, and his face is half hidden in darkness.

Opening my mouth to speak, his lips unexpectedly press to mine with bruising force. Gasping in surprise, swallowing the sound, he takes that as a means of encouragement.

My body reacts to the heat and earthy cedar scent of him. With a forceful tongue, he wrestles mine into submission. The grip on my hips, nearly painful.

I become all need and sharp desire, but pulling away from my mouth, he nuzzles into my neck. Wetness pools between my legs as his kisses send shivers down to my core.

I moan and in the next second, he bites me. Hard. His fangs don't break the skin, but I will have a bruise for sure.

My cry of pain is muffled by his tongue as I push at his chest and the hand he has around my back holds me tighter as his other hand makes its way into my hair.

Yanking my head back to expose my neck, he licks down to the crest of my breasts peeking out of my dress. His growl rumbling through us both.

I'm not willing to take this next step with him yet. Especially not like some shameful dirty secret to be had in a dark storage closet.

Pushing on his chest again, his knee forces its way between my legs, rubbing up and down my sex. The hardened length of him smashing into my thigh repeatedly.

"Prince Ayxian, I need a minute," I gasp between panted breaths.

Reluctantly, he releases his hand from my hair and rests his forehead against mine, but stays in place, not removing his leg. No longer rubbing me with it though.

After another minute, standing straight, his hooded eyes flutter with their dark lashes and a meek grin dances at the edges of his swollen lips.

"Lady Piper, I always seem to lose myself in your presence." Leaning in, he takes a long draft of my scent from the crook of my neck. "You are an intoxicatingly beautiful creature."

We made out several times when I'd first arrived in Anavrin. Each time it became a bit more intense. Each time he's referred to me as a beautiful creature.

Maybe it's weird but I feel like he might be more attracted to the thought of my panther side than to me as a person. That can't be right though. Can it?

Last night, I simply thought it was because we were drawing closer to doing something more that maybe he'd misread my willingness. Or his animalistic beastly gifts had snapped their reins.

Now, I wonder if there is a different underlying reason. The feeling unnerves me, but that unhinged excitement also drives me to him time and time again. Good gods, I need help!

Breathlessly, I find my voice again. "You wish to discuss something with me?"

This time, he fully steps back like I'd thrown a bucket of cold water over his head. The contrast in his personality is astonishing.

Where a minute ago there had been a pouncing lion, now stands a stoic prince. Maybe I imagined all of that brutishness. Perhaps Anavrin is making me crazy.

"The point seems moot now. I wanted to offer my regrets for my behavior last night." One corner of his mouth turns up. "I don't usually act this way. You bring something out in me that I never knew existed. And for the boredom of immortality, change like this is difficult to cope with."

Relieved, a smile plays at my lips. I'm not so crazy after all. The way he'd growled and stalked towards me last night is an image I can't escape. Part of it gets my motor revving. And part of it scares me deeply.

When I don't say anything, he raises his hands in surrender and takes a step back another foot. With the small bit of light shining across his face, there's a piece of lint in the scruff of his beard, and without thinking, I reach up to touch it.

Mistaking my intentions, Ayxian reacts by pressing my hand against his cheek and closing his eyes. After a breath, he steps away.

"Until next time, Lady Piper." He turns and sweeps out of the small room. I'm once again left confused and aching.

Collecting my thoughts and smoothing out the hems of my skirt, I exit the anti-chamber.

A shadow cast from the torches along the corridor reveals a figure leaning against the opposite wall with their arms crossed.

Roxalus.

Chapter Eighteen

Our eyes meet and if I could have crawled under a rock, I would have.

Ayxian and I hadn't done anything but that doesn't stop the embarrassment of being caught coming out of a storage chamber with flushed skin and a guilty conscience. My cheeks heat even more under Roxalus' scrutiny.

"It appears that you are more fae than I first imagined." A shadow of a sneer dons his lips, but his eyes hold mine with their ferocity, a small twitch in one of them.

"And what is that supposed to mean?" It infuriates me to have this undercurrent of desire playing with my emotions right now.

Roxalus and Ayxian can't be more different, but my body reacts to both with equal parts longing and loathing.

"Am I supposed to take that as a compliment or a condonement? I assure you; I do not seek your validation." Or maybe I do. Gah.

Taking a long breath, in through the nose, out through the mouth. Then another. Neither of us says anything else. Me fuming. Him seething.

Turning in opposite directions at the same time, we leave each other's sight before any embers ignite.

I can't be the only one who feels this inexplicable pull. He hates me. That much is for sure. But everywhere I turn, there he is. Mucking up my mind. Making me feel things I shouldn't.

As I exit the castle, the fragrant lavender hits my senses like a punch to the gut. After the scents of earthy cedar and peppermint & pine needles, the flowery smell feels accosting instead of calming.

The sun is hidden behind a few sparse clouds. All of the princesses are waiting for me under the gazebo.

I'm tempted to turn right back around, go to my rooms. Maybe read for the remainder of the day and night.

A tug at my sleeve draws my attention. Amalie has her hair pulled back in a messy bun and holds a cup of coffee out to me. "I thought you could use this."

The gesture is so kind and so wanted that I have no words. Her smile is sincere and her motives honest. I can *feel* it in every square inch of her being.

"You are a breath of fresh air, Amalie. Has anyone ever told you that?" Her cheeks redden as she smiles and curtsies.

"No, My Lady. You are the only one who has never made me feel like I'm too extra." Beaming up at me, I feel like I'm seeing a soul take its first steps towards self-acceptance.

I know what she means all too well. Too often, females especially, are made to feel that boisterous or forward personalities aren't respectable.

I lived meekly for most of my life, trying to fit into everyone else's mold. Fuck that. We gals need to sing each other's praises, not tear each other down.

"Have you thought about what we talked about? I'm getting ready to throw myself into the lions den." I say with a wink. "Now would be the perfect time for me to press the issue if you are so inclined to my proposal." I want her to come with me from court to court, but I've left the choice up to her.

"As much as I would love to, I think you should give some other handmaidens the same kindnesses that you have extended to me, My Lady." Biting at her bottom lip, a small smile turns up the corners of her mouth. "Maybe after the competitions are over, I could take you up on your offer after you've settled in whichever place you've decided?" Fidgeting with a string hanging from her sleeve, the insecurity reminds me so much of how I use to be. "That is, if you still want my services."

Finishing my coffee, I hand her back the cup, feeling rejuvenated. And with a lightness in my heart, I turn towards the princess's direction. Over my shoulder, I call back, "That sounds just about perfect, Amalie. You have yourself a deal."

A fae deal is binding and the magics shimmer in the air around me before I hear her squeal with delight. The sound filling me with joy, making this day just the teensiest bit better.

I know I made the right choice in my initial offer to her, but the one she presented was better. She's right. Getting to know other servants will help strengthen my connection to these lands and help me with the task Max set for me.

They're the backbone of Anavrin. They're the ones keeping things running smoothly and the ones that the royals need to prove worthy of ruling.

Walking with a little more bounce in my step, I saunter towards the gazebo. It's strange not to see Lord Davian present or Nydin, for that matter.

It's just the twins and Princess Elodie. All of the usual courtiers are in the gardens but not lounging around the gazebo as they normally do.

It has to be Princess Embla's doing. She really doesn't like the classes to mix with the royals, does she? What a sad little life she leads.

Going to her court is going to be oh so fun. *Not.* I can already feel the dread simply from the thought of how high her step ladder had to be to get on that particular horse.

I know I should be approaching it with an open mind, but she's been making it difficult to do that from the first moment Max introduced us when I came to stay with him at the kingdom seat castle during the third competition.

"Lady Piper, how good of you to finally join us." Embla's tone puts my hackles on end, but I don't rise to the bait. What would be the point?

"Princess Embla." I say, inclining my head.

Her pursed lips speak volumes. She's not happy that I don't fully curtsy to her. Secretly, it makes my spirits lift a little to egg her on without fully being a bitch myself.

Looking towards Princesses Emenda and Elodie, I give a more respectful curtsy. The glee I *feel* coming off of Elodie has me fighting the urge to laugh. "Your Highnesses. I beg your pardon for my tardiness. Prince Ayxian required a word."

Elodie cocks her head to the side trying to gauge my feelings. I school my expressions the best I can, but I know she can *feel* the confusion and desire marring my emotions.

The corners of her mouth turn up. "Oh, Embla. You shouldn't be put out. Lady Piper may very well be Queen one day."

If looks could kill, Elodie and I would be goners. Emenda nearly spits out the tea she'd brought to her mouth. Embla's gift of electricity sparks at her fingertips.

"And why would a lowbee like her ever be queen?" The venom in her voice sends a chill of ice down my spine but with a ping of fortitude from Elodie, I steel my nerves.

I almost want to respond. My human raised side is at constant war with my fae hierarchy side and it's exhausting.

All of the curtsying and pomp and circumstance is giving me such a feeling of homesickness to be back with my silly cousin and her sarcastic granddaughter.

I've been tempted time and time again to show them all what it truly means to be a lowbee, but I've wanted to fit into their society.

I've made myself act the way that the upper class fae act. Here in Anavrin, the overpowering sense of self has unlocked every precaution I've put into place over the years.

If I knew the exact vision mother had, it would be easier to judge for myself whether hiding behind Inara's coattails and denying who I am was worth it.

All I know about it is what Aunt Eowyn and mother had whispered when they hadn't known I'd been hiding in the bushes.

The only words I'd caught for sure... fae prince, panther, war and a cage. It's extremely frustrating.

It's still my hope that Inara can uncover more details in that book of shadows she'd inherited. If Eowyn wrote it down anywhere, it'd be there.

"Dear sister," Elodie's tone teasing but serious. "If Ayxian wins and becomes king, it is very possible that he will court our Lady Piper here. Or Roxalus for that matter."

It's my turn to spit my tea. Princess Embla glares daggers in Emenda's direction, but Emenda is studiously averting her eyes.

I would have bet my left arm that Emenda and Embla shared everything in that special twin way of theirs but apparently, Emenda had kept some secrets for her own.

These fae and their games! When am I going to learn that all tea doesn't need to be spilled in a single afternoon?

"How is that brother of ours, Lady Piper?" Elodie turns in her seat to gleam my reaction full on.

How am I supposed to answer that? It's a loaded question. Elodie's smile holds all of that underlying fae mischief. Traitor!

If playing their games is how I am meant to live out the rest of my life, I'm going to have to make a decision.

Stay in this Bridgerton style of talk and etiquette or embrace the hidden parts of myself I locked away all those years ago?

Throwing my hands in the air, I exclaim. "Fuck it... He's confusing. And honestly, a bit frightening. One minute he's all desire and longing, the next, he's distant and driven for the crown. I don't know where we stand."

Uh-oh. That dam I'd built around my mouth is finally crumbling. It's freeing and terrifying and exhilarating.

Royalty still deserves more respect than the rest of us but my inner panther purrs at me letting it off its leash and I don't think I can bring myself to chain it up again.

Elodie's all smiles and honest thrills. Emenda gasps, but Embla looks smug. "There she is!" she says. "I knew that crass lowbee was in there somewhere."

My panther circles inside my head, begging to be freed. Snarling to get to the surface. A bit of that snarl sounds from my chest with my next words.

"Be that as it may, if Ayxian does win and we marry, I'll be your better." I feel that wicked fae mischief coat my tongue and this time I don't shy away from it.

Gasps go up from all three of the princesses this time. It's Elodie's *feelings* that help to ground me.

"That's not to say that he will win, or that we will be a couple, but the fact of the matter is that if you're not the one to win this competition, Princess Embla, you may want to be kinder to the..." I slur the word in that disdainful way of hers..."*lowbees*. One of your brothers or sisters may make one of them a king or queen someday."

Emenda is the first to find her voice. "Lady Piper." Her tone is false shock. A hand placed over her heart to further the effect and a smirk graces her face. "I knew you had a forked tongue under those bonny lips."

Elodie and I laugh but Embla purses her lips so tightly, I fear she'll give herself wrinkles.

"Oh Emenda. I do know how much you love your tea," I say with an exaggerated, opened mouthed, wink.

Grabbing her sides Elodie laughs with her whole body. With its infectious nature, Emenda and I follow suit.

Embla seethes once again, her face red and blotchy. Her lips pursed even tighter. I'd cut her to the quick and I know I'll pay the price for it eventually.

Today, however, is not that day. I take what feels like the first real breath I've had in months.

Maybe being me, unfiltered, is how I should be. As much as the warning mother gave me plays over and again in my mind, I'm tired of hiding myself away from the world.

"And what of Prince Roxalus? Does he also find that tongue suited to his liking?" Embla asks the question to unnerve me but surprisingly, it doesn't.

Relief washes over me. I've been wondering if it's my imagination, the things happening between me and Roxalus, but hearing her speculations, something unlocks.

"He never mentioned it after our kiss," I say boldly without remorse. Fuck her!

Emenda and Embla mirror each other as their hands fly up to cover their mouths. Elodie snickers at them and it solidifies my liking for the youngest princess even more.

Friends are hard to come by when everyone is scheming all the time, but I can already believe that she and I are well on our way.

Sighing, I let them drink from my cup. If being fae means playing the games, then call me thirsty.

"Getting a read on his intentions hasn't been easy. If I am being honest...well, he does kiss better than Prince Ayxian. I suppose I should make friendly with Prince Noxian and Prince Loxias at some point, ya know, just for comparison."

Wicked glee fills me, and I smile conspiratorially at Elodie. She's contented herself with my unspoken words, letting her *feel* what I'm not saying.

"Now, if you'll excuse me, I'm going to go freshen up." Lifting the hems of this ridiculous skirt, I stand to gather them. "I feel ridiculous in these outfits. I'm going to go scrounge up something more suited to what a lowbee finds to be comfortable attire." Dipping my chin in deference, it's time to make a change. "Princesses. I will see you all at dinner."

Chapter Nineteen

As the week moves on, I'd run into Ayxian and Roxalus in the corridors of the castle only a few times.

They'd both been too busy trying to write their poems for the competition, hurrying by without acknowledging me at all.

Neither of them ate in the dining room with the rest of us, choosing to spend their time in their rooms or in the study when no one else was in there to bother them.

All of the royals are tense and have basically sequestered themselves in various parts of the castle, working away diligently.

They aren't supposed to have any outside help, but I've noticed several of them relying on the fae in their entourages to research this or give their input on that.

Roxalus and Elodie are the only two that I haven't seen asking for help. The thought makes my necklace warm briefly before cooling again.

Max turned up about an hour ago. The reciting of the poems is today. Crowds have gathered all around the land and throughout the castle.

I'm beginning to feel claustrophobic from the influx of bodies. I've made great progress in controlling my gifts, but with this many people around, I'm struggling.

"I hear that you've come out of your shell." The twitch to Max's mouth leaves me feeling exposed. Like a child being scrutinized under a parent's tutelage.

I've stayed true to myself since that day in the gazebo with the princesses, allowing my human raised side to shine. In doing so, I've felt the weight of all the other lies I'd been living slipping away.

"You've only been here an hour. Who told you?" It doesn't matter really. I'm simply curious.

Max isn't to blame for my anxiety. He's never made me feel bad for a single choice I've made or thing I've done. It's all my own ingrained insecurity that projects this shit. I need to get a grip.

"Inara. She said that she hasn't seen you this lively and free since you were young children."

Inara popped in for a few hours with Faelan three days ago. She and I gossiped and laughed over coffee, and she filled me in on all of the pack's goings on.

I really thought that I'd miss it more. When she was here, she'd said that she noticed a difference in me. In a good way.

I filled her in on everything... the stolen kisses, the standoff with Ayxian and Roxalus, and on the fact I'd decided to be thoroughly me from now on.

Her only response... "I'm glad you're back."

It meant the world to me that she'd remember who I'd been when we were children. Who I'd changed into after my mother's death wasn't something we'd talked about openly that often.

Inara loves me, not just the carefully curated version of myself that I've always presented to the world in my mother's wake.

"Is that where you were? In the Lupian Forest?" I have my suspicions about if Max will take up residence with his family after the throne's secured. The decision will be hard for him.

He'd only found out that Inara is his daughter with his lost mate just before he took over as King Regent.

On the other hand, he'd only found out that Leif is his son around that same time.

He had been with a fae woman before he'd ever met Eowyn. He didn't know she was pregnant when he was shipped off on a mission by his father, King Zyoden. By the time he'd returned, he found out that his lover had died but he'd never known it was in childbirth.

Max's life will never be contented until Inara and Faelan come to live here. It's hard enough for him to accept that his granddaughter, Faelan's mother, will pass in the human realm.

Inara and Faelan are having their own issues with it, but no one is going to force it upon her. So, they are enjoying her company for as long as they can in the human realm.

"Yes, but only just recently. There was a disturbance on the roads leading here from the southern courts. Another human realm fae death." Wringing his hands in front of him, he sighs, exasperated. "I'm at a loss. I don't know where to look next. I feel like we're missing something crucial, but I can't see it."

Taking a moment, I think about everything that's been found out. "You said that the first murders were in the kingdom seat, right? And that the murder before happened here?"

"Yes. And this one was not far from here." Scrubbing at his face, the frustration leaks from him to me. "Piper, I don't know how to keep them safe. Keep you safe. I feel like I have failed. I..."

I don't how to comfort him. Raising my hand to cup his face, I wait until he looks at me instead of his feet. "It's not your fault. You can't be everywhere at once, Uncle." A long breath escapes his control as he acknowledges the truth of my words. "Perhaps we're looking at this wrong. Perhaps it's not someone following the competition. Maybe it's someone in the competition."

"What do you mean? One of my siblings?" Dropping my hand, I reach for the book I've set down.

The hum of activity coming from the kitchens is loud today. Smells of all types of food permeate the air. Fresh baked bread and smoking meats. The sweet scent of sugar and fruits hang throughout the castle.

A feast will follow the poems and tomorrow I will head out to Loxias' court. It's the farthest away, close to the entrance of Anavrin, so the trip will take a few days.

"Maybe, but I think we'd be better to look into one of those in their entourages. If I were you, I'd find out who here amongst them hates the lowb... human realm fae."

Arching a brow, he shakes his head. "Not you too? Why would you call them that?"

It's a question that the *me* from a week or so ago would have weighed the answer and went with the safest route... but that isn't who I want to be anymore.

"Because I own it. Someone can only make you feel bad calling you a name if you allow the name to have that connotation. Instead of it meaning below them, I am allowing the term to float right over me. I've changed the way I look at it to mean lower realm. A direction. That's all. I took away their meaning and replaced it with one that can help give us lowbee's a sense of self in the face of their negative term."

Rubbing his chin, he digests what I've said. I *feel* it take root, first in his mind, then in his heart. A smile that touches his eyes beams back at me.

"You are amazing. Do you know that?" Heat rising to the apples of my cheeks at his praise.

I know his thoughts wander to Inara and Faelan. They will be living here eventually, and he worries about that from time to time.

"Alright then. I shall have Leif and a bunch of trusted fae around the lands spread the word of the new meaning. The next time someone tries to use it as a slur, they'll be in for a surprise," he says, chuckling to himself.

Holding out the elbow of his pro-offered arm, I take it. "Shall we? I'm dying to hear these fools give poetry a go. It should be quite interesting."

Smiling, I instantly see the shimmer of magics as he teleports us to the stage set up for the readings.

As always, it's a beautiful day, with just the right amount of cloud cover. It is around seventy-five degrees, and a gentle breeze blows the ends of my hair that have escaped my braid around my face.

Black leggings that Inara brought me on her last visit cover my legs. I've paired them with a flowy blouse. My cleavage is exposed but not in a sleezy way. It's subtle. The sides of the blouse hug my figure until it reaches my hips. There, it cascades out and away from my body like a dress.

It hardly goes halfway down my ass, but I love that I don't have to wear dresses all the time. If it upsets the royals or etiquette or the fae, no one's said anything. Though, I won't care if they do.

The fact of the matter is, over the last week, I've seen a few of them following my lead. Their outfits are handmade and not quite lowbee style, but it lifts my heart to see that they are trying to imitate me.

Max and I take our seats in the front row along with the other royals. They've all drawn numbers to decide the order in which they get to present their poem.

Princess Embla is up first. A hush falls over the chattering crowd as she takes the stage.

It's finally time to find out what being King or Queen will mean to each of them. And to us, their subjects.

Chapter Twenty

"I have been brought up to see things in the terms of status. My people will tell you that I am a good ruler to them. I try to listen to their concerns and hear their disputes with a fair and just ear. If I were to become queen, I would extend my ears to the whole kingdom. With that being said, here is my poem..." Princess Embla's hands shake slightly.

I'm compelled to believe her words due to her nervousness, but there's a small ping of self-righteousness hitting me in the heart as she speaks.

"A queen isn't just a figurehead. She is the epitome of her people.

A leader without enemies is not seen as a formidable threat to an opposing kingdom.

I shall walk with the grace that I have been blessed to carry.

The cruelty that I will deliver to our foes.

<u>And determine the course of our future that ensures our lifestyles remain consistent.</u>

<u>That is what my reign will mean.</u>"

I *feel* the weight of her words like an anvil in my gut. When she said that she'd *ensure our lifestyles remain consistent*, I *feel* the meaning behind them.

There's a sharp ping from my gifts, metallic on my tongue. I know what she means by those words, and I hope the others of the lower class can decipher their meaning as well.

"Thank you, Princess Embla. That's quite enlightening." Lord Davian is conducting the proceedings.

I haven't seen much of him since Nydin was caught by Max outside the doors of the study. Nydin is now sitting a few rows back and he gives me a weak smile when I give him a subtle wave.

"Next up, we have Prince Ayxian," Lord Davian announces.

Ayxian takes the stage. His muscular form cast a large shadow on the seats of the front row. I smile up at him as his eyes meet mine, but he looks quickly away.

If I thought I might be more important to him than the task of winning the crown, I've be deluding myself. His sights are set, and I am... how had he put it? Oh yeah, a distraction.

<u>"Formidable as a lion. Solid as a stone wall. My rule would be prosperous. Our enemies would all fall."</u>

Oh great. Rhyming... how poetic.

Maybe I'm being too harsh. He did tell me from the get-go that winning the kingdom was his goal.

It stings that our interactions didn't mean as much to him as his quest for power, but I can understand. The need to win and conquer is who he is.

I've never wanted to be in control of anyone but myself. That wasn't something that was in my grasp in the past.

Now that I am the one in control of me, I don't think I can give it up again.

"If I were your king, you would not want another.

If you chose not to have me, I'd still honor my sister or my brother.

I am royal, through and through.

My blood, it does run blue.

If I were to be made your king. I'd save this land and it's fae.

My actions will ring true."

He leaves the stage without another word, and I honestly don't know how to feel about his poem.

He's clearly tried his best. The broad muscles of his arms glisten with sweat as he walks by. It's not hot so it must be from nervous energy.

Being king is obviously important to him but I can't decide if I think he's worthy of that position.

After finding him in the gardens when his predatory nature took hold, I can't see Ayxian as the same caring person I'd picnicked with on the hillside or taken long walks through the pine forest with.

Does he wear that darkness just under his skin or is it simply something that only comes out when he isn't in full control of the animal within?

Will he be a just king or will he be one that is biased and unmoved by the problems of his people?

While I've been speculating about the handsome warrior prince, Noxian and Emenda have gone on stage and given their poems, and I've missed them entirely.

My daydreaming about Ayxian's caring side and then fantasizing about his primal side gives way to irritation with myself and it floods my system as Roxalus takes the stage.

A hush descends over the chattering crowd. Prince Roxalus had been named king's heir when Max disappeared, and the kingdom holds a collective breath, waiting to hear what he has to say.

"Lonely is the head that wears the crown.

Heavy is the heart in ways that can never be seen, only felt.

The greatness of a kingdom resides firmly on the shoulders of the righteous."

My heart aches with the weight of his words. I can *feel* the sadness emanating from his soul.

Roxalus cast his eyes over the crowd, down one side and coming back up the other.

"That's what my tutelage led me to believe.

If the heart is full of woe, then power can be grasped with both hands."

I can't tear my eyes away from him.

"... but power doesn't come from magics.

It doesn't come from control or placement.

True power is derived from having something worth fighting for."

His eyes snap to mine and hold me firmly in their depths. Is he is talking to the crowd in general or solely to me? I can't tell, but I drink him in.

"I was unworthy."

Gasps and jabbering run a course around the audience. My ears are ringing.

"If nothing moves me, then how can I be fair?

If no one challenges me, how can I be just?"

Air refuses to enter my lungs. He won't release me from his gaze, but I find that I don't want to be pulled away. I want to drown in the depths of those cold blue eyes.

"If I have no room in my heart for love, how can I find love for my people?"

Dropping his eyes to his hands, the air rushes back into my constricted lungs. I *feel* pings of anger and jealousy and awe from every direction.

With a glance over to where Ayxian sits, his fists are in a tight ball, but he won't look at me.

Roxalus' voice is now barely above a whisper.

"I am unworthy, but I am hopeful."

Exiting the stage, he does look at me... like he is trying to see into my soul but doesn't say a word as he passes.

Lord Davian trips up the steps to the stage to announce the next contestant. I peer around and everyone appears as dumbstruck at the stoic prince's poem as I am.

"That was very..." Lord Davian struggles for words. "... thought provoking, Prince Roxalus." After gathering himself together, he announces Loxias and the prince comes bounding onto the scene.

After a whispered conversation, Loxias begins.

"First, I must say, that I am not using my gifts. I have no need of them to sway you my way."

The crowd gives a little chuckle but takes to heart his words. Faeries can't lie, so he is being smart, putting it out there that we aren't being influence unduly.

"Secondly, while being king would be marvelous, I don't know how to be regal."

The fae around me, including Max, laugh again at his light-hearted speech.

"And thirdly, I have no idea what constitutes a poem so the one, two, three thing is all I've got."

Winking out at the audience, he bounces back off of the stage. Quill and Leif clap him on the back as he comes down the steps.

I can't decide if he's brilliant or a lunatic, but I feel lighter after his performance. And that saying something.

Would it be a good thing, or a bad thing, to have a young jester like him as king? In charge of the lives of an entire king-dom?

The last of the royals to speak is Princess Elodie.

Honestly, I may be a bit bias myself now, because Elodie has wormed her way right into my heart with her bold, unabashed honesty.

It's refreshing in a land of omissions and half-truths. She never puts on airs. Her sense of justice and the need to be fair oozes from her like clean water from a natural spring.

"The fae of Anavrin are half heart and half hate.

A land without limits in power and fate.

A beautiful land with colorful lives helps create balance for all to thrive.

A thrown and a crown must be for the whole.

A leader without limits for status or prole.

Honesty, balance, and fairness a must.

As queen I will strive to be impartial and just."

She finishes with a little flourish of her hand. It doesn't come off as silly. It's quite endearing. And how she rhymed and told a story didn't feel fatuous, like Ayxian's poem did.

Max stands, going to the stage after giving my hand a quick squeeze.

I hadn't eaten much before the competition and now that it's over, my stomach grumbles with hunger.

"That was amazing. You all did a wonderful job. And before you ask, NO." He looks to the front row that holds all of his siblings. "I won't be announcing a winner. At the Feast of Sol, the points will be tallied, and we will all know who the sovereign will be at that same time."

Gesturing towards the castle, that radiant smile of his has me smiling in return. "Princess Emenda's staff has been working overtime to bring us a delicious feast. Eat, make merry, and sleep well. Tomorrow, we part ways for another couple of weeks before journeying to Prince Loxias' court."

Some of the crowd meanders around the lawn and gardens, but others head to the castle straight away. Max hears my stomach growl loudly as he descends the stairs and laughs.

The corner of his elbow is already extending my way. "Come on, Peppercorn. I can get us there before everyone else."

I love how he's picked up my mother's nickname for me from Inara.

Glancing over towards Ayxian and then to Roxalus and taking a deep breath, I let Max teleport us away.

Chapter Twenty-One

The carriage ride to Prince Loxias' court had been un-eventful but had felt never ending. His was the farthest away from Princess Emenda's.

It's so close to the Anavrin Arch that leads into the human realm, I keep feeling the urge to sneak off in the middle of the night to go see Inara.

Then I remember that the Arch is magically sealed. Only King Maximus, Inara, and Faelan can pass through it at will.

Faelan's spell sealed the fae in this realm and the only way for us to come or go is with assistance from her blood line. Direct bloodline.

Inara and I are cousins but on Aunt Eowyn's side, not Max's. I have to rely on them if I want to visit the Lupian Forest.

I'd been so upset by all of it at first. All of us fae or half fae had been sucked back into Anavrin during the Blood Moon when Faelan performed a ritual to break the curse that limited the fae's power and their ability to connect with their mates.

In doing so, she re-worked the spell to help keep the humans safe from the faeries.

It was the only way that she'd been willing to break the curse and give them back all of that power.

And while I understand her reasoning, it had still upset me. I hadn't even known that I was a fae until that day. I'd thought that I was simply a gifted shifter.

Loxias has given me a room fit for a princess. His court is beautiful. The air around the castle is crisp and homey. There are many items that the prince has brought back from the human realm.

Antique furniture, mirrors, satin sheets, books. I nearly cried when I saw my rooms. Homesickness hit me like a ton of bricks.

His hospitality has been more welcoming and refreshing than I'd ever have dreamed him capable of when I'd only known him as The Hunter; a fae prince of legend.

It turns out, he's a big softy.

He hunted magical creatures in the Lupian for centuries. My kind included; wolf and panther.

Growing up, we all heard the stories of the lives he'd taken for sport. We all feared the Hunter as much as human children feared the Boogie Man.

On my first night here in his castle, we had a small dinner with just him, Quill, and a few of his friends.

It was so different from the dinners I'd had at the kingdom seat and at Princess Emenda's that I was taken aback.

Loxias is down to earth when his mischievous side is kept tucked away. He laughs and drinks and makes no demands of his staff or his courtiers.

Halfway through dinner that first night, he leaned in towards me. "Aren't you having a marvelous time, Lady Piper?"

I couldn't feel any underlying meaning behind his words. It *felt* like he genuinely wanted to know.

"I'm still a bit tired from the journey, but I must say," I'd lifted the honey mead to my lips and took another drink. "I honestly am. You're so much different than I thought you'd be."

His tipsy smile broadened. "And how did you think I would be? Hmmm?" His eyelashes batted down once.

I knew he hadn't been truly flirting with me. I'd come to understand him a little better over the last several encounters since my arrival in Anavrin.

He wanted to find his mate and live a simple, happy life. The truth of that beamed from every bit of his playful personality.

"Well, I thought that you would be a blood thirsty savage. You've hunted my kind for centuries." I hadn't stopped my bluntness simply because I'd left Princess Emenda's court.

I was me, only more so. The fae version of me. All of my observations. All of my forwardness. All of my spirit without the limitations of being human.

Loxias lifted his glass in a toast. "May your days be filled with joy and nights be filled with passion." He downed the rest of his mead before anyone else realized the toast was finished and the snort of laughter that left me had been extremely unladylike, which made me snort again.

Quill hadn't taken his eyes off of the prince all night as we'd sat around the table making merry. Their friendship was more than brotherhood, but Loxias didn't appear to notice the longing in Quill's gaze or the jealousy that I'd seen on several occasions from him.

Poor Quill didn't know how to bridge that desire into something more, but it was none of my business. Unless asked, I was staying out of it.

Two weeks breezed by. We'd laughed and drank and hadn't talk politics or problems.

Only one time did the prince need to address a dispute from two villagers about too much water use by one of them. He handled it in that carefree manner of his that I've come to know.

He gave them both a bucket of rocks mixed with dirt. He had them place one plant from each of their crops in the bucket and water it the way they would water their entire crop. At the end of one week, he had them bring their buckets back.

"See, both of your crops are thriving. Perry, you grow basil. It doesn't need the same amount of tending to that Hammond's potatoes do. Neither of you are in the wrong. You have differences and that is what makes a community strong. Perhaps, Perry, you could spare more of the stream with that in mind."

Loxias gave them both a dip of his chin and glared at Perry until he conceded.

"Yes, Your Highness. Thank you for hearing us out."

He simply smiled and waved their thank you away but I noticed a small glint in his eye at the debt. Faeries were nothing if not mischievous.

That's been my only excitement since arriving here... Until now.

A messenger came with the next challenge and that means tomorrow the other contestants and their entourages will start to join us.

I've been enjoying my lackadaisical days here and haven't given much thought to the two princes who'd left me confused and wanting since leaving Princess Emenda's court.

Except at night.

Often, my mind had flashes of Ayxian's strong, broad shoulders or Roxalus' chiseled jawline and soft lips.

My hands tended to wander along my body when those thoughts pressed themselves to the forefront of my mind.

I don't have a handmaiden here to interrupt me, so giving in to those fantasies a few times without worry of interruption is the only relief I've found.

With the new arrivals, I'll have to be mindful of personal space again. People tend to tread where they like, whenever they like when the royals are around.

Lazing by the front doors, the sound of approaching hoofbeats pulls me from my daydreams. Prince Roxalus horse canters into view a few moments later. Two figures accompanying him.

A male who appears older, maybe fifty human years. The fae age extremely slowly. This fae must be ancient.

The other was a beautiful female. All fae have beauty but hers required me to look away. Not quite the goddess beauty Elodie has, but right up there.

It's bright and alluring and there's a haughtiness that makes me feel like I am an ant under her glare. She's wearing riding leathers, and a sword hangs at her side.

"Prince Roxalus. We weren't expecting you until tomorrow." Loxias' demeanor changes completely from how it'd been just moments ago.

I've heard how Roxalus and the twins treated their siblings that were not born of Queen Ombriana before Max's return.

Queen Leyashna had been King Zyoden's second wife, and they've been inclined to believe their siblings are lesser in the line of royalty because of it. The thrown was Queen Ombriana's. King Zyoden had married into it.

He took a second wife because the people demanded it after Queen Ombriana was killed by his mistress. If he wanted to keep the throne, he had to comply.

Max is the oldest but when he'd gone missing, Roxalus and the twins are said to have been cruel and wicked when it came to their treatment of Loxias, Noxian, and Elodie.

Ayxian can hold his own against them, but he didn't intervene as often as he should have.

Sneering down at his youngest brother, the sound of his voice ripples through me. A brush of heat flares in places it has no business being.

"I'm sure you have my rooms ready. It wasn't a hard journey." His eyes briefly meet mine and I swallow the lump that has formed in my throat. "Tell your staff that we will be requiring only two rooms."

Quill looks from me to the female at Roxalus' side and shakes his head. I've been observant of him over the months, but it seems he's been observant of me too.

Well, that's sobering. Geesh!

Loxias must have caught on to the situation quickly too. "I assume your riders will need two beds in their room?"

Clever wording. Loxias and I have developed a friendship over the last couple of weeks. He may not be privy to everything going on, but he's proving to be far from clueless.

"Lord Beartach will be in need of his own room." He spares me the briefest of glances before waving his hand towards the beautiful female. "Commander Mystiance will be sharing with me."

Chapter Twenty-Two

Heat burns in my cheeks. From behind, there's the brush of a hand.

Quill's trying to comfort me, I realize, but I don't know why it matters to me that Roxalus is sharing his room with this beautiful fae warrior.

She glares in my direction for half a second, then turns her nose up but says nothing.

Loxias calls for the castle seneschal, Tomas. After whispering in the servant's ear, he turns back to face his brother.

"Your rooms are waiting. The others will be here in the morning. Or perhaps the afternoon. Enjoy my lands but brother," his tone is pure defiance, "refrain from your usual iniquity. My people are all equals here in their homeland."

"Oh, you poor little fool. When have I ever given your words any thought."

Loxias pales but doesn't cower. Hopping down from his horse, Roxalus casually offers his arm to Mystiance.

"Mysti and I would like to be alone to freshen up. Do call us for dinner."

Loxias hasn't moved. He stands between Roxalus and the front steps. The tension's thick enough to almost see.

Or maybe my mind is hazy from this irrational jealousy I'm feeling.

If Loxias is struggling in his desire to use his gifts of persuasion, he's hiding it well. Quill steps to his side and Mysti's hand goes straight to the hilt of her sword.

I've been quietly fuming since the sleeping arrangements were made but my body's frozen to the spot.

Later, I'll think back on it and wish it all went differently, I'm sure... but from the moment the unusual cold blue fire dances at the tips of Roxalus' fingers, my reactions are nothing but primal instinct.

I hate bullies. I've been made to do things that I didn't want to all of my life. Even if my mother and family had the best of intentions, it was still hurtful to be made to feel small. To feel helpless.

From one second to the next, I'm in front of Prince Loxias in my black panther form.

Mysti takes an involuntary step backwards before drawing her sword. Roxalus' eyes widen but he keeps his composure. Lord Beartach draws a quarter staff which holds a large stone at one end.

Pacing back and forth in front of Loxias, I don't allow them within a few feet of the castle. Quill's crossbow is drawn, aimed at the opposing prince.

Mysti raises her sword and takes a step in my direction, and I let the loudest roar of rebellion rip from my throat.

She swings it through the air like she can't wait to try and take my head. Quill looses a bolt that hits her sword mere millimeters above her hand, knocking it to the ground.

"I tire of this," Roxalus says lazily as he extinguishes his flames. "We shall freshen up and see you at dinner. No need to have a pissing match here. I'm sure Lady Piper knows who wields..." his eyes rake over my fur, and a shiver runs clear down my spine, but I shake it off. "... the bigger piece."

If I had been in my other form, my face would probably have burst from the heat of the embarrassment at what he's implied. I've never been anywhere near his *piece*, but that doesn't mean I haven't thought about it more often than is healthy.

He looks Loxias up and down one more time before proceeding into the castle. Calling over his shoulder, the arrogant bastard's words are meant solely to rile me up.

"Lady Piper's jealous outburst will require more food, so make sure your staff is accommodating."

I shift back to my normal form to retort but Roxalus, Commander Mystiance, and Lord Beartach are already inside.

Grabbing my shirt and pants from Quill's outstretched hand, he chuckles under his breath.

"Stuff it, Quill! That asshat needs to be taken down a peg or two." I look over to the message from Max still in Loxias' hand. "Let's see if we can arrange that, shall we?"

The hours until dinner pass slowly. I'm trying to keep myself busy and not think of what Roxalus and Mysti might be doing, but my freaking mind keeps wandering to things I'd rather not imagine.

If I had any sense, I would be relieved that whatever has been happening between the prince and me is over. That he's moved on from me as prey for his attention.

It's only my fool pride that's hurt. That kiss we shared still roils under the surface of my skin. I should be glad to be as far away from him as possible... so why am I unable to stop thinking about it?

Arriving at the dining room before Loxias, I take in the empty space and steel myself for this dinner. There will only be a handful of people. Leif went back to his father's court a few days after I'd arrived here and I miss his company more than I thought I would.

Even though he and Inara are siblings, they'd never met until after the curse was broken. It didn't stop them from being a lot alike.

She and her brother see each other more than she and I currently do. I'm missing out on all the sibling picking and I dare say, I'm a tad jealous.

I can't help but to feel cheated out of their company. Inara has been a sister to me since we were young. Hopefully, once she and Faelan come to live in Anavrin, we'll be thick as thieves again.

Leif and I got to know each other well after I went to live in Max's castle. Leif took over running the court while Max is at the kingdom seat.

He's been doing a wonderful job. He's worried that the fae there won't accept him because of his mother's commoner blood, but they love Max. And Leif has been welcomed with open arms.

I keep telling him that he's being silly. This stupid classist bullshit only happens when we let it.

After punching him playfully on the arms a few times while we'd all been drinking did he relent and accept the fact that he's a damn prince.

Honestly, Maximus is an amazing king. The fact that he doesn't want the position doesn't negate the fact that he's the perfect person for the job.

He's fair and beloved by his people. He always tries to find the best solutions to any problems that occurred. And the love he has for all of the fae of Anavrin can be felt in every action he takes.

The doors to the back of the dining room pull open, drawing me out of my thoughts. No one enters but I can hear breathing from the shadows.

"Hello. Who's there?" There's a sounding of thuds along the floor in a clip clop manner. Sudden trepidation flows through me.

I don't want to be alone with Roxalus. At least, I don't think I do.

As the dark figure steps out into the light of the wall torches, an unnatural wind breezes around the room.

Lord Beartach taps his staff on the floor as he approaches the table. The closer he gets to me, the more difficult I find it to breathe.

"Piper." Arctic cold slinks down my spine at the sound of my name coming from his rough, grizzly throat. It's nothing like the cold shudders from the prince. "Alone, are we?"

That doesn't sound like something I want to answer. Looking a little more carefully at the staff he carries, there's a slight glow inside of the crystal on top.

"You're a sorcerer!" It's so obvious to me now. I don't know how I missed it before.

There have only been a handful of them throughout history.

I know of the first, Tobias Isbith. The First Witch's son who killed her and attempted to kill his three sisters and take their magics for himself.

From the books I've read since coming here, and what Inara's found in the family grimoire, there is only one bloodline. His.

And in that line, only one sorcerer lives during the duration of that time to keep the magics pure, together, and untainted by imbalance.

"I am thee Sorcerer." A wicked grin lights up all around the wrinkles in his face. Seriously? That's not creepy or anything.

Before I ask him anymore, the doors to the front of the dining room open and Loxias, Quill, Roxalus, And Mysti file in.

No one willing to break the ice. Lord Beartach's gaze is practically burning a hole in the side of my cheek.

I've had enough of this arrogance from these royal assholes. Loxias has been nothing short of fantastic company since I arrived.

Knowing he and Roxalus don't get along has me questioning why Roxalus decided to show up early, unannounced, and wanting this extra time in this close setting. It makes no sense.

Deep breaths. I'm not going to put all of my focus on the problem. Instead, I'll take on the best solution. Play buffer.

"Prince Loxias, Prince Roxalus." Curtsying, I bow my head.

Mystiance smirks from her place at Roxalus' side. She's wearing a low-cut long dress that accentuates her more than ample bosom and curves.

From this angle, I can see she has on boots, hidden from the elegant style of clothing.

If I was betting person, I'd venture to say she's also probably wearing a blade somewhere under that ensemble.

"Lady Piper, you needn't do that for my benefit." Loxias grins, but Roxalus raises an eyebrow at the friendliness we share.

"As a prince in my own right, I do require my lessers to show respect, brother." Amusement dances across his face.

Standing straighter almost instantly, a snarl tears up from the back of my throat before I can stop it.

Roxalus' eyes flash with heat for half a heartbeat. Desire stares straight from their depths. It's there and gone so fast I might have imagined it.

That doesn't stop the heat in my core from making my mouth suddenly go dry.

"I suppose that means that you should be curtsying, Mysti. Lover or not, you wouldn't want to upset your superior."

The air goes out of the room. Quill's hand twitches at his side, above the crossbow strapped to his thigh.

Mysti's lip curls up in defiance. Loxias moves a small step in front of me protectively, and his brother's eyes shoot straight to the movement.

A few tense seconds pass before the servants begin filing into the room, trays laden with food and drink, like they have every night since I've been here.

The air rushes back in, and the tension eases at the sight of the feast that now covers the table.

Lord Beartach breaks the silence. "It's been a long journey and I, for one, am famished." He says, gesturing to the table. "Shall we eat?"

Chapter Twenty-Three

It was the longest dinner ever. No one had been jovial or drank too much. We'd eaten in near silence. And after the food was gone, I excused myself from the table and headed straight to my rooms.

Looking back over the evening, I fixated on all of the stolen glances.

Prince Roxalus was stealing glances in my direction almost as often as I was in his. Why does he confound me so much?

I need to stay clear of him and his pine and peppermint scent. I should stop thinking about his hands in my hair and soft lips brushing against mine. I should...Ugh! Enough already.

Sleep hadn't come quickly but it did come, and it was full of tormenting dreams.

I am tangled up with Roxalus when a hulking shadow appears to our left. He pulls his lips away from mine and pushes me roughly towards the shadow with a regretful snarl in his voice.

The next thing I know, I am tangled up with Ayxian. There's a sense of disappointment at the loss of Roxalus' presents but it grows increasingly more faint with every swipe of Ayxian's lips across the skin above my collarbone.

He drags his calloused hands along my neck, my legs straddling one of his as he grinds against my center.

A noise from the shadows snaps me out of my lustful drive to climax and as Ayxian continues to nip and lick his way up and down my neck, my eyes lock with Roxalus'.

He hasn't gone anywhere. There's fire, rage, and frustration in his expression. My chest aches with the draw towards him as my core throbs at the pleasure Ayxian is bringing in the moment. I'm almost there...

Awaking abruptly, I'm feeling unwarranted guilt and thoroughly unsatisfied. These princes will be the death of me, I swear.

The sun is starting to turn pink outside my window. A few stars still have yet to wink out of the sky.

It'd be fruitless to try and return to sleep. These fae males are more of a pain in the ass than any of the humans or shifters I'd been drawn to over the years.

Maybe it's time to take matters into my own hands before I self-combust.

With that thought in mind, I conjure up the bulge in Ayxian's pants from when we'd been the that anti-chamber back at Emenda's, closing my eyes to the feel of it pressed against me.

Allowing my hands to run down the side of my night shift and towards my throbbing center, I picture Roxalus coming up from behind me. Broody and dangerous, snarling darkly.

Putting his arm around my waist, he grinds his hard cock against my ass. My core throbs as my fingers slide through my slick center.

Ayxian drops to his knees before me kissing my navel. Dipping lower and lower until his tongue meets my erect bundle of nerves with long, languished strokes.

Sucking in a breath and letting out a moan at the fantasy my overactive mind is displaying, I spread my legs wider as my fingers work in circles around my center.

Roxalus' hand moves upward, cupping my breast, and pinching my sensitive nipple as I do so in real time. His clothed, hardened length rubbing more and more forcefully against my wet entrance from behind fueling the lust building with every new conjured image.

My fingers skim my entrance as my mind has me rocking against Roxalus' cock. The press of him demanding as he nuzzles my neck, just to the back of my ear.

My fingers are Ayxian's as they plunge inside and work furiously towards my climax. Pressure pushes, pulls, and fills me with need. With want. With... with... with... Oh gods! Yes! Yes!

I lose the vision of the princes as I shatter over the edge. The release leaving me panting, wet, and mildly relieved.

I hadn't meant to fall back asleep. A knock at my door draws me out of a dreamless rest.

With the sun shining high in the cloudless sky outside the large window, it has to be close to afternoon. I'd slept through the night and well past the morning.

Grabbing the robe hanging by my bed, I slip across the floor to open the door.

"Well, it must be nice to have no responsibilities." Princess Elodie smiles as she pushes her way into my room. "I arrived over an hour ago and couldn't fathom a reason that you wouldn't want to greet me. Now I know that you've been lounging about, I can put my insecurities to rest."

"It's nice to see you too, Princess." I can't help myself. She's asked me to call her Elle and the little dig of using her title is all I can manage before coffee.

Making herself at home she heads straight over to sit on my bed instead of the chair beside it. Her faint scent of honey and vanilla has become a comfort in the weeks that we've become friends.

"Are you just going to sit there while I dress?" I'm not modest in the least but it does seem awfully forward for me to disrobe in front of royalty without a care for decorum.

Looking me over, she gives a sniff and smirks. I know that she can scent and see beyond my disheveled hair. The real mess underneath.

"We've got the same parts. And besides that, I came to bring you down to lunch. Most everyone has already arrived, you know."

Walking over to the wardrobe, I pick the first thing to touch my hand. It's a pair of slacks that flows out from the knees down. Grabbing a blouse with flowing sleeves and a subtle dip in the chest area, I walk back over to the end of the bed beside her to put them on.

"I'm not going anywhere before I have my magic bean potion." Staring up at me mischievously without a word, her intentions smack me in the face. "That's why you're here!"

We'd been sharing a cup of coffee together every morning when in the same vicinity since I'd stayed at the kingdom seat. I'm her freaking supplier. That's not friendship! It's addiction. Gah!

My supply is running dangerously low now, but I can't help but feel the bond of friendship that our little ritual has created. I almost want to laugh at her unrepentant attitude.

"Guilty. I've missed it almost as much as I've missed you." Pinkness in her cheeks shows at her words. I return the sentiment because... well, it's Elle. How could I not?

"Well, get out the supplies while I get dressed, at least. We can have a quick cup before heading down. I wouldn't want to bite someone's head off simply because I haven't subdued my inner beast."

We both laugh. I know how my panther longs to sink its teeth into anything that keeps me away from that magical roasted bean goodness.

Elle is easy to get along with. No bullshit. No scheming. She's straight forward. Open and honest. It's refreshing in the land of faeries. And I am truly blessed to have her as my friend.

We arrive in the dining room a half an hour later. Leif's returned with Max and all of the other princesses and princes, except for Ayxian.

Elodie brushes past me, grabbing my hand as she goes. She's practically dragging me towards the table.

We take the seats that are left. To my dismay, those seats happen to be across from Roxalus, Mysti, and Lord Beartach.

As the prince looks up, my face heats at the reminder of my earlier fantasy. Elodie tugs me down into my chair and whispers in my ear, barely loud enough for me to hear, even with my excellent fae hearing.

"When we leave, you will be spilling whatever is going on!" Her glare promises pain if I don't pour the tea. Heavens forbid she go thirsty. Giving her a slight dip of my chin, the tightness around her eyes smooths away.

Honestly, it'll feel great to get this off of my chest. Inara can only understand so much because she doesn't live here amongst these treacherous creatures.

Inara's been sympathetic, but it's nice to have Elle as an ally here. She can relate to the way things are here. They're her brothers, so I won't do her the horror of detailing anything too specifically, but still... it'll be nice to have a sounding board.

The food is brought out, and everyone begins eating. Mysti keeps giving me dirty looks at the most inconvenient times; when my mouth's full, when I'm mid conversation with someone, when she catches me staring at Roxalus. It feels intentional.

The amount of venom that fills me each time she casually lays her hand on his arm, or leans in to whisper in his ear, or laugh at something he says, is rapidly eating away at my carefully guarded mask.

Roxalus' smug face makes me want to scream but Elodie's picked up on my emotions. She immediately takes an offensive position, and I've never appreciated her more.

"Tell me, Brother, is it your intention to bed every member of your guard?" Gasps go up from most of the lords and ladies at the table but none of the other royals show any dismay at her bluntness. "Or are you simply making sure your commander..." Elle's eyes trail over Mysti with low regard, "...fits your needs?" It's so unlike her, that a huff of laughter falls from my lips before I can rein it in.

The smirks slide from Mysti and Lord Beartach's faces. Roxalus' nose twitches but that's the only indication he gives that her words irritate him. If anyone else notices, no one calls him on it.

"I didn't know you cared so much, dear Sister." The twins giggle from the other end of the table.

There are only twelve seats down each side and one on each end. The gathering is only meant for the royals and their one or two top ranking court members.

Twenty-six people is still a lot. Enough for the rumor mills to churn if something juicy enough to be spread warrants it.

"If you're that jealous, Elodie, perhaps my commander would be so inclined to escort you instead if you ask her nicely."

His voice is like velvet over crushed ice. I know I can't be the only one who hears it that way, right?

A light, pastel pink color rises to the apples of Mysti's cheeks. She doesn't say anything directly to Elodie. Instead, she speaks to me. The spite dripping in every word. "Or maybe Princess Elodie is graciously trying to cover for Lady Piper's jealousy?"

This fucking bitch! I want to rip her to shreds and I don't even know why.

If not for Elodie's hand gripping my arm, my panther would already have its jaws clamped around her throat. She'd *felt* it before I'd even been aware of my failing composure.

That gift of hers is something else. I need to take pointers.

"What's that? What are you saying?" I forgot Max is here. Shit!

He's been laughing with Loxias and Quill at something Leif said but now, his attention is centered on our group's little back and forth.

Roxalus' now droll voice cuts through the chit chat that had started up after Mysti's proclamation. "Come now, Maximus. Surely you've been paying attention the last few months." I bristle at his words. So does Lord Beartach. "Lady Piper has been..."

The doors to the dining room fly open. Prince Ayxian comes traipsing in like he's in a hurry, but he stops abruptly as he takes in the room.

"Apparently I've missed more than the beginning of the meal." Walking with assured steps, he leans down next to me, kissing me squarely on my heated cheek. A wave of his hand and the Lord that had been sitting next to me moves down a seat without any protest. "What have I miss?"

Chapter Twenty-Four

Roxalus huffs and shrinks back in his chair. Max isn't going to let Ayxian's sudden appearance deter his earlier question. His focus lands squarely on Roxalus.

"I asked what you meant about Lady Piper?" Max's tone is clear.

He's not currently their brother. He is King Maximus Suilari, first of the royal line, leader of the Anavrin fae. And he looks more imposing than I've ever personally witnessed.

Ayxian glances in my direction but doesn't say anything. Heaping food onto his plate, he digs in.

Elodie pats my arm sympathetically but has no words of encouragement. That can't be a good sign.

The whole of the table figuratively trembles under the weight of his commanding voice. Not just the courtiers, but the other royals as well.

Max truly is the fae king, whether he wants it or not. He is what every leader should be, and they all *feel* it, empathy gift or not. Each and every one of them.

"Humbly, your Majesty. If I may shed light on the situation." Lord Beartach's staff lays against the wall behind him. A faint glow emanating from the stone atop it that wasn't there a moment. "It seems over the last several months, Lady Piper has positioned herself to ascend the ranks and maneuver into possibly becoming queen."

Distain coats his tone as his head bows in respect to Max. It's false though. The comment and the respect. I can *feel* it and Elodie's stiffness beside me tells me she's senses the same.

My mouth pops open in disbelief. What the fuck is going on? Am I being set up?

"I never..." I begin but, once again, Elodie takes up my charge.

"It isn't a bid to be a queen that Lady Piper has made. Your words are meant to instill fear and anger."

No one here doubts her or her abilities. She can see through the crux of any situation. She doesn't pry on a personal level, but that doesn't mean she's oblivious to what I have yet to tell her.

"She's merely fallen for the charms of two different princes. I can assure you..." She stares into the eyes of every person at the table before continuing. "...that her intentions are heartfelt. Chasing emotions. Driven by desires."

The heat of that embarrassing revelation has risen inside me at her words. It's almost worse than people thinking I'm seeking to put myself on a throne.

If I could teleport, I'd have disappeared in this instance. There is nothing I can say that will make me look better or feel smaller than I do in front of all of these watchful eyes.

Ayxian stops eating. Scooting his chair slightly towards mine, his hand rests atop my clenched fist.

"Is this true, Piper? Are you torn between me and that box of rocks over there?"

Roxalus snarls and stands, drawing his sword as he does. "I will not have you disrespect me, Ayxian! Stand and face me. May the better male win."

Ayxian still hasn't looked away from my face. He barely glances at Roxalus. Every time Ayxian touches me, a low growl rumbles in his brother's chest.

"Enough!" Maximus gets to his feet, challenging both of the princes to defy him. "Piper, a word."

Dropping my hands to my sides, I stand too, hanging my head and following Max out of the dining room.

We don't speak until we are outside, winding through the hedgerows maze to a bench at its center.

"Max, I swear I never meant for this to happen. I don't know how I..." but I don't know how to finish that sentence.

I can't deny my feelings for either of the two princes. I can't lie, even if I wanted to.

I've never had a father figure. And being around for as long as I have, it's strange to me that "Uncle Max" might be interested in my love life.

That only leaves the queen thing to be the reason for his concern, right? Would it be too much to ask for the gods to hide me before Inara's dad blows a gasket?

When he finds his words, the softness in them surprises me. "I know that what Lord Beartach fears isn't you. You're not that conniving fae sort."

Lowering my gaze to my hands, shame inches its way along my skin.

I hadn't thought about how it would look to the fae. They're so used to this kind of behavior from each other they probably won't believe anything to the contrary.

He continues with a touch of sadness in his voice this time. "I'm concerned for you, not that queen business. I know you and Inara have always been each other's compass, but I guess I'm a tad hurt that you felt you couldn't come to me if you were having difficulties navigating through your new life."

A dull ache winds its way around my heart from his words. I hadn't considered his feelings of rejection. He's missed out on so much with Inara and Leif. Here I was, a pseudo daughter, shutting him out of something he felt in his heart that I should be comfortable with telling him.

Mistaking my silence for further rejection, his toned turns melancholy. "I thought maybe you could use an impartial ear. That's all."

Bless his genuinely good heart. Tears well in my eyes. "I never had a father, Max." Sniffling, I wipe the tears on the back of my hand.

The sun shines down from the afternoon sky and the fragrant azalea flowers make my head feel lighter, my thoughts less befuddled.

"I don't know what to say. Ayxian was kind to me when I'd first arrived but then his ambitions rose to the forefront. And Roxalus..."

I don't know if I can get the words right. Taking a steadying breath, I blow it out in a long, frustrated stream.

"He's so frustrating. He acts like I am beneath him but then he does things like noticing my needs." That sounds wrong, I rush to clarify. "Like yesterday, we had an altercation, and I shifted." Max's brow arch's but he doesn't comment. "Before he walked away, he told Loxias to make sure that I got some extra food. Why does he pay attention to the little things like that if he's going to keep toying with my emotions?"

A plethora of emotions filters over his face. Bringing his hand up to scrub through his hair, he brings it away, shaking his head.

"Listen, I can't tell you who you should be with. What I can tell you is that Roxalus was spoiled by our mother. And when he was named heir in my absence his self-righteous attitude only intensified from what I've been told."

A piece of his dark hair hangs across one eye. It's not often that I've seen it out of place.

The realization that this "talk" is hard for him, but he's doing it anyway, brings a smile to my face. He's going to be in for it when Faelan finally comes here to live. Though, with Inara still single, navigating those waters will be fun to watch.

"With that being said, the fact that he's showed concern for you? Even if it's not obvious to everyone else." Shaking his head again, he chuckles. "The fact that he's brought Mystiance here to make you jealous, well, that's got to mean something, right?"

I try to consider what he's saying. It makes perfect sense when he puts it that way. "Why is Lord Beartach here, then?"

"That's something that I've been asking myself as well. I've never been particularly fond of the sorcerer. He has a penchant for malevolence when it comes to those he sees as lessers."

Quiet for a moment, he's deep in thought. The hedgerow maze blocks out most sounds but a group of tiffy scuff fairies flying overhead brings the sound of tiny laughter to the sky's just above our heads.

"As for Ayxian, he's a warrior. I don't know why he wants to be king so badly, but other than a few brawls and orgies driven by his primal gifts, I don't have any advice I can give you about him. I think that he would defend you to his last breath if you were together if the need ever arose. Other than that, I've got nothing."

Giggling softly, I laid my head on his arm, taking in his smoky oak and leather scent. It's nice to have Inara's dad as a confidant.

Not as good as it would be to have her here though. As much as I like him trying to help, I need to find out who I am all on my own.

I have to admit, he did a wonderful job giving me a shoulder to lean on and advice without judgement or pushing an agenda of his own.

My necklace heats with a light thrum below the surface of the metal. Forgetting I was wearing it, it startles me a bit.

"Thank you, Uncle." Thanking a fae is not a good idea, but in this moment, he's simply family. And he feels that too.

"Any time, Peppercorn."

Chapter Twenty-Five

The next two weeks go by without too many problems.

As promised, I've told Elodie everything. And I mean everything.

She giggled and scrunched up her face over the sexual stuff, because eww... they are her brothers. And she'd given me her own version of advice.

I don't know if it's bias or not, but it feels like I can trust her fully, the same way I trust in Inara's advice.

Loxias, Leif, Quill and I drank a bit too much last night. Loxias really means it when he says he doesn't care if he becomes king or not.

We shouldn't have indulged so much the night before a competition but watching Roxalus shuffle off towards his rooms with Mysti in tow had made me see red.

Ayxian had come walking down the corridor last night and when he'd noticed me there, he'd turned around without a word and headed in the other direction.

Feeling spurned, I'd taken Leif up on his offer of honey mead and a game of two truths and a lie.

The whole night's pretty much a blur. I can't recall details but there are a lot of small things that stick out.

Like how Quill kept casually dropping hints about his feelings for Loxias while we'd all gotten more and more sloshed as we played the game.

Leif and I would grin at each other the more blatant he became, but Loxias hadn't paid him any attention and is still either oblivious to it or unwilling to acknowledge his long-time friend's obsession.

I remember giving a few honey mead induced answers to their questions myself. Those involved the princes and my past experiences. None of them could guess between my truths or my lies.

Well, omissions would be a more accurate a term here in faeryland, so my secrets are safe.

All of the courtiers are chittering excitedly throughout the halls and the grounds about today's competition.

The smell of fresh baking breads and roast and an array of different foods waft through the castle for tonight's feast.

My head aches, but it's manageable. What I desperately need is to hydrate. My morning coffee was Luna sent, but it isn't nearly enough to save my poor mouth and tongue from feeling raked over a desert at high noon.

Reaching the veranda that hosts the various pastries and breakfast foods, I make a beeline for the honeysuckle tea pitcher at the end of the table. All the food smells wonderful, but my stomach groans at the prospect of eating.

I've never gotten sick from drinking in excess before. Shifters heal quickly, so it's usually out of our systems before it can take root for too long.

This has to be the effect of faery made spirits that I'm not used to because the boys all step out of the castle and head towards me looking none the worse for wear.

"It's good to see that you can hold your own, Lady Piper." Loxias winks while Quill studiously avoids mine and Leif's gazes. The poor guy. I feel bad for him.

Loxias wears his axe at his side this morning. For the month that I've been here, this is the first time I've seen it on him. If the point is to make him appear more imposing, it's working.

He is the ruler in these lands. He doesn't need to prove himself to his own people. It must be for the sake of his brothers and sisters that he's put on the air of an enforcer.

Quill has his crossbow strapped to his thigh, like usual, and Leif wears a sword at his side. His shadow gift is all he needs in any regular circumstance.

My senses are irritatingly overactive this morning and have me wondering if they are expecting trouble today or if they're just being overly cautious.

Noxian comes running out of the castle without looking around. His eyes land on me for half a second before striding over to whisper in Loxias' ear.

Whatever he's told him makes the prince of the castle's face fall. A stoic expression shutters over his features as, he too, glances in my direction.

"What? What's going on?" I don't like the way they're keeping me out of the loop.

Leif comes up beside me and takes my elbow, leading me off to the side as the others follow a step behind us.

"There's been another lowbee murdered," Noxian says. "As far as we can tell, it must have happened about two weeks ago. The body was hidden in a barrel down in the cellar. The kitchen staff reported a foul smell coming from there early this morning, so I sent my right hand to look into it. I wasn't expecting it to be a dead body."

Shaking his head, he scrubs a hand up over his face, into his hair. He is such a mirror to Max, it's a wonder that they don't have the same mother.

"This makes me certain that the murderer has followed the competitions for sure. Two weeks ago is around the time that we'd all arrived here."

He's right. The hairs on my arms stands on end. I understand their looks in my direction now. These males and I have become closer somewhere along the way. They are my friends, and they are concerned about my safety.

My heart warms at the thought. I relish in it for a moment before I remember the reason for their concern and my blood turns cold. Another innocent faery has been murdered.

Who amongst us can hate lowbees so much that they feel eliminating us is a promising idea? Killing because they feel themselves to be superior? It's unconscionable to fathom hating someone with that amount of venom in one's heart.

Maximus, Elodie, and Ayxian are gathered at the table along the far wall in the throne room when we enter. Max's eyes slide to mine for a brief moment, assessing.

I give him a nod to let him know that I'm okay and continue to blend in with the crowd.

Courtiers from all of the different courts and the kingdom seat have traveled a long way for today's festivities. I know the royals didn't let any of them know about the murders and part of me wonders if that's for the sake of the people... or the need to keep them under control.

No. I refuse to think like that. Max is a good male. Maybe I should take a break on reading the mystery novels for a while.

As Loxias' voice carries over the crowd to call us all to attention, Roxalus slips in through a door off of the side from where the servants bring in food.

Why he's coming from the servant's area, I can't begin to venture a guess.

"We've all gathered here for the next leg of the competition, but I feel that it is time that we divulge some tragic information that may help to keep the public safe." Loxias doesn't sway in his resolve.

Max and Ayxian look like they want to storm the stage to stop him. I can't help but to admire his commitment to his people. Their well-being means more to him than whatever wrath his brothers have planned.

When the crowd quiets down, he continues. "There has been a string of murders." A shocked chitter of energy runs throughout the crowd harder this time.

"All of them being..." he glances in my direction, and I give him an encouraging nod. "...lowbees. I know that term was first coined around the land to mean something derogatory. It has since been taken back by the fae who've come from the human realm. I want everyone here to know that I see you. I don't disregard you because of your status or your line of work. I see you. And the person responsible for these murders has to be blind. If telling you that you should be on your guard helps you to stay safe, then I will shout it from the rooftops."

Awkward energies flitter through the air. Some of the upper-class courtiers in Princess Embla's entourage shift their weight from foot to foot or pick invisible lint from their clothes or studiously find their surroundings fascinating.

There are some from other courts who appear uncomfortable with the inclusion of us lowbees, but I don't know which courts they are from.

Max makes his way to the dais and Loxias waves him onward. "King Maximus. The floor is yours."

"Thank you," he says through gritted teeth. A false smile is plastered across his face before he addresses the gathered crowd. "We have every resource across all of Anavrin looking into these murders. Prince Loxias is right. You should have the right to know and protect yourselves. We didn't want panic to ensue but it's better to be prepared than to be caught unawares."

His eyes find mine as I stand hidden in the crowd. A tick in his cheek gives away his emotions. I'm too crowded to feel them for myself.

The smell of pine needles and peppermint drifts towards me from behind and I don't have to turn around to know who's there.

Heat from Roxalus' skin sears through my light blouse. His closeness sets every nerve tingling. Shuddering as he brushes the hair away from my neck, he leans in to whisper in my ear.

"Watch yourself, Lady Piper. You never know who wants you..." He pauses, then blows the last word across my overly sensitive skin. "...dead."

Chapter Twenty-Six

I turn quickly to look him in the eyes, but he's already out of range, moving with the speed of the fae.

A large, calloused hand grips mine, giving it a squeeze. "There you are Piper. I was worried that the news of the latest murder would frighten you into hiding." The light bounces off of Ayxian's eyes as he rocks back and forth on the balls of his feet.

My attention's drawn to a small brown spot on the collar of his cream white shirt. It's barely noticeable if you aren't staring at him like I am.

"I don't frighten that easily." Winking up in the direction of his head, my eyes haven't adjusted to the dim light yet from the corridor. "I have claws of my own."

This earns me a hearty bark of a laugh. My hand landing on his muscular forearm without me giving it permission to move.

Ayxian's earthy cedar scent is warm and tantalizing, like a pleasant day in the canopy of the forest while the sun beats down on the tops of the trees.

Leaning in, inhaling a long breath, his lips hover below my ear. "You smell like hunger and bad decisions, Lady Piper."

Umm, what? That doesn't ring any kind of alarm bells or whistles or anything. Crazy beast man! Why am I so damned intrigued?

"Would you care to escort me while I practice for the competition? I need to warm up before my turn."

Biting at my bottom lip, I contemplate my options. On one hand, watching the fluid way he moves makes my center throb. I could use more arsenal for my alone times.

On the other hand, I don't want to miss the other royal's attempts at the challenge Max has set.

This one is about defending and de-escalating a situation. I can't be sure how the king will instigate a problem to begin with, but I'm more than interested in watching it unfold.

"As lovely as that sounds, I am due at King Maximus' side for the start of the competition. Good luck, Your Highness."

Letting my hand fall away from his corded arm, I take a step towards the main chamber where everyone is still gathered, but Ayxian's hand flies to the back of my neck. Fisting my hair and drawing me closer, our lips meet.

He is nowhere near gentle, and I can't bring myself to care at the moment. Our tongues wrestle as he tries to get the upper hand. As tall as he is, my tiptoes won't grant me the full access that I crave.

This kiss is more than enjoyable... that is, until his other hand snakes around my waist, yanking me roughly into his possession. The hand in my hair pulls to the point of pain.

Try as I might, I push against his chest in attempt to break the kiss, but the mass of male that he is, he doesn't budge... Then, he bites me.

His fangs sink into the flesh of my tongue, and I squeal around his lips. Blood trickles out the sides of my mouth and the shock of the situation, along with his massive hands, keep me locked in place.

My mind starts to panic. No one will be able to hear me. All eyes are on the front of the room where Max is running through the rules.

I claw at him, desperate to get free. My brain won't think straight enough to shift into my panther form.

Breathing is starting to become a problem. I can't get in any air. He's so caught up in conquering his prey, I'm going to die by suffocating on my own tongue.

Feeling like this might be where I meet my end, here, ten feet away from hundreds of fae, my eyes start to drift shut.

Then suddenly, there's open air. I inhale deeply through my nose, and I've never been more grateful for the rush of oxygen in my life.

I can't make my eyelids open. Weightlessness replaces the tight arms that had caged me, though no pain comes from me hitting the wall.

Shouts go up from the people closest to where we'd been standing. A chatter buzzes around the chamber like the screams of cicadas across a field.

Something wet covers my fingertips as I bring them to my mouth... copper and tangy. Blood.

Finally locating my eyelids, my brain still can't process the scene in front of me.

Roxalus stands defensively five feet from me, sword drawn and pressed against Ayxian's chest, hovering it over his heart.

Ayxian's fists clench and unclench, itching to draw his own sword but Roxalus' doesn't give him the room to maneuver without puncturing his ribcage in the process.

He looks at me, still huddled in a heap on the floor. Pain and anguish fill me, but it isn't mine.

Giving his attention to Roxalus takes all of his effort. Ayxian speaks, but only to me while he stares daggers at his brother. "I beg your forgiveness, Lady Piper." His hands still clench, inching towards his sword.

The murmurs of the crowd grow louder all around. Max is shouting. Loxias is calm but angrier than I've ever seen him.

"I seem to always forget myself in your presence," he says, hanging his head in shame. If I wasn't in so much pain, I might have felt sorry for the big oaf.

"Then maybe you should no longer **be** in her presence." The venom in Roxalus words can ignite a wildfire.

His hand doesn't shake. If anything, his sword presses harder. A trickle of blood surfaces from beneath Ayxian's shirt.

"Lady Piper, I didn't mean to..." Ayxian rubs at his eyes, a hand going roughly over his face. "If you command it, I will allow Roxalus to run me through. I am undeserving of your company."

I can't believe that he's telling me it's okay if he is killed. I don't like what he did but that doesn't mean that I want him dead for it.

The bleeding in my mouth stops, but it still hurts where his fangs have pierced my flesh. My words don't come out the way that I want them to around my swollen tongue.

Fae venom doesn't affect fellow fae the same way it does other beings, but it still has an effect. "I don'd wand you dead, Aythian."

Roxalus snarls as I get up and take a step towards them. I can *feel* his anxiety and anger as if it is my own. Laying a hand on his shoulder he snarls even louder but doesn't move away or stay his sword.

The hilt of it dances with icy blue flames, freezing it to the tip. Ayxian's shirt is singed at the point where it touches, but he doesn't shy away from the burn.

My fae healing's already helping take the swelling down but not quite enough. "I can'd say that I forgive you... not yet at leath, but your death ithn't warranded."

Trying to push passed Roxalus to touch Ayxian's arm, his swordless hand comes up quickly around my waist, tucking me into his side.

I want to protest but it feels... nice. Like a puzzle piece I didn't know was missing. His pine needles and peppermint scent soothes my frayed nerves.

Ayxian looks between the two of us and snickers. Why? I have no idea.

"I see." His large, calloused fingers wrap around the freezing hot metal of the sword. Shaking his head, he still eye fucks me. There's no other way to explain his gaze. "I never had a chance."

I try to pull away from Roxalus' side, but he holds me tighter. "I don't know what you mean by that, but I athure you, I care about you Aythian. I like spending time with you... At leasth, I did."

This beast he becomes is making me rethink every encounter we had. There's an underlying animalistic quality to him that is more savage than normal for any animal I've ever encountered.

Skimming me up and down one more time, he snaps at Roxalus. "You should tell her."

The tip of Roxalus' sword pushes harder against his chest, drawing more blood.

"No. It's none of your concern, Brother. My destiny lies elsewhere." Relaxing the pressure from his chest, Roxalus glares at the fallen prince.

The smirk that spreads across Ayxian's face is one of nightmares. I shudder into Roxalus side before thinking better of it.

"In that case, fates be damned. I do love a challenge." As Ayxian gets to his feet, Roxalus snarls but steadies his breathing and loosens his grip on my waist.

I don't understand the exchange between them. And before I can ask any more questions, Max and Elodie arrive at our little party.

"What's going on here?" Max demands.

Lacing her fingers with mine, Elodie gives them a hard squeeze that I wasn't expecting.

I'm going to have to ask her later what in the seven hells she knows that I don't. It's clear her gifts are seeing right to the crux of the situation that I can't see, and it's more frustrating than chewing on my swollen tongue.

"A misunderstanding," Ayxian says. Inclining his head to me, he steps back from under the blade that Roxalus has yet to drop. "A most unfortunate error on my part. Lady Piper has my regrets."

Without another word or glance at any of us, he leaves. Roxalus drops his arm from around my waist like a boulder.

"Someone better tell me what's going on." Max glances from me to Roxalus, and then to Elle. No one says a word. "Piper, you're bleeding."

Wiping my mouth with the back of my hand, it's just left over blood. My tongue is already almost normal size again and the puncture wounds are closed up.

When we continue to not say anything, his frustration leaks through. "Very well then, I think we should get back to the stage." With a final beseeching glance my way, he leaves us standing in the corridor.

Roxalus eyes meet mine. A ping of regret hits my heart that I don't understand before Elodie pinches my arm. Hard.

"Ouch." I turn to tell her off. "What was that for?"

The heat at my back disappears and I know without turning that Roxalus has gone. Suddenly, I feel all alone.

"We need to talk." I open my mouth to tell her to get on with it but... "After the competition."

Steering me towards the stage, she never let's go of my hand. It is such an Inara move. We truly are becoming the best of friends.

And I, for one, need a true friend here like I need coffee.

Chapter Twenty-Seven

B oth Ayxian and Roxalus only show themselves again when their time comes to participate.

Max had lived in the human realm for almost two centuries. The competition consists of a board game; part Monopoly, part Stratego, and part Risk. It's one of his own creation and has a time limit of fifteen minutes. I dare say, it's fascinating.

Each prince or princess takes the seat opposite Max. He gets to make the first move. And I've figured him out. If he's losing towards the time limit, he plays dirty.

It's to see how each of them will react to not getting their way. I wonder if anyone else can see the mind games he's playing with his siblings? Pure genius.

Princess Embla has been winning during her turn and Max buries her under a lot of faux bureaucracy. Poor spoiled princess. She actually flips the board over in her anger and I barely manage to stifle my laugh.

After the competition, we all head outside where a huge banquet has been set up by Loxias' staff.

Strings run around trees and crisscross over the tables. Dusk sets the scene with beautiful yellows, pinks, and purples before the sun set.

People from all over Anavrin have come to see the royals and Loxias is a gracious host. I can't believe I ever bought into the whole big bad hunter persona he used to maintain. The guy's a huge softy at heart.

Twinkling lights flicker in and out along the strings. It's the most enchanting thing I've ever seen.

There's no electric here. When I look closer, there are hundreds of firefly looking teeny tiny faeries along each string.

"I had my staff put nectar on the strings. It attracts the Beagwisps to the sweet meal and provides us with a pleasant atmosphere." Loxias has thought of everything.

He's happy. I can *feel* it. It has made all the difference in his personality. I'm glad Faelan gave the fae back their ability to find their mates. She made the right call.

Leif appears out of thin air, and I gasp, clenching my chest. "By Luna! You scared me."

Loxias and Leif roar with laughter at my outburst. Those shadows of his sure do give him a step up on the rest of us.

"That was not funny!" My exclamation only makes them laugh harder.

I guess it was a little funny. If I'd seen it happen to someone else, I'd have laughed myself silly too.

"I sometimes think you forget what we are, cousin." Shadows coil around Leif's arms and legs.

I didn't forget. My coy smile is all the warning he gets.

From one heartbeat to the next, I lunge at him, shifting to my panther form, before I land on his chest.

Loxias is laughing so hard, I'm worried he'll bust at his sides.

With both paws squarely on Leif's chest, my wet tongue whips out, drenching him from chin to hairline.

"You had it coming, Son." Max stands ten feet from us by the head of one of the long tables. "Piper and Inara are going to eat you alive once they're reunited full time."

Trying my best not to give my nudity a second thought the moment I shift back, Uncle turns his head, but he doesn't need to. Leif's shadows envelope me as I find my clothes and put them back on.

Over the years, modesty has gone by the wayside, but since coming here, I've become more self-conscious of prying eyes. At least, to those of my close friends and family. I find it strange to be bare in front of them.

Maybe it's that I lived a more savaged life back in the Lupian Forest. The civility here in Anavrin is rubbing off on me. Castle suites and banquets have taken the place of my leaf bed in the den and raw meat eating habits.

When I look up, I happen to catch sight of Ayxian staring in my direction. His eyes are dark and he licks his lips before noticing that I can see him.

I thought he would quickly look away, but there is a hunger lurking in the features of his face, unnerving me to my core. Like prey to a predator.

Maybe this behavior is a normal fae thing or maybe it has more to do with him and his gifts. Either way, I'm finding, with increasing trepidation, that I no longer want to be in his sights.

The smell of peppermint and pine needles drifts to me from behind as the wind changes direction. Turning to locate the source, he's nowhere in sight.

"You okay?" Emenda's concern is warranted. I hadn't even realized she'd approached me. My observation skills have become shit since coming here. "Should I fetch someone?"

"I'm fine. I thought I..." What? Smelled your arrogant brother close by? "I'm fine. We should eat."

Max disappeared just before I sat down with Emenda. Elodie sits on my other side. While Leif, Loxias, and Quill sit across from us.

The banquet fair is grand. The wine flowing freely. Honey mead makes an appearance somewhere along the night.

I'm having a great time and tipsy enough to not even realize that the other princes have come to sit close by our little party.

Embla's next to her twin because, of course she is. I can hear all of the snippy comments she makes as the night wears on.

Quill and Noxian are having a lively conversation about the other fae kingdom, Sidhterra, and I can't help but wonder what the fae are like there.

I catch tidbits... like, wildings and uncivilized, but I'm too far into the bottle to give it much more thought than passing curiosity.

As the others attending the festivities retire to go back home or to their tents, all of the royals, except Max, are left drinking and making merry at the table.

Nydin, along with Leif and Quill are merrily chatting casually to one another.

Mystiance is in deep conversation with Lord Davian. He purses his lips at something she says, and she tinkles a delighted laugh at his discomfort.

Lord Beartach sits quietly. Observing.

The sorcerer gives me the willies, but I don't know if that has more to do with the fact that his ancestor was a power-hungry murderer or that he is the only one of his bloodline and his self-importance shows how must distain he holds for the rest of us *beneath* him.

Every once in a while, I'll laugh at something someone says, and I'll *feel* a ping of irritation from him.

Ayxian and Roxalus don't speak. Ayxian merely sits, sipping his mead without merriment.

And Roxalus drinks nothing, sitting stoically, hardly taking his eyes off me or his beastly brother. He'd motioned to one of the servants and whispered something in their ear as the sun fully set and night settled in completely, but that was the only time I'd seen him look away.

Desserts were laid in front of us at some point during the evening and we all absentmindedly pick at them as we drink.

I have taken four or five bites of the pastry in front of me when I catch Ayxian's eyes growing wide and rapacious.

I don't miss the low snarl that comes from Roxalus' direction when he notices.

Again, I can't help but to think to myself that these princes will be the death of me. One wants me dead. The other wants to devour me. Only, I can't be certain which is which. And for the life of me, I can't decide which intrigues me more.

Oh man... these must be those damned euphoria pasties. That's all I need.

Pushing the cakes away and grabbing a pitcher of moon water that some thoughtful servant has placed on the table, the first sip is heavenly. There hasn't been a time in my life when mere water has quenched my thirst so well.

I'm still tipsy and those pasties are still playing havoc with my senses, but I feel a bit steadier than I did a moment ago. I'll have to find the servant responsible and thank them personally in the morning.

"Now that we're all well soused, how about a few rounds of two truths and a lie?" Emenda's idea of fun is wickedly fae. And surprisingly, I am all for it.

Wording is everything when you can't lie, and that makes this game all the more fun for faeries.

"I'll go first." I can't seem to help myself. "I haven't found pleasure since arriving in Anavrin. I like venison. I've never pictured myself wanting to be with royalty."

Oh, dear Luna. What did I just put out there?

Elodie pats my arm but doesn't give away my secrets. I think I love this blessedly beautiful faery even more now.

Loxias has other plans. The bastard. "I say the pleasure thing is the lie. A charming beauty like you must have had some trysts here in the last few months."

"Well," Ayxian takes a long draft, finishing off his mead. His eyes blazing bright and glassy. "I've never been granted the chance to taste the nectar of the pepper plant."

The heat of his gaze burns through my cheeks and a flush runs along my jawbone. It isn't as wanted as it had been once.

If we were alone right now, I would bet the kingdom that he would take me. Permission or not. That thought alone makes me anxious more than intrigued.

Distractedly, I nibble off the end of the pastry again and Elodie slaps it out of my hand. "Half a euphoria pasty is more than enough for you my dear."

Well shit. I might as well have wrapped a bow around my head and gifted myself to these sharks.

Lord Beartach sneers in my direction while the end of his staff glows a little brighter. There's a pull in my throat and my mind forces my lips open.

"I am a peasant, below all of you." My eyes flash wide. It's my voice, my mouth, but the words coming out of me are not my own. "I shouldn't be allowed to dine with royalty. I deserve no more hospitality than a serving maiden."

Embla claps her hands together in glee and Lord Beartach smiles a cruel, black toothed grin.

My eyes search frantically for my friends understanding and Loxias notices the staff, shimmering with magics.

Surprising the sorcerer, his hand touches Beartach's arm and without hesitation, the sorcerer throws the staff hard against a large oak tree. It shatters in half, but the crystal still glows from the broken top.

Beartach stands quickly, fuming at what Loxias has made him do, but he knows he can't make a stand against a prince and still keep his courtly status.

Ayxian huffs out a dark laugh that I don't understand. Is he being a jerk, happy about my humiliation? Or is he purely acting on his fae instincts to find pleasure in the cruelty of the situation?

"If you've come to my court to sow discord, I will take it out on your hide, Lord Beartach. My lands are a place for all to prosper, and I will make you regret every choice you make to the contrary." As Loxias speaks, I remember why I feared him when first coming to Anavrin.

It's easy to forget that behind that carefree jovial side, there is a highly gifted fae prince who has a firm backbone.

"My regrets, Your Highness. I meant no harm. It was all in good fun." His tone belies his words as the sorcerer seethes just below the surface. I can *feel* it. Elle can *feel* it too.

Embla cackles loudly and Emenda smacks her on the arm playfully, but Elodie takes my hand and gives it a gentle squeeze of support.

Roxalus clucks his tongue. "Gather your things. Ride out ahead. I will find you when I return home." He looks down the table at Mysti. "You go with him."

"But my Liege," she starts and stops quickly at the look on his face. A silent conversation passes between them in just a few short seconds. "Yes, Your Highness." With one last hard look at me, she leaves.

I am still in shock at the whole ordeal. Everyone sips from their cups, but no one mutters a single word for several awkward minutes.

"You don't like venison." It takes me a minute to realize that Roxalus is talking to me. His deep voice does things to me I'm not prepared to deal with on honey mead and euphoria pasties.

"Excuse me?" If nothing else makes me dizzy tonight, the sound alone could push me over the edge.

Butterflies flap their wings in a frantic bid to escape my stomach, bringing heat to the apples of my cheeks that travels down to between my thighs. Those damn euphoria pasty get me every time.

Glancing up from the plate he's been studiously staring at, his eyes drift to mine, a slight upturn to his lips on one side. "You don't like to eat deer meat."

I'm a mess of emotions, blushing like some silly schoolgirl again. Being seen by anyone is still all so new to me. Being seen by a male who I can't get a good read on is a whole other conundrum.

"What gives you that impression?" I bite at my bottom lip and Ayxian grunts, a beastly animalistic sound, under his breath.

Roxalus fingertips flare with cool blue flames in response. Two elements? Interesting. I hadn't thought about it before.

Distantly, I remember him wielding ice when I'd arrived in Anavrin. Seeing the cold blue flames isn't new but it isn't right either.

"I feel it may embarrass you if I divulge my deductions, My Lady." He glances around the table.

Not one of the people sitting here has said a word, too enthralled by our interactions apparently.

With an arch to my brow, flourishing my hand, I motion for him to lay it on the line. I want to hear why he thinks that's my lie.

"If you insist." A coy smile plays at the edges of his lips and eyes, but glancing towards Ayxian, he schools his features. "You know the lips that have been met with yours since coming here." He isn't giving away that he and I kissed but everyone knows about me and Prince Ayxian. Maybe he's unaware that his sisters have already sipped that particular cup of tea. "So never wanted to be with royalty makes sense, even if that's no longer the case."

Smiling into my cup, I try to hide my expressions. My core tightens with every word he speaks.

"And you've found pleasure." I start to protest. His cheeks pink slightly in the most delicious of ways. It's such an unusual thing to see on the prince that I find myself leaning towards him. "Anyone one of us can smell your arousal from time to time. That pleasure may have only been at your hands, but it is pleasure none the less."

Would anyone notice if I crawled under the table? I hadn't once thought of that before giving this stupid game a go. The pasty's effects are beginning to wear off and I'm not so keen to keep playing this stupid game.

Embla leans forward past Emenda to stare between me and her brother. Shutters close over his eyes under her disapproving glare.

"Okay. I don't like to eat deer," I reluctantly admit.

"Piper, you lived as a werewolf for over a century. How do you not like deer?" Loxias says this like one and one must equal two.

"I'm not a wolf. I'm a panther. And for too long, I did what I was told or what was expected of me. If the pack ate deer, I ate with them. I didn't really have a choice in the matter." I took another sip of wine. "When I first got here, Max kept having deer made for me, bless his heart. He thought that it would help me adjust better and back then, I wasn't accustomed to having a mind of my own that I was allowed to voice yet." Pack mentality and all. "Once I realized that this was a permanent situation, I started trying new foods and making sure it was something that I actually liked. Me. Piper. Not something that I was expected to like."

Roxalus holds his glass high in a salute. "To Lady Piper. A force of her own making." My cheeks flush again. "May she find exactly what she deserves."

I can't tell if he is being an ass or sincere, if it's a threat or a blessing. I lift my glass anyway. I'll make it my own, this life and this toast. No more following along to play it safe.

Ayxian stands. Then wobbles. "Lady Piper, would you care to travel with me to my court? There's plenty of room in my carriage."

Roxalus posture stiffens at the idea, and I don't know why. He is so damned flummoxing.

Ayxian's court is the next leg of the competition. I'll be spending two weeks there with him. It unsettles me now whereas it hadn't before. I don't know if I should trust him... or myself.

"Thank you for the offer. I think that I will travel in my own carriage." His smile falters but Roxalus relaxes. "I tend to snore." To that, Ayxian laughs his husky bark of a laugh.

"I shall see you at home then." He sways and shifts his position to steady himself.

I don't like the way he makes it sound like we are together. Neither does his brother.

"Travel safe. I shall see you when I arrive at your court, Your Highness."

The grip on Roxalus glass looks half a second away from shattering the thing.

I can't explain away Roxalus' attitude or actions when it comes to me. His arrogance doesn't match his defensiveness.

There's nothing I can say to make him less worried. There's nothing I can do to make *myself* less worried.

I still have the fingerprint escape on the necklace Max gave me, but enduring two weeks of Ayxian, not knowing his intentions, sets my nerves on end.

Chapter Twenty-Eight

The next morning, both Loxias and Elodie come to see me off.

Roxalus, I was informed by Elle, left just before daybreak. Her subtle wink had brought heat to my cheeks.

I wanted to talk to her about what had happened in the corridor with the two princes, but I hadn't had the opportunity.

Between the drinks and the euphoria pasties, I collapsed into bed last night and didn't wake until mid-morning.

The late start will have my carriage coming in several hours later than I'd hoped for in a few days time.

Ayxian's court is in the north, close to the twin's courts. The journey will be long and with the murderer still at large, I'm not keen on all of the nighttime travel.

On the plus side, Loxias has lent me a couple of books to keep my mind occupied during the journey.

He's also gifted me a lantern that never needs oil and burns without the heat of a normal fire. It won't make the carriage overly warm, like a normal lantern would in such a small, enclosed space.

I asked him how it was possible, but he gave me that coy smile of his and simply said, "Why, magics, of course."

My small entourage has been on the road for nearly a full day before stopping to eat and rest the horses.

Max had provided a driver and two guards to escort me from court to court originally, but now there are four guards, and the driver has been replaced by a male with a sword as well.

If I had felt unsafe before setting out, that feeling has been quashed by all of the precautions taken.

There are four males and a female. The driver wears no helmet, but all of the guards do.

I haven't seen any of their faces and when we had stopped to eat, they'd made a circle facing away from me before they removed their helmets.

It wasn't that they were stand-offish. On the contrary. They'd laughed and made jokes and included me in their merriment, but I was never allowed to see their faces or have their names.

The male who was in charge explained that they are an elite unit, and their identities are secret.

I didn't push the issue. If keeping our perimeter watched and not getting to see their faces meant I didn't have to worry about dying, then they could wear Leif's shadows, and I would have been okay with it.

We'd finished up our meal and relieved ourselves. Thank Luna for the female that accompanied me. And we got back on the road with the horses rested and ready for the next leg of our journey.

Night had fallen before we made it another few miles. The cooler air carried the scent of the pine trees through the window of the carriage and my heart shudders at the scent.

I won't be seeing Roxalus for nearly two weeks. And Ayxian has become dangerously unpredictable.

After what feels like hours, I can't keep my eyes open enough to keep reading, the book falling to the seat with a soft thud as I drift off into a fitful sleep.

Sounds of metal-on-metal rouse me from a deep slumber. Peering out the curtained window, I can just make out two of my guards clashing swords with five other figures.

There is a guard on the ground, unmoving and covered in blood thirty feet away. My driver and the other guard are nowhere to be seen.

One of my guards, the broad-shouldered leader, fights three on one. A kick to his leg knocks him off of his feet but he puts his sword up just in time to deflect the one swinging for his head.

The female guard holds her own, but she is wearing down. A flash of light shoots from her hands and throws her two opponents ten feet away. Finding her footing, she runs to help her leader.

With a quick blow to the back of the one standing over him, she gives him the time and the opening he needs to end one of the other attackers.

A crack of thunder in the cloudless sky sends both my guards to their knees. There is definitely magics at play.

I'm frozen with indecision. Should I shift and try to help or stay put and hope for the best?

I'm not a trained fighter and if an Elite guard can't best these attackers with unknown magics, what chance do I have?

Even with claws and powerful jaws, I won't be able to take on this many fae at once. And if I do leave the safety of the carriage, is it disrespectful to the people trying to protect me?

An unnatural swift wind blows, and the carriage rocks. The moon is new, and the stars don't provide enough light to make out a figure clearly from this distance, standing to the side of a massively large tree up on the hillside.

I can smell fresh earth, burnt sugar, salt, and pine. Energy buzzes in the air like bees at a hive.

The tree line to the woods along the road is less than forty feet away and a movement catches in the corner of my eye.

Another gust of wind hits the carriage. My head bounces off the wall hard enough to make my eyes swim with dots, blurring my vision.

A lone figure breaches the copse of trees, but I can't make out more than a cool colored glow as they head straight for the fray.

With vision is blurry, I fight to keep myself from being pulled under into the darkness of unconsciousness. The pounding inside my skull is growing increasingly painful though. I don't know how much longer I can hold out.

More metal clashes as the lone figure swings his sword through one of the attackers.

Literally through them. It's a sickening sound. Barely a scream has the time to rip from the dismembered body before it crumples in two pieces to the ground.

I would have thought, for sure, that the lone swordsmen would have been another fae trying to end my lowbee life.

He raises his sword over and over again. Metal on metal. Cutting through the attackers until no more stand.

My two remaining guards bow their heads slightly to the figure dressed all in black. My head swims, pounding harder as I try to concentrate on the scene in front of me.

A flash of in the sky lights up the area again. That distant person by the large tree swings their arms in a full arc and another gust of wind blows against my carriage, and I scream as it goes tumbling it end over end, landing on its side.

I manage to climb up onto the bench to look out of the window, but there's an enormous pain in my leg and my head feels as if it's about to split open.

Before I lose consciousness, I make out a roar of pain, a spot of light, and the faint scent of... Christmas?

Chapter Twenty-Nine

The sun is shining bright through a window onto my face. Gods, my head and body hurts. Maybe I slept too long. I can't bring myself to open my eyes yet.

Soft sheets and a fluffy mattress cradle my body, making me sink into the feeling of the plush pillow under my head.

I can't find my eyelids to make them open properly but the comfortable spot of half sleep that holds me doesn't care if I ever leave its embrace.

A bustling noise reaches my ears from my right and I stiffen. Why is someone in my room?

All at once, the attack rushes to the forefront of my mind as I quickly sit up. The movement making my head pound and my leg throb. Nausea roiling my stomach.

Some of the details are fuzzy but the last thing I remember is passing out in the carriage, still a two day's ride from Ayxian's castle.

An older female sits beside the bed I'm in, dipping a cloth into a basin of water. Wiping it across my skin.

Jerking out of her reach, she gasps, finally noticing I'm awake.

Without a word, she jumps to her feet and flees the room. Spry for someone of her advanced years. I'll give her that.

Looking around at my surroundings, the room is enormous and adorned with a large, four poster bed that I'm currently laying in. A huge wardrobe. Lavished curtains. And an over-sized settee. There's a bookcase on one of the expansive walls that houses hundreds of tomes.

My head begins to pound harder the more I move around. My eyes refusing to fully focus.

A great bathing chamber sits off to the back of the room. Light comes from in there too, so it must have a window.

As much as I want to get my bearings, I'm not willing to get up just yet.

Laying my head back down and wondering at the rooms I've been put in, I close my eyes on instinct to try and alleviate this constant throbbing in my temples.

They snap back open at the scent wafting up from the pillows under my head. Pine needles and peppermint.

I had assumed I'd been brought the rest of the way to Ayxian's castle but... Shit!

The door flies open with a bang. Prince Roxalus comes bounding in from the corridor followed closely behind by Commander Mystiance.

Trying to sit up, the dizziness in my head forces me back down. And when I meet his gaze, it's all consuming. There isn't enough air.

His eyes scan over every inch of my face, down my bruised arms, and linger on my legs that are thankfully covered by a soft duvet.

"Lady Piper." The look on his face speaks the words he doesn't. Concern. Pain. Anguish. Anger.

"Prince Roxalus. My regrets in assuming, but I thought I had awakened in Prince Ayxian's castle."

With a twitch from the side of his mouth, concern and pain are replaced instantly with loathing and anger.

Honestly, what was he expecting me to think? Maybe those shouldn't have been my first words to him but what else should I say?

Thank you is out the window. I can't owe him a second boon. Why am I here seems like a slap to the face.

If he hates me more than I intrigue him, I might as well have stayed crumpled and bleeding back in that carriage.

Maybe I'm a coward but I take the easiest route to navigate. "How long have I been out?"

The older maid comes back into the room, pushing past Mysti and bumping Roxalus as she goes. Her brazenness almost makes me want to giggle if not for the fierceness of her commanding presence.

Without preamble, she picks up the duvet on one side and takes my leg in both hands. I gasp at the intrusion and then at the pain that shoots out in rivulets from where she's touching me.

"Ouch! What are you doing..." Sucking in an audible breath, I see it. The giant slice running from my calf to right above the back of my knee.

"When the carriage flipped, it broke your leg. Eskay here...," He motions to the fae I'd thought was a maid. "She's had to force your protruding bones back in and set the break."

Ah, gotcha. She's a healer. I had met an amazing healer the second week I'd been back to stay with Leif.

There had been an accident with some kind of harvesting tool on the castle grounds. The fascination I'd felt watching the magics heal that fae had been a wonder, but tables turned? I shouldn't have gawked at what I'd witnessed now knowing the pain firsthand.

The prince's stare unnerved me... but not in the same way that his brother's did. "I didn't want to risk heading all the way to Ayxian's with your body so broken."

Looking over a Mysti, she isn't smirking or gloating as I would have expected. Her face is a forced mask of indifference. There's a wall around her feelings that my gifts try to push through, but it won't budge.

"I'm sure you have more important things to attend to, Commander." I don't know why I felt the need to voice that. She'd irked me at Loxias' court. I don't want her to see me in this weakened state.

The wall suddenly crumbles, and her next move stuns me. Emotions flood my senses. Sorrow, guilt, shame.

Dropping to the floor beside the bed, she bends her head in supplication. A dagger raised in her flat palms as an offering.

"My apologies, My Lady. I failed you. I except whatever punishment you deem fitting." No tears fall but they sit heavy on the bottom lids of her beautiful eyes.

Mouth popping open, I try to scoot away from the dagger like it's a venomous snake, but I cry out in pain as Eskay dabs ointment to my wound.

Roxalus glares at her but says nothing of Mysti's humbling. I can't think. I have no idea what to make of any of this.

"I don't know what you're thinking." My breathing's too fast. I can't get enough air.

Between the pain in my leg and aching body and the pounding of my head, the shock of her proclamation has me hyperventilating.

"Why would you be punished? I was attacked by lowbee haters in the middle of the night. Were you responsible for sending them?" Gods, what if she says yes? My leg is too fucked up to try and get away.

I truly am helpless right now. The side of my cheek is sore and tender, under my right eye and there's bruises along my arms that my fae healing hasn't worked its charms on to remove yet.

If it's still this bad after who knows how long I've been out, I had to have been in an absolute a horrible mess when I'd first arrived.

Panic begins to settle in. "What happened to my driver? The guards! Are they okay?" If I don't get some air into my lungs soon, I'm going to pass out again.

Roxalus inches towards the bed. His bed, I realize.

Laying a hand beside my good leg, his fingers graze the side of it above the duvet and I shiver. My breathing begins to calm, but only slightly.

After a deep breath, he leans in quietly, like he's scared that I'll spook. He's never been this close to me in the company of others.

"One of the guards was killed. The driver and the other guard were missing when I got there and haven't been found. Admiral Biscott is in severe condition, but Eskay won't let my top-ranking elite unit member die."

He arches an eyebrow in her direction in challenge, and she scoffs. I like her all the more for it.

"I don't let anyone die, if I can help it. Your Admiral is no more special than any of the others I care for." Her curt manner brokers no room for argument. She's fascinatingly feisty.

It shocks me that Roxalus allows the disrespect from someone who is supposedly below him. A gentle warmth touches his eyes at her chiding and my heart softens. I can *feel* his admiration for her.

"And what of the female? The one who'd been with the other guards? She was nice to me. I saw her fight to help the Admiral, valiantly I might add, but she went down just before that sword wielding male arrived on the scene. Is she okay? Oh gods! Please tell me she's okay."

Mysti still hasn't raised her head, but she does lower the dagger.

He chuckles and I find it incredibly irritating at first. I start to chide him for it until he shakes his head and looks to his commander. "Mysti is alive... for now."

What? It had been Mysti? She'd been the one to guard me so ferociously during that attack? Oh, by the Gods! That means that he's the one who...

"Mysti?" I turn to look at her and Eskay yanks my leg back, keeping me from pulling from her grip as she works. "You were the female on the road with me? The one who watched my back as I peed and laughed with me and told me jokes along the way?"

I can't believe it. The helmets might have kept me from seeing their faces, but her voice sounded so different. Maybe because there hadn't been any animosity in it when she spoke, unlike when we were guests at Loxias' court.

She still has her head bowed. I'm not sure what the protocol is here. I go with the human thing. It's all that makes sense to me right now.

"Just get up." Her mouth purses at the command. Standing straight, looking ahead, her body is stiff. "What do you want, a formal decree or something? I don't punish people. I'm just a fae shifter who happened into a courtier's title."

"I owe you a debt, Lady Piper. My failure to do my job has caused you injury. Allow me to pay you my due."

Rubbing my temples, I try to hone in on her intent. There's no hostility or falseness in her heart. She really does feel I'm owed something for her short comings.

"Okay. I have a request." Roxalus looks pleased. For some inexplicable reason, pleasing him pleases me. "I will need help getting around until this heals." I turn to Eskay. "How long do you suspect that will be?"

"I'd say about two weeks, give or take, My Lady. I've done what I can but a snapped bone, ripping through flesh, needing re-broken and mended takes time." I cringe at her imagery.

I've never had an injury take more than a day or two to heal. This isn't going to be easy. I am grateful for the excuse to use Mysti's help.

"I call in my boon, Commander Mystiance. You shall escort and assist me around Prince Ayxian's court." Glancing at Roxalus, the corners of his mouth twitch but he doesn't comment. "Hopefully, I will be fully healed by the time the rest of the royals arrive at the castle."

"Yes, My Lady. I will ready a new carriage and gather supplies. We shall be off in a few hours." With a low bow, she turns and leaves. No sass. No complaints. It's plain weird to me but I'm not going to look a gift horse in the mouth.

Eskay mumbles something about needing more supplies and no one cares what she thinks but she re-adjusts the position of my leg and leaves without haste.

The prince doesn't remove his hand from the side of my leg and heat from that barely there touch sends an ache to parts that haven't any business aching under the circumstances.

In a gesture I would never have considered when I'd first arrived in Anavrin, I pat the bed invitingly. "Sit... if you wish."

My nerves are already frayed. Him being closer can't do much more damage. Right?

Taking a seat beside me, he does his best not to jostle my body around. My leg gives a pang of pain anyway.

My mind wanders to that kiss we shared over two months ago. How pathetic that that small amount of affection has me in its grip?

There isn't anything I can say to make this less awkward. The hot and cold prince works me up and grinds me down with his flip-flopping emotions.

"I should have been there sooner." His voice is soft, tone sorrowful. "I never should have left you alone to deal with the murderer or those rebels out there. Noxian and I found out that there is a small faction against lowbees rising up in different areas of Anavrin. We rode out ahead to look into them. I entrusted my top people to your care, but it wasn't enough."

His people? I thought the extra guards were Max's doing, other than Mysti, of course.

With his head hung to his chest, I ache to caress his face. Instead, I let my hand fall to his forearm, and he shudders at the contact.

"Why?" My voice is a mere whisper in my own ears. "Why did you save me?"

The cool blue of his eyes brim with sorrow and his pine needle and peppermint scent all around me helps boost my resolve.

"Why do you feel the need to protect me, Roxalus?"

Shaking my head, I immediately regret it. The thumping has been a dull ache, but now it's more of an insistent flicking.

My frustration spills over. "I can't understand you. Half the time I think you hate me. And the other half I think I might go crazy not knowing how you truly feel about me."

Standing abruptly, running a hand over his face and back through his hair, frustration seeps into the room from us both. The air thick with the onslaught of emotions.

Thinking he won't answer, I start to turn away. I can't be left in a riptide with someone who won't tread the waters of emotion to save me from my own thoughts.

"It's not what I feel about you! It's what I feel for no one *but* you!" He blurts out as if he's unable to contain the words inside anymore.

The air's sucked from my lungs in one fell swoop. My heart beats hard against my ribcage.

Not allowing himself a moment's reprieve from the raw emotion, he cuts the distance between us. Bending low, fingers gripping under my chin, he places a soft, plush kiss, just grazing my lips.

My body reacts before my mind has caught up. As he begins to pull away, I bring my hand to the back of his neck, deepening the intensity of the kiss.

Careful not to jostle my injuries, his strong arms encircle my waist. A pleasant rumble settles deep in his chest, and I sigh into his opened mouth.

We are lost in one another in the most delicious of ways as the world fades away.

The door bangs open, hitting the opposite wall with a hard thud. Eskay and Mysti come bounding in, arms ladened with clothes, food, and bandages.

We jump apart like two kids caught with our hands in the cookie jar. With swollen lips, I brush my fingers over the trail of heat left in his wake.

"My regrets, My Liege. We must be off. Admiral Biscott is awake and has asked to see you at your earliest convenience."

Nodding to her with a long glance in my direction, reluctance to leave me is written all over his face. "Be wary, Lady Piper. Stay safe."

With that, he's gone, and I feel his absence like a missing limb.

"Don't worry, My Lady. Two weeks will fly by quickly enough." The commander doesn't smile but I can *feel* her sincerity.

I'm not sure if she's trying to comfort me or herself, but I know that Ayxian won't let the time slip away so easily.

Chapter Thirty

We arrive at Prince Ayxian's court around midday. Mysti has insisted we take a short cut not many people follow between Roxalus and Ayxian's lands.

It only takes us one full day. We are still behind the time I should have arrived, but only by one day. Not Two.

A small party of servants greets me at the entrance. The prince is nowhere to be seen, and I am secretly grateful.

His right hand has the staff fetch my bags. Glaring at Commander Mysti, Lord Hadence doesn't address her. He focuses on me only.

A beat late, he asks about my limp and the marks on my face. Mysti comes to stand beside me and I'm grateful for the solidarity.

"Where is Prince Ayxian," I say to diffuse the tension. It must be the wrong thing to say.

Lord Hadence extends his arm to me, and I take it. He was cordial but not warm during my time here in the beginning. I'd overheard him and Ayxian discussing me more than once. It was one of the reasons I'd decided to go stay with Leif.

I'd never gotten a welcome feeling from him. Some of the staff and I got along famously, but there'd been a few courtiers and servants that were cool towards me.

"He is off training. You were due to arrive yesterday, Piper. Should the prince wait around?"

Well, the prince's concern would have been nice, but I don't say that.

Mysti raises her chin. I can *feel* her indignation on my behalf. "**Lady** Piper." She says to Lord Hadence, taking a half step in front of me, hand on the hilt of her sword.

"What?" It's clear that he heard and understands what she'd said. Feigning ignorance is unbecoming.

"You will address her as Lady Piper, **Hadence**."

His nose scrunches like he's inhaled a big whiff of blue cheese. I know he's a great fighter from my time in this court, but he doesn't appear to want to challenge Mysti.

"Her title is no less than yours." She doesn't remove her hand from her sword or lower her gaze.

A long moment of tension passes between the two of them while I'm caught in the pull of their stand-off.

Standing here, leg throbbing, I wait for it to be over. This is one pissing match I don't need to be a part of.

After sitting for so long, standing all of this time is sending blood rushing to my toes. There's wetness on my pant leg.

"Oh shoot." They both break their stare at the same time to look at me. "My leg is bleeding again. Lord Hadence, can we see our rooms now?"

"I have yours ready. We weren't expecting Commander Mystiance. I will have to find her accommodations... perhaps in the staffing area." His sneer makes me want to slap him.

I want her close. Need her close. He probably suspects that. If my legs both worked well right now, I'd be tempted to shift and snap at his stupid face.

"No. She will have a room adjacent to mine." He starts to protest but my tone brokers no argument. "Prince Ayxian will want me comfortable and that's that."

Reluctantly, a dip of his chin and a wave of his hand later, we are on our way to the rooms Prince Ayxian had originally put me up in.

Lord Hadence doesn't walk us there. He whispers to a few servants who scurry about frantically. My former handmaiden, Keyara, shows us to our rooms.

It's more of a suite rather than just rooms. There is a front sitting room, a large bathing chamber, and two rooms that house beds. One large. One a moderate size. Both as luxurious as lavish as any grand hotel in the human realm.

Mysti takes the larger room. I could have protested but I'm exhausted. It's been a rough few days. The journey was long and full of peril. I'm just grateful to have a place to lay my head and rest my injured body.

Keyara makes her way back into my room sporting fresh towels. A fruit and cheese platter has been laid out in the sitting room, along with an assortment of nuts and some blueberry wine. She remembered about my penchant for sweet wines. Bless her heart.

"My Lady, the prince requests that you dress and meet him for dinner in an hour. Shall I pick out an outfit?"

"That won't be necessary, Keyara. I don't wear a corset anymore. And my leggings go pretty well with all of my dressy tops."

Dresses and corsets were the bane of my existence when I'd arrived. I'm glad to be doing my own thing now.

"Oh, but Lady Piper, you must wear a dress." Commander Mystiance entered my peripheral vision. She leans against the door jamb smirking. "Prince Ayxian will not be pleased if you're not dressed properly."

"Well, the prince can wear a dress if he likes, but I will not be." Her head dropping in dismay, I try to comfort her a bit, but I won't be but back into anyone's box. "I will make certain that he knows it's my doing. Not yours, Keyara. You needn't worry." This still doesn't seem to cheer her up.

Forty-five minutes later, Mysti and I are being led to the dining room. With her sword hanging low on her hips, she peers into every shadow as we pass.

Once we arrive at the table, she takes a breath after scanning the room for threats. I don't know if this is normal behavior for her or not, but I appreciate her thoroughness after the attack.

Ayxian enters the dining room slapping his hands together. "I'm starving. Ah, Lady Piper. Good of you to join us. I was beginning to think you'd stood me up for our allotted time together."

Making his way passed the few courtiers that have come to dine with us tonight, his eyes finally notice Mysti.

With a grimace overtaking his features, there and gone so fast, I might have imagined it. "Commander. To what do I owe your unwelcome company?"

Ouch. Harsh. I don't know if they have some sort of former beef, but that was rude.

"I owe Lady Piper a debt, Your Highness. She has requested my assistance for the next couple of weeks."

If I weren't paying attention, I would have missed how carefully she worded her answer. It appeared to please the prince. His former smile returned with a huff of laughter.

"Caught you up with a boon, eh? Lady Piper is a clever one." He winks at me like we are sharing some private joke. "Pass the turnips."

Lord Hadence steers the conversation after everyone's plates are full. The meal isn't grand, but the foods themself are hearty and filling.

"Lady Piper wondered at your absence upon her arrival this afternoon, My Liege. I told her that your training kept you away."

The way Lord Hadence fills him in on what passed between us isn't suspect by outward appearances, but I wonder if there's something Ayxian's doing that his right hand is covering for? He hasn't had time to inform him before we all gathered.

"Yes, yes. It couldn't be avoided. The kingdom is on the line, and I need to be at my peak if I'm going to win the throne." Taking a huge bite of turkey leg, mouth full to the brim, he doesn't bother to swallow before taking offense to my injuries. "Dear Luna. What happened to your face?"

It kind of feels like an insult that he's only now noticing the cut on my forehead and the bruising on my cheek. They're mending quickly. Yellowing with only a tinge of purple. There are shallow scabs where deeper lacerations had once been. But to not notice something amiss before now? He really is an unobservant oaf.

I open my mouth to respond but gleaning Mysti out of the corner of my eye, she gives the slightest of head shakes.

Changing tactics, my brain works double time. "I'm not adept in traveling. Horses are more beast than I expected."

None of that had anything to do with what happened. The facts were all true, so the omission doesn't halt on my tongue.

"My leg is worse for wear. It will take weeks to heal. That's why Mysti's boon came at the perfect time." The corner of her mouth lifting nearly imperceptibly in amusement.

"Pity. Your legs were perfect. I have admired them greatly each time we've come together."

My cheeks heat at the insinuation he's attempting to give the table at large. If I could die of embarrassment, now would be the time.

"I do hope you'll allow me to help you as well. After all, we're supposed to be spending time together, right? Getting to know each other. You, getting to know my court."

My first instinct is to reprimand but I switch to a more playful response, letting a meek twinkling laugh escape. "Prince Ayxian, don't play games. Your wicked tongue already knows the taste of mine."

That draws a big grin to his face, and I pull back, not wanting to overdo it. The lug doesn't know when enough is too much as it is.

Lord Hadence's frown tells me that perhaps the prince hasn't let him into his confidence as much as he thinks.

The dinner concludes without much else of importance taking place. Ayxian does comment that, because of my delayed arrival, he'll only have a week and a half of my company to himself. And I point out, once again, that we've had time together before.

After that first night, I haven't seen much of him. The first week blinks by in what feels like no time.

Mysti is more of a help than I thought she would be. I don't worry at all about being attacked with her around.

She's helped change my bandages. I realized that I couldn't manage them on my own. And embarrassingly enough, she's also helped me at bath time.

With her perfect face and toned body, I initially felt self-conscious, but her gentleness and quick smiles soon had me forgetting that I'd once despised her.

When we're out of these rooms, her laughs and smiles are nearly nonexistent. She's all duty. I admire her dedication.

I'm not sure when it happened, but somewhere along the way, I found that I enjoy her company. Maybe it isn't friendship, but it's at least camaraderie.

On the night after we'd arrived here, I'd more than my share of the blueberry wine. She'd had some, but not a lot. It was then that I asked questions about her prince.

I'd been fascinated by all of the tiny details that she'd divulged. She never spilled his secrets, but she'd been more than willing to paint him in a glowing light.

I learned that he hated mice. She'd told me that when they were younger, a field mouse tried to snatch a piece of cheese from a platter that had been between them and a few other fae in their inner circle. He batted at it, and it scampered off.

When they'd all settle into their tents for the night, Roxalus came screaming out of his. Apparently, two of their party scrounged up all of the mice they could find and stashed them in his bedroll.

I laughed along with her and by the time midnight had rolled around, our cheeks hurt, and stomachs ached from laughing at the prince's expense.

I've only seen Ayxian three times since that first night. His training is of the utmost importance to him.

Max said that me being at each castle and spending time with each ruler was crucial to the competition, but I couldn't bring myself to care enough to seek Ayxian out.

My leg's healed nicely over the last few days. There's only a bit of an ache around the puncture area. If I would have shifted at some point, it would more than likely have healed nearly instantly, but selfishly, I didn't want Mysti to leave me alone here.

I feel safer with her nearby. And the daggers that Lord Hadence stares at me now since he found out about Prince Ayxian's and my precious entanglement sets my nerves on end.

News has reached us about two more murders and the anti-lowbee faction is growing louder every day. It's also been made known that the murder victims had been sexually assaulted prior to their deaths. The very idea of that level of depravity shakes me to my core. Hating lowbee's enough to kill them but forcing them into giving a piece of themselves away before taking their lives is sickening.

If I could somehow trick Mysti into another boon, I'd keep her as my personal bodyguard for the foreseeable future.

Today is only a day or so before the others are expected to start arriving. Tents and vendors began filing in yesterday. Excited chatter has been carrying throughout the courtyard and to the fields along the castle's main road.

Mysti had hung back to take a bath this morning. Since my leg is pretty much healed, I'd told her that I wanted to take a walk around the castle before breakfast and that I would meet her there.

This castle isn't as dim as Emenda's had been but there aren't enough windows to let in as much natural light as I crave indoors.

Coming around one such dark corner at the end of the corridor on the east side, the hairs on the back of my neck stand on end. Then I spot it, a darkened figure looming in the dark shadows.

Chapter Thirty-One

Tensing all over, the smell of earthy cedar wafts my way. Being caught unaware and alone by one of the rebels would have been a horrible mistake. Not as bad as if I'd run into the deviant murderer though.

I should be relieved that it's only the prince. For some reason, I'm not. I don't think it's a good idea to be alone with the beastly portion of Prince Ayxian. I can never tell which version of him I'll get until it's too late.

"Mmmm..." I hear him inhale loudly. "Lady Piper." Stepping out of the shadows, his hulking form stands statue still in front of me. The torchlight casts his face in an eerie glow and there's a hungry gravel in his voice. "I was hoping to find you alone. That bodyguard of your is always looming."

Suddenly, I'm not so sure leaving Mysti back at our rooms was such a good idea.

"I'm here. What do you wish to discuss?" Proud that my voice doesn't shake, I take comfort in my false bravado. "Shall we go down to breakfast, My Liege?"

Leaning forward, he inhales again and goosepimples rise to the surface my skin. He's a tower of bulking muscles and testosterone.

Once, I had desired nothing more than to be wanted by him. Now, I find that all I want is to be in the safety of a crowd. Away from him.

"In here." He motions to the room off the corridor I hadn't even noticed I'd wandered to in my meandering.

His private gym. There are stones for lifting. Benches for sit-ups. And various other contraptions made from stone and trees that are similar to those in the human realm.

"I've wondered all week if you'd come here to visit with me." He motions for me to sit at one of the equipment stations.

It has a bench-like seat and there are stones in buckets attached to ropes. He lifts them, repetitively. The muscles along his arms glisten. His white tunic hangs open, exposing the curls of dark hair across his bare chest.

"I hope you like what you see, Lady Piper. I have great plans for us."

Um, what? After our last... encounter, how can he possibly delude himself into thinking I'll so easily fall back into our flirtatious routine?

"You flatter me, Your Highness, but I don't think it wise for you to deviate from your course. The throne is important to you."

The stone buckets drop to the floor with a loud clatter. He snatches my wrist and yanks me up and into him. "If you're through telling me what course of action is best for me, let me show you what I have in mind for us. For our future."

Spinning me around, his front to my back, his firm arm around my waist pulls me close to his taut body. Nipping through the clothing at my shoulder, he pushes it aside, making his way to the nape of my neck.

Frozen in shock, caught between the desire to be touched and the fear of his beastly side, Roxalus' face pops in my head.

Grinding his hardened length against my backside, a little moan escapes through my pursed lips without my consent. Small bites to my ear are followed by rougher tugs against my restrained torso.

I need to get control over the situation. This isn't what I want... I don't want *him*. Not anymore. Not since...

Trying to think around the acidic emotions churning in my stomach, I attempt to pull away but the cage of his arms holds me tightly.

Before I can break free, his large, calloused hands yank at my leggings, attempting to pull them off.

"I love it when you wear these. They're less restraints to the conquest, but I'm always up for a challenge," he growls close to my ear.

Trying again to pull away, he holds me fast. The tips of his fingers brush my entrance. "Stop, Ayxian! I don't want this..."

"So wet." he murmurs without listening to me. I can't be sure, but the noises he makes from behind me sound like he's sucked my juices from his hand.

"Ayxian," I breathe harshly. "Stop. Please stop! I'm don't..." He isn't responding to my pleas. The beast I've glimpsed in the past is in full control.

Pressing between my lips, he pushes one finger inside and I panic. Then a second pushes inside and my body clamps down on the sudden intrusion. An involuntary moan slips through, and it only encourages him further.

The arm banding around my waist splays his fingers down towards the apex of my sex, brushing the soft tuft of hairs there. Pulling away again as hard as I can, he yanks me roughly back into him with more force. "Stop, Ayxian! I don't want this," I cry out. "Get off of me!"

Thrashing, pulling, and twisting, using all of my fae strength, only makes his fingers sink deeper in, over and over again. Panic and fear tear at my mind as I attempt desperately to get away.

His fangs dig into the soft fleshy part of my neck. No venom comes but hot blood flows freely over my skin as the arm around my waist moves down to undo the pants restraining his hard cock.

"Stop, Ayxian. I can't..." He isn't listening, biting hard to hold me in place like prey as I thrash about.

My mind reels at the vulnerability. At the helplessness I feel. Seeing red, rage takes its place quickly.

Through my fear, time slows briefly, just enough to clear the cobwebs of panic from my mind.

Before he can push himself into me, I shift.

He growls but doesn't stop his attempts. He is singularly focused. His predator side in full control, not accepting the loss of his game.

Swatting him in the face with my powerful tail, I use the strength of my panther's hind legs and kick with all my might.

Growling louder this time, he cradles his stomach but reaches for my tail, which has slipped from his grip.

Now's my chance to seize the opportunity to turn. With a swipe of my large claws across his chest, he falls back.

The desire still heavy in his gaze makes me sick. He is willing to take me in my panther form. The fact that I don't want him in any form doesn't seem to matter to this beast.

The claw marks I'd torn across his chest run from one shoulder and down to his navel, bleeding profusely. The open flesh knitting itself closed slowly, but surely. It'll scar. Wounds left on a fae by a shifter leave their mark but that is no comfort right now.

With the nerve to chuckle, amusement is clear on his face. "Come now, Piper. You don't think that a little thing like your animal side will turn me off, do you? If anything, the fight in you turns me on more, kitten. I want every piece of you."

Gross! I want to scream in his face, but I refuse to shift back to do that. I won't give him the satisfaction of my ire while I stand here naked.

The fact that he is in control of himself enough to speak so plainly of his depravity tells me everything I need to know about this horrible prince.

Instead, I back up towards the door and once out in the corridor, I run to my rooms as fast as my legs can carry me.

Not out of earshot yet, Ayxian calls to me. "Where are you going? I thought we were going to have some fun."

Arrogant asshole!

Chapter Thirty-Two

Shifting halfway across the sitting space, Mysti looks up from applying her makeup at the vanity. "You okay."

The blood that had been on my neck disappeared when I'd first shifted into my panther form, so it must be the set of my demeanor that's giving her a cause for concern.

I don't reply. I can't. Shame is a living beast inside my chest. I'm humiliated and I feel like, somehow, what happened is my fault.

Closing the distance to my bed chambers, I slam the door shut behind me. Bangs and shouts make their way through the wood repeatedly, but I can't face anyone. Not now.

Throwing myself across the bed, I finally let the tears flow. And flow. And flow until I have no more liquid to give.

Time is moving forward but I'm stuck in a loop of despair. At some point along the day, I'd climbed under the duvet and fallen asleep. A fresh round of banging on my door waking me from a fitful slumber.

Throat dry, stomach grumbling from hunger, I don't give in to the demands of my body.

Blood still crusts my fingers where my claws had scraped across the prince's chest. My neck is sore from his bite. There's bruising from the force he'd exerted.

Stretching the ache from my bones, I finally get up and walk to the window, closing the curtains to the light shining in from the early evening sky. The darkness of the room is the only comfort I can claim.

Not bothering to light the lantern, I feel my way to the wardrobe and throw on the first nightshift that touches my hands. I need to rest. My entire system is exhausted.

As I'm climbing back in bed, disappointment, distrust, and shame coil in the pit of my stomach. Burrowing deep into the duvet and covering my head, sleep claims me once again.

More banging comes a few hours later. Or possibly a few days. I have no idea of how long I've been hiding in this room, and I can't muster a fucking care one, but I am stiff and sore all over. I need to at least let in some light.

Opening the curtains, the midday sun shines bright in the sky. No wonder I feel so thirsty and achy all over. A soul aching tiredness creeps back into my body the moment his face flashes in the forefront of my mind.

Not bothering to cover myself up, the bed rises up to meet me before the door bangs open and Elodie, followed by Mysti, comes walking in. Throwing the cover over my head, I groan in their direction.

"I was worried that I did something to offend you, seeing as how you didn't bother to greet me this morning." Elodie's hand grazes my arm as she pulls the duvet back.

Wincing at the unexpected touch, tremors rock through me unexpectedly.

Mysti's gasp is more than I can bear. "Who bit you?" The demand in her voice is more than concern. It's rage.

Fae bites to the neck, wrists, or stomach don't heal quickly. They are a marking. A claiming.

It makes sense that she's concerned after the way I'd come back here and not left the room.

"It doesn't matter. I just want to go back to sleep." I can't face them. I'm not ready.

Elodie sighs loudly. I don't know if her gifts will show her the truth of the situation or not and I can't muster the will to care.

Shame is a creature living in my chest. Moving from this room seems an insurmountable task. "Let me be."

She and Mysti are whispering, pointing at my thighs, at my neck. Anger coursing off of them both. I try to build a wall to block their emotions but I'm useless right now. A weakling. I don't deserve their pity.

"You need to eat. And you definitely need to drink something." Elle's voice seems far away but she's standing right next to the bed.

As if summoned by the princess's words, Keyara bounds into the room with a tray laden with food, wine, and coffee. When I make no move towards the coffee, Elle's tone changes.

"Who?! I want to know who did this to you and I want to know now!" I wince at her demanding tone. "Not only as your friend, Lady Piper. I want to know as a royal princess of Anavrin!"

I've never heard her so cross, so angry, and when I try to pull the duvet back over my head, she grabs my wrist and I wince again.

The contact will give her the scene if I think of it. And in this moment, it's all I can think about.

The blood under my nails has caught her attention. Mysti's too.

They talk to each other, but I don't try to ascertain what they're saying. I'm too absorbed in my humiliation.

I'd blocked out what had happened the best I could when Elodie had made contact, but my wall is shit in my current state.

Catching words like *mixed scents* and *blood* and *distinct bite pattern*. None of it matters.

The helplessness I had felt when it happened, the hopelessness that I feel now, it's all marrying together in a feeling of disgrace.

It's an unwarranted emotion. I've done nothing wrong, but that doesn't stop me from feeling like, somehow, this is my fault.

I've carried a torch for the two princes. I've kissed them both. Ayxian may be a beast, but I'm a monster for toying with their feelings.

The princess and the commander leave. Keyara is still in the room with me. Her soft voice cutting through the haze of my self-loathing.

"Lady Piper, if I may speak freely?" I glance up unwillingly at her meek tone. Pink coloring her cheeks, her hands wring in front of her.

"Okay." I don't care to listen, but her vulnerability *feels* kindred. My gifts are pushing me to learn what she has to say. "What is it, Keyara?"

It's the second time I've spoken since my pleas for him to stop. All of the boons I'd made, I can't remember any shimmering magics, but my mind isn't right now, and my throat is dry.

After fidgeting with the food on the tray and picking at the hem of her skirts, her tearful gaze meets mine.

A ping hits me and when no cold or warmth meet it, I realize that the necklace Max has given me isn't around my neck. It must have fallen when I'd shifted. Shit.

"It was Prince Ayxian, was it not?" She isn't asking. She knows. It's a kind of firsthand knowledge that is making her so bold as to ask. "His beastly warrior gifts make him lose himself, My Lady. Many of the females, and some of the males, in this court have kept this secret for a long time."

The pleading in her eyes brings tears to mine. Unaware of giving myself permission, I reach out and squeeze her hand.

"Being royalty doesn't excuse anyone's actions. Why do you all hide his nature?" I'm not angry with her. Just frustrated.

I can honestly say that never in my life would I have thought I'd react to an assault like this the way that I have. Hiding away. Feeling shame and guilt.

Pouring a glass of wine, she pushes it into my hands. Nodding for her to do the same, we both take long draughts of the sweet berry wine.

I won't push her for answers. If she needs time, that's what she'll get from me.

After a few deep breaths, she finally finds her voice.

"He's a good fighter. Our court is safe from most attacks. If he were made king, he would defend Anavrin to his last breath." She finishes off the glass. "I can't speak for the others, but me personally, I felt ashamed. For not fending off his unwanted advances. For not being worthy of royalty. For thinking that I was anything but a means to keep his beastly needs met."

At the hanging of her head, a rage like I've never known flitters inside my chest. Attempting to pat her shoulder in comfort, I know the feeling all too well. Now, I'm beyond angry!

"We should always have a choice when it comes to our own bodies, Keyara." Downing the last of my wine, it hits my empty stomach and revolts. Grabbing a hunk of cheese off the tray, I chew it without tasting it and swallow. The crusty edges tear threw the dryness in my throat that has yet to be satiated. "Enough is enough!"

"Please, My Lady, don't tell him that anyone here has ill feelings about his dominating needs. I don't know what will happen to those of us he's had his way with. Please!"

Her pleas left me even angrier. At him.

For the fae that he thinks are nothing but a game. For the fact that he believes he's entitled to anyone's body without their explicit consent.

For myself. By gods! I'm finally angry for myself.

My self-loathing burns away into full blown rage. He should be grateful that I don't have Faelan's power for particle manipulation. I'd tear him into teeny tiny pieces, only to make him whole again so I can rip him apart, limb by limb, over and over and over again.

"It's not my place to divulge your stories. It is my place, however, to avenge my violation. I won't let him get away with what he's done. I won't allow him to steal my peace, my self-worth." Getting up out of this wretched bed, I go to the wardrobe. "Has lunch been served yet?"

"Yes, My lady. It's actually closer to dinner time."

It's much later than I'd thought. I've hidden myself away in this room long enough. Ayxian has probably thought no more on what he's done to me.

And here I am, wasting my sorrow on his hedonism when what I should be doing is figuring out a way to exact my retribution.

"Wonderful. The others have arrived?" I need a plan. To send a message to Ayxian, but also the murderer, and the anti-low-bee faction while I'm at it.

Nodding her agreement, I can *feel* her weariness. "All but King Maximus. He's not meant to be here until the day after tomorrow."

"Splendid. Will you fetch me a bit more coffee, a hairbrush, and the most beguiling dress in my arsenal. I have a prince to ensnare."

Chapter Thirty-Three

Waiting until I'm sure all of the royals and guest courtiers are seated at the high table, the food has already been served and merriment is underway.

There's one remaining seat. It's been left open for me. And it happens to be next to Roxalus, a few chairs down from Ayxian at the head.

Keyara found me the most enchanting gown. It has a low bustline, an open back, and cutouts that allow most of my sides to be exposed. She's also found the most intoxicating perfume I've ever smelled. I wear my hair up, with long pieces hanging down the sides of my face.

If beauty is considered a weapon, I am going to wield it with brutal efficiency. If he can use my body for his wants, I can use it for my own needs. Vengeance without violence will still cause pain.

All eyes flash up to take me in as I enter the room, slowly gliding across the space.

Roxalus' eyes lock onto mine and I smile.

Ayxian's growl speaks of wanting, pure desire. It's heard above the scraping of utensils and chatter around the table. He stands and my steps falter briefly before I recover myself.

Seating myself beside Roxalus, he stiffens out of the corner of my eye. If I had felt exposed before, I really feel it now.

Elodie sits across from us, and Mysti sits to her left, avoiding Roxalus' glare.

"Lady Piper, I didn't know if we'd see you here this evening. You're looking loads better than earlier." I'm sure Elle can feel the nerves wriggling around just under my skin.

I don't envy her gifts tonight. I can barely make out my own emotions when around a large group. She's ten times as powerful as I am. It must have taken her centuries to learn to wield that power properly.

"I wouldn't miss it. It's an honor to dine with royalty. I don't take that for granted."

Elodie can see through my intent. All the more reason not to show weakness in front of this lot.

Ayxian's eyes roam over my bust. Roxalus' eyes are firmly on the bite mark still highly visible on my neck. I'm only now realizing that he may misinterpret the situation.

"Lady Piper," Ayxian calls down the table to me, his voice gravelly, holding up the strip of material that ripped away when I'd shifted. "You left this in my private gym."

The bastard has the audacity to taunt? Whether it's meant for me or Roxalus, I don't know.

The color drains from Roxalus' face. As he inhales deeper, pain blazes behind his cold blue eyes.

He's good at keeping his mask in place, but several long seconds pass before he schools his features. "Excuse me."

Throwing his napkin to the table, he storms off towards the door behind Prince Ayxian who grabs a hold of his arm.

"Off so soon, Brother? I thought we might share dessert."

Roxalus' nostrils flare. The meaning clearly not lost on him. I want to rip Ayxian apart for his tormenting.

"It would be best if you removed your hand. If I do it, it will not grow back." His anger seething just beneath the surface.

The beastly prince chuckles, putting his hands up in a mock surrender. Without a glance back, Roxalus exits the dining hall with anger pinging in his wake.

A painful ache tugs from a spot inside my chest as my hand comes up empty when I reached towards his retreating back.

Mysti and Princess Elodie both stare. Not at the princes. Their sights are set on me, identical expressions of horror. Embla and Emenda look up curiously from the far end of the table where they sit with Prince Noxian.

Loxias saves me from the mortification I'm enduring. "What's going on, Piper? Are you well?" Nothing but concern in his tone. "Anything I can help with?"

I have a friend in the youngest prince. Our time together has solidified that bond and I am Luna blessed for it.

"Nothing to worry yourself about." His eyes catch on the bite mark. "I haven't been myself for the last day or so."

Taking the time to pivot in Ayxian's direction while speaking to Loxias, but also to Elle, Mysti, and all of those in attendance, my voice carries down the table.

"I'd forgotten my worth for a moment." Ayxian's smirk falls briefly. Lord Hadence's smile is like poison on the tip of a dagger. "That won't happen again. I assure you; no one is above comeuppance."

The rest of the dinner passes without incident.

Ayxian's making merry, trying to engage with me, to which I deflect his attention with the skill of a sashimi chef.

Mysti looks ready to rip his throat out right here at the table and I'm grateful for her loyalty and for her protection. If she weren't here, I don't know if I'd have the courage to face him so closely already.

Studiously ignoring the prince in favor of Elodie's male courtier, Lord Nalan, I laugh at one of his jokes, touch his arm, and engrossed myself in his conversation.

Ayxian's huff of annoyance is music to my ears. Jealousy might be rewarding for his behavior, but it's also dangerous.

When I've had my fill and the hour has grown late, I rise to leave.

He begins to stand but Mysti, Elodie, and Loxias all link arms with me, and we walk out of the dining room together.

Quill is astute. His glances to Loxias have been fewer tonight than any of the nights past but that could be that he's being watchful of the situation. Bringing up our rear, his hand rests at his side around his crossbow.

We go down a few corridors. The prince and Quill go left at the stairs and Elle heads to the right. Mysti and I continue walking in silence for several paces before she shifts then says, "Excuse me, My Lady. I'll be right back."

I have no idea where she's going or why but her sudden abandonment makes me feel naked without the safety of her company.

From out of the shadows to my left, awareness of a male sends unease skittering across my skin. The stars shine through the window of his curtainless room behind the opened door. The smell of pine needles and peppermint engulf me and I instantly relax.

"Prince Roxalus. You startled me."

"My regrets, Lady Piper." The stiffness in which he speaks has me taking a step back. I've had my fill of unpredictable males for the week.

As always, he notices. "You thought that I'd bring you harm because you chose my brother?" Hurt and disbelief color his tone.

Chose? Yeah, right. When I say nothing, he clicks his tongue against his cheek, his gaze boring a hole straight through me.

"I would never harm you, Piper...Never." Despite how hot and cold he's been since I first arrived in Anavrin, I don't doubt that the way I once had.

When I still don't say anything, he turns to excuse himself, but I catch him by the crook of his arm, and a light sigh escapes his lips at my touch.

My voice won't work above a whisper, but his presence a balm to my frayed soul. "I didn't choose him. I didn't choose anything."

My voice sounds wounded, even in my own ears. It leaves my throat raw to say the words out loud as heat flushes my cheeks at the admission.

"I can see his claim clearly. His bite mark mars your beautiful skin." Gods, he thinks I'm not being fully truthful. That I still want both of them.

Fingers gently grazing my skin just above the puncture wounds, dark emotions swim in the depths of his eyes.

"I can smell him all over you, Piper. I could smell you all over him. That's why I had to leave the room."

Irrational embarrassment creeps into my system. Swallowing back the bile at the thought of Ayxian's advances, I try a different approach.

"Yes, I'm sure you could." My throat constricts. "Let me say it again. I didn't *choose* anything." My eyes plead with him to understand. I can't bring myself to say any more than that.

Clarity finally rings in his eyes and a primal growl ushers from his chest. With his body shaking from anger, he tears away from me down the hall.

Attempting to catch his arm again, I'm already too late. He's heading towards the dining room.

Shuffling my clinging dress, trying to chase after him, it's no use. Calling loudly to his back, I feel the weight of the world fall to his center. My center. "Where are you going?"

Without turning to face me, his growl echoes off the words. Before he rounds the corner at the end of the hall, he glances over his shoulder, and I shudder with a sudden possessiveness.

"To kill that wretched brother of mine."

Chapter Thirty-Four

With my head pounding. My heart racing. I'll never be able to stop him.

The tug at the center of my chest is persistent, an ache. It's being pulled taut with every step Roxalus takes away from me. The ridiculous desire to protect him from harm floods my every cell.

Taking a breath, I redirect my angst. Ayxian deserves punishment for his actions. Not only for what he's done to me, but for all of his subjects that have had the same or worse experience at his hands.

Whether death is justice or vengeance, I don't know. Only the king of Anavrin can make that call.

The king! Max. That's it. My pendant. I have to find it.

Taking off in the opposite direction, I arrive at Ayxian's private gym quicker than I thought possible. Frantically searching for the fallen necklace, I don't allow myself time to think about the last time I was in this room.

The floor is bare. The equipment still in its place. Nothing stands out to me.

Dropping to my knees and ripping my dress in the process, I search as quickly as I can. My insides frantic.

There's nothing to be found. It has to be here. I have to find it. I just have to! I need Max here.

Distraught and frenzied, I'm sure I'm missing something. I have to be. It has to be here!

Calming myself through several steadying breaths, I let my eyes roam over the entire room.

Then I see it. A glint of metallic color on the small table in the corner of the room. Snatching it up, I press my finger to the back like Max showed me and take off at top speed towards the dining room.

Nearly there, I run smack into Mysti and Elle. "No time." I call back over my shoulder, but I know they'll be following me. Mysti won't leave me unprotected running through these corridors.

This dress I've chosen tonight is the same heavy contraption that I'd been wearing when I'd first arrived in Anavrin. It definitely isn't made for full on sprinting through the halls of a castle.

I make it another five paces before the sounds of clanging metal on metal hit my ears. With Elodie and Mystiance bringing up my rear, and I skid to a halt as I round the corner.

The twins are in the corner shouting, being held at bay by Noxian. Ayxian's smile grows wider the moment he spots me.

Roxalus uses the momentary distraction to knock him back, his brother's sword clanging to the ground. He stands over him with the tip of his sword pressed squarely over his heart.

"Roxalus, wait!" I shout. Hesitating to run his blade through him, he turns to me. Concern for me warring with extracting retribution.

Ayxian booms a laugh like they are merely sparring and Roxalus has gotten the better of him. "That was great, brother."

Holding out his hand for help up, Roxalus presses his sword harder, blood seeping from under the white tunic Ayxian's worn to dinner.

"I'm going to carve that beastly heart from your unworthy chest, *Brother*." He snarls the word like a slur.

Loxias and Quill come out of the servants entrance, axe and crossbow raised. They must have stolen away to the kitchens and been informed of the commotion.

Max pops in in a sudden blur ten feet from where me, Elle, and Mysti stand. With one look at the horror on my face, his attention darts to the two princes. A blast of pure heated power throws Roxalus against the wall and Ayxian back into the table and a scream rips its way up and out of my chest.

"What in the name of Sol is going on here?" Anger and concern exuding from his every pore.

The smell of burnt sugar and musk climbs its way up my nose as his magics filled the air. Neither of the princes rushes to fill him in. "Piper?"

There's a light squeeze on my arm and I'm realizing, for the first time, that Inara is here. She's teleported in with Max. My focus had been so intent on the fighting males that I hadn't noticed her at all.

I can't bring myself to voice what Ayxian has done.

Elodie looks between her brothers and shakes her head. "Ayxian needs to be detained, Your Majesty. We'll need to have a royal meeting. Our brother has things to answer for."

Max doesn't question Princess Elodie's assessment. I know he has confidence in her gift to see through the situation. "Prince Ayxian Suilari, you are hereby detained under royal decree. You will be escorted to your rooms and will remain there until we convene for your judgment."

I think the prince might throw a fit or refuse but he does neither. Four guards march into the dining room with swords drawn. Lord Hadence behind them. His sour face making it clear that he disapproves of my involvement in any way.

Ayxian stands and walks alongside of the guards without protest. Eyes landing on me, on the rip in my dress that shows my leg all the way to my upper thigh, they linger there. His desire thrums audibly as they approach us.

Mysti draws her sword and steps in front of me as they file out the door.

Shaking off Inara's hand, I run to Roxalus, dropping to my knees. The back of his head has hit the wall hard, and blood crusts his hair even as the wound is healing over.

My hands fluttering aimlessly over him, I can't to figure out how to help. That tight rope in my chest nearly to the point of pain now.

"I'm sorry," he says. He knows what he's saying. It's no accident the boom he's given me. My eyes water as his hand comes up to cup my face. "I will never fail you again."

Max clears his throat. "Will someone please explain to me why two of my brothers were about to commit fratricide?"

Roxalus and I never look away from one another. I can't move, not even my eyes. They belong to him. Every part of me belongs to him.

"Ayxian assaulted Lady Piper. He has sexually assaulted many of his subjects." Elodie's voice is firm, factual. She can separate emotions and distance herself from feelings when logically looking to serve justice. I admire that about her greatly.

Inara gasps and Max swears. Frenzied chattering starts around the room from those who are still in attendance.

"This will need dealt with swiftly." Noxian has come to his side, whispering something I haven't a care to hear. "Emenda, please ask Lord Nydin to send word to Queen Mother Ombriana that I will collect her in a few hours."

Max's anger and disgust sit heavy in the air, but my focus is solely on Roxalus. The heat of my face under his touch. The feel of his fingers against my skin.

Rubbing his chin, Max shakes his head. "That still doesn't explain why Prince Roxalus didn't call for a council meeting."

"Open your eyes, Max." Elodie's voice holds a smile. "Can't you see it? Piper and Roxalus are mates."

The air catches in my lungs. Inara claps her hands together with glee.

I hadn't known for sure what this tug towards him had been, but I'd had my suspicions, no matter how much I'd pushed them off.

Roxalus doesn't move. Doesn't so much as breathe at the revelation.

I'm realizing that he knows. He knows and has been allowing me the time to decide for myself if this is what I want.

Leaning forward into his touch, my lips brush against his. The salt from my tears resting upon our tongues.

"Why didn't you say anything? I thought that it was just me. I thought that..."

Hand coming to rest in my hair, he pulls me in, lips brushing softly together. Opening my mouth to allow him better access, the kiss is sweet and tender and claiming.

When we pull apart, he still holds my face in his hand. Looking up at me through sad eyes, his sigh breaks me.

"I don't deserve you. I have lived hundreds of years and caused the discontentment of thousands of fae. Before I met you, I was resigned to live in the dark halls of loneliness..." His words burrow deep within me... "but from the moment I first saw you, your light cut through the dark shadows of my weary existence. The ice in my veins and coldness of my long disused heart melted away from your mere presence."

As his hand comes away from my face, I feel its absence like a wound as he turns his head away. "If having you means that you'll suffer for my pernicious soul, I can't allow it."

When he looks back at me, my breathing hitches. He's trying to pull away from the mating bond. His intentions to keep me safe, to keep me whole, have led him to keep himself at arm's length from me.

Oh, my foolish prince. I'm having none of that. He can't get away that easily.

There is a connection. A ribbon of sorts, deep within. Connecting his soul to mine. It's not something I can see, but I have to try anyway.

I am a descendant of the First Witch, Mab. Magics run deep within me. If there has ever been a time to call on them, it's now.

In the center of my mind's eye, I imagine a cord. It glows cool blue. My heart on one end, his on the other.

Wrapping my metaphorical hands around it, I yank with all of my might, until Roxalus' side of the rope slams into mine, visualizing it glowing brighter, thicker.

With a heady excitement, I push down the bond all of the emotions and longing that I've built up for him.

Gasping, his heart gallops under the weight. With a push to me now, the images send sparks cascading over my mind.

The rope is a solid steel chain, forged through our intentions, unbreakable.

The room has gone quiet in the few moments of silence that I've been concentrating. Or maybe it hasn't but I don't care about our audience.

Roxalus scoops me up into his arms and I vaguely register Inara and Max talking as we pass by. Elodie is giggling something to Mysti but none of it matters.

The only thing that matters is my prince.

My mate.

Chapter Thirty-Five

Roxalus is carrying me all through the corridors, placing kisses on my forehead, my cheeks, my lips. Servants scurry along, some whispering behind their hands, others with incredulous sideway stares.

Not paying much attention to wear we're going, he's brought us to my rooms. I would have thought that he would have taken us to his.

"Mysti can take my room." After I say nothing, he explains. "Ayxian and I have never been close. He gave me a smaller royal room on the west side of the castle." Dipping his head to kiss my forehead again, he opens the door without jostling me. "Besides... I want you to be comfortable, Piper. There are two bedrooms in here. I won't force you to share a bed with me, but I will be staying close to you, for my own piece of mind about your safety."

I'd thought he'd been carrying me here to bed me. Heat had pooled low in my stomach with every touch along the way. The way that he's taking my feelings into consideration, my heart skips a beat.

Roxalus had been a brut when we'd met. All hard edges and sharp tongue. The way he glared in my direction. The way he looked down on lower class fae. The angst that I'd *feel* coming off of him in waves from time to time... it had given me the wrong impression of the male before me.

I understand it now. The front. The need to make others believe power can only be maintained by coldness.

The truth of my prince is that he's kind and trying to be better, even if it's only with me.

Setting me down on the settee in the common area, he begins to move away, and I wrap my arms around the back of his neck, caging him in. "I don't want you to go."

Placing another kiss to my forehead, he kneels before me, laying his head in my lap.

"I'm lost, Wildfire. I'm floundering." Stroking my fingers through his hair, I relish in the pet name, letting him say his piece without interruption. "I've never been a happy male. I've had privileges and luxuries beyond what most can fathom."

Raising his head to look me in the eyes, those beautiful blue orbs search the inner most parts of my soul. Encircling my wrists with his long fingers, his chin drops to his chest.

"I find myself thinking about you at all times of the day. I cannot rest at night for the circles you run around my head. I will sleep at your feet if that's all that you'll allow."

The raw words move me to comfort him. Cupping the side of his face, he leans into my touch.

"My Prince." His head snaps up to meet my gaze. "I will have all of you." Bending down, I press a kiss to his lips. Fire erupts inside of me. "I will take every part of you." Grabbing onto the hair at the back of his head, I pull him back so I can look at him properly, needing to make myself perfectly clear.

Tightly winding my fingers into his hair, I yank on it so that his chin comes up, exposing his neck to me. The pulse there beating fast, his throat bobs.

Without giving myself time to think about it, my mouth opens wide, fangs exposed, and I bite him... hard.

I've never bitten anyone with my fae fangs before. The venom throbs in each one.

A shuttering sigh slips from his throat. I am marking what is mine. There will be no undoing my claim to him. A mate marking creates a tattoo of sorts. It links the soulmate cord to the surface for all to see.

Leaning back to admire my handiwork, lines appear in swirls of fire, smoke and vines with leaves. It's only half visible, like ink under tracing paper.

It turns me on more than I thought it would. "Prove to me that I'm yours to claim." Where my boldness has come from, I have no idea.

With a growl issuing from deep within his chest, he scoops me up once again, and we can't get to the bedchamber fast enough.

This damn dress is restricting but the tear up to my thigh helps. Gently laying me down, he steps back. All of my years of self-doubt have me momentarily worrying that he's going to leave, but he stands there, just staring.

"You're so damn beautiful, Piper." Unfastening the clasp of his pants, the huge bulge below the surface pulses in anticipation. "I will never let anyone touch you again. You're mine! Do you understand me?"

Freeing himself of the clothing, his hard cock is on full display and dear gods, the thing is enormous. A deep blue vein pulses along the side, wrapping towards the front.

With one hand wrapped around the shaft, he pumps it up and down a few times. Pre-cum glistens at the tip and I purr.

My dress is torn but not enough. Using both hands, he rips it off in one swift motion and a startled breath escapes me. The top half is still in place, breast overflowing the cups as I lay before him exposed from the navel down.

"Spread those magnificent legs for me like a good girl." The deep velvet of his voice is enough to do me in. My nipples harden at the command, and I do as he asks.

Another slow stroke up and down his shaft fills me with an aching desire. It's the most delicious of torments and I long to feel him inside of me.

Placing a hand on each of my knees and spreading me wide, he stares his fill. "Mmmm, that honey's already dripping. Are you ready for me Wildfire?" I can't find my vocal chords. Non-committal sounds usher from my lips. Moans, whimpers. "Ah ah ah," he says as I arch my back, trying to get him to touch me. "I need to hear it. Say the words, Piper."

My name falling from his lips is the sweetest sound the heavens have ever produced. The longing for his touch making me wet from his mere presence. My clit is so erect that the air stings.

"Please, Roxalus. I want you inside of me. I need to feel you fill me." I've never been so verbal. It's freeing. Exhilarating. The warm connection in my chest to the male in front of me gives me courage to let go of my inhibitions in the safety of his gaze.

With a quick inhale, a lustful breath rushes in through his teeth. With one hand still on my knee, the hand stroking his cock comes away to rub my center for the lightest of touches. Pulling his fingers away glistening, he suckles them into his mouth.

"Oh no, sweetpea. I missed out on dessert tonight. I'm going to need a bit of your delicious honey to satisfy my cravings." When his mouth closes over me in the next breath, I moan at its luxuriating feel. His tongue circles my clit agonizingly slow. Flattening it against my lips, he makes a long lap down towards my entrance that has my back arching off of the bed. "Mmmmm. You taste so fucking good, Wildfire."

"Yes. Gods yes." He's barely begun, and I'm already at my limits. That velvety voice will be my undoing, for sure.

Sliding his head between my thighs, his tongue makes its way inside. In the human realm, we call kissing with our tongues "French Kissing". That's the only way to describe what he's doing, and as he devours me, I can't get enough.

Arching my back in an attempt to gain as much friction between us as I can get, I'm gripping the duvet to the point of pain, my knuckles turning white. As I get closer to orgasm, they make their way to his hair and I pull, curling and knotting what I can get a hold of. My knees shake and my muscles begin to quiver.

Replacing his tongue with two fingers, he curls them over and over again. I moan loudly, almost there. Bringing his thumb down on my clit, he rubs gentle circles around and around, his fingers curling in time with my undulating. Oh gods, it's too much... and not enough!

"Let go, love," he commands. My back arches again at his assiduous touch. It's too much for me hold back any longer. "Cum for me, Piper. "

Moving his fingers faster, my walls clench around them. Liquid, hot and pleasurable, flows over his hand. Roxalus brings his mouth down on me again as I explode in rapture.

Aftershocks rock my body, one after the other, as he studiously laps at my sensitive flesh. Never have I ever cum so hard in my life.

Licking his lips as he sits up, he brings his wet hand down over his hard cock, using my juices to stroke himself. "That was a *very* good girl."

The praise does funny things to my core. I could drown in it over and over again.

Motioning for me to come towards him, my muscles quiver as I try to use them. The bed is high, but he's tall. Crawling to the end, I kneel on all fours in front of him. His cock sitting at chin level.

"Do you want a taste?" Again, that wicked voice. This sinfully sexy male will be my ruin.

The sight of him in his own hand strokes my desire. I've been eyeing that pre-cum from the moment his cock emerged.

I only nod, knowing he will reprimand me for it. It gives me a secret thrill to hear him make commands.

"You know that won't do, Wildfire." My eyes widen as flames dance along his free hand.

Squashing them, he wraps that same hand in my hair, gently tilting my head back to look him in the eyes. "I asked you a question," he says with devious smirk. He strokes himself again, torturing me with yearning. "I can just as easily put this away if you don't want to play anymore."

"No! I'll be good. I swear." When he lets go of my hair, I immediately spring forward, taking him into my mouth before he has the chance to drop his hand away.

His moan urges me to gorge myself on his length. On all fours, I slurp and suck and try to breathe around his girth while his long arms reach over my torso, cradling my ass.

Cupping his balls and gently kneading them, his legs wobble slightly where he stands at the end of the bed.

Pulling me impossibly closer, I choke, gagging on the length of him. My throat so full, I start to panic.

"Shhh, shhh. You're doing so well. You can handle me, baby-girl." Sliding one of his fingers inside me from behind this time, I'm grateful for those long arms of his. The distraction helps my throat to relax enough to continue.

Firmly squeezing my ass with his free hand, he pulls it back, only to swing it forward with a loud thwack. The shock and sting of the smack makes me jump and I choke on his cock again, drool sliding down my chin.

Pumping his fingers in and out and swirling his other fingertip over the heat from the print on my ass, I race towards climax while I suck him down my throat over and over again.

"Mmmm. That feels amazing," he snarls. The breathy thrum of his praise stroking my own desire.

Fingers sliding out of my entrance, he begins rubbing my juices over my backdoor and I panic, bucking to pull away while trapped between his cock and his arms.

My jerking motions have my throat closing around him, drawing a guttural sound with the next push of his hips. "I think it's time, wildfire," he says breathlessly.

He never breached my behind. I'm realizing now, it was a mere ploy to have me thrash about.

Letting go of me, he pulls his cock from my saliva dripping mouth.

I start to protest that I haven't gotten my fill yet, but I don't get the chance to before he flips me over onto my back and his weight comes pressing down as his cock lines up with my entrance. Waiting for me to adjust to his body, a deep sense of need has my skin zipping like a live wire. I need to be filled with him already.

"Roxalus, please," I beg. I'm not above it at this point.

That brings another smirk to his handsomely devilish face. "Please, what?" The tip of him sits ready, pressed in only an inch. Squirming beneath him, I try to force him where I want him, but the bastard won't be moved. "Are you sure you want all of this? If I claim you this way, there's no going back. I will end anyone who tries to touch what's mine."

Gods, that's hot! Wiggling the tip around, the rest of his shaft nestles between my thighs, hard and throbbing, waiting for my reply. I can't believe he thinks I don't want him. *Or maybe the **bastard** simply believes it should always be your choice.* Damn that inner voice. Right, as always.

"I'm yours. From now until always." Attempting to scooch myself down his length, he pulls out all the way. "Noooo..." I start to protest but he slams back into me at full thrust. The moan ushering from me is like that of a different creature.

Slow and tortuously, pumping into me hilt deep, he stops, placing a passionate kiss on my lips and sliding achingly slowly out again. The absence leaving me feeling hollow.

Sitting back on his heals, his eyes roam over my body. "This just won't do, Wildfire." Adjusting his body, the light growl stiffens my nipples. "I want to see every square inch of what's mine."

The top of my dress rips as easily in his strong hands as the bottom half had. A sudden thrill rushes through me a half a second before he's sucking my nipple into his mouth, and I lose all thought. Pulling back and settling back between my legs, he groans deeply, satisfied with the exposure. "Mmmm, much better."

Lifting one of my ankles and placing it over his shoulder, he slides all the way in again. The ecstasy of it brings stars to my eyes. Our bodies connecting at the muffs, our hair mingling in the most delicious of ways.

Bringing his thumb down on my clit, he rubs it in time with each thrust. All of the way in, I still need him closer. Dropping my leg from his shoulder, he comes up to kiss me. My shoulder, my neck, my lips.

"Do you want me, Piper?" Placing chaste kisses my neck and slides almost all the way out again, I moan loudly.

Pumping back in slowly, he hits bottom with the ache of perfection. We fit together like two pieces of the same puzzle. "Am I yours, Wildfire?"

Another slow, agonizing thrust. I'm going mad with the torment. His lips at my ear, he whispers seductively. "Are you my mate, My Lady?" The next thrust is hard, claiming my body, mind, and soul.

Crying out from the pleasure building steadily inside me, I scream. "Yes. Yes, I'm yours, Roxalus. And you're mine. No one's but mine!"

With the next thrust, his fangs sink into the soft flesh of my neck. Venom courses its way into my system and euphoric bliss erupts in every cell.

Pulling his head back, he growls like a beast and then pumps faster. I can't contain myself. The sound of slapping flesh on flesh heightens my arousal and the emotions of the moment bring joyful tears to my eyes. With the next thrust, my walls tighten, holding him in with the strength of my claiming.

Bringing his lips to mine with a gentle but firm demand, tremors course along his cock, and he shouts his approval into my open mouth. "Oh yes. Fuck yes. Fuck... Piperrr!"

The moan of pleasure escaping him sends me tipping over the edge with him. Sweat covers us both from head to toe. It's blissful and wholeness and everything I never knew I craved.

Still seated inside me minutes after we've spent ourselves, neither of us willing to move. Our mingled juices seeping down our legs, our breath coming in short bursts.

"That was..." he starts, panting hard.

"Everything." I finish, slowly catching my breath.

Chapter Thirty-Six

After rolling off of me and onto his back, I turn onto my side to face him, arm cradling under my head. His eyes are closed. A look of pure elation rides his face.

Placing my finger on his lips, I trace their shape, and he twitches. "What are you doing, Wildfire?" That pet name makes me giggle.

"Why do you keep calling me that?" I'm not that feisty. At least I don't think I am.

Turning on his side to face me, he rests his head on his arm looking completely contented. I've never seen him this way. So relaxed and not broody.

"My fire gifts have been under control for centuries. Fire was my mother, Queen Ombriana's element. When she was killed, my heart turned cold. I found it harder to use my fire without a surge of unwanted emotions. I locked it down. The ice from my water element kept me on task, helping me be able to keep my distance from everyone. After a while, it was my only element. And as I ruled with ice, I didn't feel the suffering of those around me. I didn't know how to let people in anymore."

Reaching out, he boops my nose. It's the most playful and unexpected thing to see from the brute that my cheeks ache from smiling. "Then I met you. Someone who I've spent the last few centuries looking down on... your kind, I mean. My mind is like everything else fae; slow to accept change." His fingers graze up and down and around my breast absentmindedly and I luxuriate in the sensation. "I find you intoxicating."

Thinking he'll continue, I wait. And wait. My nipple becoming more erect under his touch with each passing brush... then he flicks it.

Fuck! That hurts so good I moan. The sting making my center throb again, heat pooling low in my belly, ready for more.

"That still doesn't explain why you call **me** Wildfire." Sucking the nub into his mouth, my back arches. When he pulls back, his cock is stiff again.

"Doesn't it? I am drunk on you, Piper." He caresses the side of my face. "When fire mixes with a flammable substance, it goes wild. My ice melted every time I tried to use it. You changed the very make up of my being. I can no longer use my ice without your wildfire shaping it into flames. They burn cold. Colder than any of the ice in my past. They burn hotter than any of the fires I've ever conjured. You've made me evolve, My Lady. I've never been more aware of my gifts and less in control of myself. You consume my every thought."

Lightly grazing my nipple with his teeth, a sigh of pleasure escapes my lips. "You are my every desire." His fingers graze the spot just below my ear. "Simply put..." He trails his hand down between my thighs. "...you're mine. From now until the end of existence. And if I can't follow you beyond the heavens, I will raise the seven hells to claim you once more."

The bite I'd made on his neck is now dark, no more tracing paper look. The mating bond marking is completed. Dripping with every craving of possessiveness, my whimper of longing seizes the cool blue ribbon inside my chest, and I yank with the intent of knotting us so thoroughly, even the gods won't stand a chance in keeping us apart.

Eyes widening when he feels it, I snarl when the tug reaches his end and his eyes darken with desire. Grabbing me around the waist and pulling me up to straddle him, I'm trembling with anticipation as his erection settles between my legs.

"Ready for round two?" The growl rumbling through his chest, burrowing itself deep within my core.

Without waiting for an answer, using my hips, he slides me all the way down his shaft, seating me like a queen upon her throne.

Chapter Thirty-Seven

Several rounds later, sleeping on and off through, who only knew how many hours, the sunshine coming from the balcony window wakes me.

I'm thoroughly sated laying here in Roxalus' strong arms. My mate. With his chest rising and falls under my head, light snores send a sense of true completeness to my core. I realize what this feeling is... Happy. I am consummately happy.

Not just contented. Not just existing in the background of my own life. My mother's vision can't touch me here, and I never want this moment to end.

As with most things in life, the second you think them, they find a way to rush you to the next problem on the horizon.

There's a clanging noise coming from the common room. A creak at our bed chamber door has me sitting up, pulling the covers over my bare chest. Roxalus wakes with a start, jumping from the bed in a defensive pose, his nakedness on full display. And by the fate of the gods, I think I might actually swoon.

Keyara drops the serving tray to the floor with a loud crash. Her whole body turns in the opposite direction, but not before I see the pink rise high up in her cheeks.

Placing a hand on Roxalus' bare back, he relaxes, but only slightly. It's not just his naked body that's turned me on, but the pure primal instinct he has to keep me safe revs my engine.

"My regrets, Your Highness. Lady Piper." I hand him a pillow to cover himself and he arches an eyebrow.

Giggling at his amusement, I pinch his ass. Mine!

"No worries, Keyara. Can you bring us another tray of food and definitely a huge mug of coffee? I need my fix."

Turning around slowly, her eyes never leave the floor. "My regrets again, My Lady, but your presence is requested by His Majesty." She sounds like she's been crying. "Yours too, Your Highness."

Wrapping the sheet firmly around myself, I push past Roxalus and he snarls at my lack of protection against my oh so scary handmaiden. With a hint of amusement, I shush him as I approach her anyway.

"Keyara, are you alright?" Her glance at Roxalus tells me she's uncomfortable talking with him here. I can *feel* her anxiety like a living, breathing thing. "My Prince, would you excuse us for a moment? I'd like to speak with Keyara alone."

A look of wonderment and incredulity slide over his face. As nonchalantly as I can, I brush a strand of hair behind my ear, motioning with my finger for him to listen in." A subtle dip of his chin tells me that he's caught on that I'm holding no secrets from him.

"Of course, My Lady. I'll be waiting for you in the shower." That mischievous fae smirk has the blood rushing to my cheeks, along with other areas.

With a dip of his chin to Keyara, he tosses the pillow back onto the bed and heads out the door. Her face turns beet red, but I growl, surprising myself with the territorialness.

"Lady Piper, I would never have barged so carelessly into your bed chamber if I knew you had company." Her earnestness hits me like canon fire. "The king asked that I make sure you've eaten and tell you that he wishes to see you. I swear I meant no harm."

It takes me a few seconds to realize that she thinks I'm going to have her punished for the intrusion. The poor girl. Ayxian's rule is worse than I've ever imagined.

"My goodness, Keyara. Whatever have I done to give you this horrible impression of me?" Her eyes go wide. "I would never have you disciplined for fulfilling your charge." Tsking, I sit down on the edge of the bed and pat it for her to do the same. "Sit. Tell me why you're so upset... beside the accidental tray dropping." Lifting a knowing brow at her, she sighs.

"Am I that obvious?" Taking her hand in mine, I give it a gentle squeeze. Sighing heavily, she finds her bearings. "Okay. The king has asked that anyone who has had any unwanted advances from Prince Ayxian to come forward. And Lady Piper, I want to come forward. I do, but if the prince isn't held accountable or worse, if he becomes king, then he'll come after those of us who have spoken up." Hanging her head to her chest, she speaks to her feet. "I'm scared, Piper. I want justice, but I want to live my life without always looking over my shoulder."

Pulling her against my chest, too late I realize the scent of sex and sweat cling to me, the sheets, and the room, but she doesn't shy away from my stench.

"Listen, I know His Majesty would never force anyone to come forward, but if he doesn't hear enough of the reasons for punishment against the prince, then his hands will be tied in delivering a reasonable justice." Stroking the hair at the back of her head in comfort. "I, for one, will be testifying for all of Anavrin to hear. I want to see him removed from a position of power. No one should ever feel obligated to let him use their body however he sees fit."

Her sinus's fill with her sob, tears running in rivulets down her cheeks. "Yes, My Lady. I can see your point. I will think on it." Getting up and picking up the tray and its spilled contents from the floor, she straightens to look at me.

My sheet is still draped over my naked body from the top of my breasts down. "By the way, your mated mark is beautiful. It compliments you well," she says, pointing to the spot where Roxalus bit me during his claiming.

My hand rises to my neck with heat in my cheeks. I'd forgotten all about it as we tumbled over and over again in the night. Walking over to the mirror, stretching my head to the side to get a better look, I can see what she means.

She's right. It is beautiful. It speaks of his icy fire and weaves pepper plant vines with what look like a large cat's paws mingled in, hidden amongst the mix. A seamless combination of us both, intertwined forever.

"It is special, isn't it?" Turning back around to face her, there's a genuine smile brightening her face.

"I would never have believed that Prince Roxalus could be tamed, My Lady." She curtsies and scurries towards the door to fetch us a fresh tray. "I must say though, he looks good on you too." With a wink, she exits the room, and warmth rises high on the apples of my cheeks.

Roxalus peeks his head out of the bathing chamber. "Coming, Wildfire?" Holding out a hand to me, I let the sheet drop to the floor and cross the room at a near run.

"Not yet, My Prince"

Not yet... but I will be.

Chapter Thirty-Eight

R oxalus and I are the last of the royals to arrive.

I'm wearing a blouse that hangs around the tops of my arms, leaving my mate mark exposed in full view. My pants are just a casual pair of capri bottoms that flow out a few inches below the knee.

Walking hand in hand, we enter to hushed whispers and staring eyes.

Inara and Leif are at the end of a high table that has been set up in the front side of the throne room. Giddy with newfound love, I wave to Inara, and her smile beams back at me.

There are two empty chairs at the table waiting for us. Loxias, Noxian, and the twins are already seated.

At the front center table sits King Maximus and to his right, Princess Elodie. Her gifts will be crucial in seeing justice through. From everything I've gathered over the last several months, not one fae in the entire kingdom doubts her word. That is a true feat amongst faekind.

In front of their table stands Prince Ayxian with two guards on each side. The way his features light up when he sees me is unnerving. He's throwing an arrogant smile my way, setting my teeth itching, and every muscle I possess tightening.

Roxalus squeezes my hand reassuringly and I relax into his touch. His scent. Our scents. Mingled and intertwined. A solid front to bear witness to justice.

Approaching our seats next to Inara, Max stops us before we get to them.

"Prince Roxalus, Lady Piper. So good of you to finally join us." His tone reprimanding, but his eyes twinkle with amusement. "Congratulations on your mating. I wish you both centuries of bliss. Now take your seats."

Smiling for what feels like the millionth time in the last twenty-four hours, there's a pleasant ache in my cheeks. If anyone knows what the first few days of being mated are like, it's him.

Aunt Eowyn rarely spoke of Inara's father, and she never let on that he was her mate, but when she did speak of him, love exuded from her complete being. She practically glowed with it. I can't imagine what she went through at his loss.

Roxalus and I have only claimed the mating bond in the last day and a half and I feel so tied to him in every way that it breaks my heart for Max and Eowyn's loss all over again.

When Max and I would speak of my aunt in the beginning, I didn't know how to help him through his pain at her loss. He still grieves her. Two hundred years later. That kind of devotion had been unfathomable to me before Roxalus and I claimed one another, but I understand it now. I wanted to make things better for Max but that would be an impossible task.

"Let the chosen courtiers and commoners in," Max addresses the two guards standing as sentry at the door.

Whispering over to Elodie, whatever he'd said makes her laugh. The sound is a whimsical chiming. The pressure in my chest releases some of its hold to hear the levity for the briefest of moments.

The fae file into the room. Some look around nervously, others chatter like they don't have a care in the world. The energy throughout the chamber is charged with excitement and dread in equal measure.

I put the necklace Max had given me back on before we left our room. There are a lot of people in here and right now. The poor magical metal can't decide if it wants to be hot or cold, making me shiver from its pulsing. Roxalus stared at it when I'd first put it on but didn't ask me any questions. And for that, I'm grateful.

Max calls the room to order. "Before we get started, I have some tragic news. There has been another lowbee murder. It appears to have happened a day or so before the arrival of the royals and their entourages."

Elodie's watchful gaze makes its course around the room, pausing briefly from time to time. Being more observant than most, my attention is drawn to Ayxian's second hand. Lord Hadence's face has the look of someone smelling bleu cheese. His lips are puckered, and his nose is scrunched in distaste.

As Elle's gaze lands on Lord Beartach, her focus is intent but when the crystal to the top of his remade staff glows dully, she looks away without further inspection.

Ayxian's eyes crinkle in the corners, but his face remains unreadable. I never know what's going on in that brain of his. *Feeling* through his emotions isn't a walk in the park either. He's more animal like than any other fae I've tried to read. Nothing sticks more than surface level with him.

"Roxalus," I pull him over to whisper into his ear. His scent of pine needles and peppermint shove themselves up my nose in the most wonderful of ways. "What do you make of your sorcerer? He just used some kind of mojo to force Elodie away."

Taking my hand and brushing a kiss across my knuckles, his warm breath stirs the fine hairs along my arm, sending a small shiver that makes its way to my neck and down into my core.

"Lord Beartach is old. A lot of people misunderstand him. It's not easy to change your ways as a fae but I've trusted him for the majority of my life."

I don't want to argue but there is a gnawing feeling in my gut telling me that trusting the sorcerer is a mistake. Instead of pushing the issue here with everything going on, I snap my lips together and nod sharply. We will be revisiting the subject later because I'm not going to give in to doubt or start discrediting my own intuition now simply because I'm mated. We are meant to be a compliment of each other, not a completion.

Max continues his proclamations, and I tune back in. "The murderer will face his karmic justice as soon as he is apprehended. The fae of Anavrin will be safe in this kingdom from the likes of a bigoted snob with a penchant for odious sexual assaults and violence. Princess Elodie here will use her gifts of insight, and I have another fae who's gift can burrow into the mind to seek the truth and project it out for all to witness." Voices ring out in shock, protest, and some in relief. "I will **Not** be making this fae known. They are a secret weapon. At their request, their gift will be used only by the royals of the court upon the permission of the King Seat approval. No exceptions."

The crowd dies down a bit. If what Max has said is true, and since the fae can't lie I assume it has to be, then no one who is brought before this secret fae can get away with anything.

I have nothing to hide but I understand their outrage. No one wants their inner most private things rooted through and perused at leisure. I can also understand Max's stance on what this fae will be doing and with whom he will allow it.

"Now, on to more pressing matters. It has come to light that Prince Ayxian Suilari has abused his power and forcibly assaulted one or more of his lessers. Advances of unwanted nature and bodily possession are taken seriously here in Anavrin. Since before the days of Queen Ombriana, the laws have always been made quite clear on consent, and justice will be dealt to offenders."

Motioning for Queen Leyashna, she takes her place at his side. His stepmother is hardly seen in public anymore. She's been enjoying a laid-back life, reading most days, not having to worry any longer about the responsibilities of running a kingdom. As Ayxian's mother, it's only right for her to be present during his trial.

It's a sound tactic. Putting her front and center to bear witness. If Ayxian feels guilt at the accusations against him, then it'll be clear to everyone he knew he'd done things he shouldn't have. If he feels no guilt, then he is more dangerous, because he doesn't see fault with his actions.

Giving her mother's hand a squeeze, Elodie solemnly nods and the queen resigns herself to hear the truth.

"Would anyone with a complaint please step forward. This court would like to hear your side." No one moves. The entire room is holding its collective breath. Max's eyes meet mine and I drop my head briefly. My resolve wavering for a moment as guilt and shame claim me.

Roxalus places a gentle kiss to the temple and starts forward to address the sitting nobles, but I grab his arm and steel my backbone. Taking a deep breath, calm washes over me at the contact from my mate. "I need to do this."

"That doesn't mean that you have to do it alone." Emotions welling inside of me, I realize I will never be alone again. And that is the most comforting realization I've had since finding out I have a mate.

Ayxian has hurt good people with the acts he's committed. Good fae who don't have anyone. Good fae who don't have a voice or the fortitude to stand up against a prince of faery.

Reaching back to take Roxalus' hand, I tug him forward with me. "Okay. Let's go make our world a safer place."

Chapter Thirty-Nine

Elodie addresses the crowd. "I would like to remind you all of my gifts. Not only can I *feel* the true emotions of others, but I can also see through to the truth of any situation placed in front of me."

Those in attendance nod and chatter in whispers to their neighbors in a buzz of commotion. Not every person in Anavrin has met or encountered the royals personally enough to know the measure of them firsthand. It's clear that some appreciate the reminder of her abilities. It's also clear that a few are more than upset by this little piece of information.

"This is all just a misunderstanding." It's the first time I've heard Prince Ayxian speak since he was detained. "I like to have fun. And I thought that my needs were made clear with regards to Lady Piper."

Roxalus snarls from beside me, but I won't let him fight this particular battle for me. I need to stand up for myself on this one. It's the only way that I'll be able to push past the feelings of vulnerability that still creep into me from time to time since it happened.

I read up on the fae of Sidhterra on the first leg of the carriage ride here. Loxias leant me a few books and there was one on their culture in mix. They are a realm of fae that are freer in giving their bodies. And they express their sexuality with desire or dominance. No isn't generally heard in their society. And one enforces laws of self, other than the ones kept in place for their royals and noble fae.

"I accuse Prince Ayxian Suilari of sexual misconduct. We fae of Anavrin are not like the fae of Sidhterra. No and stop means just that. And Prince Ayxian forced himself on me, even after my pleas not to be touched." My chin's high but my entire body shakes with the recollection. I can barely hear over the blood rushing in my ears.

King Maximus looks to Elodie, who nods for the whole court to see. Not one of the royals or nobles doubt that she has heard the truth from me. A few don't like it, but they don't doubt her.

He then looks to Queen Leyashna, tears swimming in her eyes. Her gift of words notwithstanding, I don't know what her other gifts are. She gives a small dip of her chin.

"Prince Ayxian, tell us what happen from your perspective." Max holds up his hand to quiet the crowd. "Care to defend yourself against these accusations?"

My heart pounding, I whisper into Roxalus' ear as his snarls grow louder. "Omnia Meum, let him talk. We'll have our justice." His arm comes around my waist, pulling me closer possessively in response. With a kiss to the top of my head, he nods but still growls low in his chest.

"I had just left my private gym. Lady Piper came around the corner, and we went back into it for some privacy." The arrogant bastard is grinning, turning to smirk at the crowd. "We were engaging in some light flirting, and I scented her arousal. My inner warrior beast responded to her needs." Shaking the hair out of his eyes, he tsks condescendingly. Like somehow, I am the one who is in the wrong here. I feel small and cringe back into Roxalus. "Honestly, I don't know why she ran off before we were finished. It left me with blue balls that needed promptly taken care of." The bastard actually winks at me. Then he turns to look into the crowd. "Anayelli there can vouch for me on that fact."

The young female that he refers to hangs her head, clearly uncomfortable. As she looks back up, our eyes meet, and I know that he's bedded her without her true consent. Fury makes me see red. I want to throat punch him. I want to use my panther claws and wipe that smile from him so that he can never feel comfortable enough to show his stupid face again.

Before I can voice what I *feel* from her or enact retribution, Elodie chimes in. "King Maximus, their tryst was not consensual." No bias. No emotions. Just facts presented before the court.

"Nonsense. She loved it." Ayxian is more animated now. His hands aren't bound, and he's standing in front of his mother, pleading with her for understanding. "It was a bit of fun to alleviate the frustration I'd been left with in Lady Piper's sudden absence."

With the facts presented for all to hear, four more women step forward and two males. Max decides to ask the court as a whole about their ordeals. "Raise your hand if you have a similar story to Lady Piper or Anayelli's." Hands go up throughout the room. At least a quarter of those in attendance have been assaulted at the prince's whims.

"Unreal." Prince Ayxian is shaking his head, disgust clear in the lines around his eyes and mouth. "I've been good to you all. I've protected you and listened to your inconsequential problems. I've been a good prince, and I will be a great king." His glare in my direction can melt steel. "You've ruined my good-hearted nature with your lowbee opinion. I should never have given you a chance to climb my tree." Shaking his head again, as if clearing away the sudden fury, he speaks directly to me like I'm the only one in the room. "Piper, we can still move forward. I can forgive your little tantrum. I can't have my future queen thinking the worst of me."

Roxalus is pushing me behind him before I can wrap my mind around what's going on. "You touch her, you die!"

With a quick scan of the room in slow motion, my sights land on Lord Hadence and a group of others who have iron daggers at the throats of several fae around the chamber. Realization slams into me. They are all lowbees and these dagger wielding fae are part of the faction of hate that's made its way through Anavrin.

"Guards. Seize them!" Max is trying to take control of the situation, but the guards are made up mostly of Prince Ayxian's court.

Half of them turn on the other guards around the room. Chaos ensues as the sounds of clinking metal runs around the chamber. Screams tear from the throats of the lowbees caught in the mayhem for brief seconds before they are silenced for good. Bodies litter the floor.

Orange flames dance at Max's fingertips and cold blue ones at Roxalus'. They throw them at the guards who are killing without discrimination. Loxias' axe flies passed Ayxian's head, wedging into the skull of one of the rebel guards. The twins are both jumping in place, electricity coating their skin but aren't helping anyone in their panicked state.

Noxian has forced his way to Queen Leyashna's side, sword raised at the ready, while Loxias has commanded Quill to stand in front of his mother and protect her with his life. With Quill sure shot abilities, his crossbow bolts find their marks easily but without poison tips, they're more of a nuisance than they are life threatening.

Elodie swings her sword up just in time to block an arrow coming from one of the nobles in the faction. I recognize him from Ayxian's court. The fear and hate emanating throughout the space is making my head throb.

Feeling helpless for a split second, I glance over and see fur erupt in my peripheral view. Inara snarls and her teeth close around the arm of the fae who's lunged for her. She is one of the fiercest alpha wolves I've ever known. Seeing her join the fray snaps me out of my stupor.

The roar that leaves my lungs startles half the room as my panther form meets their eyes. Pouncing on the rebel guard closes to Elodie, my teeth sink into him, tearing a chunk of his arm clear off.

Roxalus is shouting something from where I left him throwing freezing fire at a few guards who went after the twins. Turning just in time to see where he's pointing, Ayxian's sword comes swinging for my head. Jumping back, I circle the prince as he continues to take swipes at me with that deadly blade. He's delusional and has run so hot and cold within the span of a blink, I'm not prepared for his assault after he has declared we can still be together.

"You cheeky, teasing little bitch! I offered you a prize that most would give the world to have. Instead, you turn against me?" Swinging his sword in an arc, it connects with my tail. Pain explodes through my entire body and blood drips from the cut as I roar. "You may not live to see what becomes of the lowbees or of your precious mate, but if you do, I hope you can forgive me my transgressions, love. Ours will be a union of great admirability soon enough."

The smirk on his face says it all. If he can't have me, he plans to kill me. He'll enjoy it too. How could I have been so blinded by this neandertal?

"Your lack of receiving me has caused me to do it! It's your fault they are dead!" If I hadn't witnessed that beastly look from him in the past, I sure as hell can't miss it now. He's gone way passed mischief and into full blown madness.

What in Sol's depths was he talking about? My fault all of them are dead? What is he going on about? ... Oh my gods! He can't be!

"You made me do it! You, with your womanly wilds. I need-ed release from your grip and got carried away, is all. Couldn't be helped really." Bringing his sword high, he uses my momen-tary distraction to slide a step closer. Snarling, I swipe out with one of my giant paws but miss.

He killed them! He assaulted and murdered those poor, innocent fae! How could I have ever cared for this heartless beast? Gods! Is he the leader of the anti-lowbee faction, or are they merely rallying behind him for power?

An ice cold, blue fireball flies past his ear and he turns. The distraction causing him to lose sight of me and step towards my mate. Time slows slightly, giving me the opening to pounce with my claws extended. He will not have Roxalus! I didn't mean to slow time. I still have no clue how to do it on purpose, but I will take full advantage of it while it's happened.

Swiping across Ayxian's face from the top of his left eye, across his nose and ending at the tip of his collarbone, a tingle of energy passes through my claws as they go. I have no idea what it is or what it can do other than sending that buzz beneath my nails as they make contact. Blood spatters over my fur. It gushes from Ayxian's wounds without stopping. The instant healing of the fae isn't working on the three long cuts marring his skin. They are my justice. A marking to show all who see him that he is a threat.

Fingers wrap into the fur on the back of my neck as Roxalus comes up to my side. Quill is letting loose bolt after bolt trying to protect the queen and defend Loxias at the same time. Leif is nowhere to be seen. Neither is Inara or Queen Leyashna, who I'm certain is standing somewhere behind Quill's general area.

He must have hidden his sister and step-grandmother away in his shadows, and for that I am grateful. Inara will be pissed but it still makes me feel better to know that she is safe.

Lord Hadence runs forward and bends down to Prince Ayxian's side. As he motions to a couple of his rebels, they come rushing up to help the prince to his feet. Chaos is reigning throughout the chamber. A flash of a glowing staff catches my eye as the sorcerer saunters through the crowd, glee etched in those cruel eyes.

I tense but Roxalus relaxes beside me. "Lord Beartach, bind these fools. It's time we bring them to heel."

Beartach sneers, looking through Prince Roxalus to me. "My regrets, dear princeling. I don't see any fae here worthy of this trouble." The light on his staff glowing brighter with every word.

Prince Noxian is creeping up behind him, but there is little in the way of nature for him to wield inside the castle. Potted plants could have sprung forth with vines to secure the enemies, but there's nothing. Loxias' abilities to influence the room should be working but only half the fae here appear to be effected.

It takes Roxalus a full minute to come to grips with the reality in front of him. Lord Beartach is ancient. He's resided in his court for centuries. He's trusted him. The betrayal stings so hard that I feel it, not only through my gifts, but through the bond.

With a flash of power like a sonic boom, everyone in the room flies back, knocked down by its force. My panther form rips away, leaving me naked in the midst of the battle scene.

Roxalus lands on top of me. Max flies back into the wall, hitting it with a crunching sound loud enough to reverberate in the suddenly still space.

All of the insurgents are only momentarily stunned. The blast was a targeted attack. Beartach's stone glows faintly now that it's expelled so much energy. Magics demand balance.

Moving my head to the side, I can see them backing out of the room. Prince Ayxian is slumped in Lord Hadence and a few guard's arms. He's an enormous male. Even with the strength of the fae, they seem to be having a difficult time hoisting him out the back door of the room.

Ayxian lifts his head, blood seeping in long rivulets down his front, meeting my gaze. "This isn't over. I will have my throne. And I will take whatever queen I desire." With a creepy smile spreading over his face, a shiver runs down my naked spine.

Looking around the chamber, I nearly throw up. Bodies lay strewn over the concrete. There's blood everywhere. Smeared on the walls, covering the still fae from cuts and assaults, running to drains in the floor meant for cleaning the mop run off after a banquet.

There are no more insurgents in the room so it surprises me when Embla screams. Her throat raw, she's wailing in sobs. "Help me. Someone, help! Oh gods! Help!"

Roxalus' weight lifts from me instantly. Hurt or not, he's across the room before I've even registered the movement.

She's not calling for help for herself. Covering my mouth at the sight before me, the sight grips me in a cold embrace.

It's Princess Emenda. She lays still and quiet on the floor, blood flowing freely from a gaping wound in her chest.

Chapter Forty

Max recovers enough to sprint across the room in two long strides. Roxalus bends down and places his hand over the opening in her chest, ice blooming around the hole, momentarily sealing off the flow of blood. The panic in his eyes nearly does me in.

"This won't hold long. We need a powerful healer!" The look on his face tells me all that I need to know. Princess Emenda doesn't have long if something isn't done swiftly.

Inara races forward quickly. Reaching her hand out towards Emenda, an electric current hits her square in the chest, knocking her to the floor. Even in my human form, my growl is loud. How fucking dare she?!

Her fingers dancing with sparks, hate spews from her wretched mouth, "You will not touch her, you lowbee scum!"

A blast of explosive fire throws her against the far wall, head smacking into the stone and blood trailing down the side of her face. Embla teeters in and out, on the edge of consciousness, slumped in a heap on the floor.

"If you **ever** hurt my daughter again, I won't hesitate to end you, dear sister," Max snarls through gritted teeth.

The restraint he's showing is one of a million reasons why he is the best candidate for the throne. No matter that he doesn't want it. I am barely holding myself back as it is. If not for the fact that my mate needs me at his side right now, I would have gone after her myself for hurting Inara, princess or not.

Inara pushes her way off the floor, and I rush to her side. Leif's shadows cover her modesties from view, not that Inara will care. It's still nice that he does it for her sake.

She's been practicing witchcraft for as long as I can remember. Her studies intensified when Aunt Eowyn died. She wanted to learn everything she could from the book of shadows her mother had left her.

"What do you need?" If I can help in any way, I will. I'm not knowledgeable the way she is, but I can gather things for her.

Placing her hand over the frozen wound, closing her eyes, she concentrates. "Her heart still beats, but barely." Looking around the room, her gaze landing on Prince Noxian. "Fetch me wild lettuce, burdock root, and penny royal."

Dashing off without hesitation, his gift of nature will lead him right to the plants she needs. I find myself, once again, in awe of Inara's ability to think clearly and quickly no matter what situation she's thrown in to.

Her eyes meet Max's, and my breathing ceases in my chest. "I can't save her. I can only prolong her life for a bit. I need you to get Faelan."

Yes, of course! Faelan's gifts are all consuming. With being able to see and maneuver particles, she'll be able to manipulate them to whatever end necessary as long as he can get her here in time. Retrieving her from the Lupian Forest in the human realm will take him longer because of the ward, but it's Emenda's only shot.

Max's eyes are dark swirls, swimming in unshed tears but he nods once, glancing to me, he blinks out of existence. He knows keeping Inara safe will be my priority.

Noxian comes back quicker than I thought possible, but his gifts of nature will have led him exactly where he needed to go. Still, he's speed is impressive.

"Good. Meld those into a paste for me." Inara is direct. She doesn't kowtow under pressure. Her alpha side rings the commands and everyone follows her lead without question. She may not have been born under a royal blanket, but she was born to command. "Roxalus, Melt the ice slowly." Taking the paste from Noxian's hands, she smears it over the hole as Roxalus' ice begins to recede. "Embla's stirring," she says with a glance over my shoulder.

Turning my head to look at Emenda's twin, her presence has always felt large and menacing. Now, laying here still and crumpled, my heart aches for her. The bitterness of her usual personality is gone. Sadness and a deep-seated loneliness pours from her every cell. It's almost overwhelming.

Roxalus comes up behind me and pulls me close after stripping the shirt off his back and wrapping it around my naked form. I'm still new to this mating bond, but I'm guessing he feels my anxiety through it. I'd felt his earlier, so it makes sense if he's picking up on the emotion around the room from my gifts.

Yeah, it has nothing to with you being on display before the entire kingdom, or anything. Gah, well I guess there's that too.

"What are... You... Doing to... Her?" Embla gets to her feet with significant effort. The wound on her head is already healing over but blood crusts the side of her face and has dried in her hair. "Heal her!"

Her demands are met with hung heads. Loxias pushes solace out over those of us hovering in the room. Emenda has wormed her way into my heart and accepting the outcome that she may not make it lodges a stone behind my ribcage.

Princess Embla screams. She can't be consoled. She won't be subdued. Sparks dancing along her skin. Roxalus braves them to lay a comforting hand on her shoulder, but she pulls from his touch.

Before she can make a move towards her twin's still form, Max and Faelan return without haste. Dropping to the floor beside her grandmother, Faelan closes her eyes and holds her hands over Princess Emenda's chest. While she concentrates on mending the wound, we all hold our breath. Leif coming up beside Inara, he rests his hand on Inara's shoulder in support.

Quill slinks back into the room, trying subtly to get Loxias' attention but Loxias is solely focused on his dying sister. He won't look away or acknowledge his second's presence, and I can't shake the feeling that Quill has something of importance to tell him.

My curiosity and angst are screaming at me. I'm not able to contain my inquisitiveness for more than a few heartbeats. "What is it, Quill? Spill it."

Max turns to look at him and all of the prince's follow suit. Only Embla, Inara, and Faelan's attention remain on Emenda.

Realizing for the first time that Princess Elodie isn't in the room, worry gnaws at my insides. Her sister lays dying a measly five feet away from me and she is nowhere to be seen.

"It's not good, Your Majesty. Princess Elodie took a group of her elite guards and rode off to stop the rebels." He bows his head. "They were met with extreme force. Only a handful survived. I only just managed to pull the princess to safety before the sorcerer sent a wave of his magics across the field. It was a blood bath, My Liege."

Commotion out in the corridor draws all of our attention. Bloodied and disheveled themselves, two of Elodie's guards carry her in between them. She's awake but isn't able to stand on her own.

Running to her, my hands flutter uselessly over her wounds. "What can I do? How can I help?" My heart feels a ping of amusement as she huffs a breathy laugh.

"Well, my back's broken. I can't move anything from the waist down. So, maybe you'll need to help me pee later." The jovial tone doesn't match the surrounding atmosphere, but I can't help but smile at her. My friend is nothing, if not straight forward.

The sound of Princess Embla sobbing catches my attention, and we all turned to see Princess Emenda sitting up and staring around at all of the turmoil. "I don't know about all of you, but I could use a drink."

The room, as a collective, lets out a sigh of relief and breathes for the first time in the last half hour. Faelan makes her way to Elle, and I fall back to let her work. Grateful for her presence doesn't begin to cover it. Not that I wouldn't help Elle pee or anything. I'm simply relieved she'll be whole again.

Searching the room over for any survivors we might be able to save, the prince's go around the room doing the same. In the end, I found three. With all the chaos that erupted during the insurgence, most fled the room as quickly as possible, but the fae who were herded and murdered in cold blood never had a chance to escape. There're more than thirty bodies scattered around the chamber, the stench of copper digging its way up my nose.

Max calls for his guards to remove them with care and ushers in servants to help with the clean-up, but only those who are willing to volunteer. He then teleports Inara back to the Lupian Forest. Faelan hangs back for a moment to make sure I'm doing okay. After many reassurances that I'm coping the best that I can, she finally teleports back to her pack as well.

Max advises us to all get cleaned up. After all of the evidence of the attack is cleared away, he wants us all to meet in the dining chamber to discuss the competition and the attack. I've never had such a roller coaster of emotions in such a short span of time in my life. I'm exhausted, elated, distressed, and want to fall in bed with my mate and sleep for the next week but I know he's right. We need to hash out a line of strategy to keep the kingdom safe.

Chapter Forty-One

We're cleaned up and feasting on a meager meal of cheeses, breads, and fresh fruit. Ayxian's staff has been given the rest of the day off. Loxias, Quill, Leif and I scrounged what we could to make a decent meal without having to cook. Maybe it wasn't the most filling or savory foods but if the others wanted to go fend for themselves, that'd be up to them.

Quill informed us as we gathered the foods that he had secured Queen Leyashna before pursuing the rebels with Elodie. She's safely away, heading back to the kingdom seat. He and Leif leave after they help out. This meeting is only for the princes and princesses.

I begin to leave too, but Max stands firm on the subject. I am mated to a prince. That makes me a princess, like it or not. He tells the room at large that if Aunt Eowyn were alive, she'd have his balls if I were to be excluded. I want laugh, because the visual is on point.

Without preamble, Max begins. "Prince Ayxian is no longer one of us. He has taken it upon himself to decide who and what fate should befall Anavrin. I would like each of my sibling's input on how we should proceed." No mixing of words. No false platitudes. Simple and to the point. "Let's go around the table. Shall we?" He motions to Loxias, who is seated to his left, to start.

"I've made my feelings known about being king. I am more interested in finding my mate than ruling the kingdom. It seems like a lot of work," he gives a gracious nod in Max's direction. "I would rather spend my time doting on my other half. Seeing as how our brother is a traitor and nearly killed two of our sisters, I must say that squashing this rebellion should take precedence over the race for the throne. Just my few thoughts." With a swig of his mead, giving a small raise of his glass in the king's direction, he settles back into his seat.

Embla is the next to voice her opinions. "I am ashamed of Ayxian's actions to an extent, but the sentiment behind them isn't off base."

A loud growl escapes my throat. It's one thing to think herself better than commoners or lowbees, but to stick by the evidence of Ayxian's casual use of his subjects against their wishes is okay? It makes me see red. Roxalus interlocks his fingers with mine and gives a hard squeeze. He loves his sister. Logically, I know this. That fact doesn't negate the desire I have to rip her apart right now.

"I felt that way once too, sister." Glaring at Embla, he addresses the elephant in the room. "I might still feel that way if the stars didn't adjust my vision." Bringing our linked hands to his mouth, he brushes a kiss along my knuckles. "Perspectives can change, Embla. I hope that you will one day quell that loneliness that impairs your sight." Turning to Max, he dips his chin in respect. "I think that King Maximus Suilari should remain king for the unforeseeable future. His stability and well-tempered hand will serve Anavrin greatly in the coming conflict."

Embla tsks and turns to her sister. "What are your thoughts?" Her voice is gentler with Emenda than I've ever personally heard it. "Are you still willing to take the throne and see to it our way of life is upheld?"

Emenda is physically healed but that doesn't mean she's feeling one hundred percent yet. Shifting in her seat, I *feel* a ping of discomfort at her sister's words. "I think Max should stay king until Ayxian is dealt with, and the rebel faction is eliminated. I believe royals should be held in higher regard than our subjects, but that doesn't mean that our lessers lives don't matter."

Embla purses her lips and sits straight backed in her chair. "I see. And just when did you come to this conclusion? Was it when Lady Piper came to stay at your court or was it when she bedded our formerly agreeable brother?"

I want so badly to knock that smug look from her face. I'm red again but before either Roxalus or myself have an opportunity to say anything, Emenda fires back. "No Embla! It was when our brother, a prince of Anavrin, thought himself so much better than anyone that he forced himself inside of his victim's bodies without their consent." Reaching over Roxalus, she takes my hand, and I *feel* the earnestness of her words. She looks back to Embla. "If someone were to force you to splay your mouth wide, or spread your legs or ass cheeks without you wanting them to enter you, wouldn't you want someone to stand up for you too?"

Princess Embla turns fifteen shades of pink. "No one would dare. I'd have them executed."

Max arches an eyebrow and Elodie laughs mirthlessly. Noxian's frustration with his sister's ignorance spills over. "That's the whole point! You are royalty. You can do something about unwelcome advances. You consider everyone beneath you and yet you don't see how it's your job to protect them. You will never be queen, Embla. I would rather cut my court off from the kingdom seat than see you upon the throne."

It was the most I'd ever heard Noxian speak at once. Her eyes have widened but she has no reply. Her younger brother isn't one of many words. What words he does speak on occasion hold great weight.

Loxias and Quill snicker but not at him. Their amusement is directed at the less than understanding princess who cares more about status than justice. Max simply shakes his head. Elodie and I can *feel* the disappointment he holds in his heart for his sister like a living thing.

It takes me a few precious seconds to rein in the emotions swimming around the room. I can't let my gifts take control and heighten everyone else's. That wouldn't be fair or just when making decisions that will affect the kingdom.

Seemingly disgusted with Embla's lack of caring, he turns his attention back to the others. "Princess Elodie, what say you on the matter?"

He initially turned down the throne, wanting to spend time in his court and with his son and daughter. After the last seven or eight months, I wonder if he's changed his mind. It is his birthright after all. No one can take it from him. If he wants to be king, it's his for the taking.

We all know he's proven himself to be a great king already as regent. And Inara and Leif both get to spend time with him in the quiet moments. Somehow in the mayhem of all of this, he's managed to find the balance that he was looking for in his life.

Eowyn would never deny him a new queen if he so chose. That I know for sure, but I also know that he will never take one. Mated pairs are the end all, be all. If one died, the other never longed for anyone but their missing half. I read it in a tome months ago. Now experiencing the bond firsthand, I can confidently attest it to be true.

"Well, dear brother. I believe that Roxalus has the right idea. You should stay king." He starts to protest but she holds up a hand to quell him." Hear me out. Our father, King Zyoden would never make this..." she gestures around the table... "a discussion. Our input meant nothing. You, on the other hand, not only ask us for it, but will seriously take anything we have to say into consideration before making the final decision. If you will consider doing that with each major decision about the kingdom, I for one, will follow your leadership to whatever end."

Clearing his throat, Max is clearly touched by Elle's heartfelt words. "Noxian, your thoughts on the situation?"

Tapping his finger to his lips, I can *feel* the cogs turning in his heart and mind. Elodie quirks a half smile. That's about as much conformation as I can hope for.

"I think Princess Elodie makes a fare point. I can't say it won't be disappointing. Being king would have meant a great deal to me. I'm most regretful about the fact that we never got to meet your mate, brother." Max's eyes tighten ever so slightly. I only see it because I'm always watchful of things that others aren't. "With that being said, none of us, other than Roxalus here, has had that opportunity yet. And like Lox said, devoting yourself to your mate should take number one priority in your life." His smile broadens. "I say, all Hail, King Maximus Suilari. First born of the namesake, Leader of the Spring Court, Ruler of the Anavrin Fae."

Hails go up around the table. Mine amongst them. We all lift our glasses and toast to his honor. Embla is quiet, arms folded over her chest, bottom lip pouting, sitting amongst a room full of family and utterly alone.

Pulling me closer, Roxalus warm breath brushes over my ear. "I guess this means you won't be queen." I can hear the smirk in his voice. "I'm guessing that this also means you won't have to travel to Embla's court." His throaty purr in my ear sends goose pimples to race across my flesh. "I can't wait to have you all to myself. By my side. In your new home. Spread across *Our* bed."

I love the sound of that. Swallowing the lump in my throat, I quiver with anticipation. Max clears his throat again. Realizing that he's caught onto our little interlude, a flush of embarrassment raises heat to my cheeks.

"As I was saying, I am honored. I didn't want this position after losing Eowyn due to father's disdainful biases. I will do my best to run the land as efficiently as possible, keeping the people safe from outside threats and inside rebellions." His chin dips in respect to each of his siblings. "I do think, however, that this subject should be revisited once all of this turmoil is over. No one should remain in control for longer than their goals match the goals of the whole. Immortality gets boring. It can make you bitter or complacent."

Emenda begins to protest his addendum, but a pointed look from Noxian hushes her. The prince still would like an opportunity to be king one day. That much I can *feel*. Elodie even gives off a little of that same aura. Maybe they can all take turns at some point. A change in regime or rotating speaker type deal. I've never looked into how different types of governments work.

"Now," Max looks around the table again. "How should we deal with Ayxian and the sorcerer? I'm open to any suggestions."

I can't tell if he's pleased with being king or if he's accepting the position because he knows he can rein his siblings in. Either way, I'm more than thrilled to have him as my king. He has a way about him. Justice and fairness shine through with every decision that he makes. He isn't boastful or too wickedly fae. I see a lot of Aunt Eowyn's temperament in him, and I wonder what he was like before he met her. It also makes me wonder how much of him had become her personality. I'd never known her before they'd met. I hadn't been born yet. It begs the question if perhaps he changed her in ways too? Maybe that's why he and I have gotten along so famously since we met.

Roxalus has been cold and indifferent to the people of Anavrin for centuries. It makes me think about how I've shut out my panther side. He's made me more bold. I've softened some of his edges. Even before the bond was claimed, it began to reshape us. make our puzzle pieces mesh perfectly together.

If this is how my mother's vision is coming to pass, maybe it was inevitable, and I could have stayed true to my shift in the past. I meant to ask Inara if she's found out anything more in her journals, but it slipped my mind through all of the chaos.

Roxalus runs his hand up my thigh under the table. He's fully engaged in the conversation with his siblings over how things should proceed, but he can't keep his hands off of me. I feel wanted, accepted. I don't crave being hidden away anymore. My heart is my own, and yet it belongs to my mate. Running with Inara's pack of werewolves, I'd made friends with each of them, but I never felt like I was a part of them.

With Roxalus, it all feels natural. I fall into his arms and the depths of his eyes every time he's close. I felt the pull towards him, the tug in my chest way before we'd fulfilled the mating claiming and now that tug is a solid connection to one another. We will be able to communicate emotions and stay connected even when we aren't in the same place. That thought alone gives me hope for the future.

I am his and he is mine. Forever.

Chapter Forty-Two

We ate and drank, and the royal's all discussed strategies for handling the insurgents. It's nearing midnight when Max motions for me to come talk to him. "Hey there, Peppercorn."

I do a half-assed mock curtsy. "Your Majesty." His shining smile shows all of his teeth. "I suppose that I have a new home now." The drinks I've had tonight work a blush readily to my cheeks knowing he had caught the scent of arousal from me and my mate earlier. "I should give this back to you."

Undoing the necklace, I start to hand it back to him, but he closes my hand around it. "You need to keep that on. You're still going to visit each court, sweetpea."

Why in the world would I continue to each court when we've agreed him to be king for the foreseeable future?

"Look guys, I accept being king until the kingdom is secured but we're still continuing with these competitions. There are those who will not see lowbees as anything but foreigners from the human realm. We need to force them to see them as fae. By continuing the challenges, the crowds will be gathering and mingling. We'll be able to send the elite teams from each of our courts to scout out any potential rebels. The best way to do that is to proceed as planned. Each court will have a few haters, for sure. We need to weed out the rebels from the haters. Everyone is entitled to their own opinion, but they are not entitled to acts of violence. To get the upper hand, we're going to move forward with the competitions. Agreed?"

"I don't want her staying in my court." Princess Embla points her boney finger in my direction and Roxalus viciously snarls. The way she jumps back from the malice in his glare is almost comical.

Max is having none of her antics. Emenda scoots an inch or so away from her sister and Embla blanches at the distance. Not only physical, but emotional.

"You will accommodate PRINCESS Piper accordingly. In case you have forgotten so quickly sister, Prince Roxalus has found his mate in my niece. I understand that in your empty heart you have no idea how to receive mated pairs but that is a lesson you will learn quickly or find yourself more alone than you already are. And as your king, it is my wish to have her visit each court."

Fire coating the tips of his fingers, light bouncing off the stone walls. He called her sister, but he was nothing but her king in this moment. As lonely as I imagine her to be, most of it is of her own making. She'll get no sympathy from me for her hatefulness.

"Fine. I'm not going to argue against good taste. You either have it or you don't." She turns to me, and my stomach drops. "It would be my pleasure to have you in my court." The wicked smile playing at her lips tells me everything I need to know. Fae can't lie. Her idea of pleasure and my idea of pleasure will be vastly different. I'm sure.

"I will be accompanying her." Roxalus brushes a kiss across my knuckles. "We'll need a room far away from everyone else if you don't wish us to be heard."

Embla tsks and Max clears his throat. "Rox, I know that feeling you're having, but I need Piper to have the two weeks with Embla by herself."

Roxalus' posture stiffens beside me. "You cannot ask this of me! I will Not leave her unprotected! If Ayxian or any of the other insurgents come calling, I will show no mercy for anyone trying to harm her!"

I don't know how to comfort him. Parting from him won't be any easier for me than it is for him, but I have to trust that Max has a plan. Ayxian and the rebels need to be dealt with swiftly. I'd told them all while we'd ate and discussed things about the revelation Ayxian imparted before he'd left. He was the murderer. He wanted me and when I couldn't be had, his beastly side went too far with each of his victims. It hurt to know that I had a small hand in each of their demises.

Max is in full king mode now but making an effort to be more understanding. He knows first-hand what it's like to lose a mate. Though to carry out his agenda, and try to keep the kingdom safe, he'll stick to his guns about this. It's there, in the set of his eyes.

"Accompany her to the castle, but do not stay. If it makes you feel better, Mysti may be with her. Your Elite commander still owes her a debt. That can't be denied by any courtier or commoner." Running a hand through his hair, he appears to have aged ten years since this morning. "I'm asking you, brother. Will you trust me?"

I give his hand a gentle squeeze, Roxalus looks down into my eyes, searching for something. There's a tug of anxiety from the bond, and I push back as much reassurance as I can. If anything happens to me, Roxalus is likely to lose himself to the cold all over again.

"If you all are finished preening over the lowb... princess," Embla knew what she was saying, and I find myself unable to care. "I need to retire for the night. Tomorrow's trip may only be a half days ride, but I'd like to arrive early enough to make sure everything is in order for our newest guest." Without waiting for a reply from anyone, including Emenda, she turns and leaves without so much as a glance back.

Elodie watches her go and I make a note to ask her what she's glimpsed. Loxias and Noxian move forward to embrace Princess Emenda before departing with their seconds. Max embraces Roxalus' arm in one of those hand on each other's forearm moves I've seen in warrior movies before he leaves too.

"I will protect her with my life, My Liege. I swear it." Mystiance kneels in front of him. I *feel* a ping of nervousness from her and a ping of anger from him.

"You have been charged with her care twice now. And twice now you have failed to keep her from harm. There will not be a third time, Commander." Pulling her to a standing position, her chest slams against his as the cold words whisper across the shell of her ear. "For any mark that's made on her, I will give you an identical one that will not be healed." Cold blue eyes stare intently into the depths of her bright green ones, and I shudder as frost seeps down the bond.

"Roxalus!" I grab his shoulder, and his arm comes around my waist, placing a gentle kiss on top of my head.

"This is not up for discussion, Wildfire. You are the most important thing in the world to me and I will make any who aim to hurt you pay in flesh."

Okay. That's... kind of hot. The threat of harm shouldn't turn me on like this but damn!

"He's right, My Lady. I don't deserve another chance, but if you'll have me, I won't let you down again." She breaks away from his glare and hangs her head.

I want to protest that she hasn't failed me, but the fact is, I have been harmed. Not that it's her fault. I don't see it that way but neither of them will see it any other way.

With an exaggerated sigh, placing my hand on her shoulder, all of this feels like overkill. Her overwhelming beauty doesn't fit the profession she's chosen, but who am I to judge what someone wants to do with their life?

"Commander Mystiance, I charge you with my life. If harm befalls me, it befalls you threefold. Your debt will be paid by your protection. Do we have an accord?"

Her hand shoots forward and a magical flare rises up between our palms, sealing our agreement. A binding contract. I wish that I hadn't said that harm her threefold thing, but what's done is done.

"Now," Roxalus says as he scoops me up into his arms. "I shall like to see you off properly, Princess Piper." Heat rises from every spot where our bodies touch. "I have about eight hours to show you all of the ways that you're mine before we depart."

I giggle. I never used to do that in the forest. It's become my go to laugh since coming to the faery realm. If it wasn't for the fact that I promised myself I would do what makes me happy, I might be embarrassed by it, but I'm not. I like to giggle. It makes me feel wonderful so I will own it the way I've accepted every other aspect of myself that I was taught to hide away.

"We have to get some rest, Starbear." Running my fingers through his hair and tucking a lock behind his ear, he shudders.

Leaning into my touch, he nibbles on my lobe before the heat of his breath whispers across my skin, "Is there a meaning behind *that* particular pet name?" His eyes smolder and I clench my legs together at the aching taking up residence at my center.

Blushing, I trail my fingers over his lips. "Well, you see..." Stumbling over the words that'll make me seem hopelessly pathetic, I settle on the straightest point forward. "There's this coffee that I'm, sort of, addicted to. And the best pastry to pair with it makes my mouth water."

The look in his eyes is one of pure amusement. I can't bring myself to say the rest. "Go on... I'm a coffee and some sort of pastry." The smile playing at his lips pulls a laugh from mine.

"You have to understand... coffee and bear claws are my dark obsession." Pleading my case feels oddly like confessing to some nefarious act, like popping the heads off of dandelions for fun.

Sweeping me up into his arms and chuckling, those luscious lips of his find that sensitive spot along the nape of my neck. "Hey! We need to rest." My protest sounds half-hearted even to my own ears.

"You can rest in the carriage." Eyebrows shooting up, biting his bottom lip, he nuzzles his face into my neck, and I purr with pleasure. "Tonight, I'll be making sure that my scent is the only thing that anyone approaching you over the next couple of weeks will smell." Wetness pools between my thighs at his words. "You are mine, Piper."

Chapter Forty-Three

I try to wave to Mysti as Roxalus carries me from the room, but her eyes are averted to the floor. As we walk quickly through the corridors, any servants we pass do the same thing.

"Why won't anyone look at us?" I know he has a reputation for being not so nice, but this behavior suggests something else entirely.

Nuzzling into my neck again, he growls and the throbbing in my center intensifies. "We're a newly mated pair. Your arousal and mine greet them before we're even in view. If they meet my eyes, I might not be able to control the need to defend what's mine."

I want to tell him that all of this is silly but when a pretty servant girl heading in our direction doesn't avert her eyes to the floor for a few steps, a snarl escapes my own throat, and I clamp a hand over my mouth as she passes us. His chuckle rocks through me everywhere we're touching. Cheeks heating with embarrassment at my lack of self-restraint.

"See? It's not easy to control yet." Leaning in, he kisses my lips, and lust explodes throughout my body. "I'd known quite a few mated couples centuries ago. After the first ten years or so, they said it gets slightly less difficult to rein in the possessiveness."

Ten years? Surely, he has to be pulling my leg. I can't imagine a decade of snapping at anyone who looks at him wrong.

"Oh, is that all? A decade to *slightly* get it under control?"

I've never acted irrationally before. I've been an observer. A creature of habit, sticking to the shadows of others and only speaking out when absolutely necessary.

Since coming to Anavrin, my life no longer perceives the world around me in black and white. Brilliant colors from every facet of the rainbow sweep me in and make grey obsolete. My moods, my words: they all live in full HD mode, and I'd never known that was an option in my old life.

We arrive at the door to our rooms. I have no idea who will take over Ayxian's court now that he and his second, Lord Hadence, have been ousted and joined the rebellion. This room he's given me is fit for a queen. I don't like thinking of him while here in Roxalus' arms, but the image of him accosting me lodges in my brain like a tick.

Taking a deep breath and leaning into my mate, his peppermint and pine needle scent scratches the itch under my skin, relaxing every part of me. Our lips meet and my mouth opens naturally for him. This male is all mine.

The taste of his mouth. The fire in his eyes. The strong muscles that clutch me tightly to his firm chest. They're all that I didn't know to ask for in life. My other half.

And if that truly is the case, then I must be meant for more... I don't know to what end, but more of something. That hope brings me joy. And I haven't had hope in so long. It's a relief, a blessing, and I plan to cherish every second of it to the fullest.

Roxalus is powerful and his presence commands either fear or respect. Me, on the other hand, I've always hidden myself away in the background of my own life. As scary as it is, trying to step into the limelight and be worthy of such a mate will be my goal for the future that lies before us.

Butterflies flitter around low in my belly. Sensing my growing desire, he quickens our pace. His corded arms squeeze gently as I nuzzle into his neck. I feel safe and want to be held by this perplexing male. Need rises to the forefront of my desires, and I stop fighting the urge. Just a small bite.

With fangs sinking into his skin like a hot knife into butter, venom seeps from my teeth along his mate mark and the taste of his skin heats my core to a raging fire.

Snarling at the hiss of pain and pleasure, his growl is the pitch of velvet over glass, smooth and raspy all at once, like whiskey over ice. The sound is the single most alluring thing I've ever heard.

Kicking the door open with his foot, we barely make it to the bed before his strong arms rip the top from my breasts, and his mouth comes down squarely on one of my painfully erect nipples.

The gasp that leaves me is quickly cut short as his hand wraps around my throat. Panic sets in, not because I think he'll hurt me. The firmness of his grip isn't painful. I've just never been in a tryst where I've felt safe enough to explore the less than standard sexual acts.

Sensing my anxiety, his grip loosens but he doesn't remove it. "Piper, are you scared of me?"

The hurt in his voice creeps into the darkest parts of my subconscious. Shaking my head, I place a hand on his chest. The hand holding my throat loosens a fraction more, but I hold his gaze until he can read the desire in my eyes. Squeezing just a little tighter, reaching down with the other hand to undo his pants, he angles himself between my thighs. I've worn no undergarments this evening. I had a feeling we'd end up here and didn't want to waste the time disrobing. Feeling bare flesh beneath my dress, his breath hitches.

"You dirty little vixen." The dimple on his cheek, that I'm sure I'm the only one who gets to see, lights up my entire world.

Intensity reigns in his cool blue eyes as I stare back. Wiggling his fingers for a better grip of pressure, the tip of his erected length settles into my entrance. With firm intent and purpose, he slides fully inside of me, squeezing my throat as he does. My eyes lock onto his and I gasp in pleasure at the feel of him filling me to the brim.

Releasing my neck, my hair's his next target. A gentle tug from behind my head angles my mouth with his. Our lips meet, tongues tasting one another, as thrust after thrust works every bit of angst and worry from my system. It's gentle and beautiful and gloriously perfect.

The rest of Anavrin may think of my mate as a brute, but they can't possibly understand this magnificent male the way I do. He is mine. And together we'll make sure that the rest of the kingdom witnesses him walk in the light rather than the shadows.

The touch of his fingers trailing down my side in such a loving way do me in. Our pace quickens, still tender. Still passionate. I meet every thrust of his with one of my own. The building pressure is almost too much. With the flat of his thumb, he rubs circles in place at the top of my clitoris, and I see stars on the next thrust.

Fireworks spark throughout my body, lighting me up from the inside out. With an almighty roar, Roxalus throws his head back and follows me over the edge, twitching and jerking with the potency of his own undoing.

Exhausted and pleasantly spent, wrapping his arms around my middle, he pulls us down into the plush pillows. Fully sated, my head drops to his chest, and I fall fast asleep. Safe. Wanted... Loved.

Chapter Forty-Four

It's a while later that a knock comes to the door. Mysti's voice calls quietly through into our little bubble of serenity. "The carriage is ready for our departure, Lady Piper." Roxalus growls from the depths of his semi-conscious state. She hears him though. "Apologies... Princess Piper," she corrects.

Scrunching my nose up at the new title, it dawns on me that I'm going to have to get used to it. My mate, however, has already adjusted to my role and settles his arms around me like he is overly contented by its use.

"We'll be just a few minutes, Commander." Her footsteps trail off and Roxalus grumbles something about bullshit and I giggle at his sleepy ramblings.

Dressing in comfortable travelling attire, I slip on some leggings and an oversized t-shirt with a Stars Hollow decal on the front. Inara had brought it to me the last time we'd had tea. Her favorite show also happens to be Max's favorite from the time he'd spent in the human realm. It's only fitting for me to wear it as a personal tribute to the now and foreseeable future king. Uncle King Max. It has a nice ring to it.

"Wildfire, what are you grinning about over there?" Sitting up, the cover falls to the floor, exposing his chest and the rest of his handsome form in all of his wonderous glory. Noticing the direction of my thoughts, a mischievous grin creeps over his beautiful face. "You should return to bed. Commander Mystiance can wait."

The thought is so tempting. At half a day's journey, it won't take long, but the thought of arriving after dark makes goosepimples cover my arms. Embla is a hateful shrew, but I can't believe that her lands are anything but breathtaking. None of Anavrin has let me down so far. I'd like to see the castle at sunset if we can make it there in time.

"Tempting. If there was ever a time for me to give into lazing about, it'd be in bed with you. I'd like us to arrive before sundown, though. Even if Emenda's not the best company, surely her lands are splendorous enough to hold my heart light."

Snagging my hairbrush off the table, my thoughts wander to Keyara. She hasn't been herself since the massacre. I'd told her to take some time to heal the hurt. She'd lost her best friend in the chaos of the fighting, and it didn't seem right to ask her to tend to my needs when she deserves time to grieve.

"You are amazing, Wildfire." Pulling on a pair of trousers, he fastens them and reaches for the white shirt I've laid on the bed. I can't lift my eyes to meet his when nothing hides him from view. Even if I am fully sated, the sight of Roxalus well-toned body does funny things to my insides.

Snapping his fingers out in front of him, he chuckles. "Hey! My eyes are up here." Heat rushes to my cheeks as my teeth sink into my bottom lip. If I could have had any other gift, I'd have wanted teleportation. Travel time would be irrelevant then. And that time saved could be well spent in other ... endeavors.

"Amazing, am I? Why so?" The smell of fresh brewed coffee drifts in from the common room and I abandon our conversation mid-sentence, reaching for the knob and heading out the door. The coffee is hot, and the scent reaches deep inside my soul, dragging the last vestiges of sleep away with ease.

Trailing out after me, his hair disheveled, his shirt wrinkled, he looks most unprincely. Gorgeous, but not regal in his current state. Shaking my head, I close the distance between us.

"You truly are addicted, aren't you?" He says while smirking. His arched eyebrow brinks what I just did front and center in my mind. I'd left him behind without a thought once the coffee lured me out of the room with its glorious aroma.

"Oops. Apologies, your highness." Swirling the cup under his nose, I mock his chiding. "This potion does funny things with the mind. Want some?"

Wrapping his hands around my waist, pulling me close, amusement dances in those cool blue eyes of his. "I see it now." Taking the cup from my hand, I begin to protest but he places a finger over my mouth to quell my little rebellion. *That's how you lose a finger, Mister!* "I have serious competition from those magic beans."

Brushing a kiss to the top of my head, the contented sigh that escapes me has me questioning if I really need to see Embla's castle in the light of day.

The blue sky peeking through the large window frames the balcony with a pleasant light. Bird songs flutter through the open curtains. The sounds of people bustling about outside the castle create a pleasing background to the atmosphere in our own little world.

"I might be inclined to agree with you if it weren't for the fact that I won't be able to obtain those beans forever." That thought sobers me up to the reality of being stuck in Anavrin. From his quizzical look, the lack of understanding is clear. "Once Max and Faelan close the borders for good, I won't be able to get anymore. It may be a hundred years from now, but it will feel like all too short of a time."

Jutting out my bottom lip in an over exaggerated pout, he reaches over and tugs on it. "Well then, we'll just have to figure out a solution, won't we?" Leaning down to face level, kissing me softly, I shudder. "We can't have my wife wanting for any-thing."

My heart beats in double-time as I absorb those words. "Wife?" Holding my breath, I don't think I can manage my emotions, keep them under control, if he takes it back now.

"Of course, Wildfire." Pulling back to look me in the eyes. "Unless..." I sense the fear in his hesitation. "... you don't wish to be my wife." Turning his head away quickly, I reach for his arm before he can get away.

"You are my mate, Starbear, but I didn't want to assume that you'd want me to have a throne in your court." Hanging my head in embarrassment, I *feel* his hurt. It courses down the mating bond, amplified and raw.

Way to go, dunderhead. How could I have been so obtuse? He's been cold hearted and alone for a long time. I would never reject him, but he's been conditioned to think that way over the years.

Taking both of my hands in his, he drags me to the settee under the window. "Piper, if I have given you any reason to doubt me, spell it out in plain terms so that I may rectify it." I try to speak but he covers my mouth with his finger once more. "Let me be perfectly clear... I am yours. You may have all of me or none of me. It is your choice. It will always be your choice."

I attempt to mumble under his hand, but he clamps my lips shut with his fingers and I giggle. "I am your mate," he kisses the knuckles of my one hand. "Your friend," and then kisses the other. "Your lover," he places a gentle kiss to my forehead. "And if you'll have me, I will be your loyal husband."

With his lips coming down on mine, I can't catch my breath. And the gods know, I don't want to. Oxygen is inconsequential right now. My prince is rough around the edges and tender just for me. Mates are for life. The stars choose them for you... but a husband? That is a choice I get to make for myself. And there isn't a single one reason to say no. He'll love me. He will protect me. Roxalus will grant me the space to make my own decisions and stand by me when I make them.

Tears rim my eyes from the joy filling my heart. With the softest brush of a touch, I place a chaste kiss upon his lips. "My prince." Another kiss. "It is my honor to be your mate." A third one. "And it will be my privilege to be your wife."

Scooping me up into his arms, we take two long strides towards the bedchamber when Mysti comes into the common room with Elodie and Loxias before we get there.

Oops. Once again, we've forgotten about the world outside of our bubble.

Elodie is smiling fiendishly. "And just what do you think you are doing?" From her coy expression, I know she's gathered the gist of what's going on.

"I am taking my fiancée, in every way possible," he says with an onery snarl. No embarrassment. No care for their presence.

I smack at his arm playfully. The forwardness bringing my own smile to my lips. A thousand years will never be enough. Hell, it won't even scratch the surface.

"I insist you put my soon to be sister-in-law down so that we may congratulate her properly!" Loxias demands waggishly, taking a step in our direction. Roxalus growls, showing all of his teeth, and Lox steps back with his hands up in mock surrender. "Geesh, lighten up, Rox."

He sets me down but keeps one hand around my waist. Mysti looks torn between wanting us to get a move on and wanting to celebrate our announcement.

I know he's still not thrilled with her right now. Honestly, I can see it from his point of view. If I'd entrusted her with his safety and he'd been harmed twice, I'd be more than willing to rip her a new one. But as it stands, I'm the one on this side of things. I need her with me if I'm to feel any semblance of safety. I might as well save her from Prince Grumbles a Lot before he gets angry.

"One drink. And then we must be off. I hear Princess Embla's castle is a sight to see in the colors of twilight." Mysti gives me a small smile and dip of her chin ever so slightly. "I wouldn't want to miss the sight of the shackles and the dungeon without the light because we arrived after dark."

Roxalus tenses under my teasing, but Elle and Loxias smile appreciatively at my jest.

The real question is... is it really a jest if it turns out to be true?

Chapter Forty-Five

Forty-five minutes later, we're all loaded up in our carriages, going our separate ways. Roxalus is journeying with me to Princess Embla's court and after I'm settled in, he'll return to his court... our court, to begin the preparations for our wedding. The commander will be by my side for the foreseeable future.

Mysti keeps glancing in my direction when she thinks that I'm not looking. I have no idea of what she's thinking but I do remember how we met. It has me pondering why Roxalus brought her to accompany him to Loxias' court in the first place. Making a mental note to get her to spill the tea once we're alone, I give my full attention to my mate.

"You're staring." It isn't a question. Lifting our interlocked hands, he kisses my fingers. "Is there something that you wish to say?"

Scooching impossibly closer, practically putting myself in his lap, it's still not close enough for my liking. I'm all too aware that we'll be apart for two whole weeks. That thought bothers me more than having to endure Embla for the next month or the possibility of attacks form the rebels.

"I'm just counting the hours until we're together again." I've only just found my mate, and it feels plain wrong to be apart from him in any way. Pity for what Max and Aunt Eowyn must have gone through tears at my heart.

Bring my attention back to him, running a hand up my thigh, I quiver. My arousal is a living thing. From that one act, every cell in my body is now on fire as his thumb inches higher.

Mysti clears her throat. She's sitting on the bench seat directly across from us, not three feet away, and I had totally forgotten she was there. "Please, don't." Rolling her eyes, a small smile draws her lips up at the corners of her mouth, as she averts them.

Roxalus chuckles but doesn't stop rubbing his hands on my legs. His peppermint and pine needles scent threaten to overwhelm me. It will be torture to be away from him for these couple of weeks but Max has been adamant that I try to see Embla without bias. If I understand him as well as I think I do, then his underlying goal is to suss out potential risks to the kingdom. And that may include her. She's proven herself to be a known elitest, but would she go as far as to go against the crown? That is the question at hand.

"What flowers would you like to be the most prominent at our handfasting, love?"

The way he takes my needs, wants, and desires into account is still new to me. I never realized having your other half also meant having everything that you've never thought to ask for yourself in life.

Loxias was right to want this for himself. He's proven himself to be a good male. I want this for him too. He deserves it and I hope he finds it sooner rather than later.

The mention of our ceremony sends heat high into the apples of my cheeks. Not from embarrassment but from pure elation.

I never *Fell* in love with him. When the marking occurred during our claiming, our love was set. It wasn't a choice. The gods had split souls in half out of jealously for all the happiness they themselves would never have in that way... but the Fates worked in mysterious ways. They intervened when the gods proved themselves selfish. After all, the Fates are devious creatures and perhaps more mischievous than the fae. They allow you access to your other half. But only if you happen upon your divided soul, recognize and accept them, and then claim them completely. It is said that the gods secretly root for the hope that mates bring to the world. They are both the loving embodiment of the whole and the hateful resentment of the unconnected.

Our love is a feeling of joy and protectiveness. An understanding on a soul level. It's right and circular and all encompassing. I never want to be without him, and I will never want another for the rest of my days.

"I think roses and flowering pepper plants would be appropriate," I say, and Mysti scoffs. "What? You don't like them?"

Roxalus stiffens next to me. His desire to keep me happy bringing a defensiveness to his posture.

Her beautiful face turns away from the carriage window to look at me. "It's not that, Princess Piper." Again, I scrunch my nose up at the title. It's really going to take some time to get used to the royal address. "I just don't think you should compromise what you actually want for what you think is expected."

Aww, fuck. Way to call me out, Commander. Though I'm not surprised that she sees through me so easily. She obtained her position for a reason.

"Is that true?" Taking my hands in his, warmth and compassion shine back at me in a way I'd never thought a male like him would be capable of showing. "Wildfire, I want you to be happy. I don't ever want you to do what you think is expected at that expense. I mean it."

"Thanks a lot traitor." I glare at her, and she hides her smirk by looking out the window. I'm not as upset with her as I am annoyed. If I can make his life easier by not pushing his people... our people... then I should have some give in me. Then again, I've sworn to never to diminish myself to appease others again. Ugh! I have to find a balance.

"Lavender, honeysuckle, and jasmine are my flowers of choice. I don't want to put anyone out but as it is our day, perhaps they won't mind?" Kissing his knuckles, I add, " Ohh, and if we could have some cacao covered flakey pastries, that would be amazing."

Smiling down at me, that rare dimple making its appearance just before he kisses my forehead. "Anything you wish, love."

Glancing over to see a satisfied smirk coming from Mysti, mine brightens in response, realizing that she has my best interests at heart.

We stopped only one time to eat and relieve ourselves. The journey would be over all too soon and with it, Roxalus' departure. My chest aches at the mere thought but I plaster a smile on my face to save him from seeing my distress. I can feel his through the bond. At least we're undeniably matching each other's energies.

It's twilight when we arrive. The castle is as I imagined... exquisitely stunning. The trees surrounding the lands drip with colors so beautiful, they take my breath away.

"She always has had a flare for the extraordinary." Strong arms wrap around my waist from behind and I lean into his touch.

The commander's on full alert. Her eyes rove over every nook and cranny searching for any threats. With a dip of her chin to Roxalus, he ushers us forward, keeping our hands linked between us.

I'd expected the princess to meet us here at the front entrance, but she is nowhere to be seen. A guard approaches our little party a few moments later. "Prince Roxalus, Lady Piper."

Roxalus growls at the slight and the guard rolls his eyes ever so slightly. I must have been the only one paying attention though, because neither of my companions seem to notice. "Princess Piper. Your room is ready if you will follow me." He turns towards Commander Mystiance. "Your room is in the guard's quarters. You know the way?"

"Commander Mystiance will be in the rooms with Princess Piper." Roxalus' tone brokers no room for discussion.

The guard gives me a once over. I can't help but to feel like gum on the bottom of his shoe. Grabbing Roxalus' arm in mine for support, I find my backbone and address the guard. "Do you have a problem with me?"

The guard stumbles up the steps as Roxalus stiffens again. The corded muscles of his upper arms tense. He does that a lot when trying to control his emotions. It's a turn on to know that he censors his responses to give me the opportunity to handle myself. It's empowering. It bolsters my resolve and makes me feel brave.

"No." The guard says no more but Mysti steps up to my other side. Having her here is the best thing for my safety, yes. But it also gives me a lifeline in a sea of unwelcomeness. And for that, I am immensely grateful.

Without another word, the guard leads us down a long corridor with beautiful stone sculptures that sit in little niches off of each side. The artwork is fabulous. There are sprites dancing around a faery with wings. There is another sculpture that looks like a family of pigs, but they are huge and have tusks that appear sharp enough to maim.

The last statue to catch my eye is one of some sort of water fae that I've never seen before. I've heard of their existence but have yet to meet one. It's said that they can grant you a boon, any boon, if you can guess their riddle right on the first try. If you fail, you will sink within their waters for a year's time. No one could tell me what happens during that year, but I don't think I want to know anyway.

We arrived at my room and Roxalus tsks, shaking his head in displeasure. It looks fine to me, but he and his sisters are close... or at least they had been in the past. He'd know if this room was meant as an insult or not.

"I'll be back, love. You and Mysti get settled in, just not too much." Before I can respond, he grabs the guard by the arm and forces him down the hall, a small flame under his palm singeing the guard's uniform.

I'd nearly forgotten his brute side. I've had the pleasure to see the tender side of him that no one else ever gets a glimpse of, except maybe Eskay. From the look on the guard's face, he's never forgotten the demons that live just under Roxalus' skin.

Turning to Mysti, she's smirking again. I don't hold my tongue this time. "What sort of trouble is Princess Embla in for this?"

Her mischievous smile broadens across her entire face. "The most wicked kind from the Prince of Nightmares."

Chapter Forty-Six

Prince of Nightmares? "What is that supposed to mean? Does Roxalus have another gift I should know about?"

The fact that he's never mentioned but the two, I wonder if he perhaps hasn't told me something on purpose.

"No, Your Highness." Mysti looks to the bag she's carrying over to the vanity, not looking me in the face. "My Liege has had many years to hone his cruel side." Her voice dropping to a whisper, I hear what she isn't saying.

"Before mating with me." It isn't a question. I know it in my bones. That's what she means. That I've worn away some of his edges. Brought light into his dark, cold heart.

It has been nagging at me for some time. How can we be the other half of each other's soul when he is known for his cruelty, his brutishness. I've never thought of myself as violent or mean, but maybe I'm missing something.

"Commander, why did you accompany him on his trip to Loxias' court?" I let the end of the meaning hang there in the air. Does she have an interest in my mate? This might not end well for her if that's the case and I can't get myself under control. I'm doing my best to force the rumbling snarl in my chest back down before it gives away my jealousy.

She smirks and I let loose a growl without meaning to, taking a small step in her direction before giving my feet permission to do so. Her hands flying up in front of her in surrender.

"Easy, your Highness. I have never wanted Prince Roxalus." Looking to her feet and taking a casual step back. "I... well..." The way she's stumbling over her words isn't like her at all and it makes me irrationally irritated.

"Spit it out, Mysti." I say, with another step in her direction. Exhaling a long breath of discomfort, her grunt of annoyance brings me up short. Once I *feel* the ridiculousness of my re-action with my gifts, the nonsensical way that my body has risen to the challenge to defend what's mine, I relax my posture slightly.

Sitting down in the chair next to the vanity, she puts her head in her hands, shaking it back and forth. "May I speak freely?"

I'd forgotten that formality was the norm here for a moment. No wonder she's having trouble articulating what it is she wants to say.

"Of course. I want you to always speak your mind, Mystiance." From the look on her face as she raises her head, I know what's coming next, so I cut her off first. "At least, speak freely when it's just us," I say with a wink.

Quickly grinning, she understands what I'm dancing around. Roxalus may be a big softy for me, but no one wants to see his *nightmare* side if they can help it.

"Okay, then. Here's the thing... Prince Roxalus was supposed to inherit the throne once King Zyoden died. Prince Maximus had disappeared nearly two hundred years prior. Most all of the fae in Anavrin had loved Max dearly. He had been just and kind. He still has that underlying mischievous quality that all fae have come to expect but without being cruel. He was..." she dips her chin. "... is the king that they wanted. King Zyoden named Roxalus heir in Maximus' absence, and no one took him seriously. The king began tormenting him, taunting him, trying to toughen him up. King Zyoden taught Roxalus that being cold and shutting yourself off from caring for others was the only way to rule without objection."

My hands fly up to cover my mouth. How could a parent do that to their child? Granted, he was several hundred years old at the time, but to instill in him the need to cut off his heart? King Zyoden was one sick bastard!

"I'm glad he's dead," I say under my breath, but she hears it. The corner of her mouth turns up with a wicked gleam in her eyes.

"Right there." Pointing at me and waggling her finger, she shakes her head. "That is the fae way. You are kind, Piper. And Roxalus has been cruel for ages. Soulmates are about tempering each other's dominant traits."

"You **want** me to be harsh? To be mean? I don't want to lose myself to cruelty, Mysti. Roxalus can still be kinder and worthy of love without me having to come over to the dark side." My eyebrow remains arched as I wait for her response.

We're losing the light. It is already dark outside the lone window in the room and Roxalus will be back at any minute. Casually going about the room, she begins lighting the lanterns. Excruciatingly slowly. Driving me crazy in the awkwardness of my question's wake.

Just when I think she isn't going to address my statement, she begins speaking low. So low that I have to use my fae hearing with all the concentration I can muster.

"I love your kindness, My Princess." She turns to face me, eyes glistening. I can't explain it, but she looks smaller somehow. Resisting the urge to hug her, I allow her the time to gather her thoughts. "If the world were a softer place, then I wouldn't want any part of the sharp edges to touch you in any way... but it isn't."

Walking over to the small table that holds a bottle of amber liquid and a few glasses, she pours us each one with a small nod for confirmation. Taking a sip from the glass and handing me the other, she downs hers in one go. I've never seen her composure shaken. Always standing with her back straight, confidence exuding from her like air, it's unnerving to watch her falter.

"Beauty can be a curse." The beginning of her tale is already starting out with a foreboding *feel*. I attempt to brace myself, but I don't know that I have the kind of strength needed for her to relive her past. "All fae have qualities that make them attractive, but when beauty is beyond even fae standards, no one takes you seriously."

There's nothing to say to that. She's speaking the truth, not boasting, just stating facts. There isn't any denying how absolutely radiant she is. My stomach drops further when I *feel* the dread coming from her through my gifts. "You don't have to tell me anything that you don't wish to, Commander."

"You know, I've not talked about this in centuries. The only one to know my story is Prince Roxalus." There's a level of reverence in her voice for my mate and I find it brings me joy.

He has people. He has those who care about him. He just needs to open his heart back up to accepting the love he's shut out because of his horrible father. I'm going to make sure that he feels the love he deserves again.

"I wasn't strong enough when they came for me. I was meek and kind and did what was expected of me all of my life up until that point." It had been centuries, and her emotions were as raw as if it had happened yesterday. Males like Ayxian can't be allowed to get away with what they do. The way they think is unacceptable.

Reaching over, I take her hand in mine. "I hope you made them pay." A wicked sneer dons her full lips. It's so at odds with her beautiful face, I cringe back slightly. "I take it that was when you decided to start training?"

"No, actually. I came to Prince Roxalus and stood before his throne. My eyes where still blackened. I wore a dress that showed my bruised thighs and the cuts on my arms. I wanted justice."

Suddenly, I don't know if I want to hear the rest, but I listen to her bare her soul to me anyway.

"He sneered at me after giving me a full once over and I kowtowed under his cruel gaze." Seeing my distress, she pats my arm like I'm the one who should be comforted. I need to get a grip. "The look on his face said that he didn't care about my pain, but what he asked spoke to something inside of me."

I was practically biting my nails to the quicks. "Well... what did he say?" With my demand of her waiting on an anxious breath, she chuckles.

"He asked me if I wanted vengeance *or* if I wanted it to never happen again?" Understanding fills me. That brilliant, wonderful mate of mine. He gave her the choice to have her retribution, but she'd have to earn it for herself. Even though his heart was meant to be turned cold, he'd still found ways to serve his people without letting it show.

"So, you see Princess, having a little cruelty in your heart will help you to keep yourself safe. Fire burns. Ice freezes. It's about balance..."

Taking another swig of my drink, I let the sting in the back of my throat help me rein in control over the emotions swimming through me.

"...He is the Prince of Nightmares, not due to extra gifts. He is the Prince of Nightmares because he has a way of figuring out how to exact the most delicious reckonings."

I can't help the green headed monster that keeps sneaking up on me. "Have you... never mind." I wanted to ask if she's fucked my mate in the past. The woman has bared her soul to me, the first time in centuries letting it come to light, and my selfish need to claim Roxalus in every way won't let me let sleeping wolves lie.

I've had past lovers. I can hardly begrudge his centuries of them. But thinking of her with him makes my blood boil and I have to take a few deep breaths to get my temper under control.

"No, Piper. I swear it. I don't... I haven't. That is, I mean to say." She's looking up at me with imploring eyes, but I have no clue what she's getting at. Inhaling through her nose and out through her mouth, she tries again. "I don't cavort with the opposite sex. Not since..." Leaving the sentence hanging, I get the message all the same. "Speaking frankly," her sudden bashfulness has me shifting towards her instinctually to comfort her.

"Go on. We're friends, Mysti. I'll keep your confidences." It's silly to feel giddiness at the prospect of this beautiful fae as a loyal friend. I have always had Inara, but rarely do I make connections with others. Not lasting ones. This feels nice. Elodie has become one. And I'm still getting used to the idea. And Loxias, Leif, and Quill have become my buddies, but I guess you'd call them friends. It's kind of amazing to go from relegated loner to shining socialite in the span of less than a year.

"Well, I've had a hideous crush on Princess Elodie for so long that it's embarrassing." The way her eyes twinkle speak to the depths of that crush, and I playfully bat at her arm.

"I bet if you spoke up, she might take you for a ride." It's her turn to smack my arm just as Roxalus comes bounding through the door.

Jumping to her feet, she bows to him immediately. "Your Highness."

His face is stoic, unsmiling. A snarl resounds through the air. "Did I just see you raise your hand to my future wife?"

Chapter Forty-Seven

"My Liege, no. I was just... we were..." Stumbling over her words, Mysti takes a step away from me and towards him. The scowl he levels in her direction sends a visible chill rushing down her spine... but I can *feel* his jest and the one corner of his mouth twitches with the effort to hold back a grin.

"You're terrible!" I push passed her. "That wasn't nice."

"I haven't a reputation for being nice, Wildfire. Or did you forget?"

Mmmm...That crushed velvet voice of his. It brings me up short. I would have protested the statement, but the aroma of coffee drifts in from behind him and I'm rendered dumbfounded.

A servant carrying a tray of meats, cheeses and fruits is followed by one carrying a tray with cream, sugar lumps and...

Yes! Coffee. Rich, dark roasted sex in a mug. My hands reach for it before the poor girl can set the tray down.

Roxalus laughs, actually laughs. It is the best, most thrilling sound my ears have ever heard. A full turnaround from the apathetic prince I'd met in the beginning.

"What?" Feigning ignorance, it's easier for me not to acknowledge my addiction. "If you are quite through, I'd like to get settled in for the evening."

His arms snake around my waist and Mysti and the staff make themselves scarce. "So eager to be rid of me, Love?"

I nearly drop my mug. Almost. It isn't like I didn't know that he would be leaving tonight. It just never sank in that he wouldn't be, well, here. I'm such an idiot.

"I didn't mean it that way. I want to be rested enough for whatever Princess Embla might have planned." Sheepishly, I set the mug to the side and twist in his arms. His eyes sparkle with fire from the hearth and the scent of peppermint and pine needles envelope my being. "I wish you didn't have to go. The bed will feel enormous without you hogging all of the covers."

Squeezing my hips, he pulls me flush with his hardened length. Hot breath blows across the nape of my neck as he bends to whisper in my ear. "Is that all that you'll miss, you rapscallion? Are you sure that there isn't anything else that might make that bed more comfortable?"

Heat is rushing its way up my cheeks as goosebumps raise over my arms, but giving in, here in the castle of the princess who hates me, doesn't fit the agenda Max has laid out. It takes all of my willpower to quell my rising desire. The opportunity to see her people without influence is what I've been tasked with, and I have to take that seriously. My life isn't the only one on the line with those damned rebels.

Reluctantly, I pull back slightly, putting a little bit of space between us while still there in the circle of his arms. "I want to do this right, Starbear. Your sister already despises me. And as much as I hate that we must be apart, I do think Max has a point."

His arms fall from my sides, and he takes me by the hand to sit on the settee. Popping a grape into his mouth, chewing slowly, eyes narrowed in concentration at some hidden puzzle.

Reaching for a grape myself, he smacks my hand away playfully. "I wanted that one." A mischievous smile crinkles his eyes in the most heart stopping of ways. "So, let me get this straight... you want to spend two weeks without me, in the company of someone who doesn't like you and you don't seem to like either, all the while enduring whatever misery she decides to inflict upon you? And you don't want to give me the pleasure of a proper send off so that I can make the perfect arrangements for our upcoming nuptials? All because you think that it might offend her?"

Oh, this trickster. That wording was deliberate. My mate is definitely a crafty one.

"You're planning our wedding while I'm stuck here?" No wonder he's peppered me with so many questions on the carriage ride here. Brilliant bastard. "Do I get any say on the matters?"

That crooked grin he gives just to me pulls up the side of his mouth. Waggling his eyebrows, he leans towards me and practically growls. "That depends on how proper my sendoff is."

Heat pools between my legs, and I have to clamp my thighs together. He knows he has me. Nostrils flaring as he scents my arousal, I hold up a finger to stave him off for a moment. "Three rules. We can't destroy the room. We can't be heard. And most importantly, we mustn't be too long."

Before I've barely finished speaking, my knees are knocked out from under me, and I giggle. Heading towards the door with me in his arms, I begin to protest but he leans into my ear. "I do not agree to these rules. This isn't a room fit for a Princess. I will make sure that you are heard and claimed as mine before I ever leave you in the care of others. And Wildfire, I'm going to be as long and thorough as I need to be to ensure that you are fully satisfied before I even consider burying myself balls deep inside of you."

After several hours of satiating ourselves, we throw on a couple of robes, and he scoops me up into his arms. Striding down the hall, he calls back to the servants and Commander Mystiance. "Bring the princesses things to her new room in the morning. Mysti, stand guard outside of our door... but I wouldn't advise listening in." That roguish smirk donning his lips. Smacking his arm, I grin. I'm more than ready to make a mess in every room of this castle if that's his goal.

Considering Princess Embla has chosen that particular room for some reasons unbeknownst to me, I didn't initially want to make waves. However, if Roxalus doesn't get his way on the matter, I can't be sure if it's worth the risk of furthering the growing rift between the siblings. She may be a lost cause already. I guess I will just have to wait and see.

"You sir, are incorrigible." We arrive at a set of rooms that are as grand as they are unnecessary. At least these have two bedrooms, a sitting area, and an oversized bathroom. Mysti will like that. I've noticed her pension for long soaks in the tub.

"I haven't found the words yet, Piper." My name on his lips explodes fireworks in my chest. "I don't want to leave you at all. And I can't stand the thought that there are fae out there that want to hurt you." His arms tighten around me, but I don't know if he's conscious of it.

Setting me on the large four poster bed in the larger room, his hand running its course through the top of his hair, it stays on the back of his neck. The tension in his face is enough to have me pushing off the bed and wrapping my arms around his midsection. Corded muscles lay just beneath the loose-fitting fabric of his robe, and I want to lick them, but I give my attention to his angst.

"You don't have to worry. It's only a couple of weeks." Lessening my grip, I look up to see the hard set of his eyes. Wars were started with less emotion than I behold there. "By the time you get home, get all the arrangements underway, and then travel back here, it will have all flown by so quickly that you'll question why you ever worried in the first place."

My hair is a tangle of knots from the day's travel and our earlier love making but the fingers he trails through the strands never snag on a single one. Taking my chin between his forefinger and thumb, he brushes the gentlest of kisses to my lips. "I have waited my entire life to find you. I will not hesitate to harm anyone who tries to take you from me. You are mine."

A tear runs down my cheek at the feeling in my chest. I am his. I am worthy. I am finally wanted for being exactly who I am. I'm loved for being simply myself.

The depths of those beautiful blue eyes call to me. He needs to know how I feel about him too. "I want you to know something. I won't shy away from your cruel side. I won't be frightened by it. I won't see you any different when it rears its ugly head. I accept that it is a part of you, Roxalus."

"...But?" The skepticism in his tone undoes me. The way he waits for something negative breaks my heart.

"No but. I see you. I accept you. If you are less hardened because of our union, I will love that too. I am making no demands of you or giving you any ultimatums. You are perfect to me. You are mine as much as I am yours."

A relieved breath shudders through him. He can feel the sincerity of my emotions through the bond. He is worthy. He is enough.

Our passion is intense. It's a living thing breathing in life and love and it will not be contained. Minutes turn into hours. And the hours drift by quickly. Several times I accidentally slow time around us. My emotions are apparently the key to that particular gift, and I realized it was happening whenever I was trying to prolong an exceptionally good moment of bliss.

The higher the intensity of emotion, the more likely I am to trigger this gift until I learn to control it.

All too quickly, it's time for us to say goodbye. He dresses, kissing my forehead with whispers of devotion, and leaves me exhausted in the most delicious way.

He and Mysti are exchanging words in the front room. Something about being right and perfume and other, inconsequential things I can't make out in my half sleep. A small laugh escapes from both of them before sleep fully claims me. My eyes have been closed for only a few moments before my dreams take hold.

There's a figure shrouded in darkness. The shadows of the trees are too thick to see into the woods.

Stepping out onto the path, the moonlight illuminates the side of the face hidden under a cloak. Reaching up to take its hood down, it speaks. "Hello, Peppercorn."

Taking a tentative step forward, I squint at the person before me.

"Mother?"

Chapter Forty-Eight

Her thin face and the bow of her lips look like they did before she passed away all those years ago. If this is a dream, then my memory should have restored her features to their past glory.

Before she had gotten sick, my mother's beauty shone through every aspect of her life. She wasn't only fair of face, but the light of her sweet soul shined so bright that it was a bit intimidating at times. Living up to what made her so radiant was what I aspired to and more often than not I failed miserably.

"As happy as I am to see you, I have to ask why you've come?" A warm breeze blows across my face dragging her long-forgotten scent of gardenia and cucumber through my senses.

Nostalgia claws at my chest, and I reach a hand towards her. Without explanation, she swivels away from my touch and smiles.

"I had hoped to make my plea to you without sounding remorseful." Her gaunt figure sits on a bench and pats the spot beside her for me to join. *"I understand now what I was seeing back then. That we are fae, Peppercorn."*

It strikes me only now that she is referring to her vision from all of those years ago, but that doesn't tell me much.

"Mother, I never got to learn of your vision." I say hanging my head. *"You died before you could tell me. And Aunt Eowyn never divulged it before she died either."*

My internalized rage rakes at the carefully maintained fence I've erected around it after it began to grow.

"I became a wolf. My panther never had the chance to bloom. I kept quiet and I did everything that you asked of me!" If talking to her like this upsets her, she doesn't let on. *"I deserve to know, Mother, what was in that vision you had that made me shut myself away from the world and live as but a shadow?"*

I thought that she would chastise my outburst, but I was wrong. Slowly, her eyes turn towards the light. I can see the dark circles beneath them and itch to run my fingers down her face like I used to when I was younger.

Words fail me when I notice the lone tear that runs the length of her cheek. In all of her days she lived, I'd never seen her shed a single one. Tears would never compromise her strength in my eyes, but I know that she held them in many times for my benefit before she passed.

"Oh, my sweet child. If only I had known the things I know now." Her forefinger and thumb grip gently under my chin and bring my eyes to meet hers. *"I thought that the fae would kidnap you. You are the last of the panther shifters, Peppercorn. I thought*

that if you hid who you were that perhaps the future events I saw would never come to pass."

Dropping her hand none too harshly, she turns her body away from mine in what looks to be disgust.

"I don't understand. What future, Mother? What did you see?" Even though I am asleep, my patience is running thin. I have the urge to shake her, to rattle her bones with my frustration.

Standing and striding several feet away before looking at me again, disappointment is clear upon her face. My chest aches. A hollow feeling carves a chasm just beneath my ribcage. My whole life, all I ever wanted was to make her proud.

"I foresaw the fae princes vying for your hand. I saw one win it and you bound to him without revoke. He was cruel and you belonged to him. Piper, I saw you in a magical cage, unable to shift out of your panther form. When out of that cage, magical chains bound you. You were his pet, my sweet girl."

Relief washes through me. It isn't disgust for me I realize. It was disgust for what she'd seen the fae do to me. A small bit of warmth begins to seep back in to fill the hole that her perceived waned confidence in me had left.

"It's okay, Mother. I'm okay. I am bound to Prince Roxalus by way of the mating bond. We're mates." Taking a step forward to reach for her hand, her dark figure begins to blur before I can grasp hold of it. "He would never harm me, Mother. You must know that."

The cloak around her shimmers as she speaks. "Beware, my lovely girl. Beware of the prince who has chosen you." Disappearing from one breath to the next, all I can do is stare at the spot by the edge of the trees where she had been and wish she would have stayed a little longer.

Waking abruptly, my mind is reeling as anxiety coils in my chest. Roxalus would never lock me away. Would he? What lengths would he go to in efforts to keep me safe?

My head swimming with visions of my mother and Roxalus and cages for the rest of the night, I've finally settled into a dreamless sleep right before dawn when a loud knock sounds on the bedroom door.

"Princess Piper," Mysti calls without opening it. "Princess Embla is demanding that you make your way down to breakfast without haste."

Rolling over with a huff of frustration, I yell back a retort that Embla can shove something somewhere and Mysti laughs through the door.

Fine. Time to play keen observer. Pushing the covers off of the bed, I slip on my slippers and robes and head for the common area. If Princess Embla is going to make demands of my time, then she will receive me just how I am. Pajama clad and hair unbound with Max's necklace in place.

Time to let my inner animal show. The thought makes me giggle. Lowbee for the win.

Chapter Forty-Nine

"Ah, Princess Piper. How good of you to grace us with your mediocre presence." The room is full of courtiers that sit to either side of a long table ladened with fruits and pastries. "What in Luna's name are you wearing?" she demands.

Mocking flattery, I lift one side of my robe and flutter it about. "Oh, this old thing? It's all the rage in the lower realm." Looking up at her astonished face and seeing the distain gives me a thrill of cruel satisfaction. "I could ask that you be brought one with my next delivery of goods if you'd like."

I waste no time sitting down and scooping heaping amounts of food onto my plate. Chancing a glance at Embla, her mouth remains hanging open in shock. Smugness settles around me like a comforting blanket. If she's going to be a bitch, there's no way that I'm going to back down from her challenges anymore.

Princess Mightier than Thou can take her bullying and shove it where the sun doesn't shine for all I care.

The first bite of some sort of flaky baked item touches my tongue. It's light and fluffy with just a smidge of honey. The flavor is absolutely divine. I haven't had a chance to have my coffee this morning. The rush to get out of the room and down to breakfast has put me in a foul mood but I give credit where credit is due.

"Princess Embla," the look she gives me for addressing her directly is worth the hassle of being here at her beckon call right now. "Your staff have outdone themselves. This pastry is marvelous."

Several of the servers beam with pride but the princess purses her lips with distaste. Perhaps she doesn't think that praise is something her lessers should be given. What kind of wanker cares so little for the lives of others?

"It's just a pastry, Princess Piper." The way her mouth curls around my title makes it feel like a slur. If I had been granted the time to be caffeinated, maybe I wouldn't bite back but...

"It's a lovely breakfast. Your staff is brilliant, Princess Embla," I say, using the infliction for her title in return. Mysti stiffens beside me, but I pay her no mind. "What's on the agenda for today, Sister?"

Maybe antagonizing her isn't the best idea. This is her court, her castle. And these are her people. Even if she is a pretentious twit. I'm surprised that she can see where she's going with her nose so far up in the air.

Play nice. The voice inside my head speaks so loudly that I nearly jump. It has a rough timber to its quality now that I'd never noticed before. I feel a tug at the center of my chest and realize that I have heard that voice for many years now... only, I never knew it wasn't mine. It had been a keen feeling, not an actual tone. Now, it's clear as day that it was never my own.

Roxalus... he's been my internal guide down the mating bond that I never knew existed. Maybe it has always been a connection to him. Even before we met. Even before we mated. A part of me that I never questioned as being my own. I wonder if I've influenced him over the years without knowing it as well?

Taking a fan from the sleeve of her dress, the princess makes a show of being overheated as she waves it about in front of her face. "That depends, are you planning to wear clothes or are you going to lounge around in pajamas all day?"

I get the feeling that my appearance matters to her. And my subtle reminder that we are to be family in law brings her thoughts back around to her brother.

"I will change, Your Highness." Upon standing from the table, I notice the male next to her. He's sneering down his nose at me. I can only assume that he's one of the Lords of her court sitting here at her table.

His right hand rubs down his left forearm over his shirt and then raises in a fist pressed to his chest. It's a small movement, and it wouldn't have stuck out to me... except that two other courtiers at the table do the same motion in response. If I was a less observant person, I might never have noticed.

Filing that away to tell Mysti later and stepping towards the door before turning back to Embla, giving her a half-assed curtsy, I smile my most winning grin. "I shall return to you after I put myself together."

"I hardly think that's possible." Her courtiers give snickers and chortles, but her staff's lips turn down. Not one of them find her jibes endearing. As far as I can tell, they find her lacking. This is why Max has sent me here. He wants the truth of her rule. And so far, she is failing. The necklace heats and I know what it's taking in. My feelings.

The rest of the week pass much the same way. Embla is tight lipped in my presence. I worry for her mouth. She's pressed it so hard closed that wrinkles are beginning to form around the edges. The only time she speaks to me is to toss a loathsome remark aimed at making me feel small.

Twice, I've had to bite the inside of my cheek to keep from throwing out retorts of my own. Whenever I'm about to lose my composure, I feel a tug from the mating bond. Reassurance and a reminder. Embla might be a piece of work, but she is also the sister of the man I love. That thought alone keeps me from shifting into my panther and ripping her head clean from her shoulders. A gal can fantasize though.

Her staff and I get along splendidly. I made my way to the kitchens on my second day here. The entire buzzing atmosphere stopped. After I assured them that I didn't need anything and I wasn't there to scold them for anything, they looked confused at my continued presence.

"I just needed a place to hang out without..." I'd made a grand imitation of the princess and a few of them lost their composure with fits of belly laughs and giggles.

I was right when I'd thought that they didn't care for their monarch. She doesn't see them as people. She sees them only as lesser beings who are meant to service her needs. Emenda and Embla might be twins, but their personalities couldn't be more different in that regard.

Over the last two weeks I've made many observations. That first day, we'd run into the guard from the night before and he had bruising and a huge gash that was slow to heal above his left eye. When he saw our approach, he rubbed his forearm and brought his fist to his chest as he turned to the other guard on duty. I told Mysti of the nonchalant signal I'd seen quite a few times since coming to the castle. The forearm rubbing followed by the fist to the chest and she began noticing it too after that.

"I sent a message to General Biscott. He will let me know what Prince Roxalus thinks after they discuss it." Her words were said casually but her attention to our surroundings has increased tenfold. I'm never more than a few feet from her except in our rooms. I like her being here. I feel a bit safer than I would all by myself.

Roxalus is supposed to arrive tomorrow. It's been an end-lessly long couple of weeks and knowing I'll see him soon provides a lightness to my chest. Loxias, Leif, and Quill all arrived earlier today. Their kingdoms are the farthest away, so they wanted to get a little rest before the others are set to arrive. I haven't seen any signs of Elodie yet. And Noxian is a mystery to me. From what I can tell, he's very much about keeping the fae of Anavrin safe. Though he is quiet, that doesn't make him any less formidable. I'd like to get a better grasp on that particular brother-in-law, but he's hard to pin down.

Today was, yet again, a beautiful day. Sunny and in the seventies as usual. When I lived in the Lupian Forest, I loved the spring. The buds were in bloom. The earth was waking up from its winter slumber. Everything was fresh and new. Here in Anavrin, we're stuck in a perpetual spring. I never thought I'd miss the trees being bare or the press of snow and cold air. I can understand why immortality becomes boring after a while when there is no change to highlight the passing of time.

Mysti and I decide to spend some time lounging about in the solarium. The glass roof and outer wall are tinted but let in all of the sunshine. A pitcher of cucumber water and a few euphoria pasties have made for a pleasant way to pamper ourselves before the next competition.

Inara brought me a couple bottles of nail polish on her first visit to me all those months ago. It's time I put them to use. Mysti was reluctant to let me paint her toes but in the end, her female side and my charm win out.

A loud bang startles us coming from down the hall. She jumps to her feet, knocking the polish from my hands. It spills over the rug, and I just know that Princess Embla is going to crucify me for the stain.

"That wasn't..." I start to protest but Mystiance is in full commander mode. Bringing her hand to her lips, she motions for me to be quiet and hide. I don't know what she thinks is happening, but I trust her. Making my way to the drapes behind a tall potted plant close to the window, my mind slips to the massacre at Ayxian's trial.

Drawing her sword, she falls into a fighting stance, making the hairs on the back of my neck stand up. Creeping towards the door and turning the mechanism, the tumblers lock in place. There's a large wooden shelf housing an array of knick knacks and books to one side of the door. Pushing it to cover the entrance as quietly as she can manage, it bars anyone entrance to the room without it being knocked over.

Voices shouting and the sounds of metal on metal meet my ears. Then it's quiet. Too quiet. Footsteps make their way towards the solarium. The sound of a sword being dragged against the stone floor sends fear rushing to every part of me.

A deep muffled voice floats into the room from behind our barrier. Mysti glances over her shoulder to make sure I'm hidden from view as pounding begins on the door. Whoever is out there is beating against the wood hard enough to break through.

The door practically explodes in splinters on the next hit. A male figure stands just out of the light. I can't make out their face. The scent of earthy cedar shoves its way up my nose, hitting me like an unwelcome intrusion, making my stomach roil.

Ayxian.

Chapter Fifty

Entering the room, Ayxian's eyes fall to the sword in Mysti's hands. He huffs out that deep chested chuckle of his and my hands have to cover my mouth to keep from vomiting.

"Where is Lady Piper?" The dark glint in his eyes tell me all that I need to know about why he's looking for me. The scars from my claws stand out in stark relief, marring his otherwise handsome face.

"That's Princess Piper. She is My Liege's mate, and they are to wed next month. Her whereabouts are no concern of yours." Slipping her foot nonchalantly around the shelf that's pushed aside, she maneuvers it between them as casually as she can.

"Ah well, that's where we have a problem, Commander." He doesn't even look down. His large bulking form struts forward, and the heavy wooden shelves push away without any thought.

"Lady Piper is who I have chosen to be my queen, and I shall stake my claim in her before I ascend the throne as king." Mysti doesn't move an inch. I can't imagine standing toe to toe with a beast the size of him.

His eyebrows arch incredulously, like he can't believe there is any problem with what he's said. "Surely, you wouldn't want to deny a prince of Anavrin his just due."

With her back to me, I can only imagine the incredulous look on her face. It has to mirror my own. The way her shoulders stiffen paint a picture clear enough. Sword held high, her legs widen into a defensive stance.

"And there is where we have *our* problem. You are no longer a prince of Anavrin. The king and other royals have stripped you of that title. My Princess will be going nowhere that she doesn't consent to go, you pompous asshole. Do not even think about touching her!"

For the first time since entering the room, Ayxian's face looks crestfallen. His arrogance is truly a sight to behold. If I could go back and scar that mug all over again, I wouldn't stop until I mangled the entire thing.

Lifting the sword in his hand, he growls as he takes a step towards Mysti. Having to lift her head to look up at him throws her balance off. With a quick glide to the side, she swivels around, the point of her sword presses firmly against his ribs just below his heart and he falters in his overbearing confidence.

I gasp at the deftness of her fighting abilities. It's one thing to know she's Roxalus' commander for a reason, but it's quite another thing to witness it first-hand.

Recovering quickly after his momentary lapse, he presses forward. "I mean to take what's mine, Commander. Whether you live or not is the only question." The vitriol spitting from him like a viper poised to strike. Shifting positions just as quickly as she had, he falls into a fighting stance, towering over her lithe form.

His sword comes down in a swift arc. The sound of metal on metal this close is loud and more than a little disturbing. I don't dare to move. She's risking her life to protect me. The least I can do is make sure that her efforts aren't in vain.

I hadn't realized I'd been holding my breath until I began to feel dizzy. Gulping in copious amounts of air, it won't fill my lungs. Anxiety grips me, my limbs are frozen in place.

They go round and round. His enormous size doesn't matter. She is nimble and moves agilely, matching his swings blow for blow. A hard downward swing nearly connects with her neck but she rolls to her side at the last second, bringing out a dagger from seemingly nowhere and stabbing it into his side. Blood flows freely from the wound. With an abrupt jerk, she thrusts her sword between his legs and slides around to his back. A long rivulet of blood runs down his pants leg from the second wound as he roars in pain.

A half second of hope rises in my chest before she turns to stand and slips in the blood, landing hard on her back. It's all I can do to throw my hand over my mouth, stay in place, and not call out to her.

Ayxian stands over her with his sword above her chest and hate in his eyes. "You nearly cost me my manhood, you bitch!"

I've only heard him lose his cool once before. The beast within rearing its ugly head, he steps closer. The smell of copper filling the room, I can't move fast enough to stop him. He slides his sword deep into Mysti's chest and my scream won't be stifled.

Jumping out of my hiding spot, his eyes snap to mine. "Stop it! Stop it, you fucking asshole!" It is only a second that his attention is distracted by my outburst. He's caught off guard.

With blood seeping all over the stone floor, the commander pushes him back and stands with a horrible grunt of pain. She shoves him through the glass wall of windows with all the strength she can muster.

Shattered shards rain down, and I have to duck and cover to avoid being sliced apart. They both land bodily on the lawn, guards and rebels clashing all around. Loxias, Quill, and Leif taking on more of them than the rest of the guards put together. Princess Embla's guards appear to be here more for show than actual fighting. Or maybe they don't care if us lowbees die.

At the sight of us appearing in the midst of glass and debris, Loxias turns and runs towards us, sword at the ready, axe hanging poised at his side. In this moment, I see the fierce huntsman readying for a kill and I've never been more pleased with that aspect of his personality.

Quill glances up from his own fight and aims his crossbow directly at Ayxian's head. Leif's shadows creep across the grounds to cover me and Loxias from view. Once again, I foolishly allow hope to fill me. Maybe things won't be so bleak.

Then reality settles in. Mysti's eyes are closed. Her chest is barely moving. Blood is blooming across her armor.

Ayxian meets his sword with one he can't see while Leif's shadows are keeping Loxias under cover. With his fighting instincts honed, he doesn't need his eyes to be lethal. Slicing through a guard to his right, he readjusts his sword to meet Loxias' blade again within the next breath. Quill looses a bolt and Ayxian bats it out of the air just before it hits him.

I turn my attention to Mysti and crawl to her side. Leif covers us both with his shadow magics. The fighting is still going on behind me, but I can't tear my eyes away from her.

Holding her hand, I kiss it gently and sob. "I forbid you to leave me, Commander." Her chest rising and falling only once. "Do you hear me? You have to stay. I need you." Tears run down my cheeks. The salt leaking onto my lips is bitter on my tongue. This beautiful, brave warrior lays bleeding in the grass all because of me. "Mysti, please!" I beg. If I owe her a boon, so be it. I will give it freely. "Please don't leave me."

Anger replaces my sadness. I don't give my body permission before it is standing and heading towards the two fighting princes. I am not strong. I don't know the first thing about fighting. I have no plan, buy my goal is set. Stop Ayxian by any means necessary.

As my anger builds within, things around me slow. Loxias' sword is on its way down to meet Ayxian's with brute force. Pushing Ayxian's sword aside, I swivel his massive body as best as I can into the direct path of Loxias' blade. I haven't stopped time, but it is creeping forward in slow motion.

Quill has loosed another bolt, and it's heading towards Ayxian at the perfect trajectory to imbed itself into his chest. Ayxian's eyes widen and it gives me great satisfaction to know that when time starts back up, there'll be nothing he can do to stop the blade to his neck or the bolt to his chest in time.

Stepping back to admire my handywork, I let go of the anger. The rage. Taking a deep breath, I push away the feeling of congealed air.

The bolt flies true. The sword comes down. Only...

Neither of them connects.

Leif's shadows remain in place but are not swirling. Loxias' sword arm is still poised for the kill but not making the deadly contact. Quill's bolt presses into Ayxian's chest but isn't penetrating.

Taking in my surroundings, a blurred figure comes into view from the edge of the field. A figure with a tall staff. The stone atop glowing brightly.

The sorcerer. Lord Beartach.

Chapter Fifty-One

"Tsk tsk tsk. We can't have that. No murder for you, lowbee wench." He steps to Ayxian's side, plucking the bolt from the air. Taking the end of his staff, he pushes Loxias to fall on his ass, sword laying several feet away. "For whatever reason, King Ayxian wants you by his side."

"King? Are you deficient, Lord Beartach?" Ayxian will never be king. I can't fathom the thought. "Ayxian doesn't even have prince statis anymore. He was stripped of that title when he decided that his wants overrode common decency! His sister was almost killed in that little rebellion, did you know that?"

Casually walking over, he steps on Loxias' wrist. The crack resounds through the eerie quiet of the field. Unlike when I had slowed time, there is no awareness in any of the figures around me.

"I can continue to do this until they are all in pieces, or you can come quietly with the king. Which shall it be?" Carelessly strolling towards Mysti, the end of his staff pushes down and twists on her open wound. Blood coats the wood as he pulls it away.

"Alright... Alright." I raise my hands in surrender. "Just fix them and I will come with you."

Taking a few steps towards Loxias, I slip off my mate's ring. He's given it to me as a place holder until mine can be forged. Dropping it into Lox's pocket, I know he'll get it to Roxalus for me.

If evil has ever existed, this fae sorcerer is the embodiment of it. A vicious grin lights his face, and a new fear blooms internally.

"I won't be fixing anything. I am not a healer." Walking over to Ayxian, the stone on top of his staff glows gold for a brief second. The ground around him brightens and the smell of tilled earth meets my nose. Ayxian is stirring. His gaze meeting the sorcerers, then his brother, and finally landing on me.

My stomach roils at the desire written on his face and my heart clenches. Unconsciously, I tug on the mating bond... hard. Fear and anger tug back. Roxalus is coming... but I know he won't make it in time. I am on my own with the brutish dethroned prince and an evil sorcerer.

It doesn't scare me as much as it once would have back in my old life. Pack life had been a blessing at the time. But wolves depend on each other. They thrive in the unified mind setting. I, however, am not a wolf. I am a panther that can rip muscle from bone. In that form, I am powerful. I am dangerous. I am deadly and will not suffer the demands of these arrogant males.

I've scarred Ayxian's body, his face. There is something about the First Witch's bloodline that makes any shifter's marks unhealable to the fae. Inara, Max, and I had debated it for a full afternoon once during one of her visits. It isn't poison or venom. It is magics itself that remain left behind. Only Faelan has the ability to manipulate particles completely, but Mabs bloodline allows us to slide our intent in when we attack, holding it in place forevermore. I had gotten away back at his castle. I will get away again. And I will mar anyone one of these assholes who touches me.

"There's my sweet girl." He honestly believes his delusion, thinks I'm his. My mate mark on my neck shows the truth of Roxalus' claim on my heart and still, he thinks that I'll be with him. The bastard is crazy!

Holding out his hand to me, I shake my head no, but he doesn't care. "Come, my queen. We have a ceremony to perform."

"I will come with you if you promise to keep them safe. All of them. Every lowbee." Stepping towards me, I hold up my hands to stave him off. "I will never be yours, Ayxian. I am Roxalus' mate. I love him and only him."

Anger flashes across his face for the briefest of seconds. There and gone in a blink. "After Lord Beartach removes that hideous mark from your otherwise flawless skin, you'll feel differently, my queen."

Remove my mate mark? Oh, Hell No! I won't let him. I do the only thing I can think to do. Shift. In a fit of fury and fur, I explode.

Turning and growling in his direction, he laughs like I'm putting on a wonderful performance that he's all too willing to watch. His arrogance knows no bounds.

I don't move away when he comes towards me. I said I would go with him to save those I cared about, and I will. That doesn't mean his close proximity doesn't make my skin crawl.

"Lord Beartach?" Holding his hand out to the sorcerer, I can't see what he's placed there until he rushes forward with fae speed and clamps a glowing collar around my neck. "Sorry, pet. If and when you see reason, I will take off the magical collar. I like to look at you in this form anyway."

His hand comes down and runs through the fur behind my ears. I'm going to be sick. I forgot just how twisted he can be with his desires. Going with them is a bad idea.

I don't know what this collar is capable of but the magics drain is the first thing I take notice of. Stopping time isn't working. I can *feel* the emotions around me, but barely. Shit! I can't change back. Panic is setting in quickly at that realization. If I can't shift back, I can't slip out of this collar and break away when I have an opportunity.

"I have prepared the cage for our departure, My King," Lord Beartach says as he smirks in my direction.

I want to wipe that smug look off the old fae's face. I'm going to take pleasure in ripping him apart one day. I snarl at him, and he has the good sense to back away a few feet.

Ayxian cautiously inches forward to look me in the face. "It's only for transport right now." I don't miss the *right now* part. "Hopefully, you will accept our bond soon. Then you will be free to rule by my side in whichever form you like." He chuckles under his breath, and I get the feeling I'm not going to like what comes next.

Leaning down and nuzzling into my neck, I growl, showing all my pointed, deadly teeth but it doesn't deter him in the slightest. "In the meantime, I'm going to enjoy learning what makes my kitten purr."

Gross. Can he be anymore disgusting? His hand slides down my back and scratches a firm caress at the fur on my ass, just before my tail. With a couple of pats, his trousers swell. Oh, fuck no!

Reaching under my belly, he yanks me up into his arms like I weigh no more than a tabby cat, fingers brushing against my underside as my massive weight settles into him. I snap and snarl and try to connect with his face to no avail.

The door to the cage is open and waiting. There is a velvet plush cushion inside, a hunk of raw meat, and a bowl of water. Parading me through the streets as his pet must be some sort of fantasy of his. The twisted fuck!

There's a hard tug from the mating bond... love. Roxalus is getting closer. The bond is less strained. The line has less slack. Anger and rage war side by side with the love. He's frantic. I can feel his anxiety as if it's my own.

I am anxious enough without feeling his emotions or feeding him mine. Making the decision for us both so he won't have to feel everything that happens to me, I sent as much calming energy and love through the bond as I can.

Then I throw up a thin wall from my side. I can still feel his emotion like a dull ache but not as sharply as a knife prick. That should help him in the same way. If Ayxian attempts to...

well, whatever he attempts to do, this wall will be the least I can do to spare my mate.

I won't let Ayxian win... but just in case, Roxalus has to be spared from the horror of feeling whatever awaits me.

As the cage door locks, dread fills me and even with the wall in place, I can feel Roxalus' fear pounding across the expand.

Epilogue
Roxalus

My horse gallops his hardest, but I never let up. The moment I'd felt her fear and her pain, I grabbed General Biscott and his soldiers and took off towards Embla's. It's normally a couple of hours ride but I am pushing my steed to his limits.

It's all I can do to not fall from my mount as feelings down the bond intensify. There is fear and rage. Then love that makes my cold heart ache. Then... nothing but a dull sense of dread, loathing, and disgust.

We arrive at my sister's castle within the hour. Bodies lay strewn about. Blood and cries of pain come from those littering the ground soiling the otherwise perfect looking day.

As we approach, it's evident that someone has busted through the solarium wall of glass. Loxias is standing over a bloody figure with Quill and Leif at his back. As I get closer, I can see who he's leaning over and my heart faulters.

Commander Mystiance would never leave Piper's side. Not if there was anything left in her. She knows how I'll react. Knowing this is her final chance at redemption for her past failures, it can only mean death is hovering.

Luckily, when I'd hopped onto my horse and took off, Eskay was close by. I didn't ask her to make the journey. The old stubborn fae never listens to me anyway. When the General and I were half an hour away from my court, I glanced back and saw her riding quickly behind us, nimble as ever.

It takes her a full ten minutes to catch up to us once we arrive on the scene and I still haven't been able to make myself walk forward. I'm standing here, stunned. Piper is gone. Mysti is laying in a puddle of her own blood with a gaping wound in her chest. The grounds reek of Lord Beartach's magics. And yet, I just stand here.

"What are you waiting for? Go on. Walk to your soldier." Eskay's voice rings with authority that she doesn't possess. Since my mother's death, Eskay has been by my side. She'd said her former position in the king's seat no longer felt right.

Personally, I think I'd been her favorite since she delivered me into my mother's arms. It was a difficult birth, so I've been told. My mother was worn and too tired from blood loss to care for me for many months. Eskay took on my tending and has had a hand in my life ever since.

Bending down, I place a firm grip on Loxias' shoulder. He turns to look at me but doesn't take his hand off of Mysti. I realize he's trying to apply pressure to the wound to slow the bleeding and using his gifts to comfort her as much as possible. The angle of his one wrist is odd but it's healing before my eyes.

"I've got her, Lox." I can't remember the last time I've spoken kindly to him. Piper adores him and if I am to be a male worthy of someone the likes of her, I need to start appreciating those around me who care for her as much as I do.

A long laceration down the side of his neck and across his arm are slowly healing. He backs up and Eskay comes pushing forward with a basket of her herbs and salves.

"Oh dear. Prince Roxalus. I'm going to need a lot of food if I survive healing a wound of this magnitude. It may just kill me, just so you know." I begin to protest but she holds up her hand to silence me. "Shush now. I need to work." Blue light pulses under her fingers. Growing brighter with every pass. "This could take a while. Go, make yourself useful elsewhere."

I nod my agreement and grab Loxias by the elbow, pulling him a few meters away. Quill and Leif step to his side. I don't miss how Quill's crossbow is casually aimed at my chest. Or how Leif's shadows swirl at his fingertips, ready to defend him. What must it be like to have friends like that? Not people whose job it is to protect you, but people who will defend you because you matter to them.

"Brother, what happened? Where is she?" It comes out a lot angrier than I mean for it to and he takes a step back. Understandable. I'm barely holding myself together at the moment. I'd promised her I'd never let anything, or anyone harm her ever again. I've failed miserably. Again.

Glancing towards his friends, Quill gives him a small nod and Loxias exhales a long breath. "It was Ayxian and lots of his rebels. I swear Roxalus, we gave it our all to defend her. To defend all of them." Shaking his head, he scrubs at the back of his neck. "I don't know what happened. One minute, we were poised to kill him and the next..." He trails off, at a loss of words.

Reaching up to clap my hand on his shoulder for a second time, he cringes at my touch. I deserved that but... Damn. It still stings my newly, slightly softened heart.

"I know you did. It's not your fault." Loxias looks at me like I've grown three heads. "I know you care for her. All of you. I could smell Lord Beartach's magics when we arrived. He is the reason that you couldn't win, brother."

The copper scent of blood tinged the air as the breeze blew through the trees on the grounds. Stepping away from Loxias as General Biscott comes back from reconnaissance, he drops his head to whisper in my ear, but I motion for him to tell the group, and he looks at me the same way that Loxias had.

"Ayxian and a group of rebels stormed the castle. Princess Embla was in the throne room with her guards. When Ayxian came in, he told her that he was looking for Princess Piper. She directed him to her whereabouts like they were discussing the weather, with no care for his trial, crimes, or stripped title. A few of her guards accompanied him but broke off to meet the rebels outside when they'd heard a commotion."

I see red. The rage is palatable on my tongue. Something wet covers my palms and I realize that my nails are biting through them. Blue fire coats my fingertips, and all sense of reason goes out the window.

Loxias holds up his hands. "Woah, brother. I'm not happy about any of this either, but you can't go attacking Embla. Max and the others will need to bring her to court so that justice can be served."

His words are falling deafly on my ears. I know he's right. I know that Piper wouldn't want me to harm Embla, even if only for Emenda's sake. I know, and yet I can't stop myself from fuming. From flaming. My gifts of fire and ice cover my body in tandem. I'm not able to get myself under control. The ground is shaking. No... It's me. I'm shaking with vibrant tremors all over.

I can't reach Piper through the bond. Thoughts of what Ayxian might do to her taunt me and I'm coming undone. I have tried it Piper's way. I've tried to be a better person but, in this moment, I want to watch the world burn at her feet to bring her back to me. I want to kill anyone who glances wrong in her direction. I need to feel their blood boil with cold fire in their veins and taste the ash of their corpses on my tongue.

"General Biscott?" He comes to my side but stays several feet away from my freezing flames. "We are going hunting... but first, I'm going to need help," I force through gritted teeth. My proclamation makes them all gasp at once. I've never asked for help. The Prince of Nightmares has never even admitted to *needing* help before. Their concern is warranted.

Loxias steps forward and Quill is at his side in an instant. "What do you need us to do?"

Piper's right. Loxias is a good male and now I am going to test that theory.

"I need you to take away my drive to kill Embla." I look to Quill. "I'm going to need you to shoot me in both knees. And General Biscott, I'm going to need you to send a message to our armies. Find and dispatch any and all rebels. I want their heads on pikes. No exceptions. No excuses. We did it the king's way. Now we do it mine!" Loxias shakes his head but doesn't try to contradict me. "Leif, shield Loxias while he uses his gifts and yank him away if I resist."

My control is slipping further away with every passing second. It amazes me that I've gotten through my instructions without losing it. With a quick nod, I raise my flaming hands towards Quill. It takes everything in me to keep them on me alone. "Now, Quill."

Two bolts leave his crossbow in rapid secession, one embedding in each knee. The pain is more intense than I'd anticipated. I fall to them immediately, painfully, just as planned.

Loxias darts forward and lays both hands on my face as I cry out in agony. Both physical and from the tear of failure radiating through my chest at her loss.

"You are angry with Embla, but you won't hurt her. You need to find Piper as quickly as you can." His words burrow into my mind, making connections. Redirecting my emotions.

My flames are freezing his hands, melting away skin with each passing second, but he doesn't stop. I've never given him the credit he deserves. It strikes me in this moment that Loxias is my saving grace in my current state. I will find a way to repay him once my world is righted. This I vow.

"Ayxian is a threat. A threat that you must deal with." I can feel the push of his powers warring with my strong will. "You will stop at nothing to get Piper back. Do you understand me?" That last little push felt different. That wasn't for my sake. He cares about my mate. Family means something to him and she is family.

All at once, my flames go out. Yanking the bolts from my knees, I stand, pushing through the pain as if it doesn't exist.

I know I've been raging but my heart is cold fury now rather than hot anger. I am focused with one task.

"I understand. I will kill anyone who stands between me and Piper's safety." Running towards my steed, knees bleeding, my need to find and save her overrides everything else in my mind. Glancing back, Loxias' incredulous face falls. "General Biscott, you have your orders."

"That's not what I meant! Roxalus! I didn't mean for you to..." The sound of his voice fades away with every stride I push my horse to take.

I'll become that villain again. I'll be that ruthless fae who strikes fear into the masses. I will slaughter anyone who dares to get between me and my mate.

If she feels anguish, so will every fae around her. I will make all of Anavrin bleed if that's what it takes to get her back.

Piper is my salvation, and mercy will play no role until she is again by my side.

The gods may have mercy, but as me... I will show none!

About the Author
Anexa O. Saphire

I was born in Maryland and love steamed crabs. I moved to Florida for a few decades but have moved back to Maryland recently. I love to write, create art, read, and sing. I've become extremely introverted as I have gotten older, but I do still love going out for an occasional night of karaoke. My hubby and I live a simple, quiet life with our furbabies. Life becomes simpler once you let yourself dream and let go of whatever holds you down.

Acknowledgements

Firstly, I would like to give a huge shout out to my husband, Tim. This year has been riddled with stress and strife, loss and floundering in a sea of uncertainty. Without him, I would have drowned in self-pity and relished in self-loathing like a warm blanket. He's been the hero I needed and the villain that kept us going.

Secondly, I want to thank the few people in my life that were always there when I needed an ear to vent to, words of encouragement, and solutions to problems that plagued me. My mom, Sandra, at the top of that list. Along with Ashley, Laura, and Keay.

A huge thank you to Melanie Elkins for all of her help. She has been my eyes when mine have failed me. I am so grateful for her. She has stepped up and been in my corner in a time when I truly needed a friend.

I would be remiss if I didn't acknowledge my furbabies. When I was down and need hugs, they were there. When I needed a reminder that I matter to someone, they were there. And whenever I was not willing to push myself to do something, anything, through the stress of the day, they picked up on my needs and dragged me to whatever end.

I've made several friends through social media, and I want to give a shout out to them as well. Especially Evie, Angelic, Brittney, Ash, Mir, and Little Raven for these last few months.

I am an author, but more than that, I am an avid reader. And a book dragon to boot. It's an addiction that I refuse to kick!

9 781970 300000